THE SEX QUEEN

Marek had w... a great love. ... million men'... dise. A woma... ...he had shared a married hell. A beautiful, talented, tormented woman who destroyed herself at the height of her Hollywood career.

Now on the stage he saw the girl who was trying out for this, the greatest part he had ever created with his mind and his heart and his pen. It was like seeing a ghost—yet at the same time he knew it was no ghost.

Only a very live woman could make him feel like this . . . could make the old madness begin again . . . a madness he could not resist. . . .

"A BLOCKBUSTER"—Oregon Journal

4 931-5821

JEFFERSON
SQUARE

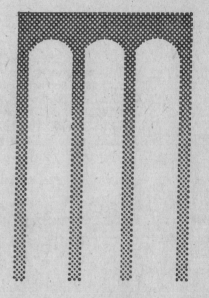

NOEL B. GERSON

A DELL BOOK

Published by
DELL PUBLISHING CO., INC.
750 Third Avenue
New York, N.Y. 10017
Copyright © 1968 by Noel B. Gerson
Dell ® TM 681510, Dell Publishing Co., Inc.
Reprinted by arrangement with
M. Evans and Company, Inc.
New York, N.Y.
Printed in Canada.
First Dell printing—May 1969

The cultural explosion
currently rocking
the United States
is a phenomenon
unique in the long history
of the arts.

—*The New York Times*

PROLOGUE

Hopkins Towers
April 28th

Memorandum from Benjamin Hopkins
To: All Jefferson Square Board Members

As a number of you know from our telephone conversations of the past forty-eight hours, I believe we have, at long last, found the right man to direct and coordinate the artistic activities of Jefferson Square. I am pleased that so many of you concur.

Our exhaustive search convinces me that Daniel Robertson has the professional and personal qualifications necessary for the supervision of operations at the world's largest, and, we hope, most distinguished culture center. All of you who were in the city during Professor Robertson's previous trips here this past October, and again in January, have interviewed him at least once. May I urge that you who have not as yet spoken with him avail yourselves of the opportunity this week?

I would like to suggest, also, that committee chairmen hold final interviews with Professor Robertson, at your own convenience, preferably in separate meetings, at such times and places that will be mutually satisfactory. I scarcely need remind members of this board that all of us are investing large sums in Jefferson Square; this is a cultural, not a philanthropic enterprise, per se, and its success is vital to the stature and dignity of the community.

A few of you have questioned Professor Robertson's suitability for the post because he is young. I believe the presentation of culture to a popular audience is a young man's "business"; with a man in his thirties in charge, Jefferson Square will reflect the tastes of the generations for whom we are building the center.

I refer those of you who may not recall Professor Robert-

1

son's credentials to his personnel file, #14-B, and to the Confidential Investigation Report of the same number. Copies of the former are already in your possession, and copies of the latter may be obtained from my office on request.

It would be negligent of me to fail to take this opportunity to thank Chancellor Carl of Seaboard University for calling Professor Robertson to our attention.

Finally, I cannot resist adding that I have, in recent days, read portions of Robertson's much-discussed book, The Quandary. Although not qualified to discuss its literary merits, I find him the clear, incisive thinker we have needed ever since the idea of creating Jefferson Square was first conceived.

BH: el

Late afternoon sunlight still reflected on the glass and chrome cliffs of the new skyscrapers and shone less brilliantly on the older office buildings, but the financial district was almost deserted. Here and there solitary men with attaché cases headed toward taxi stands, but the hordes of pedestrians had vanished, as had the cabs and busses and private cars. For three-quarters of an hour, while the banks and brokerages, exchanges and counseling services had emptied for the night, there had been a form of organized bedlam in the streets. Secretaries and clerks and the junior executives in their conservatively-cut suits had headed for the subways like lemmings pushing toward the sea. The second wave had been smaller and, on the surface, less frantic, as the older, more substantial men had walked toward the subways, hailed taxis and gone off to garages and parking lots for their cars. But now, only a short time later, even the limousines waiting near the entrances to some of the bigger buildings were gone.

The May afternoon was warm, and Dan Robertson pushed his hat back on his head as he walked rapidly up the unexpectedly narrow street. Like so many out-of-towners, he was still surprised to discover that most streets in the financial district were narrow. Glancing at his watch, he calculated quickly: his next appointment was at the Metropolitan-National Bank in ten minutes; it was about five blocks away, so that would give him time to call Phyllis at the hotel. Provided he could find a telephone.

He moved with the long, limber strides of one who kept

himself trim with squash in the winter, tennis in the spring and fall, and swimming in the summer. At each intersection he paused to glance up and down the street, but not until he was only a block from the Metropolitan-National and saw a sign on a small side-street establishment saying *Ed's Diner*, did he feel reassured that he would be able to make his call before the meeting.

It was dingy and cramped, with a single, long counter, imitation-leather stools and a small work-area. The fluorescent lighting gave the place an antiseptic appearance, but at the same time emphasized the dirty walls and cracked plaster of the ceiling. In all, it didn't seem appropriate to the affluent financial district.

A counterman in shirtsleeves and a long, once-white apron was leaning against the refrigerator, reading a tabloid, and barely glanced up as Dan entered.

"Do you have a telephone?"

The man jerked a hand toward the far wall and resumed his reading.

Dan hurried to the instrument, fished in his pocket and was annoyed with himself when he found three quarters and a nickel. "I'm sorry to bother you, but I wonder if you could give me some change."

The counterman stared steadily at his newspaper. "Mac," he said, "I could spend my whole life making change for people, and I'd starve to death."

Dan glanced at his watch. He had six minutes before his appointment. "How much is your coffee?"

"Fifteen cents."

Dan slapped a quarter onto the counter.

The man returned his grin. "Hell, Mac, you don't have to buy the coffee." He handed Dan two dimes and a nickel.

"Drink it yourself. On me." Dan slid fifteen cents toward him, and turned to the telephone. He had called the Sheraton-Plaza so often on the many trips East he and his wife had made that there was no need to look up the number. He dialed it rapidly, and asked for Room 814.

Phyllis always sounded a trifle breathless when she answered the phone.

"It isn't official yet, honey," Dan said without preamble, "but we're in."

Endless months of interviews, investigations and delays had made her dubious. "Are you sure?"

"Only fools are positive, but I'm positive. Mr. Hopkins confirmed it this afternoon, and his public relations people got my background and took some pictures of me for a news release tomorrow." The words came out in a rush, and although he knew the details could wait, he couldn't stop talking. "Jefferson Square is still in such a remote planning stage that it doesn't have its own publicity setup yet."

There was a silence so long that he wondered whether they had been disconnected.

At last Phyllis said, "Well, the suspense is over. Congratulations, darling."

"And to you."

"I haven't done anything."

"You're as important in this deal as I am, Phyl."

"Hardly. Where are you now?"

"On my way to the Metropolitan-National for a meeting with Keeper of the Purse Emory."

"Another interview?" Phyllis sounded dismayed. "I thought you said everything was set!"

"It is. Mr. Emory is going to show me some preliminary budget figures. We haven't fixed a starting date for me yet—first, you and I will have to decide how long it will take us to move—but I gather they're going to give me some homework to keep me busy. Emory is head of the finance committee."

"I've been up in the air so many times in the past year that I'm numb. When are you coming back here?"

"I imagine it will be a couple of hours. I don't know how long I'll be tied up with Mr. Emory, and then I've got to work my way back up to the hotel. I don't trust myself on the subways yet. Finding a taxi down here is a major project. This part of town looks like the whole population was wiped out by the Black Plague."

"We'll have to celebrate tonight, darling."

"Oh, Lord. That reminds me. We're making a command dinner appearance. Mr. Hopkins is sending a car and chauffeur for us at seven forty-five."

Phyllis became panicky. "We're invited to his house?"

"He has an estate on the river, outside the city. You showed me pictures of it in one of those decorating magazines."

"I'm not sure I want to go."

4

"I'm assured it's a great honor. Or something. They don't invite many people out there."

Her panic became worse. "What will I wear, Dan?"

He glanced at his watch and saw he was due at the Metropolitan-National in two minutes. "My dime is going to run out any second. They don't allow you unlimited time on calls here."

"Do you think my silk suit is all right?"

"Honey," he said, floundering. "I don't know any more about going to a billionaire's party than you do. And I really have to get off the phone, Phyl. See you in a couple of hours."

The counterman, who had been eavesdropping openly, was smiling. "You got a new job, huh?"

"It looks that way," Dan said.

"Welcome to the meat-grinder, Mac. And good luck. In this town you'll need it."

Dan forced himself to slow his pace as he strode down the handsomely carpeted, high-ceilinged hotel corridor. His meeting had been mercifully brief, and he was returning an hour earlier than he had anticipated, which would give him ample time to shave, shower and change his clothes for dinner at the Hopkins' estate. In all probability Phyllis was taking a bath, so he had picked up a key to the room at the desk, and a feeling of exuberance took possession of him as he inserted it into the lock.

"It's just the paper boy, lady!" he called.

There was a quick rustle, a stir, and then Phyllis, clad in the short, green silk traveling robe he had bought for her the previous Christmas, fled into the bathroom.

"Hey, come out! I didn't mean to scare you!"

The lock on the bathroom door clicked, and water began to run in the basin.

"Phyllis!"

"I'll be there in a minute, Dan!" Her voice sounded muffled, and the water ran harder.

He was slightly puzzled but still excitedly happy, and, hanging his jacket in the closet, removed his necktie. Wandering back into the bedroom, he took a cigarette from a pack his wife had left on her bedside table, and noted absently that the bed was rumpled. Apparently she had been taking a nap, or at least resting, which was wise before an important evening.

The hotel room, furnished in an ostentatious adaptation of French Provincial, was enormous and expensive-looking. The Jefferson Square Board was picking up the tab, as it had on previous trips the couple had made. Exhaling slowly, Dan looked around, telling himself that henceforth they would have to force themselves to become accustomed to opulence. His income would be roughly triple what he would have earned if, some day, he had been appointed to a distinguished service chair at a major university.

The water was turned off, and the bathroom door opened. "I've known all along they'd want you, Mr. Vice-President." Phyllis came straight to him.

They embraced and kissed, giving love and taking it, while sharing this moment of quiet triumph.

Suddenly Dan realized his wife was trembling. Holding her at arm's length, he saw that her green-flecked eyes were suspiciously luminous. Her face looked as though she had been splashing it with cold water. "Is something wrong, Phyl?"

"Of course not." She turned away from him too quickly.

"What is it?"

She walked to the window and looked out at the always-busy city. "If you must know, I wasn't expecting you for another hour."

"You've been crying." The discovery shocked him.

"There's no law says a woman isn't entitled to a few private tears." She faced him again, brushing back a lock of her dark blonde hair, and forced a smile. "After all, you did doublecross me. If you'd come back when you said you would, you wouldn't have known anything about it."

Dan refused to be amused. "What's upsetting you?"

She shook her head. "It's nothing. Really."

"I've never known you to cry without very good reason."

Phyllis picked up her gold wristwatch from the bedside table and glanced at it. "Not now, Dan. We've got to get ready."

"To hell with Benjamin Hopkins, Governor Herder and everybody else I've been seeing these past couple of weeks. Now tell me what it is."

"It isn't what you're thinking." She shook a cigarette out of the pack and lighted it with a match before he could move to her with his lighter. "I think Jefferson Square is perfect for you. You'll be teaching on a grand scale, and—well, it has all the other advantages we've talked about for this past year and more. And we won't have to deny the children anything important, ever. So stop worrying. Please."

Dan planted his feet apart. "I've heard why it's going to be great for everybody in the family except Phyllis Markham Robertson."

"It's what I want, too." Again she looked at her watch, and sighed. "Oh, all right. I'll try to sum it up quickly. It's a woman's prerogative to be silly, and I was relieved. Now, take a shower, if you're going to. I've already had my bath."

"What are you relieved *of*?"

"Dan, I've scarcely dared to breathe all these months. Any amateur psychiatrist, I think, would assure you of the therapeutic value of tears under the circumstances."

"Oh, honey, for God's sake, I didn't mean—"

"Well, I hope that satisfies you. And now I really will need your advice about what to wear tonight. The very idea of having dinner with *the* Mr. and Mrs. Benjamin Hopkins absolutely petrifies me." She removed her robe, and, attired in bra and half-slip, went to the dressing table.

Dan hesitated briefly, decided not to pursue the subject for the moment and headed for the bathroom.

When he returned to the bedroom he found Phyllis standing before the dressing-table triple mirror, critically examining herself in a two-piece suit of white silk.

"Gorgeous," he said.

"I'd better explain." Phyllis spoke rapidly, still studying her reflection. "First I thought I ought to wear my basic black, and I'm still not positive I shouldn't. But then I told myself that most women probably feel just as I do when they're asked to the Hopkins' mansion. So Mrs. Hopkins must be sick of seeing guests in black. This suit is different, and if we were going anywhere else, I know I'd be safe in it. But I don't want Mrs. Hopkins to think I'm trying too hard. After all, I've never met her—"

"You're a knockout."

"No, darling—don't come near me! This suit crushes if you just look at it!"

He held his arms high over his head, then moved them behind his back. "See, Ma? No hands. Okay?"

"I haven't put on my lipstick yet. All right."

Dan kissed her, then instinctively started to reach for her. "You're breaking the rules."

"Okay, I'll be good." Reluctantly he went to the dresser.

Phyllis was examining the effect of the one pair of earrings she had brought with her.

"This is my last clean shirt with French cuffs," Dan said.

"We'll buy you some new shirts tomorrow."

Having donned the shirt, he concentrated on his efforts to insert the cufflinks. "Hold off. We're still living on a professorial pittance."

"If you put in the cufflinks before you put on the shirt, it would be much easier."

Dan nodded vaguely. The argument was an old one, and there was no point in telling her he wouldn't be able to slide his hands through the cuffs if he attached the links first. She couldn't understand, or couldn't remember, that a man's hands were bigger than a woman's and that he couldn't use her system.

"If you need shirts, you shall have them," Phyllis said. "You have a royalty payment due soon for *The Quandary*."

"Where did you learn to look so sexy putting on earrings?"

"At the movies."

"Feet wide apart, slinging one hip, head tilted. It's very provocative."

"The Hopkins' car will be here soon. So forget it."

"I'll do no such thing. But I'm willing to be patient."

"I wish you'd stop being so screamingly funny, Dan, and tell me how I look."

"I told you. Lovely." He took a necktie from the closet rack, wondered whether to reopen the subject of her tears after learning of his appointment, and decided to wait. She was calm enough now, aside from her preoccupation with her appearance, and common sense told him to leave well enough alone.

Phyllis spread a discreet amount of eye shadow on her lids, and then applied her lipstick with far more care than usual.

A tap sounded at the door.

Dan answered the summons and a bellboy handed him a cardboard box. Dan gave him a quarter.

"It's for you, honey. Looks like a gift from an unknown admirer."

Phyllis, almost finished with her primping, glanced at her husband.

"You didn't—"

"I certainly did not. I know your opinion of corsages."

The engraved card said, simply, *"Mr. and Mrs. Benjamin Hopkins III."* There was no message on it.

There was a rustle of excelsior as Phyllis opened the box, and she sucked in her breath, looking stricken. Dan peered over her shoulder and saw a huge, purple orchid.

"If I let myself cry again," she said between clenched teeth, "it will ruin my mascara."

He groped for the right remark. "It's worthy of a Hopkins. It must have cost a few bucks."

"I loathe orchids. Or gardenias. Or camellias."

"You've got to wear it, honey."

"I know." She began to pin it on, and a smile came over her face. "I'm sorry, darling. I may not sound it or act it, but I've been as eager as you to see you get the job at Jefferson Square. I guess I've just resented all the months of interviews. Here. At home. You being interviewed. Me being studied under a microscope by investment bankers or whatever they are. It's unnerved me more than I'd realized."

"It hasn't been easy," Dan said.

Phyllis began to pull on her white kid gloves. "What really bugs me is the complete invasion of our privacy. It isn't enough for them that you're competent to run their new culture center. They'd had to dig into every last detail of our lives."

"We've nothing to hide." He scooped up his change from the dresser top, and slipped his wallet into a pocket.

"Ready to go?"

"Yes. I guess I need my coat."

"I think so. It's blowing up."

"I doubt that the Hopkins' butler has ever seen a cloth coat."

"Screw the Hopkins' butler. Just say the word, Phyl, and we'll go home to stay. I mean it."

Phyllis saw that he meant it. He was ready to reopen all the old arguments. "No, we've made our decision, it was the right one, and they've had the sense to recognize your talents. Which, now that I think of it, doesn't surprise me. I've known all about you for a long time." She slipped her arm through his, her expression calm and proud now, her smile steady. "I'm ready whenever you are," she said, and they moved together toward the door.

CHAPTER ONE

"Today, at last, Jefferson Square comes alive. As we break ground for the first units of what, we are confident, will become America's foremost culture center, the future envisaged by those of us who dreamed great dreams a few short years ago begins to come true. Here, within a time span soon to be breached, will be theaters and a symphony hall, an opera house and an art museum, schools and libraries that will enrich the cultural heritage of all the people of this city and state."

Governor Albert Herder read the opening paragraph aloud, occasionally running a hand across his wavy, dark-brown hair. As he glanced through the rest of the short speech a look of distaste appeared on his ruggedly photogenic face, and he flipped the papers aside, then reached for a key on the squawk-box beside his desk.

"Eddie," he said to his executive assistant, "this ground-breaking speech is filled with clichés. Put the new speech-writer on it right away, the fella we hired away from *Time*. Tell him to stress the national significance of Jefferson Square. But I want no outright comparisons with what other cities have done. Nothing that might antagonize my out-of-state friends. And make sure he bears down on the benefits to the state's increasing urban population. The boys who wrote this draft forgot the weight the cities are pulling under reapportionment. Got me?"

"I'm ahead of you, Governor. Staley has been working on a new draft for the past hour. He's from *Newsweek*, by the way." The metallic voice that came over the speaker sounded amused.

Governor Herder frowned. "I don't give a good goddam where he's from. I'm competing with the President this noon, and I've got to have some meat in my talk if I'm going to get even a share of the headlines. I'll talk for three minutes, no

11

more, but it'll be a waste of time unless every last word is quotable. Have it ready by eleven, and I'll read it on the way out to the airport."

"The President isn't coming, Governor. I just finished talking to the White House, and was going to buzz you when you called."

"What's his reason?" Herder snapped.

"The new crisis in the Middle East."

"I'll call him."

"He's in a National Security Council meeting for the next hour or two. The White House promised me he'll call you as soon as he's free."

"Come in here." Herder flipped the switch, stood, and began to pace the length of the huge office at the second floor rear of the state's executive mansion.

He was marching rapidly when Eddie Brown, in shirt-sleeves, opened and closed the door. It was a bad sign when Al Herder paced, and Eddie, who had been with him since the beginning of his first term, when the newspapers invariably had called him "the Millionaire Amateur Politician," or "the Playboy Governor," braced himself.

"Is the President trying to pull the rug out from under me?" Herder demanded.

"No, sir." Eddie wished that once, just once, the people of the state could see their governor without his charm-boy mask. "The Middle East fuss is genuine. The Russians have issued a statement, and the White House has promised a reply from the President before noon."

"Will Jefferson Square be knocked off the front page?"

"We'll be there, but I can't promise you column eight."

Albert Herder began to walk more slowly. "We'll have our little show, with or without the President. He's such a wily bastard. I've been counting on a joint platform appearance with him today, and he knows it."

There were times when the Governor's ambitions clouded his political common sense. "It's almost two years until the convention," Eddie said, making sure no hint of patronization crept into his tone. "You can't expect the President to endorse you as his successor this early."

"No, but he can start leaning in my direction. You and I know that he promised me—well, almost promised—"

"He may have given the same half-promises to three or four others, remember. And there was that hint in Pearson's

12

column that he doesn't want to use a culture center as a political forum. When Alsop said how clever you were, maneuvering him into a corner by using Jefferson Square, it may have scared him off."

"Nothing scares the President of the United States," Herder replied coldly. "He plays the tune on his fiddle, and everybody else dances to it."

Eddie Brown watched him throw himself back into his swivel chair, and wasn't sure he looked forward to the day that Albert Herder became the fiddler. The electorate might think of him as a gracious patrician who had become an exceptionally able governor, but everyone who worked for him knew he played such a lively tune that he exhausted his dancers. "I'll go over the speech myself, sir," he said.

"Do that. This is a big day, and we've got to milk it for every ounce it will yield." Governor Herder's good humor returned, and he struck a smiling pose for an instant before returning to the state's business, piled high on his desk.

There were days when Carolyn Emory looked far less than her thirty-five years, and she wished this were one of them. Sitting before her dressing-table mirror, she dabbed at the faint smudges beneath her slate gray eyes and examined herself critically. Her sleek black hair was intact after her few hours of sleep, thanks to the nylon and steel wire cage she had put over it, and her skin, one of her best assets, always looked fresh. She shook more lotion onto the cotton pad, and dabbed more energetically at the shadows.

It was small comfort to realize that if she failed to look her best, it was her own fault. She had always known she couldn't drink, but Warren Hopkins' liqueurs had been so insidiously smooth. All the same, she had been stupid to sit in his apartment until two thirty this morning, jabbering like a finishing school undergraduate.

Jefferson Square was *her* baby, and she was sure to receive a lioness' share of the television and news photographer coverage, so she should have known better. Only yesterday the *Herald* had devoted a full-page picture story to her under the banner, "BANKER'S WIFE RAISES FORTY MILLION FOR CULTURE CENTER. *Say She's Just Getting Started.*"

So even the out-of-town news magazines and TV people would be certain to concentrate their cameras on her. Not that she was inordinately vain, Carolyn thought, sitting back on the stool and studying the effect of her ministrations. But she had become a symbol—*the* symbol—of Jefferson Square to a great many people, so it was important that she look her best.

The telephone rang again, but she paid no attention. All three lines had been going mad ever since she had dragged herself out of bed for the unvarying ritual of eating a token breakfast with Edward before he drove off to the bank, but she had told the maids to screen the calls. She had never known there were so many people who called her by her first name, so many people who wanted seats for today's ceremonies in the temporary grandstand that had been erected on the site of the future Jefferson Square Repertory Theater.

A light tap sounded at the door, and the young Swedish maid with the too-wise eyes stood on the threshold. "Mr. Hopkins is on the telephone, ma'am. I thought you'd want to talk to him."

"Thank you, Sivi." Carolyn curbed her desire to pick up the instrument and waited until the dressing-room door closed again. If good maids weren't so hard to find, she'd let Sivi go. The girl positively smirked as she closed the door.

"Warren, you're a very naughty boy." Carolyn was surprised by the softness of her own voice.

"This is an inadequate apology." Warren's laugh barely covered up his embarrassment. "You won't believe this, but I really do know when to take a lady home. I hope Edward wasn't worried."

"I looked into his room when I came in, and he was dreaming sweet dreams about interest rates and mortgages—or whatever bankers dream about." Carolyn glanced at her reflection in the mirror, and was annoyed by the positively adolescent flush that made her cheeks glow.

"Just so everything is okay."

It sometimes startled her that Warren could sound so boyish, and then she was forced to remind herself that he was only thirty. "Of course everything is okay! I can't tell you how glad I am that we finally had the chance to go over the complete architect's plans for Symphony Hall."

There was a half-beat of hesitation at the other end of the wire. "That isn't what I meant," Warren said with some difficulty.

14

"Edward is as dedicated to the whole concept of Jefferson Square as I am," Carolyn continued a shade too firmly. "And he's quite sympathetic to the idea of my working for the cause—both day and night. I'm sure he's bent your ear about it at countless directors' meetings."

Warren was relieved. "All set for this noon?"

"Unless the weather changes, I am. If I can't wear my new blue suit, I'll have to paw through everything in my wardrobe."

"You'll look wonderful in blue. I've always been especially partial to women in blue."

Carolyn's sigh was almost inaudible. "Why do you think I'm wearing it?" For an instant she hated herself. She, who had always made a fetish of truth, was prevaricating like an expert, but there was no reason to tell him that she had chosen blue because it was the color preferred by the television cameramen.

Apparently Warren thought it best to ignore her question. "I'm picking up Betsy Callison around eleven thirty," he said, speaking rapidly, "and if you'd like, I can swing around the corner from her family's house for you."

It was absurd to feel jealous of a twenty-four-year old girl, but Carolyn stiffened. "That's sweet of you, Warren, but I'll be going with Edward."

"Of course." Again he hesitated. "None of the seats for the directors have been assigned, as I understand it, so perhaps we could sit together."

"That would be nice. But I assumed you'd sit with your uncle."

"I'm not sure he's going."

"He must!" Carolyn was horrified. "The ceremonies will be a farce without him!" The Hopkins Fund had given ten million dollars for the development of Jefferson Square, pledging ten more if it were met by another foundation grant. And Carolyn had talked Benjamin Hopkins into making a personal donation of three million, the largest sum bestowed on the center by any individual.

"Nobody," Warren replied, "tells Uncle Ben what to do. I'm not saying he won't be there. But he doesn't announce his plans in advance."

"I'll call him." Carolyn's voice was strident.

"Please don't. He admires you. His contribution to the

15

square is proof of that. But he can't tolerate being managed. If you try to pressure him, I can guarantee that he won't show."

Carolyn felt a sense of challenge, and wanted to argue, but forced herself to calm down. When the *Examiner* had asked the reasons for her success as a fund raiser, she had said, "There are two necessary ingredients. A cause worth the effort and some slight knowledge of people." Now was the time to prove her understanding of human nature. Benjamin Hopkins was one of the wealthiest and most powerful men alive, and she knew, far better than any tabloid reader, that his love for privacy and secrecy was real. She had spent five weeks of clever, hard work just arranging her first interview with him. And although he didn't yet know it, she planned to ask him for another contribution of two million.

"I'll take your advice, Warren," she said. "You're a marvelous influence on me."

"Well, I don't know about that."

She could see him shifting uncomfortably, an unusually tall, ruggedly built young man with the physique of an athlete and the tastes of a dilettante, who seemed determined to remain unaware of his magnetic appeal to women.

"But," he continued, suddenly growing bolder, "I'm glad you know I'm around." Then, aware he was treading on dangerous ground, he withdrew again. "I'll be watching for you at noon."

There was a click at the other end of the line before Carolyn could reply. She continued to hold the off-white telephone in her hand for a moment before cradling it. Restless and fully conscious of the reasons she felt disturbed, she stood, throwing aside the lace-trimmed peignoir that had been one of Edward's birthday gifts to her.

She might be growing older, but her figure hadn't changed in years, which was comforting. She had always thought of herself as a trifle too hippy for bikinis, but the real reason she didn't own one was that she wasn't the bikini type. The beautiful people of the jet set could parade in the near-nude until hell froze without arousing her envy. Mrs. Edward Everett Emory, founding patroness of Jefferson Square, enjoyed maintaining an image of dignity. And the flesh beneath that image enjoyed maintaining its secrets.

Did her figure have the youthful elasticity of Betsy Callison's, though? To hell with Betsy Callison, she thought. God-

16

damit! On the day construction was to begin on Jefferson Square, one of the most important days in her life, why, instead of savoring a triumph she deserved, was she wondering whether Warren found her as desirable as Betsy Callison?

Because, she told herself quietly, she wanted to have an affair with Warren. After twelve years of monogamous living she was deliberately scheming to lure Warren into bed.

Perhaps Jefferson Square wasn't as much the core of her existence as she had been telling herself for the past few years.

Warren Hopkins walked hurriedly from the telephone, kicking viciously at a bundle of architects' sketches on the floor. The papers scattered. Then, in penance, he moved slowly around the living room of his penthouse apartment, stooping to pick them up one by one.

Times had changed, radically, since the days of Great-Grandpa, Warren Hopkins the First, whose discovery of copper in the Rocky Mountains had laid the foundations of one of the world's wealthiest family empires. According to one of his many biographers, Great-Grandpa had been known as PP, the Puritanical Prude, and even Uncle Benjamin, who had known him in childhood, had once remarked in a rare confidence that he wondered how the old man had overcome his scruples long enough to bed Great-Grandma.

Something of Great-Grandpa's attitude had lingered as a family tradition, and until now Warren had always believed it wise for a Hopkins to exercise greater caution than ordinary men. He had worn the invisible but easily distinguishable mark of the clan with pride both at Andover and Yale. But it became a burden when he realized that he would never be able to take a girl to dinner in a public place, not even once, without reading the next day that the World's Most Eligible Bachelor was hooked.

Uncle Ben had the right idea. His private life was his own, and what happened behind the barred gates of his Oyster Bay estate was strictly his business and his family's. Uncle Ben's name appeared in print only on the financial pages, and the names of his wife and four children were exclusively in the society section, where they belonged.

Warren enjoyed the company of attractive young ladies at theatrical openings, concerts and the opera. And since his devotion to Jefferson Square was by now universally recognized, it was assumed that when he escorted a girl home after a performance of *La Bohème*, he was still in pursuit of culture. This illogical notion, favored by the press, brought joy to the sharp-eyed executives of Sims and Sims, the family-controlled public relations firm that struggled to present all Hopkinses to the public as philanthropists rather than robber barons, and above all, as gentlemen.

Although Warren's relationship with Betsy Callison was far from clear in his own mind, all the society columnists were taking their marriage for granted. Unfortunately, he didn't know whether he wanted to marry her, and was in no hurry to find out. What's more, he had no idea whether she was interested in marrying him. All he knew was that by being seen with him once or twice a week, she had virtually put herself out of circulation.

To her everlasting credit, Betsy had never complained to him about the liabilities of social life with a Hopkins. Neither of them, in fact, had ever mentioned the subject. Whenever he called her for a date he carefully outlined the plans for the evening, as he had done when he had first started seeing her, and she invariably heard him out before accepting. She had expected his invitation to the Symphony Orchestra's first performance of the new Benjamin Britten work, and to the Grand Opera Company's opening, and undoubtedly would have been hurt had he not asked her.

He had a growing obligation to Betsy, in spite of the casual level on which they maintained their friendship. But now he was coldly and deliberately intending to use her.

In his undergraduate days, one of his Yale roommates had said to him, "Warren, a guy in your position ought to specialize in married women. Rich married women. They've got husbands, so they can't squeeze a marriage ceremony out of you, and they don't want the Hopkins money because they have enough of their own. The only way you'll ever have any fun is to make your play for the women who have rich husbands."

He had known long before last night that he felt strongly attracted to Carolyn Emory. But only now did he realize that she could be his whenever he reached out to take her. Just like that. He had seen it in her eyes. He heard it on the telephone.

But what of her marriage? It was impossible to think of it without being overwhelmed by guilt. If she were married to someone he didn't know, perhaps he could dismiss her husband from his mind, in spite of the family's Puritan ethic that had been drilled into him from birth.

Not even a Hopkins, however, could get rid of Edward Everett Emory with a wave of the hand. The chairman of the Metropolitan-National Bank, a close lifelong business associate of Uncle Ben's, was neither an insignificant man nor a cardboard husband. He could buy or sell virtually anyone Warren knew, with the exception of a Hopkins, and the power he commanded in financial circles, be it on Jefferson Street, Wall Street or LaSalle Street, was impressive.

On top of everything else, Warren had become well acquainted with him during their years of service together on the Jefferson Square board of directors, and liked him. And he had taken pride in the realization that he had earned Emory's respect.

Why, he asked himself, was Carolyn ripe for an affair? In spite of his limited knowledge of women, Warren felt positive she was no tramp, and she had too full a life to be suffering from boredom. On the contrary, she was the busiest person he'd ever known. And as far as he could tell, she and her husband still loved each other.

He refused to let himself become confused. Maybe his desire for Carolyn would cool. He would try to look at her dispassionately, objectively, the next time he saw her. And that, a glance at his watch revealed, would be in precisely two hours, at the ground-breaking ceremonies.

The villa nestling in the pines of the Alpes-Maritimes above Antibes had been built by a French nobleman as a castle in the thirteenth century. Thereafter it had twice been razed and thrice gutted, then saved from final destruction by an English duke, who had constructed a new villa on the site prior to the outbreak of World War I. The duke's nephew, a distinguished novelist, had occupied it during the years between the wars. For several years it had been the requisitioned dwelling and headquarters of the Gestapo chief for the Riviera, who had been assigned to "cooperate" with the government of the Vichy French. After World War II the property had been purchased by a retired drygoods merchant from Cincinnati, Ohio, whose daughter had added a swimming pool on the grounds overlooking the Mediterranean. Since then it had become, in quick succession, the property of a French automobile manufacturer, a German actress and an Italian motion picture producer, the present owner, who was absent.

Seated at a table under a striped umbrella at one side of the pool were four middle-aged men in bathing trunks engrossed in a loud, insulting game of poker. They played slowly, savoring their hands, and the good-natured invective was as important to them as the hands they held, as was the large pitcher containing a lethal rum and vodka punch.

On the far side of the pool, opposite them, a young woman with very blonde hair, sunglasses, a heavy tan and a skimpy bikini was stretched out on an air mattress, face downward. She was doing literally nothing, but an occasional, faint movement of a slender arm or long, shapely leg indicated that she was awake.

Beside her, legs crossed on a small rug, tailor-fashion, sat Jerry Solanz. His face framed in his usual thick-rimmed spectacles, he was surrounded by a clutter of his own making, which included piles of books and play manuscripts, the heavily marked shooting script of his current motion picture, the recently arrived copies of that day's Paris *Herald* and the *Rome American,* both of them open and flapping in the breeze, packs of American, English and French cigarettes, a partly consumed glass of Scotch and water, a bottle of Scotch, an ice bucket, two ashtrays and a large, leather-bound notebook, to which were clipped pens with red, green, blue and black ink.

"Maybe," Jerry said to no one in particular, "we could try Ben Jonson's *Sad Shepherd.* The second play, of course. Not the opener. It's a hell of a good love story, if you play against the corn. We push the pastoral crap, which is very solid stuff when it's done straight, and the critics will flip."

The girl made no reply, and the men continued to play poker. "Who ever heard of a play called *The Sad Shepherd?*" one of them asked scornfully.

"I did," Jerry Solanz said, and the banter at the poker table died away. "I'm making no decisions this far ahead, naturally, but I want to consider it. With loving care. Milt, I've got a copy here. Take it into Nice tomorrow morning and have it Xeroxed. Thirty copies."

Milt Nusbaum reached for his cup of iced punch. "There aren't any companies in Nice that do commercial Xeroxing, Jerry. We been through this before."

"Then fly to Paris, sweetie. Or London. Or New York. I don't give a shit where you go. But get it done." Jerry reached for a cigarette, and his voice became gentler. "With a repertory company, you've got all kinds of angles to consider. You do only plays of lasting value. Including the opener, which I'm not ready to discuss with anybody, and I mean anybody. Also, plays within the acting range of your company. Now, if I can persuade Adams to sign with me, and he'd better, because I've got him by the balls, and he'll sign if he wants to do the picture with me in Ireland this fall, he'd be a very athletic, trim Robin Hood."

Milt, having felt the master's wrath, was careful. "Honest to God? Robin Hood?"

"That's what Ben Jonson wrote about. And sweetie here will be perfect as Maid Marion." Jerry reached out and patted the rump bulging from the scanty bikini bottom.

Berenice Tolmey did not stir.

"Fred," Jerry said, "I'm going to do you a favor. You're always the *schnook* in these poker games. The boys rob you blind. So make yourself decent, sweetie. I want you to get out the station wagon and drive down to Antibes to send off some cables for me."

The lugubrious Fred Akley had been Jerry Solanz' closest associate and assistant for more than twenty years, which gave him the right to be more daring than the others. "If you'll reach three feet to your right, you'll find a telephone. France is a modern country. Cables are accepted on the phone."

Jerry removed his glasses and, rubbing the bridge of his nose, shook his head. "When I was twelve years old, my family left Prague for the United States. We spent six months in France on the way, mostly Paris, and in that time my father sent forty or fifty cables to relatives in Chicago and Cleveland. Not once could he do it on the phone. The French refused to take calls like that seriously, and in France nothing changes." His voice became more strident. "Instead of everybody arguing every time I ask a small favor, I wish that once, just once, my friends would accommodate me. Since I put food in their mouths, clothes on their backs and roofs over their heads, not to mention paying them such handsome salaries they can afford to gamble every day of their lives, I don't think I'm being unreasonable when I ask a small favor that requires little or no effort."

Fred threw his cards on the table and stood. "It always happens when I'm ahead," he muttered as he started toward the villa.

The others, saying nothing, resumed their game.

Jerry was mollified. He busied himself scribbling in the notebook, first with the green pen, then with the red, poured himself another drink and finally transferred his attention to the girl. Reaching out again, he stroked her rump. "Sweetie," he said, "you have all the natural assets—no pun intended—for stardom."

Berenice Tolmey remained inert.

He pinched her, hard.

Although she had been prepared for the gesture, she could not control a squeal of protest.

Jerry chose to interpret the sound as a sign of pleasure. "Have part of my drink," he said, "and as soon as I send Fred off with the cables, we'll go inside."

She rolled over, propping her head on a bolster-shaped airfoam pillow, but her eyes were still hidden behind her dark sunglasses.

"I want you to read some scenes from *The Sad Shepherd* for me. And we'll do that bit at the end of the picture again that we're going to reshoot next week."

Berenice's full lips, carefully enlarged by pearly lipstick, formed in a sulky pout. "We did that this morning."

The poker players were careful to hide their grins.

"An actress who wants to be a star can't rehearse enough," Jerry told her sternly. "And how many girls have the opportunity to work with Solanz?"

"I don't mind the working part, Jerry. You know that." Her voice was high, childlike.

"When I directed Helga Borg, she took sauna baths three times a day on the set. That's how she learned to relax and become a great box-office attraction. Either you trust me to know how to relax you, or you don't. Now, take this drink."

Berenice gulped the Scotch, and made no protest when he splashed more into the glass for her. "Whatever you say, Jerry," she murmured passively.

He ran a hand across her breasts. "This will be your first chance to do a Ben Jonson play. The classics offer the best discipline for stage work. Shakespeare, Sophocles, Wycherly, Sheridan, all of them."

Her face was a mask behind the sunglasses as he continued to fondle her.

Fred reappeared in sports shirt, slacks and sandals.

With his free hand Jerry reached for the notebook. "Listen to this. You, too, Milt. 'Benjamin Hopkins, Chairman of the Board, Jefferson Square. Dear Mr. Hopkins. I offer you, your fellow directors and everyone else associated with the greatest cultural venture in human history my warmest congratulations and my prayers for our mutual success on this important day in all of our lives. I am confident that together we can make a joint contribution to the arts that will enrich the American theater. My one regret is that I cannot be with you today, but I must remain on the Continent and in Ireland for the shooting of the final scenes of my new film. My inability to celebrate with you in person breaks my heart, but I am sure you realize I would be derelict in my duties if I were to leave now, with my task uncompleted!'" Still caressing Berenice, he looked at each of the men in turn. "Well?"

The younger assistants bobbed their heads.

"You lay it on awful thick," Milt said.

"Every word is sincere," Jerry retorted. "Send exactly the same wire to Daniel Robertson, Fred. I've written his name and address in red, so you won't miss it."

"Why Robertson?" Milt wanted to know.

"For Christ's sake, do I have to spell it out to you? He's Vice-President and Artistic Coordinator of Jefferson Square, that's why!"

"Since when does Jerry Solanz take orders from some boob who wouldn't know backstage from a hole in the ground?" Milt persisted.

"Since never, sweetie!" Jerry was outraged. "You've seen my contract. I have sole and exclusive authority in selecting plays, casting and producing every goddam thing that will be done at the Jefferson Square Repertory Theater. But this Robertson has big titles and a fancy salary which he'll want to earn. That's why now, when it doesn't matter, I'm buttering him up. Later, if he gets in my way, I'll kick his ass and carve his heart out. I wish to God that once, just once, I didn't have to do all the thinking around here myself!"

"Yes or no, Mother. Please. I haven't finished making up." Bettina Callison stood in the ornate living room and fidgeted.

Ethel Callison tugged absently at the waistband of her tweed skirt and refused to be rushed. "It seems to me you're wearing more than enough makeup already, dear," she protested mildly.

"Ordinarily I'd agree with you, but since I'll be sitting with Warren, I'll get into some of the television pictures, and I don't want to look all washed out."

"Warren Hopkins knows you're not an actress, Betsy."

"I'm doing this for the sake of my own ego, not what Warren thinks. I've made a concession to him wearing this blue suit. He adores blue."

"That's one of my other questions," Ethel Callison said. "Isn't that pastel too pale for May?"

"It's the only blue I have for daytime." Bettina was aggressively defensive, and her eyes seemed to become a shade lighter, matching the suit. "I meant to go shopping day before yesterday when I went downtown, but Anton Helsing was just brilliant. By the time he finished explaining the intricacies of Schumann, the stores were closed."

"That's what happens when you wait until the last minute." Ethel glanced at her watch. "Actually, you have time to run down to Saks. The model sizes always fit you, so—"

"Impossible, Mother! You know traffic is dreadful at this time of day."

Her mother sighed. "As you will, dear. You don't listen to me, anyway, so I can't imagine why you ask my advice. But I'll risk offending you, regardless. I do hope you're going to put up your hair."

Bettina flicked back a long, blonde strand. "What's wrong with it this way?"

"You look like Alice in Wonderland, which would be appropriate for going through a looking-glass, but not for one of the most important events in years. Particularly if the photographers are going to take your picture."

There was a mischievous, elfin quality that distinguished Bettina's laugh. "If you'd heard all the plans for Jefferson Square, as I have, you'd think everybody connected with it is leaping through a looking-glass. Why, they've hired no less than nine acoustical experts to advise them on the interior of Symphony Hall, and Anton Helsing told me they're going to bring in a piano for him as soon as the outer shell is built. He'll play it every day, just for the acoustical people, you see,

24

and they'll order adjustments in the interior of the hall based on their joint opinions. It's fascinating! I'm going to try to get up enough nerve to ask Mr. Helsing if I can be a mouse in the corner." Bettina started out of the room.

"There's one thing more I want to discuss with you." Ethel stopped her before she reached the door. "Your father and I are quite concerned. In fact, Daddy is very upset."

"Oh?"

"All the newspapers printed your picture with Warren at the opera opening and at the opening of *Oedipus* when the British National Theatre company was here. That's twice in a single month. And today's publicity will be national, not local. At the club the other day, Edward Emory was telling Daddy that *Look* and *Life* and heaven knows what other magazines will be there. People are talking already, and it will be far worse after today."

Bettina returned to the center of the room and sat down in a tapestry-covered chair, carefully smoothing her skirt. "What do you suggest, Mother, that I propose to Warren?"

"Don't be facetious, dear. Daddy and I like Warren immensely, but he isn't the only young man in town, you know."

"I go out with other people." Bettina suddenly sounded very young and vulnerable.

"Of course, but photographers aren't hiding behind every pillar when you do."

"I'm delighted to say. If you didn't know it, Mother, Warren hates all that publicity."

"Then I wish he'd be more considerate of you."

"Perhaps he should have asked someone else to the groundbreaking," Bettina said. "Or I could cover my face with a brown paper bag and make myself inconspicuous."

Ethel Callison ignored her daughter's sarcasm. "At the risk of sounding very old-fashioned, Daddy and I would like to know Warren's intentions."

"Why don't you ask him?"

"That's precisely what Daddy has been thinking of doing."

Betsy jumped to her feet. "I forbid it! That would ruin everything!"

"I'm sure you know your father well enough to realize he'll do nothing to embarrass you. Please sit down."

Reluctantly, slowly, the girl returned to her chair. "Don't scare the wits out of me."

"I'd still like to know something more about you and Warren. I have a right to pry, if that's what you believe I'm doing."

Betsy was silent for a moment. "We don't lose our cool," she said.

"I've never been able to interpret cryptograms."

"All right. We have fun together. He doesn't act like a half-billion dollars on the hoof, or whatever it is he's worth. As if money mattered. And I try not to behave like a spoiled post-deb. We talk about music—anyway, I do. And he talks about Jefferson Square. Sometimes we're silly for no good reason." The girl drew in her breath, sharply. "When he brings me home, he kisses me. Gorgeous kisses they are, too. But that's as far as it goes. Satisfied?"

"Not really. What do you feel about Warren?"

Betsy was silent for a long time, then raised her head defiantly. "I love him."

"I'm sorry."

"Why? It isn't a fatal disease."

"Because he doesn't seem to show signs of loving you. Or am I mistaken?"

"I'm the only girl he's taken out more than once or twice, in years. There was somebody up in Boston when he was getting his M.A. at Harvard. But she married some professor. He's mentioned her a few times, very casually, but I don't believe he's hung up over her."

"You're evading the issue, Bettina."

"No, Mother, I'm not. As of this instant, I don't think Warren loves me. Or, if he does, he doesn't realize it. He enjoys my company—and we really do have a good time together. It's obvious he likes going out with me. If he didn't, he wouldn't keep coming back for more."

"Don't under-rate yourself. You're an exceptionally attractive girl."

"Oh, I have my plus qualities and my good points, and I'm not bashful about them. But Warren isn't the kind of man who throws himself at anybody. Being a Hopkins is a terrible strain, and he can't quite forget who he is, even when he's having a ball."

"Perhaps you'd be wise to forget him, dear."

"I prefer to wait."

"For what?"

"As of right now," Bettina said, "Warren Hopkins is mar-

26

ried to Jefferson Square. When the novelty and excitement begin to wear off, he'll wake up and look around. When he does, I intend to be right there, where he can see me, touch me—and ask me to marry him."

The familiar odors of garlic, cabbage and onions suffused the halls of the cold-water tenement, seeping into apartments and hanging like tangible solids in the stale air. The city's health and sanitation codes were strictly observed: garbage cans beside the front stoop were covered, no trash littered the floors of the hallways, and the walls, recently sprayed with their monthly dose of insecticide, were streaked and glistening.

Boys playing stickball in the street were shouting, the women of the brownstone's two Puerto Rican families were indulging in their usual morning argument, and somewhere in the building a radio was blasting the obscene promises of a new laxative. But it was quiet in the parlor of the three-room flat on the top floor, and Maria Mascaroni sat in her accustomed place before the window. A heavy, shapeless woman with a face that never smiled, she stared past the tenement on the far side of the street.

"You gonna be there, Sandra, with all those rich ladies and gentlemen?" She nodded toward the bare, rubble-littered ground broken by the craters of excavated buildings, that extended for several square blocks beyond the tenements.

"No, Mama." Sandra Masters, who had found the name Mascaroni too big a mouthful in the secretarial world, stood belligerently, feet apart as she balanced her weight on her spike heels, narrow skirt pulled taut. "That's just for the people who gave money . . . and the politicians. I don't have a ticket."

"Mr. Dougherty doesn't like you any more?" The old woman did not shift her position.

"Francis X. thinks I'm the greatest—in every possible way. He can't write a brief without me, and he'd sleep with me tomorrow if I gave him the green light. Today, even. He'd skip the ground-breaking ceremonies for a little nookie with Sandy."

"How long since you went to Confession, Sandra?"

The girl raised a hand to her strawberry blonde hair. "Last month, Mama."

"You lie."

"All right. I haven't kept count. Okay?" A gold charm bracelet jangled as Sandra lit a cigarette with a heart-shaped, jeweled butane lighter.

"Not okay." The old woman continued to stare out of the dust-streaked window. "I brought you up to be a good girl."

"I'm as good as they come, for God's sake."

"Don't you swear in this house. God will punish you."

Only one answer would prevent a long sermon. "Yes, Mama." Sandra inhaled deeply and, the cigarette dangling from her lips, straightened the suede coat draped over her shoulders. "You drive me nuts, sitting at that window all day. With half the neighborhood torn down to make room for Jefferson Square, what is there to see?"

"What to see, what to see." Mrs. Mascaroni sighed.

"I'll be glad when I can get you and Buddy out of this dump."

"This is your home, Sandra!" There was hurt as well as reproof in the old woman's voice. "Eight years ago. Nineteen years old, and my little girl becomes the *signorina grandiosa*."

"I work in a law office for a lousy hundred and a quarter a week," Sandra said wearily, "and you damn well know it. Any ammunition I needed for the great big, crumbum outside world, I got right here in the neighborhood. Brother, did I!"

"It is not good for a woman to look down on her home." There was an unyielding pride in the old woman's voice.

Sandra lost patience. "It'll be a blessing when the last of these firetrap dumps is torn down."

"I live here for thirty years. From here you were born, Buddy was born. In that bed Papa died. Nobody makes me move out of my home."

"Mama, turn away from that window and look at me."

Maria Mascaroni remained hunched before the dirty glass pane.

"I typed the demolition papers myself. In another few months this whole block is coming down. This is where they're going to build the new Grand Opera House."

"Then they will have to send the cops to throw me out! In America nobody makes an old one leave her house."

"Some house. You've seen what happened on Sixth Street, Mama, and on Seventh, only they're calling it Hopkins Avenue now. If you think you or anybody else can force men like Ben Hopkins and Francis Dougherty to leave this crumbling rat-heap standing, you've got rocks in your head."

"I got rocks."

"It's sure easy to see why Buddy is an Italian mule. When he wanted a bike, he wanted it fast. He couldn't wait until I bought him one. So he's had to report to the probation office every month for almost a year. Talk about stubborn!"

"You also, Sandra, when you couldn't wait for marriage. It helped to kill Papa when you ran off with the Bonatelli boy."

"Knock it off, Mama." Sandra flushed beneath her coating of artfully applied cosmetics. "That record wore out a long time ago. Listen. Take my word or don't. I don't care what crazy ideas you're clinging to, the ninety-day eviction notices will be sent out by summer, and the whole block will come down before snow falls."

"When I leave here," Maria said dully, "I am ready to die."

"There you go with that line again. My God, you'd think there was something grand about this place. What's so special?"

"The whole neighborhood knows Mrs. Mascaroni, and I know them. The grocer, the butcher, Mr. Goldberg in the candy shop—all. For thirty years I have good friends in this building—"

"But the neighborhood is disappearing. The people you know will all be going from here."

"Mrs. Elias wants also to die. It is not the same if we must move away."

Sandra steeled herself. "Reality may be hard to grasp, Mama, but evading it isn't healthy."

The old woman looked at her for the first time, her eyes blank.

"Whether you like it or not, you're moving. I've got a wonderful little place picked out for you—"

"I will not live in the same house where you sleep with your boyfriends. Buddy will not live there, either. He is too young to see such evil."

Sandra snorted. "Buddy knows more than I've forgotten. But don't worry. You won't be at my place. I'm renting another apartment for you. Dougherty represents the owners of that big new housing development on Jackson Drive. I used my pull, and I've been guaranteed a place for you. The living room will look out on the river—"

"If I wanted to see fishing boats, it would be better I stayed in Catrone."

Sandra changed tactics. "Millions of people are going to

enjoy opera right here where we are now, Mama. *Aïda, Rigoletto, Il Trovatore*—"

"I leave those people alone. They should leave me in peace also." Maria folded her arthritic hands in her lap.

Sandra completely lost patience and muttered a curse under her breath.

Her mother's dark eyes became icy. "You tell me you earn one hundred twenty-five dollars a week. How can you afford two apartments, one for you, one for Buddy and me?"

An expression of almost animal cunning crept slowly across Sandra's face. "I've been working on a deal for a long time. And I have an idea it's going to pay off pretty soon. In a big, big way."

"You're going to work in a better job?"

"I like it fine right where I am. Jefferson Square is going to be the hottest thing in the whole country, and with Dougherty as general counsel, I'll be right in the middle of it all. I get job offers all the time, but no dice. I'm staying with Francis X."

"You have money to invest some place?" Maria persisted.

Sandra thought of lying, but changed her mind; her mother always saw through her subterfuges. "Not exactly."

"For a long time now I pray that you find the right husband—"

"That's a gasser. I value my independence too much, Mama."

Maria slapped the dining table with such force that the cheap pottery lamp at the far end teetered precariously. "A man will pay you to sleep with him. What independence is there in that?"

Sandra made no reply.

"Will he bring you happiness? This Mr. Dougherty?" the old woman asked.

Sandra grinned. "Francis X. has had ideas since the day he hired me—and so have I. The reason I went into his office in the first place is because he represents Jefferson Square. I've had to play him carefully, but everything is coming my way now. Yes, Mama, I think Mr. Dougherty brings me happiness."

"I want to live in my home," Maria Mascaroni said. "What do you want, Sandra?"

"All the glamor and excitement of being in the big leagues! Everything that Jefferson Square promises to be!" Sandra stretched out her slender hands, her long fingers with their lacquered nails curling avariciously.

The coffee that Michele Helsing sipped was as scalding as her attitude was cold. A plain woman in her mid-thirties, she achieved an attractive appearance, in part because of her impeccable, expensive taste in clothes, in part because she still had the lithe body and movements of a ballet dancer.

"Go to bed with anyone you please, but don't bring your sleeping partners under this roof. It isn't too much to demand." As always when Michele was angry, her Belgian accent became more pronounced.

Anton Helsing leaned back in his chair at the head of the mahogany dining table, carelessly fingering his closely cropped blond hair. At thirty-eight he still looked ten years younger than his age, and when he posed, as he was doing now, he bore a strong resemblance to a "graceful monument," a description in a review of one of his piano recitals that he had cherished for years. His powerful frame and strong Nordic appearance gave the impression of a collegiate quarterback, another description frequently used in magazine interviews. "There's no need to be dramatic first thing in the morning, dear," he murmured. Satisfied with the effect he had created, he delicately lopped off the top of his three and a half minute soft-boiled egg. "This is a big day, and you know how you look when you work yourself into one of your crying jags."

"Unless we reach an agreement, Anton, I'm not going to the ground-breaking with you."

An eyebrow arched, but he did not raise his head. "If it'll make you happier to feel abused and neglected, stay home."

"I won't be here, either. I'll move out—today. And I'll take the Little Genius with me."

"You'll remove my son over my dead, broken and bleeding body!"

Michele's voice remained low. "I won't permit you to corrupt him."

"You've got to be kidding. I love him as much as you do. More, I think. And I'll do anything to give him a more secure life than his parents have had. No matter what you may think of me, I don't go around corrupting four-year-old babies, regardless of whether one of them is a stranger or my own son."

"The atmosphere in this house is corrupting," she said.

Anton sprinkled salt onto his egg. "If you want to leave me, for whatever your real reasons, get out. But don't hand me double-talk."

"I've been more tolerant than most. I've closed my eyes to your affairs with the pretty boys. But when you start bringing them here, into a room next to mine, I've got to draw the line."

His smile was sardonic. "You knew long before I married you that I'm wired for sound both ways. As a matter of fact, the first time we met, after I'd written the score for *The Bucolics*, and you were hired as our choreographer, I was living with that kid—what's his name—Billy something or other. And I was making no secret of it."

"Agreed," she said. "I'll even go a step farther. I'd been hearing for a long time that you were queer, and I was surprised to discover you like women, too."

"Life is just full of little surprises, isn't it? Now, I hope, you'll shut up! We've raked over the past, and you have all your self-righteous jealousies out of your system."

"I've never been jealous of your queens!"

His smile broadened, but he made no reply.

"I mean it, Anton!"

He held up a hand to silence her, looking like a conductor demanding *pianissimo* from his brass section. "I'm rarely at my best in the morning, but you'll inspire me. The best way to take care of this problem is the simplest. Finish your coffee and let's go upstairs."

Michele made no move.

"We don't have all day. Two of the networks are carrying the ground-breaking, so it'll begin at twelve sharp."

"This is one time we don't find the answers in bed. Either you accept my terms, or we'll pack it in."

"You're making a tacit admission that you're afraid of my love-making."

She smiled. "If you're going to become technical, I usually make love to you."

The blow struck home. "You're a genuine, one hundred percent bitch."

"So you've told me, often."

"Apparently we've got to put the record straight, even though these sessions exhaust me, and I'm giving the Jefferson Square dedication concert tonight." His breakfast forgotten, he jabbed a forefinger at her. "It was you who married me—"

"Oh, come on! It was mutual, Anton! You were afraid the public would start hearing rumors about you, so you wanted a wife and children to give you respectability."

He paid no attention to the comment. "You, my dear, knew I was going to the top, and that your own talents as a choreographer were limited—"

"I was first-rate."

"In musical comedy, maybe. But you couldn't stage *Swan Lake*. I have no intention of hassling over the point, however. Any time you want to prove me wrong, I'll not only get the Jefferson Square Ballet Company for you, but you can make up your own program. And I'll put the Symphony Orchestra at your disposal. Fair enough?"

"You know I'm rusty, that I haven't worked in more than seven years."

"Precisely, my dear. You retired to become Mrs. Anton Helsing. Through no effort of your own, you're sitting at the top of the ant-hill."

"Maybe you call it no effort. But I've never worked this hard."

He shrugged. "Nobody gets anything free. When I was little, living in that North Side tenement—"

"Spare me another recital of your life story, angel. I know every word of it."

Anton glanced at his gold watch with diamond hands, her Christmas gift to him. "I've got to shave, shower and run through the score of tonight's concert at least once before the ground-breaking."

"Will you or won't you agree not to have your affairs in this house?"

"Will you or won't you," he said in the same tone, "be good enough to tell me where to have them? Wouldn't the press just love to catch me checking into a mid-town flea bag! Besides, in a seventeen room duplex you can hardly complain about being crowded."

"I simply can't understand," Michele said, "why you reduce yourself to the lowest level of vulgarity whenever we quarrel."

"The great lady."

"I have no idea where you can go with them. My mind isn't attuned to such things. But, if you insist, I'll try to think of a place."

"Lovely! And until you do—"

"Until I do, no tricks. I hope you haven't forgotten that Broussard is still in town."

"What's that supposed to mean?"

"Figure it out for yourself."

"If I must. Henri Broussard is a meat-and-potatoes conductor. He did well enough with the orchestra in the old days, and the board retired him with charm. And dignity. He'll spend his declining years leading a band in some European *kursaal,* which is just his speed. What does he have to do with me?"

"I'll spell it out for you. You'll accept my terms, Anton, because I hold the high trumps. Some of the board, and a great many subscribers, were very unhappy when you were hired to replace Broussard. It wouldn't take much of a spark to ignite a campaign to get him back."

Anton laughed derisively. "There's no place for the senile in Jefferson Square. Broussard never did anything more modern than early Sibelius."

"I wouldn't have to go into court." Michele's calm had become maddening. "The threat would be enough. I'd ask Francis Dougherty to represent me, and I'd tell him I wanted a divorce on the grounds that my husband was a homosexual. The orchestra board would have a fit, and the Jefferson Square Board, the people who really make the final decisions, would dump you overnight. They couldn't afford to let a nasty scandal jeopardize a project that's going to cost more—the Lord in his wisdom alone knows how much more—than one hundred million dollars before the place is finished. And if you think I don't mean it, that I'm bluffing, just try me, angel."

Even when Francis Xavier Dougherty was in a happy frame of mind, his mannerisms and speech were those of a gutter fighter. When he was upset, as he was now, his whole face became florid, from the tip of his jutting chin to his gray-fringed, high forehead. He stood in the carpeted room high in Hopkins Towers, pounding a hard fist into the open palm of his other hand, and, as always, he shouted.

"Laws are made to be changed, and rules are made to be broken!"

Herbert Brookes, executive assistant to Benjamin Hopkins, was relieved that the room was cushioned with sound-proofing. He literally couldn't remember an occasion during his

34

thirty-year tenure with the Hopkins interests when anyone had raised his voice this close to the inner sanctum. "I've seen many rules broken, Mr. Dougherty, but none of them were made by Mr. Hopkins."

"I won't ask what he's doing. There's more secrecy here than there is in the War Room at the Pentagon. But the man can't be that inaccessible! I tried for an hour to reach him on the phone this morning after I got your message—"

"I know, and I'm sorry—"

"To hell with that. All I ask is that somebody tell Ben Hopkins I'm here!" Dougherty was becoming apoplectic.

"His secretary assures me that he knows. He'd see you if he could, Mr. Dougherty—"

"I can't believe that. No man, not even a Hopkins, is ever that busy."

Brookes spread his hand in a gesture that was both a plea and a flat rejection of the request.

"I don't know how much voice Ben Hopkins had in my appointment as general counsel for Jefferson Square," Dougherty continued, breathing hard, "but he sure as hell had to give his approval. Which means that he places some trust in my judgments. It's essential that he be present at the groundbreaking ceremonies! The whole country expects it. He's the biggest contributor, personally and through the fund. People all over the country, tens of millions of them, are dying for a glimpse of him. He—"

"Mr. Sims spent ten minutes with him this morning, Mr. Dougherty, presenting the public relations point of view. But Mr. Hopkins had made up his mind, and saw no reason to change it."

Dougherty hooked his thumbs into the pockets of his conservative, handsomely tailored vest. "Nevertheless, you think I'm right. He ought to be there."

"Mr. Hopkins pays me handsomely to carry out his orders, not to think for him."

"But you do agree with me." Dougherty was a sleek mongrel who refused to release a bone.

"I do, but Mr. Hopkins has his own long-range approach to every question."

"I'm thinking in long-range terms, too, for Christ's sake!" Dougherty raised his voice again. "You don't light matches in a barrel of gunpowder!"

"Mr. Hopkins never appears in public," Brookes said

quietly. "His father and grandfather followed the same rule, you know. He's aware of the importance of Jefferson Square to the community—to the entire country—but he feels that if he lets down the bars once, he'll be forced to make other exceptions. The House of Hopkins has always believed very strongly in tradition."

"There will be six United States senators, four governors and more congressmen than you can count at the ground-breaking. I understand the President was jammed up in Washington, but it wouldn't surprise me if the Vice-President shows up. Politicians are thin-skinned, Mr. Brookes. You know it as well as I do. Every last one of them is going to be convinced that Ben Hopkins snubbed him, personally."

"Mr. Hopkins has made several appearances before the Senate Finance Committee under subpoena, but the meetings were closed."

"That's hogwash. I'm not talking about appearances before Congressional committees, and you know it! It's my job to see that Jefferson Square avoids trouble. We don't deliberately court it."

"I respect your opinion, Mr. Dougherty. But my own hands are tied."

"When I was a boy up on Fourth Street," Dougherty said, "there was a gang that hung out near a little cigar store. They were laying for me, and I walked about three blocks out of my way every day to avoid them. One day I got tired of ducking, so I went straight past the cigar store. What a scrap that was!"

Brookes' smile was polite.

"From that time on, I walked wherever I pleased. Would you give Hopkins—Mr. Hopkins—that message?"

Daniel Robertson cleaned his glasses and wandered aimlessly around the kitchen, debating. Finally he called, "Phyllis!"

Phyllis Robertson looked around the side of the archway that led into the apartment's "utility dining area," and laughed. "Not again, darling!"

"Where do you keep the low-calorie bread?"

"Second drawer of the refrigerator. Dan, this is your third breakfast today."

"That's why I want the low-calorie bread. I keep remembering that funny little guy in the Anthropology Department when we were at State—I can't remember his name. He was always threatening to write a thesis on the Inevitability of the Development of Pots by Corporation Vice-Presidents. I've got to prove that his reasoning was unscientific."

"If you don't stop prowling around the house you'll make me even more nervous than I am, Dan."

"Honey, all you've got to do is look beautiful. Which you do, even with that hardware sticking out of your hair." Dan put two slices of bread into the toaster. "There's plenty of coffee left if you want another cup."

"I couldn't. You should be getting ready, Dan."

"This lush living has made you forgetful, Phyllis. When I was teaching an eight o'clock class I was able to shoot out the door three minutes after my legs went from horizontal to vertical."

"But you're not a professor at Great Lakes University any more."

"Careful. I nearly smeared butter on your hair."

She hugged him, giggling. "You've got to wear your new two hundred and seventy dollar suit, and the tie I bought you to go with it. The Vice-President and Artistic Coordinator of Jefferson Square must look the part."

"Yeah." His voice sounded unexpectedly flat.

Phyllis stood back to look at him, a flicker of surprise in her green-flecked eyes. "Nervous, darling?"

"A little, I suppose. Making a speech for live national coverage isn't the same as those interviews I suffered through after the book came out. But it's only for three minutes, so I'll survive."

"Imagine Dan Robertson showing stage fright."

He put his second slice of toast on his plate, untouched. "You're wrong, honey. I'm just wondering if we made a mistake, coming to Jefferson Square."

"Dan!"

"I know, Phyllis. We enjoy the pace of big city life. I won't even drag you into this. *I* enjoy it. *I* like associating with bank presidents and people like Anton Helsing. I get a tremendous kick out of eating lunch in Benjamin Hopkins' private dining room. This is more than the taste of celebrity living we had when the book was published. The kids have advantages I couldn't have given them, ever, on an academician's salary. I can cite all the reasons we ought to be glad we're here."

She became increasingly puzzled.

"We made a list when I got the offer, remember? Every last reason is valid. We didn't exaggerate, we didn't fool ourselves. To top it off, I have the opportunity to do more twenty-four-carat gold-plated teaching of the humanities to people in a year than I could have accomplished in a lifetime at Great Lakes or any other university. All the same, I wish we were back there."

She saw his hand tremble slightly as he lit a cigarette. "Dan, we agreed that if the pressures were too great, we'd go back."

"It isn't a matter of pressures. I take that back. Jefferson Square is one enormous pressure cooker, and I'm the guy in the steam bath." He stalked out of the kitchen.

It was one of Phyllis Robertson's clichés that she had known her husband better than he knew himself, and that she had recognized her clairvoyance when they had been undergraduates. But now, as of this moment, with both of them thirty-four years of age, she wondered if he had become a stranger.

She found him in their bedroom attaching his tie-clasp to his shirt.

"What's wrong, Dan?"

"Later. I don't want to spoil the fireworks and fandango for you."

"Now," she said firmly.

"Okay. Here's the lecture. Jefferson Square is the culture center that will make all other culture centers look like second-rate carnivals. The only orchestra in the United States in a class with the Philharmonic, and with Bernstein retiring, Helsing will be the biggest drawing card in the country. The one and only Jerry Solanz to direct the Repertory. Max de Groot is signing the finest singers on earth for the Grand Opera Company—excluding Helena Godoy who won't speak to him. The Museum of Fine Arts will be one of the most important in the country. Our library of four and a half million books on the arts will make Jefferson Square the mecca of every scholar and student in the humanities. The Ballet Company—"

"Please, Dan."

"If I'm telling it, let me do it. At yesterday's board meeting it was decided that we'll have to spend one hundred and fifty million, at least, before we're done. Stone for stone, marble block for marble block, Jefferson Square will cost at least twelve million more than Lincoln Center. We'll win the prize for one-upmanship."

"You're not being funny."

"Okay." Dan dug his hands into his trouser pockets. "Phyllis, I think I'm going crazy. You may have to send me away. Jefferson Square can erupt in an explosion bigger than the most active volcano in the world can produce. I've discovered something so—so staggering—that I can bring down the whole house of marble and stone and high hopes. I'm not being melodramatic. Or maybe I am. All I know is that I'm in a position to destroy Jefferson Square—and I think that maybe I should!"

The tall, blonde hooker with the almost masculine figure started up the stairs at the rear of the café-bar, her customer close behind her. Manuel Rios watched them, and, unable to resist the temptation, played a few bars of the "Wedding March" on the piano. If he'd been quicker, he could have had the man himself, and should have made a play for him. Manuel almost always knew when a customer in the dump was wired to both AC and DC.

God knows he needed the cash, he thought as he pounded out a medley of show tunes. He hadn't been paid in two weeks, virtually all of the tourists wanted the girls, and he knew it had been a mistake to take the job, to come to Miami in the first place.

Several burly men walked in the front door, the girls at the bar smiled at them, and Manuel, still playing the piano with nimble, slender fingers, looked up, too. Then, suddenly, he froze. One of the men was showing a badge, and the goddam joint, obviously, was being closed.

Manuel had every right to be bitter, he told himself angrily as, a quarter of an hour later, he wandered aimlessly through the half-deserted streets of the city. The early morning air was damp, and the suitcase holding his few belongings felt heavier than it was. But it was too late to curse himself for his bad judgment in taking a job at a place where the patrons wanted women rather than what he had to offer. He was almost broke, and couldn't afford to feel sorry for himself. This was a time when he needed his wits.

His legs ached and, bone-weary, he was grateful when he caught sight of a small city park ahead. The bums had been

39

chased off the benches, so the place was deserted, and Manuel sank gratefully onto the nearest seat, buttoning his sleazy sports shirt at the throat to ward off the chill.

Manuel half-dozed, but the rosy glow of daybreak jarred him awake, and he reached listlessly for the newspaper on the bench beside him. There was no point in looking at the want ads; he was sick of Miami.

Dully, only half-reading, he scanned the headlines, then became more alert as a name jumped out at him: Anton Helsing.

Helsing, it appeared, was going to become director of the symphony at the huge, projected cultural center, Jefferson Square.

Manuel, wide awake now, examined the article more carefully, reading slowly because he still couldn't make out English too easily. There were other names in the piece that aroused his interest, too. Governor Albert Herder, the man who wanted to become President of the United States. Warren Hopkins, the richest and most eligible young bachelor in America.

Reaching into his pocket for his purse, Manuel carefully counted his money. He had enough to take him North, buy a few meals, and with luck, rent a room for a few days. Prompted by desperation, he made an immediate decision, and started off toward the bus station. His mood was so grim that he forgot to walk with the mincing gait that his clients found attractive, and he concentrated on his destination, Jefferson Square.

CONSTRUCTION WORK STARTS ON JEFFERSON SQUARE

Ceremonies Attended by
Dignitaries and Crowd
of Fifteen Thousand
Governor Herder Hails
Start of Vast Project;
First Units Will Be
Completed in 2 Years

"Jefferson Square will be the cultural magnet for our city, the state, the nation and the world." With these words Governor Albert Herder today dug the first ceremonial scoop of

earth with a twenty-two karat gold spade at the Fourth Street site of what is expected to become the largest and most ambitious culture center project ever built.

In a nationally televised address seen and heard by millions of viewers as well as by an on-the-spot crowd of public officials, dignitaries from the financial world and celebrities from the arts, the Governor declared, "Everywhere there is a growing demand for culture centers. Jefferson Square will lead the way for the American people."

The same theme was stressed by Daniel Robertson, Vice-President and Artistic Coordinator of the project, who said, "We live in an era in which people are finding themselves with more and more leisure time on their hands. They are demanding something more than frivolous entertainment to occupy that time. We at Jefferson Square pledge ourselves to the provision of 'entertainment with a purpose.'" Robertson, a former Professor of the Humanities at Great Lakes University, is the author of a controversial book on the war in Vietnam that created a sensation a few years ago.

As anticipated, the crowd favorites were the noted performing artists who have become associated with Jefferson Square. Drawing the greatest applause was Anton Helsing, recently appointed musical director and conductor of the Symphony Orchestra, the controversial, brilliant conductor-composer, who was engaged when Henri Broussard retired after a twenty-three year career with the orchestra.

Also creating a stir were Grand Opera Company singers Emilio Tatti, tenor, and Edith Whiteside, soprano, who sang the National Anthem. Another in the spotlight was Walter F. Knowland, portrait and landscape painter, some of whose works have already been purchased by the Jefferson Square Museum of Fine Arts for a sum reputedly in excess of one million dollars.

Sharing honors with the artists was Mrs. Edward Everett Emory, wife of the chairman of the Metropolitan-National Bank, who was escorted by her husband.

To the surprise of no one who knows him, Benjamin Hopkins was not present. Mr. Hopkins, head of the far-flung Hopkins interests, philanthropist and board chairman of Jefferson Square, is believed to be the largest single contributor to the project. Personally and through the Hopkins Fund he is believed to have given approximately twenty-five million dollars to date.

In spite of the vital part he is playing in the development of Jefferson Square, Mr. Hopkins followed the precedents set by his grandfather and father, and distinguished himself by his absence. A spokesman for the Hopkins enterprises refused comment when asked why the "Santa Claus of Jefferson Square," as he has been called, was not in attendance.

By mid-afternoon the contractors were hard at work digging the foundations for the Jefferson Square Symphony Hall and the Repertory Theater, the first two units of the project. The Examiner *has learned from authoritative but unofficial sources that the former, according to present budget estimates, will cost something in excess of $17,200,000; the Repertory Theater will cost in the neighborhood of $9,400,000.*

Although more than $2,500,000 in federal, state and local government funds have been used for the purchase of land for the site of Jefferson Square, a sum estimated as forty percent of the total real estate cost, private capital alone is providing for the construction of the Grand Opera House and Repertory Theater.

CHAPTER TWO

Sandra Masters shuffled the papers in her lap. "Here's the brief for *Benson vs. Martin*," she said, "but Mr. Edelman says not to file it until he talks to you. He'll call you as soon as he gets out of court. I have most of the revised architect's agreements for the Jefferson Square Grand Opera House, but there's no sense in giving them to you until the rest come in. Dorothy has promised me I'll have them tomorrow, and I've already notified Mr. Brookes in Mr. Hopkins' office."

Francis Dougherty leaned back in his swivel chair, and stared across his desk at her legs. "Are you being particularly efficient today, or am I hung over, Sandy?"

"I'm always efficient, and you're hung over."

"Champagne always does this to me. What a party after the dedication concert last night."

"I read about it in today's papers. It sounded very elegant." Sandra tried to hide her wistful feeling.

"It was a blast." Dougherty chuckled. "That Helsing may be a fag, but he's all right. I don't know how he does with other liquor, but he can sure hold his champagne." He belched without bothering to raise his hand to his mouth.

Sandra returned to the documents. "Dave has worked out the details of Mrs. Chalmers' divorce settlement, but I thought you'd want to check it before he calls her in. I have all the financial newspaper clippings on the steel litigation—"

"Enough." Dougherty held up a hand. "Just leave everything, and I'll go over the pile later."

She deposited the papers on one side of the oversized desk, and stood.

"What I'd like to do is knock off early tonight, have a few drinks and a good dinner, and stay in town. I don't think I can face that goddam suburban train again."

She was aware of every body line revealed by her snug

skirt of light-weight wool and matching sweater. "Shall I call Mrs. Dougherty?"

"I'll tell her, if I should decide to stay."

She knew what was coming, and was prepared. "You're the boss," she said lightly. "If that's what you want to do, do it."

"With you."

She returned to her seat, and they looked at each other, neither willing to yield.

"You're not surprised," Dougherty said.

Sandra's smile was enigmatic.

"How does it sound?"

"It depends."

"Either you're busy tonight, or you're not. Either you'll go to dinner with me, or you won't."

"As I said," she replied coolly, sure she was in control, "it depends. I've always made it a rule not to mix business and social life."

"This has nothing to do with your job. You're the best damn secretary I've ever had, and good legal help is almost impossible to find."

She let her skirt ride high above her knees as she crossed her legs, and knew she had scored when his gaze lingered on her thighs. "I'd enjoy it very much," she said demurely, "but I hope you aren't thinking of Kelly's Steak House. I've been there at least once a week lately."

"You name the place."

She hesitated for a fraction of a second. "The Sapphire Room?" The city's most elegant and chic restaurant, located on the top two floors of Hopkins Towers, was the gathering place of the wealthy and talented responsible for the destinies of Jefferson Square.

Dougherty quickly weighed the risks. He would see friends and business associates at the Sapphire Room, all of them acquainted with his wife, but he knew enough about most of them to hang them, too. And if Ann heard rumors, he had the perfect cover story. She had heard him complain of his work burden for months, so it would be only natural for him to take Sandra to dinner for a business discussion.

"Why not?" he replied.

"I can't go there in this outfit. I'll need time to go home and change."

"Leave whenever you like, and I'll pick you up."

"Oh, there's no need for that when you have so much to do," Sandra replied, indicating the pile of documents. "I can meet you there."

He appreciated the evasion and grinned wryly. She had been elusive for months, rejecting his tentative invitations, and even though she had accepted now, it was plain she wasn't changing her tactics.

She became the efficient secretary again. "Shall I call and ask them to hold a table for you—at seven thirty?"

"Sure. But meet me in the Cloud Bar at six forty-five. I can't wait longer than that. For a drink."

The rigidly unalterable seating arrangements in the Sapphire Room had been the subject of an analytical article in *Our Town,* and regular patrons had agreed with the magazine's findings. Tables were placed on three tiers, the lowest of them directly beneath the chandelier that, at Benjamin Hopkins' personal order, had been copied from an eighteenth-century piece in the Vienna palace of Prince Eugene of Savoy. On this level sat the tourists, out-of-towners who could afford the outrageous prices, and were rewarded in return by the superb view from the eighty-first and eighty-second stories of "the world's highest skyscraper restaurant."

On the second tier, far enough from the chandelier to be spared its glare, yet close enough to be seen in its light, sat the world's famous and notorious, all of them with bulging investment portfolios. Unaware of those "below the salt," as *Our Town* had put it, they cavorted, toyed with the rich food, drank to excess with monotonous regularity and table-hopped. They, even more than the spectacular view, made it necessary for ordinary citizens to reserve tables two to three days in advance.

The third tier was small, occupying just one section of the room, and those who dined there could see only the skyscrapers south of Hopkins Tower, and, if they strained, the ships of many nations berthed in the river. It was difficult, too, to hear the string quartet that specialized in "dinner music."

But there were benefits, conferred by a maitre d'hotel who earned a salary of more than thirty thousand dollars per year because of his unerring eye.

Diners relaxed on cushioned banquettes finished in royal, purple velvet, instead of teetering on spindly chairs lacquered in gold and black. The service was slower, which the third-tier clientele did not resent, being in no hurry, and always was discreet. "The top level," *Our Town* had said, "is known to employees as Honeymoon Lane, but most of the couples who snuggle there are not married, at least to each other."

Sandra Masters and Francis X. Dougherty enjoyed the privacy of a table on the top level. The lawyer, having taken careful note of the people he wanted to avoid, was devoting his full attention to his companion. Sandra, although ostensibly returning his interest, was losing no detail of the scene she had previously been privileged to observe only from the dubious vantage point of the lowest tier.

Certainly she looked like a Sapphire Room regular, having planned for the occasion far in advance. Her red hair, supplemented by a hair-piece, was smartly styled. Her makeup was subdued, as was her simple black tent dress, which somehow called more attention to her provocative figure than a tight sheath. She wore no jewelry, and, after much deliberation, she had replaced her customary four-inch pumps with a pair of shoes that were more in keeping with current fashion.

Several martinis had preceded dinner, there had been two wines with the meal, and now, sipping her second stinger, Sandra knew she'd had more than enough to drink. But she was still in command of herself, and if Dougherty was trying to get her stoned, he had a long night's work ahead of him. A girl who had learned to handle boilermakers while still a teen-aged slum dweller knew her capacity, and rarely allowed herself the luxury of going beyond it.

While they chatted Dougherty casually let his hand touch her knee, and she pretended to be unaware of its presence there. She guessed he would become active in five minutes, and timed him on the roof clock of the Metropolitan-National Bank Building, which she could see through the huge window just beyond him. It amused her when his fingers began to move after four and one-half minutes.

When Dougherty's hand slid to her inner thigh, she reached for the package of cigarettes she had been careful to place at the far corner of the table, and in so doing moved away from him. He made a point of lighting the cigarette with a wooden match made in the shape of Hopkins Tower, and when his hand began to move toward her knee again, he discovered that it was beyond his reach.

Francis Dougherty knew women as well as he knew the

law, and was annoyed. This one had been flirting with him for the better part of three hours tonight, not to mention the innumerable poses she had struck for his benefit in the office, and if she thought he would be content to do no more than look at her, she would soon discover her error.

"I can't figure you," he said. He knew damn well he could figure her. But it was a good ploy. It occurred to him to frown.

Sandra made an attempt at dialogue. "Don't tell me I'm mysterious," she said. And then, thinking it an effective gesture, she took his hand in hers.

He stirred. Maybe she was more than a cock teaser, which is what he had thought for months. "You can hold your own with any woman in this room, but you seem content with a law office job. How come?"

"For one thing, I like to eat regularly. But a job doesn't mean I have no other ambitions or plans."

"I'd like to hear about them. I'll order a couple more stingers—"

"No more to drink for me just now, thanks. You go ahead."

"I'll wait for you. And I'm listening."

The pressure of her hand increased very slightly. "Maybe some people can talk about private matters in a place like this, but I'm not used to it." Her tone was flat, allowing him to interpret the remark as coy, facetious or leading, as he wished.

"Then let's get out of here," Dougherty said. "You got any place in mind?"

Sandra's hesitation was unintentionally stimulating. "I've got to be honest with you. This is a little awkward for both of us. If you were anybody but my boss, I'd ask you up to my apartment for a drink. But I wouldn't want you to get any wrong ideas."

"Not a chance. My ideas are sound and solid. And for right now we'll pretend I'm not your boss. How's that?"

"For right now," she said, promising herself they would return to the subject far sooner than he realized. She slid away from him, placing both her forearms on the table, freeing him to take care of the check.

Sandra's apartment, located a short distance from the heart of the downtown business district, consisted of a single, large room furnished in a quiet, modern-functional style, a pull-

47

man kitchen and a bath. She snapped on the light, knowing that Dougherty, who had kissed her once in the taxi, would reach for her as soon as he closed the door behind them. He did not disappoint her.

The agility that came with long practice enabled her to free herself effortlessly, leaving him holding her coat.

The irritated Dougherty started to protest.

Before he could say very much, however, Sandra came to him and wrapped her arms around his neck, her lips parting to receive his kiss. She pressed against him as his grip tightened, and was surprised by the strength of his arms. For someone in his late forties or early fifties who spent most of his waking hours at a desk he had great physical power.

He released her momentarily in order to get a better grip, and Sandra immediately slipped away from him. "Would you fix some drinks, please?" She could hear a faint tremor in her own voice.

"Okay." Dougherty sounded hoarse.

"There's a bottle of Scotch in the cabinet over the sink, and there's ice in the usual place." She took her handbag with her into the bathroom, leaving the door open, and began to repair her mouth makeup with a lipstick and brush.

Dougherty's hands were shaking as he mixed the drinks. He was on the verge of something. What was it? Making love to a new woman? Hell, no. He'd made love to a hundred new women since his marriage. Love, or the pretense of it, never made his hands shake. It brought out the savoir-faire; the best performance he was capable of. He made love like a man of distinction; like a Molnar hero. Or so he imagined. That was the fun of it. The performance. And, because it was usually a performance, the deep-down hunger was left unappeased. That was it. With Sandra there would be no performance. It would be like . . . like the old neighborhood.

When she emerged from the bathroom after spending several minutes rearranging her hair, two glasses of Scotch-on-rocks were waiting on the coffee table in front of the divan that turned into a bed.

"Do you mind some music?" she asked.

Dougherty shrugged. He sat on the divan watching her as she went to a record player across the room. Her wiggle was far more pronounced than it had ever been in the office. A real piece of ass . . . like the old neighborhood. He was

48

getting excited. It was like his first time out. A tough kid getting laid. He waited restlessly.

The barely audible strains of the opening bars of the *Bolero* emerged from the player as Sandra recrossed the room, picked up a glass and deliberately seated herself in a chair at right angles to the divan.

"That isn't very friendly," he said.

Her smile was innocent. "You asked me if I'm satisfied with my life. Don't you want to hear my answer?"

Sandra raised a rounded, plucked eyebrow.

"Baby," he said, "you and I come from the same part of town, so let's talk our language. We're the same kind of people."

You bet your sweet life we are, she thought, and I can read every dirty thought in your goddam head. I know what you want, Mr. Dougherty. I've been in alleys and hallways and gang basements, too.

Sandra held her glass in both hands, and shuddered at the first sip of her drink. "You've come a lot farther from Fourth Street than I have. You've got it made, but I'm still on the way up, and I haven't gone very far."

"If you think you can quit your job while I support you, you're wrong." His voice was rough.

"Guess again," Sandra said calmly.

He stared at her.

"My work is my lifeline. I'm not dependent on anybody, and if I'm not working for you, it'll be for somebody else. What's more, I'm damned good at it."

He acknowledged the assertion with a cautious, grudging nod.

"I wouldn't live the dog's life of a kept woman for anything in this world. Just the idea of groveling and taking orders from a man makes me sick."

"Okay, now we know what you won't do." He swallowed a large part of his drink, his eyes narrowed as he studied her.

Sandra sipped again. "We also know what I *will* do."

He felt a jab of increased nervous excitement. There was a silence between them, and then Sandra said, "I want to be part of Jefferson Square. I—I want to make the scene, Francis. Do you know what I mean?" Her voice was pathetic. Now that she'd said it, she realized that she herself had no idea what she meant.

She stood up then, unzipped her dress and dropped it to the floor.

What he saw was breasts in a brassiere, thighs set off by brief black panties and a garter belt, sleek black stockings, a belly just round enough, and, when she turned, cheeks of a behind that refused to be modest. Finally he assembled the parts and acknowledged the wholeness of the better than naked girl.

"Sit," he said, indicating his lap.

She knew everything that would happen next. The way he would unhook her brassiere as though it were some brilliant and dangerous bit of espionage; the way he would locate her clitoris as though he knew some stunning secret unreported to the rest of the world; the way he would crudely force her thighs apart and touch her to the point of discomfort while watching her face for evidence of being wildly stimulated; the way he would throw her on the floor and fall on top of her; and finally his exhausted triumph. Hey, gang! Dougherty got laid.

"Score," she said under her breath when it was over.

"What?" Dougherty asked.

"I said, you're good, Francis. Even better than I imagined."

"Oh. You're not bad either, baby. And remember, this is just the beginning."

"I'll remember if you do. Remember what I want, Francis."

If he kept his word to her, the doors of Jefferson Square soon would swing open. Still, she wondered whether she had made a bad bargain. She would have to submit to him again, whenever he pleased. Was admission into the world of Jefferson Square quite worth the price of being raped frequently?

"Our basic situation is sound, so I don't want to take an alarmist approach to the problem." Edward Everett Emory looked down the polished oak table in the Metropolitan-National board room at his colleagues on the Jefferson Square finance committee. A tall, ponderously solemn man in his late forties, he glanced in turn at each of the other ponderously solemn bankers, industrialists and financial counselors. "All of us have heard that philanthropy suffers when money is tight. We must prove the truism false."

The executive Vice-President of the city's largest investment banking firm cleared his throat. "Edward," he said, "with all due respect to the budget-makers, I don't understand why the figures go up every few months. We've got to establish a firm ceiling and hold it."

Emory ran a hand across the crown of his bald head, adjusted his steel-rimmed spectacles on the bridge of his nose and smiled. "We can't apply ordinary budget-making standards to Jefferson Square, Howard. That's the crux of our problem."

"I don't see why we can't! My wife and I give regularly to St. Vincent's Hospital, and the general administrator there not only predicts his deficits six months to a year ahead, but rarely varies from them by more than a few thousand dollars."

"A new culture center has its own *modus vivendi*." Emory turned to Warren Hopkins. "I've asked the chairman of the architecture committee to join us today in the hope that he can explain the mystery."

Warren opened a folder. "I think the mechanics of building Symphony Hall will illustrate the difficulty. Our original budget, based on the estimates of the contractors, builders and decorators, was sixteen million. Now we're edging toward seventeen million, five. To be on the safe side, we'll need twenty million."

There was a stir around the table.

"The costs of labor and material are still going up. Mr. Dougherty has the revised union demands, which we're being forced to put into a letter of agreement. He'll bear me out."

Dougherty's shoulders drooped wearily and his eyes were bloodshot, but he sounded alert and aggressive, as always. "The contractors simply can't do the job on the basis of their original estimates. The excavators are getting forty cents an hour more, and the steel workers fifty. So are the welders. And so on." He handed a sheaf of papers to the man on his right. "You may want to pass these around. The contractor's fee will go up by six hundred thousand, and there's nothing we can do about it."

"I'd tell them to go to blazes," a florid-faced man with a shock of white hair said bitterly.

"Unfortunately, we can't," Emory replied. "As those of you with steel and automotive associations know, private industry is always in a position to take a stand when labor makes exorbitant demands. But we cannot. A semi-public institution like a culture center must behave in the same way as a charitable institution, although it can't really be classified as one. We need public good will for Jefferson Square, so we can't do anything that might damage our image."

"I'll be interested to see how much the unions contribute to our good cause," the florid-faced man said.

Emory scribbled a note on a pad at his elbow. "I'll remind the head of the contributions committee to check on what they've given us."

Several men smiled, and one of them said, "I have every confidence in Carolyn's powers of persuasion."

Warren felt a stab of jealousy when he saw the expression of quiet pride on Emory's face. It was a proprietary look that made her would-be lover feel excluded—and cheap.

"Let's grant the extra six hundred thousand for construction workers' wages," the investment banker declared. "Let's say, for the sake of round figures, that the Symphony Hall budget will go up to eighteen million. Why earmark twenty?"

Warren forced himself to concentrate on the business of Jefferson Square. "Anton Helsing assures me that a cushion of two million for internal building adjustments won't be too much. I'm speaking of the period after the outer shell of the building is completed."

The investment banker was dissatisfied. "Helsing may be a marvel at leading an orchestra. I'm no judge of such things. But what are his qualifications for allocating other people's money?"

"That's what I felt," Warren replied, "but I've been studying the situation, and I've become convinced he's right. The Lincoln Center crowd had to increase its budget four different times when they put up Philharmonic Hall. They started at eleven million, and spent close to fifteen and a half million, before they were done. The Vienna Opera, which was rebuilt on a shoestring after World War II, had to suspend construction work six different times because they ran out of funds, and consistently needed more than they'd expected to spend."

"Poor planning," the red-faced man muttered.

"No, there's a problem that's unique in the building of symphony halls and opera houses. It's a question of acoustics."

A man with a narrow, pinched face looked up from the

labor agreements, that had just been passed to him. "They hired another consultant last week. This one is from M.I.T., and they're paying him three hundred dollars a day which is shocking. I think we have more acoustical experts than construction workers."

Dougherty, who had been thinking of Sandra, roused himself. She had been remote and impersonal in the office this morning, and he had been relieved. But the mere sight of her had sparked his desire again, even though he was tired, and he wanted her, tonight. "Including the full-time acoustical engineers and the part-time consultants, we have nine in all. They'll cost us three hundred thousand."

The investment banker's lips tightened. "There's a vast difference between three hundred thousand and two million, Mr. Hopkins."

"Indeed there is, Mr. Blackwell," Warren said. "What costs so much is following the recommendations of the acoustical engineers."

"Why don't they get together and reach a decision in the first place, before work starts on the interior?"

"They can't. Everything from the balance of the girders that frame an auditorium to the sensitivity of the silk or wood used to line the chamber affects a concert hall or musical theater."

"I can't believe," the investment banker said, "that it much matters. Music is music."

Warren leaned forward, his elbows on the table. "I'm forced to disagree with you, Mr. Blackwell. I'm a rank amateur who enjoys listening to a symphony or concerto without knowing anything of the work and mechanics that go into producing it. But even I can distinguish an acoustically perfect hall from one that has flaws. If we don't build one that is free of imperfections, it will be a waste of time for the Symphony Orchestra to move in. The musicians won't tolerate it, and neither will audiences."

The investment banker grimaced, and turned to his colleagues for support. Two shook their heads, siding with Warren; the others were either indifferent or embarrassed by their ignorance.

"Acoustical men follow a number of basic principles in their work," Warren said, "but their fine-tuning, as they call it, can be achieved only through trial and error. An auditorium wall may have to be moved. A row of seats in the front row of the first balcony may have to be removed. Hundreds of changes, from major reconstruction to new coverings for the seats, may have to be made. All of them cost money, and from the explanations I've been given, two million isn't too much."

Emory took charge again. "I won't ask for a vote until we've had a chance to study the matter. I've asked for a full report on the acoustical question and its possible costs, and I'll have copies made for each of you as soon as I get a complete memorandum. Until then, I think we'd be wise to pencil in an increase in the Symphony Hall construction budget to twenty million."

The narrow-faced man was unhappy. "That will bring the total in new, unpledged funds for the whole square to more than thirty million, Edward."

"Yes, I'm sorry to say." Emory seemed unperturbed.

"Where will we get the money?"

"The professional fund raisers are just beginning their campaign. Everyone who gives one hundred thousand dollars or more to Jefferson Square will have his or her name carved in marble blocks that will be on display in every building of the square. The solicitation of the general public—which was very effective at Lincoln Center, by the way—will give everyone who contributes one hundred dollars or more the opportunity to have his name engraved in bronze on a seat in the hall or theater of his choice. Or on a chair in the library or art gallery, for that matter."

"You're begging the issues, Edward." The florid-faced man was brisk. "We have a base deficit of forty million that we're hoping the foundations will cover." He glanced at Warren.

"I have no right to speak for the Hopkins Fund," the young man said.

"I wasn't trying to get a commitment from you. I'm merely pointing out that, in all, Jefferson Square is approximately seventy million in the red as of this moment."

Dougherty searched for a figure and found it. "Based on the experience of Lincoln Center and others," he said, "we can expect five to eight million from the individual contributions made through the professional fund raisers. The limit we can expect, realistically, will be eight million."

"Even if we get it, and even if the foundations came through, we'll still be twenty-two million in the red." The investment banker was morosely triumphant.

Emory remained unruffled. "I'm having lunch with Governor Herder today—"

"We can't bleed the state treasury for another nickel, Edward!"

"I know that. But we might be able to get another federal grant from the Artistic Endeavors appropriations the new Congress is making. Two months ago I'd have said that we couldn't expect more federal money, but the new appropriations bill changes all that."

"Why go through Herder?" asked the president of Eastern Refineries, who had been silent until now. "Why not go straight to the White House?"

"I plan to do just that. I have an appointment with the President next week," Emory replied. "But I believe that Herder is our best bet." He paused for an instant, smiling wryly. "He's anxious to appear before the whole country as the great champion of culture. And I believe we'll get our best results if he directs the operations."

The florid-faced man took the wrapper from a cigar. "That makes sense, Edward. I've never really liked Herder, but Al has proved to my satisfaction, anyway, that we can rely on him."

The investment banker agreed, but was still concerned. "There will be too many hands in the Artistic Endeavors pot for us to expect the whole twenty-two million from Washington."

Dougherty braced himself. "We'll need a new kitty one hell of a lot bigger than twenty-two million." He tried not to look at the shocked, startled faces on both sides of the table. "I've been trying to warn you, both on this committee and on the general Jefferson Square Board for months, but no one has listened to me. We've delayed too long on those additional land parcels we'll need on Sixth Street for the library and art museum. Land values have been rising astronomically in the area ever since the first Jefferson Square announcement was made, and we should have bought that real estate long ago."

"How much more than our original estimate will we have to pay?" the head of Eastern Refineries demanded.

Dougherty shrugged. "Plenty. I expect to hear an asking price any day."

The oilman was contemptuous. "They can either accept our ceiling or keep their land."

"I'm afraid it won't be that simple," Emory said. "That

55

slum property is worth more than your offshore oilfields, and every last acre has been tied up. We have literally no other place to build the library and gallery."

Eastern Refineries reputedly never evaded a court fight. "We could force them to be reasonable."

"We're a culture center," Dougherty said. "We can't slug anybody."

The investment banker shook his head. "We've dug gold out of every mine we know. Where will we get the money?"

There was an amused glint in Emory's eyes. "The chairman of the contributions committee will have some ideas," he said.

The man-made craters were growing deeper and broader as bulldozers scooped up earth that was carted away by heavy trucks. Huge cement-mixers rumbled, spewing forth the material that would become the cellars and underground garage foundations of Jefferson Square's first units. Elsewhere, two blocks away, demolition crews were tearing down tenements which would give way to other portions of the culture center. One entire wall of an aged building had been ripped off, but parts of the interior could still be seen, forming a battered and grimy stage set. In one room a broken table and several chairs contributed to the rubble, while in another a rusted tin bathtub not worth salvaging teetered near the open edge, ignored by the steel helmeted workmen below.

Dan Robertson stood with his topcoat over his arm, surprised at the progress that had been made in the two days that had passed since the ground-breaking ceremonies. He looked carefully at everything taking place at the busy scene, but the ritual of watching Jefferson Square coming to life no longer excited him. Turning away, he climbed back into his waiting taxi and gave the driver an address on Tyler Street, downtown.

The man studied him in the rear view mirror, noting his nattily conservative attire and attaché case. "You an ad man?"

Dan shook his head, in no mood for a chat with a cabby.

"So I'm wrong," the man said cheerfully.

Dan stared morosely out of the window.

"You're one of them building nuts, maybe, like me. Pretty soon, zoom! This new Jefferson Square will be finished, and fifty million people will be hollering for cabs, of which there won't be enough."

In spite of his sense of depression, Dan was amused. "Will you be there?"

"Me? Nah. I like the fights. But my wife and kid, they go for musicals. Rodgers and Hammerstein. Irving Berlin. You know. But maybe all they're gonna have at Jefferson Square is the longhair stuff."

"No. One theater will be devoted mainly to musical comedy and ballet," Dan said.

As the taxi moved boltingly forward in traffic, the driver again studied his passenger in the mirror. "You sound like you know about all this. You gonna work for these guys?"

Dan realized he should have chopped off the conversation when he had the chance. "Yes, I work for Jefferson Square."

They narrowly missed another taxi, and squeezed past a truck from the garment district. "I don't think you're a band leader or a singer. Maybe I saw you in the paper, only I don't think so. You somebody I ought to know?"

"I'm nobody." Dan took refuge in the contents of his attaché case, shuffling papers he needed for a meeting that afternoon, but not really reading them.

The driver took the hint, and remained silent until he deposited his fare at the entrance to one of the newer Tyler Street restaurants. Then he couldn't resist saying, "Watch the right side of the menu in this joint, bud. They'll clip you good."

Dan laughed as he overtipped the man. "That's okay. I'm being taken to lunch."

Harvy Simpson, who was sipping an Americano, was waiting at the table. Although his thick tweeds were ageless and his bulky necktie very modern, he fitted perfectly into the pseudo-Edwardian elegance of the place. Overstuffed, nail-head-studded chairs, hunting prints that obscured expensive pine paneling, leaded windows, waiters in stiff leather aprons and wine stewards with exaggerated, large chains hanging from their necks made it obvious at a glance that this was an establishment catering to the expense account crowd.

Tables were located sufficiently far apart to make eavesdropping difficult, captains bowed patrons to their leather chairs and thrust yard-long menus into their hands before hurrying elsewhere to wield equally long peppermills. Harvey, very much at home, half-stood up and waved, then flicked back his hand to make sure his hair was in place.

"Dan, this is good of you," he boomed. "I appreciate it. I know how hard it must be to find time even for yourself in your busy schedule."

Shaking hands, Dan realized he had come to see Harvey Simpson in a new light since moving East. He had always recognized Harvey's pomposity, of course, and had suspected there was something of the old-fashioned medicine man in his soul. But not until he had become acquainted with financial giants like Ben Hopkins and Edward Emory did it occur to him that Harvey was trying to imitate them.

Nevertheless he was a first-rate book publisher. He was president of Simpson and Smith, a universally respected company. Even more important, he was a trusted friend. But still more important, he had been astute enough to recognize the merits of a book, rejected by six other houses, by an unknown Midwestern professor. So, in a sense, he was responsible for everything of consequence that had happened to Dan in recent years.

"Mr. Robertson," Harvey told the captain, "will have a bourbon on the rocks."

"Make it a tall one, with lots of water and not too much bourbon," Dan interjected.

Harvey grinned at him. "The executive life is getting you down, eh? You were grand on the air," he continued at the same rapid pace, a trace of a British accent in his speech that Dan knew would get stronger with his second drink. "And you had a marvelous press. Too bad you couldn't work in a line somewhere in your talk making a casual reference to *The Quandary*. With the exposure you've had, I'd have ordered a new printing of fifteen thousand the same day."

Dan did not laugh.

"We're still selling, of course, although slowly and the rate of reorders probably won't climb again. But you should stay in print for years. Deservedly, Dan. *The Quandary* is one of the few books that has ever lived up to its jacket blurb."

Accepting his drink, Dan raised it. "To the questions that have perplexed the honorable, the pure—and the stupid—since time immemorial."

Harvey looked at him sharply.

"Forget it," Dan said. "Phyllis sends her love to Esther, and wants you both for dinner as soon as the new living room carpeting comes. Don't ask me why we've got to wait for carpeting."

"We have no intention of waiting." Harvey's manner was bland, but his eyes remained watchful. "Esther is calling Phyllis today to see if we can pump some fresh country air into your lungs this weekend. Bringing the youngsters, of course."

"I'd love it," Dan said. "Phyllis keeps the date book, but as far as I know, this weekend is free."

"Good. Then we can make this a purely social lunch, and I'll bend your business ear over the weekend. You know I always have an ax to grind or something hidden up my sleeve."

The self-appraisal was accurate, and Dan laughed.

"I'll just throw the idea at you now, and let it simmer until the weekend. How does a book called *The Anatomy of Jefferson Square* strike you? A blow-by-blow story of the building of America's greatest culture center—and what will make it tick. Good for Jefferson Square—and for Simpson and Smith."

"I'm afraid I can't write it, Harvey."

"Oh, I didn't think you'd have the time, Dan, although I'd love it if you could. If you approve, we can settle jointly on a ghost. I have several in mind. What I'd like is to see the place opened wide to him. You know, directors' meeting, quarrels between Jerry Solanz and whoever. Everything that happens."

Dan was silent.

"Don't give me a positive answer either way right now. Just file it in a mental corner until the weekend."

"It will take longer than that," Dan said, offering no explanation.

Harvey knew better than to probe. "Another drink, or shall we order?"

"One is enough for me. I never drank at noon when I was teaching, you know. Liquor on the breath and the classroom don't mix."

"I sometimes forget that the Puritan streak is still very strong in a good many universities, particularly in your part of the country. Why should that be?"

"Some of the more important universities—the pacesetters —were land-grant schools," Dan said. "They've been tax-exempt, and they hate the idea of state legislatures investigating them, of course. So they keep their noses clean and echo the attitudes and mores of their communities. Being large, ponderous institutions by nature, they change slowly, and are often a few beats—or even long strides—behind the current community thinking."

"Brilliant, Professor Robertson. You're being wasted at Jefferson Square. André, bring us the crêpes crabmeat. I guarantee you'll love it, Dan."

"I wouldn't say I'm being wasted at Jefferson Square," Dan said slowly. "But I've been wondering whether a square peg —and I do mean square—isn't fitting rather uncomfortably in a round hole."

Harvey oozed sympathy. "Troubles with your board?"

"They're giving me everything I want. I've never in my life met a more cooperative group of gentlemen."

"Wonderful! Then I diagnose your problem as a case of nerves. You had misgivings when you were offered the job, and I dare say they sometimes overwhelm you. Just between us, Dan, Chancellor Carl of Seaboard sounded me out at dinner before they made you the offer. He's one of our authors, you know. Anyway, I was frank with him, as I am with everyone, and I told him that your one blind spot is a lack of faith in your own talents. But it should be obvious to you that your directors believe in you, just as I do, and you don't need me to tell you there are no better judges of character anywhere."

"You're very convincing, Harvey." Dan's face felt stiff when he tried to smile.

"You authors are all alike. You swing on a pendulum of highs and lows—"

"I'm no author, Harvey. I wrote one book that happened to click."

"It had merit the reading public recognized. Our advertising and promotion helped, to be sure, but if the book hadn't been solid, it wouldn't have sold. In case you've forgotten, the Sunday *Times* reviewer said—"

"I remember every word of every good review. If you must know, Harvey, I even sneak an occasional look at my scrapbook when I'm feeling particularly down."

"Just as I said. An author. But in your case, a great deal besides. A distinguished educator, and now a man facing the greatest artistic challenge of our time. I envy you, Dan!"

"For two cents I'd change places with you."

Harvey decided to dangle a little bait. "Two cents wouldn't

buy much these days. A check for advance royalties on a new book might not be out of place, though. With as much time as you'd want to write it. Two years, three—"

"Thanks all the same, but I'm a one-book author. I literally don't have another one in me."

Harvey peered hard at him. "What the devil is wrong with you?"

Dan shrugged.

"I feel close to both you and Phyllis, and if she's having trouble adjusting to life here, I'll have a little talk with her—you can trust me not to mention that we've discussed it—"

"Good bark, Harvey, but the wrong tree. We're getting along fine together."

Harvey was about to reply, but the waiter arrived with their food. The main dish consisted of tissue-thin pancakes wrapped around delicately shredded crabmeat sautéed in garlic butter and served, garnished with mushrooms, in a white wine sauce.

Dan stared unhappily at his plate, and did not look up as the captain went through the ritual of sprinkling pepper on his salad with the three-foot mill.

"Out with it, Dan!" Harvey said, eating with relish.

"Supposing I gave you a book that would blow the lid off everything," Dan asked.

"By everything you mean Jefferson Square?"

"Yeah."

"We'd sell a million copies. Are you kidding me or do you mean it?"

"I'm kidding, Harvey. Of course, I'm kidding."

A few sponsors, most of them season ticket holders of long standing, had protested feebly when the old and distinguished instrumental organization had changed its name to the Jefferson Square Symphony Orchestra. The majority of patrons had agreed with the board of directors, however, that something had been gained and nothing lost. After all, a new era was beginning: a young, dynamic director had replaced an aging traditionalist, and as soon as its new home was ready, the orchestra would move into it.

Sentimentalists, of course, were deploring the abandonment of the hall that had housed the group since the turn of the century. They granted that it was decrepit, but insisted, hopelessly, that a relatively small sum spent on refurbishing would restore it to its former glory. And no one could argue with their contention that the acoustics were virtually perfect.

Their opponents were realistic, and Mayor Michael Burke summed up the opposition's argument in blunt if undiplomatic terms when he told the press, "It will be a miracle if the old place doesn't collapse before the new Jefferson Square Symphony Hall is ready for occupancy. I've ordered the city's Director of Buildings and Safety to make regular inspections, and I won't hesitate to close down the old barn the moment I'm told the public is in any danger. The old hall has known its days of glory, but I rejoice with our citizens that our world-renowned orchestra soon will have a new auditorium worthy of its reputation."

Anton Helsing carefully avoided the controversy, both publicly and privately, turning aside questions with a smile that was sometimes mischievous, sometimes solemn, but always charming. Secretly, as only Michele knew, he was waiting impatiently to escape from the place he scornfully termed a firetrap. As a musician he fully appreciated the acoustical properties of stage and auditorium, but the disadvantages of working in the building far outweighed the single advantage. And tradition, certainly, meant little to him. "It's the duty of an orchestra director to act as a pioneer scout," he had confided to Betsy Callison. "I'm well aware of the worth of the classics, but good music becomes atrophied if audiences are fed a steady diet of nothing but Mozart and Bach. A modern director must experiment and teach his audiences new musical values."

A few of the stage floorboards were loose and splintered, which was outrageous, and the dressing room used by the conductor was a disgrace. The hot water tap of the old-fashioned, ugly sink in the far corner of the room was capricious, and the tiles in the shower were so stained they could not be made to shine, no matter how hard they were scrubbed. Also, the concertmaster's tiny dressing room, which was located directly above a set of hyper-active heating pipes, made the cell virtually unliveable.

It was the director's office, however, that really affronted Anton's dignity. It was located on the sixth floor of the building, along with a number of suites rented to peripheral, aspiring musicians and their teachers, and the outer corridor was usually filled with the sounds of scraping violins and sopranos who either sang flat or were guilty of emitting uncurable tremolos. The ancient radiators hissed all winter and clanked unexpectedly, even in the spring and early autumn, when the building superintendent swore the heat had not been turned on. The windows leaked, making the room draughty, and their rattle was distracting when a man wanted to concentrate.

Aesthetically, the office was a mess. The yellowing, stained wallpaper had not been changed in years, and Anton couldn't understand how Henri Broussard had been able to tolerate it. The massive Victorian furniture was oppressive, and not one chair in the overcrowded chamber was comfortable. Even the rug, once an expensive Oriental, had lost its nap as well as its body, and beneath the desk it had grown threadbare after being scuffed incessantly.

One task Anton enjoyed, in spite of his homely surroundings, was that of marking the fan mail that poured in after every televised performance. He had developed an efficient and time-saving system during his years as a pianist, conductor, and composer of everything from concertos to ballets, and with a few revisions it still worked admirably. He used a standard set of nine replies to the mail, and consequently had to do no more than scribble a number of the top of each letter. Rarely did he receive a communication that required a truly individual response.

Therefore he could go through the stacks of fan letters in very short time. He scanned each one, paying little heed to praise but reading criticisms more carefully, and then jotted down the appropriate number of the reply. Now, as always, it gave him a feeling of deep satisfaction to know two secretarial assistants spent at least half their time sending answers to such mail.

The door opened, and the secretary, chosen by Michele to replace a young man she had considered too handsome, entered the office quickly and closed the door behind her. "Mr. Broussard is here," she said in an almost conspiratorial tone.

Anton leaped to his feet, almost bowling her over in his haste to reach the outer office. "Maestro!" he exclaimed, extending both arms.

Broussard, gray and stocky, with his topcoat draped over his shoulders in Continental fashion, suffered an embrace.

"I'm utterly destroyed. To think that here, of all places, you should feel you need to have yourself announced." Grasping his predecessor by the arm, Anton led him toward the inner office. "I feel like the intruder."

There was no need for Broussard to say, "You should." His eyes clearly expressed his feelings.

"I want to be disturbed by no one," Anton called over his shoulder, "no matter who it is." Nudging the door shut, he half-bowed the visitor to the creaking swivel chair behind the desk.

Broussard deliberately lowered himself into a leather chair on the near side.

Anton lacked the nerve to take the seat the other man had occupied for so many years, and took another, adjacent to the visitor's chair.

"Do I disturb you?" The old conductor looked at the mail heaped high on the desk.

"It's nothing, Maestro," Anton replied with an airy wave. "I feel honored."

Henri Broussard had no intention of exchanging flowery compliments with the man who, he was convinced, had conspired to replace him. "I thought I owed to you the courtesy of showing you the program for the farewell concert I will give before I leave on my tour."

"I'll be delighted to see it!" Anton hid his concern, and added, "Forgive my ignorance, but should I have known about a tour?"

Broussard made no attempt to conceal his sense of triumph. "There is nothing to forgive, my dear Anton. My managers have as yet made no announcement. Bernstein has invited me to conduct the Philharmonic, and then I say goodby to the rest of the America that has been so kind to me. Boston, Philadelphia, Cleveland, Chicago, all the way to California and back." His smile was as bland as it was broad.

"How wonderful, Maestro!" Anton calculated rapidly. The old buzzard was trying to steal his thunder, and a series of farewell concerts undoubtedly would bring out the tearfully nostalgic throngs. But the weekly Helsing broadcasts commanded a far larger audience every single week than Broussard could pull into concert halls if he waved his baton from now until the time he dropped dead. After suffering his first pang of uneasiness, Anton realized he had nothing to fear from the has-been. "Will I be able to hear some of the performances on the air?" Fourth down, Broussard. Punt the ball.

"Some details are still to be arranged. But each of the performances will be recorded for the American Concerts series."

First down for you on an end run, Anton conceded. "I'll be looking forward to them. Maestro, may I ask you something personal?"

"I have nothing to hide—from anyone."

"I hope you'll allow me to sit out front when you give your farewell here."

"But of course! Why would I not?"

"I must be embarrassingly honest. Rumors are the curse of the music world, as you know even better than I. But I've been distressed. It's come back to me that you and Helena feel I had a hand in your retirement from the symphony."

The cragged face became stony. "Madame Godoy sometimes talks for publication. That is her temperament, and her privilege as a diva. When the newspapers have spoken to me, I have said nothing."

Anton had to admire him for refusing to budge. Broussard had little to lose, of course, so there was no reason, other than common, surface courtesy, to paper over a feud.

"Here," the old man said brusquely, taking a folded sheet of paper from his pocket, "is my program for the farewell."

Anton scanned it quickly, and forced a smile. "Marvelous, Maestro!"

"You do not approve?"

"It isn't my taste, but I'm sure it suits yours perfectly."

"To what do you object?" Color began to rise in Broussard's face.

"Nothing at all." The last thing Anton wanted was an open break with him.

"If it were your concert," Broussard persisted, evidently determined to create a showdown, in his own way, "what would you change?"

It was impossible for Anton to side-step the direct challenge. If the old fogey wanted to call him, he'd show his cards. "I think the dose of romanticism is too heavy. If you must include Mendelssohn, why not *Fingal's Cave* instead of the *Mid-Summer Night's Dream* that's been played to death? When you put it on the same program with Chopin, you can choke an audience into insensitivity."

"You would prefer Shostakovitch, perhaps, or the nonsense of Ibert?"

The thrust struck a sensitive spot. Anton had included an Ibert work, usually reserved for "pops" concerts, in a serious program, and had been criticized severely by traditionalist reviewers. "I'm astonished how few people—and I'm speaking of musicians now, not the public—fail to recognize the ultimate purpose of Ibert's work. He's far more than a satirist, but virtually no one in the United States realizes it. What astonishes me is that he's hardly a new, young composer struggling to be heard. He did some of his best work more than thirty years ago."

"But of course." There was ice in Broussard's eyes. "It was my privilege to attend the first playing of Ibert. In Paris, where else?"

"Then we differ in taste as well as in our concepts of what may be suitable." Anton felt his temper rising. He hated being goaded by an ancient ignoramus who had spent his entire musical career looking backward to the distant past and who had never made a significant contribution to the advancement of an audience's appreciation of modern music.

"I say to your face what I have refused to say elsewhere." Broussard stood, his shoulders squared. "I have trapped you, Helsing. It was told to me by one who would not lie that you persuaded the directors of the symphony that your taste was better than mine, and that I do not know what is suitable to be played in these times. Now I hear the same words from your own lips."

"That's nonsense," Anton sputtered.

"You deny it?"

"Completely!"

"Then you lie!" First grasping the younger man by the lapels of his jacket, Broussard then delivered two stinging slaps across Helsing's face. Although Anton could easily have done serious damage to Broussard had he returned the blow, his shock and hurt were such that he felt like a spanked child.

Broussard glowered at him for an instant, spat in his face and stalked out, leaving the door open.

Everyone in the outer office had been aware of the commotion, and by the time the secretary jumped to her feet and managed to close the door again, it was too late. Everyone knew the identity of the victor and of the vanquished, and within hours the whole world of music would know of the scuffle. It would be spoken of as "The Return of David and Goliath."

Anton was so stunned he sat for some moments before his mind started functioning clearly again. He raised a hand to his burning face, and was quite surprised to see there was no blood on it. He didn't know whether to laugh at the absurdity of what had just happened, or to cry because he had been humiliated.

Gradually his mounting rage took possession of him, and his other emotions faded away. A telephone call to the record company might, with luck, deprive Broussard of much of the glory and royalties he hoped to glean on his tour, but Anton was sensible enough to realize he lacked the power to prevent the cutting and distribution of the discs. Nor could he persuade the orchestra associations of the other cities to cancel the tour; his own intuitive sense of public relations told him he would cause himself more harm than good.

Rapidly he rejected one idea after another, including that which had the greatest appeal, scheduling telecasts of his own at the same time Broussard would make his various guest appearances with orchestras around the country. None were thorough enough, none would totally destroy the man.

"The old son of a bitch," Anton said aloud.

No one deplored the "publish or perish" dictum of academe more vociferously than Chancellor Stephen A. D. Carl of Seaboard University, and few appeared more regularly in print. Every other year the Seaboard University Press brought out a new, slim volume of his most recent addresses, which he himself had selected and edited. As chairman of several commissions appointed in advisory capacities by the President of the United States, his name frequently appeared before the public as an active participant in anti-crime drives and other civic affairs that were non-controversial.

"Steve Carl," said one of his deans, "has been saved from anonymity by his support of campaigns honoring motherhood, and from banality by the refusal of a distinguished faculty to pay the slightest attention to a semi-scholar whose last serious work was a doctoral thesis called 'The Disguised

Sentimentality of Jonathan Swift.' Neither it nor its author has made any lasting contribution to American education."

Carl's detractors did him grave injustice, misled by his handsome, often-photographed profile and his seemingly ingenuous charm, which was sometimes likened to that of an automobile salesman. Carl thought of himself as a salesman, and no one could quibble with the results he had achieved. Lacking distinction himself, he had nevertheless cajoled, or persuaded large numbers of prominent academicians to join the Seaboard faculty, among them two Nobel Prize winners. He had raised more than sixty million dollars for the university's endowment fund in a little more than two years, and now, after arduous planning, intended to launch an even more ambitious expansion program.

His closest personal friend was Benjamin Hopkins, who had few intimates, and a colleague, reputedly the president of either Columbia or Chicago, allegedly had remarked that, by working his way into Hopkins' confidence, Carl had assured himself of a lifetime job at Seaboard. "The trustees wouldn't dare get rid of him," his peer was supposed to have said. "Nobody knows when Ben Hopkins might drop fifty million into his lap."

The secret of their relationship, as only Carl knew, was that he never brought up the subject of money. Everyone else did it, so he refrained, which so perplexed the magnate that Hopkins frequently made gifts to the university because his friend's silence on the subject embarrassed him.

This reticence, however, pertained only to Seaboard, and Carl saw no reason to remain quiet on other financial matters. Now, carefully stuffing his pipe as he lounged on the leather sofa in Hopkins' office, he waited for his chance. "You make it very difficult to entertain you, Ben," he said. "I can understand why you won't come to the Faculty Club, or even the Tennis and Badminton, but it upsets me when you won't come to my house for a drink or dinner."

"Don't you like my liquor, Steve?" Most of Benjamin Hopkins' acquaintances would have been surprised to see him in so indulgent a mood.

"It's as good as the meals at your house. But Mrs. Carl and I would like the chance to return your hospitality now and again."

"If I ever made an exception, I'd do it for you, Steve."

Ice in Stephen Carl's glass of Scotch and water tinkled as he raised it in salute. "You'll be an old recluse before you're sixty, Ben."

"Now you sound like Mrs. Hopkins. She says I remind her of a hermit who squats in the back of his cave, counting his gold."

"That's better than throwing it around." Carl sipped his drink.

Hopkins instantly raised his head. "Meaning?"

"Just a joke, Ben."

"I know your jokes. You never say anything without good reason."

"It's become fairly common knowledge, Ben, that the Jefferson Square budget is going to be increased again."

"News does get around."

"Within a very limited circle, perhaps. A good many of your directors are my trustees. And I've heard the opinion expressed several times in the past few days that the square threatens to become a bottomless financial pit. I'm not thinking as much of the building and decoration of the units as I am of their upkeep. The Grand Opera Company and Symphony Orchestra will run up deficits, just as they always have in the past. The Repertory Theater will accomplish the impossible if it breaks even, and so will the Ballet Company. The library will be a heavy drag, although the museum shouldn't be much of an expense once it's stocked. And I'm not criticizing Dan Robertson. I had complete confidence in him when I recommended him, and still do. But neither he nor anyone else can balance the artistic budgets of the square."

"Then the directors of each component unit will have to search for their own funds."

"Of course. But suppose they find the search difficult, Ben. Eventually all roads will lead back to you. I hate to see them taking advantage of you."

There was no amusement in Ben Hopkins' tight smile. "One of Herbert Brookes' sub-departments devotes its full time to those who try."

"You miss my point, Ben. Thanks to you, Jefferson Square is going to become the most opulent, dazzling, well-rounded culture center in existence. But the whole can't be any stronger than its parts. If they fail and close their doors, there

69

will be repercussions in the performing arts everywhere. More than that, in every university and college. The result may be the opposite of what you're trying to create."

"You're saying, politely, that my own prestige will be at stake, Steve."

"Well, as chairman of the general board and principal contributor—"

"Most of the money," Ben interjected forcibly, "came from the Hopkins Fund. I'm a director, of course, but I have only one vote. I wish more people understood that I don't control the fund."

"Even those who do know it see you as the founder of Jefferson Square." Carl took pains not to emphasize his next words. "I'm sure you remember the attempt to found a School of Music at Seaboard. You were very generous, and offered us a substantial pledge—"

"Which you turned down, cold. It was unique in my experience, and I'll never forget it."

Carl puffed on his pipe. "For one thing, as I told you at the time, I thought it wrong to ape Lincoln Center, and Seaboard would have been accused, unfairly, as it happens, of trying to use a great culture center in order to compete with Juilliard. You may recall I said I infinitely prefer to strengthen our present schools and departments, which is what we're doing. It's far more important to build a new law library, and the cancer research center the Medical School wants so desperately. All this is confidential, by the way. I'm saying nothing to anyone, including the trustees, at the moment. I prefer to complete my plans first, so there won't be any premature leaks to the alumni. They're very touchy."

"When you're farther along, give me an idea of what you intend to do."

Stephen Carl breathed an inner sigh of relief. "By no means," he said, and drained his drink.

Ben Hopkins' monumental calm was shattered. His friend appeared sincere, and he blinked in astonishment. "I will be damned," he muttered.

"I know you, Ben, and it would be just like you to make one of your block-buster pledges. But not this time. Not even you can afford to turn your pockets inside out, and you're already too deeply committed to Jefferson Square."

"That's irrelevant. You know how much the Hopkins family has given to Seaboard University in the past fifty years."

70

"I'm so very much aware of it that I'm forced to call a halt. Forget that I said anything, Ben." Carl went to the small bar in the corner cabinet of inlaid teakwood and calmly mixed himself another drink.

"Are you trying to tell me I can't help Seaboard and Jefferson Square at the same time?"

"Hardly, Ben. But I am saying you can't support both of them single-handed. The square is going to be a heavy drain on you in the next five to ten years, so Seaboard will look elsewhere." Carl sounded very firm, very crisp.

Hopkins hooked his thumbs in the pockets of his vest, his pose and expression faithfully mirroring those of his father in the portrait above the fireplace. "Seaboard was my grandfather's first love, and my father's," he said. "If you're going to build a new law library and a Medical School research center, you'll come to me before you see anyone else. Is that understood?"

"Ben, you place me in an untenable position—"

"As for Jefferson Square, if I must, I'll limit my personal contribution. I couldn't hold it together myself, any more than the Rockefellers can guarantee the success of Lincoln Center. The Metropolitan Opera isn't Radio City Music Hall!"

Carl refrained from laughter when he saw that his friend was in earnest.

"On the other hand, I can't and won't permit Jefferson Square to fail. I am committed to it, Steve. Very deeply committed."

"I hope you don't mind my barging in on you like this." Betsy Callison sounded breathless.

Warren waved her into his office, thinking how pretty she looked in pink, and what a shame it was that he hadn't fallen in love with her. "This is the nicest thing that has happened to me all day," he said truthfully.

Betsy looked around the room, an expression of surprise in her eyes.

"This office isn't at all what I'd pictured."

Warren held a chair for her. "What did you expect?" So many visitors made similar comments the first time they came into the office that he found her reaction mildly dull.

"I don't know, really. Something the size of the waiting room in the Jefferson Street Railroad Station, and very elegant. My cousin isn't much more than a clerk in his father's brokerage downtown, but his office is bigger than this."

Warren perched on the edge of his desk, facing her. "When old Benjamin Hopkins the First made his initial one hundred million, he kept the same rolltop desk he'd used when he'd been a storekeeper in a little town out in Montana. According to a family legend that's probably true somebody asked him why he didn't get himself a new desk, now that he could afford whatever he wanted. And he's supposed to have said, 'The fellow with one million has to make an impression on people. I don't.'"

Betsy laughed. "I knew I'd be put in my place."

Warren found her fresh, almost wide-eyed approach disturbing when he had been thinking of Carolyn Emory all day. "Miss Browning has a kettle and an electric burner, and I imagine she could be persuaded to fix you a cup of tea."

"I'd love some, but I'm not going to be here that long."

He picked up his telephone and pressed a button. "Don't heat the water, Miss Browning. This customer isn't buying a thing."

"How did you know she was heating water?" Betsy asked after he replaced the telephone in its cradle.

"S.O.P. Standing operating procedure. Miss Browning knows all. She decided after taking one look at you that you weren't the liquor-before-sundown type, so that automatically meant tea or coffee."

"It must be very difficult working for you, Warren." But what would it be like to be married to you, she wondered.

"Miss Browning spent ten years in my father's office before he died, and then she worked for Uncle Ben until two years ago, when they decided I'd earned a secretary of my own."

The whole process was so ordered and neat, almost preordained. "I'm in a horribly nosey mood today, Warren, so forgive me. But I can't help wondering. Do you ever curdle inside at being a Hopkins?"

He was puzzled. "I'm not sure I follow you, but to the best of my knowledge, nothing inside has ever curdled, as you put it."

"I mean, knowing in advance what will happen to you five years from now, or ten."

He laughed. "I see. That's what I thought when I first learned I'd been entered at prep school and college at birth, and that my roommates had been picked for me. But it doesn't work out that way. When I said I wanted to go to Yale instead of Seaboard, I did. And I insisted that my roommate assignments be made the same way as other guys', and that worked out, too."

"I'm glad."

"If I'm not mistaken, you decided at nine or ten, as I remember it, that you wanted to be a concert pianist."

"And on my nineteenth birthday I stopped fooling myself. I have no talent. I'll always be an amateur whose love for music is the most notable thing about her performance."

"I can't believe that anyone who practiced for hours every day could be hopeless. I hope you'll let me hear you play some day, so I can judge for myself—and prove you're incapable of recognizing your own talent."

"I'd die! But," she went on, "I will play for you, if you'd really like to hear me."

"That," he said, "is a date."

Betsy gathered her gloves and handbag. "You have more important things to do than chatter with a girl who is killing time before a beauty parlor appointment." She flushed. "Did you know that Anton Helsing is going to record *Midsummer Night's Dream,* and the most romantic Chopin? It's a really wild program for him, but he's insisting on it. Anyway, I'm invited to the recording studios. You're welcome, too, if you'd like to come with me."

"That's certainly a change of pace for him. When will he cut the record?"

"Tonight. I've never seen him in such a frenzy." Betsy stood. "He's had people on the phone for hours, rounding up members of the orchestra, and he's demanding that distribution of the record start in two weeks. Can you imagine? Anton is usually so reasonable, but this afternoon he's just bursting with artistic temperament. I've never seen him so desperately anxious to make a record—and of romantic music he's always loathed. It's odd."

Warren had half-formed a plan to telephone Carolyn, making sure he'd reach her after Edward Emory returned home for the evening, so the call would appear innocent. Then he was going to suggest they get together to discuss the projected increase in the Jefferson Square budget. "Tonight, you say?"

Betsy was aware of his hesitation, and was afraid of pushing too hard. A man usually ran when a girl began to chase him. "If you're busy, don't bother. Anton's program is so odd that I thought it might be amusing, but anyone except a music nut like me probably would be bored."

Warren shook his head as he sorted out the tangled strands. Duplicity was new to him, but he was beginning to master its technique. If he assumed Carolyn was busy during the early part of the evening, and if he himself was occupied, the suggestion of a late conference might appear innocent, in spite of his real motives.

"Really," Betsy said, "it isn't anything much."

"I'd enjoy it," Warren said. "My only problem is that I may have a meeting rather late in the evening."

"Oh, that's all right," she replied eagerly. "We can leave whenever you have to go. They'll put us off in a glass-enclosed booth somewhere, and we'll be free to come and go as we please."

"Since it's going to be an early evening, perhaps you'll have dinner with me first." He was increasingly conscious of using her, and despised himself. Furthermore he found her increasingly attractive. Maybe he ought to forget Carolyn altogether. Maybe he could succeed in forgetting her by taking Bettina to bed.

"You're making me feel dreadfully forward," Betsy said. "But I'll be very happy to go to dinner. It seems to me the least I can do is meet you here in town to save time."

"I'll pick you up at home," he said firmly. "At what time is the recording?"

"Oh, they're starting their rehearsals for it in the next hour or two, which is far too early. Anton suggested we get there around eight."

"Then I'll come around for you at six thirty." A new thought suddenly occurred to Warren. "Would it rush you too much to be ready at six? I want to make a brief stop on the way, and you can come with me."

"There you have it in a nutshell, my dear." Edward Emory handed his wife a drink and poured one for himself. "In a nutshell, Jefferson Square is going to need a far greater sum of money than any of us anticipated. The additional funds will mean the difference between an ordinary culture center and the finest in the country."

"Obviously, we'll have to raise it. After all the work and

planning so far, we can't possibly be satisfied with something second-rate. Excuse me for a moment, Edward." Carolyn rose and went into the chamber adjoining the second-floor sitting room, returning a moment later with a black, leather-bound notebook.

"Your sucker list." Edward smiled while going to inspect some huge gladiolas in a table vase that caught his attention. "Are these from the country?"

"Yes, I went out to the house this noon, and cut them. Aren't they gorgeous? I've already made my appeal to the unions, Edward, and I'm counting on their pledges in the budget I've already worked out. I don't think we can expect additional contributions from them."

"You're lucky to be getting anything. If anyone but you had gone to them, they'd have laughed."

"We can't expect more from the little contributors, either. The professional fund raisers told me in so many words not to hope for a penny more than eight million. Of course, an appeal to the public might be effective, particularly if we outlined the situation, but I think it might be wrong to ask people of modest means to dig deeper into their pockets when not one of the square's buildings has been built yet."

"I'm no public relations man, but as a banker I certainly wouldn't advise it."

"That leaves the foundations—and the big contributors. The Rockefellers were very kind, but they're carrying such a heavy burden already that it wouldn't be fair to go back to them. The Ford Foundation may open the purse strings again. You never know with them. Then I have three people listed here who may give as much as one million apiece, if I approached them in just the right way and pluck all the right strings at the right time. But with so much needed, three million won't mean much, will it?"

He raised his head from the gladiolas and smiled wryly. "Every million helps, Carolyn."

She was not amused. "How much more can we afford to give ourselves?"

"I'll have to work that out. Offhand, I'd say anywhere from fifty thousand to an absolute top of one hundred and fifty. But please don't hold me to any figure."

Carolyn tapped a pencil thoughtfully against her teeth.

"I boasted at the board meeting. Perhaps I should have

kept quiet. I told the committee I felt sure you'd be able to raise the money."

"So I shall." Carolyn snapped the notebook closed. "I'm afraid there's no choice. Benjamin Hopkins, here I come. Again."

Her husband winced.

"There's a huge floating reserve in the Hopkins Fund that must be spent this year. B. H. told me so himself. And instead of asking him for three million more as a personal contribution, I'll ask for ten—and be satisfied with seven."

"If I were Ben, I think I'd leap out the window when I saw you coming into my office."

Carolyn was preoccupied. "It's a matter of finding the right approach to him. I don't want to repeat the techniques and arguments I used the last time."

"Another drink?"

"No, thank you. I'm dining here, so I think I'll spend the better part of the evening on the telephone."

A maid appeared at the open door. "Mr. Warren Hopkins and a young lady are here," she said.

"Ask them to come up." Carolyn felt her heart race, but spoke calmly.

Edward glanced at his watch. "I'm leaving in a half-hour for a dinner meeting of Al Herder's Commission on Juvenile Delinquency."

"Oh? Go whenever you must, my dear. I'll look after them." Carolyn rose as the guests appeared, and carefully extended one hand to Betsy before she offered the other to Warren. "This is so nice."

"Forgive us for barging in unannounced," Warren said.

"We're only staying for a moment," Betsy added. "We're on our way to dinner and a recording session of Anton Helsing's."

Warren shook hands with his host.

"There are house rules here. No one is allowed to leave before taking a drink." Edward was frequently guilty of forced joviality in his treatment of guests outside his immediate circle of friends.

"A small, light Scotch for me, please," Betsy said.

"Anything that's handy." Warren glanced at Carolyn, and was startled by the undisguised desire he saw in her eyes.

Edward poured each of them a stiff Scotch.

"You look lovely, Betsy," Carolyn said, still gazing at Warren.

"Thank you, Mrs. Emory." Betsy hoped she would some day acquire the older woman's poise.

"Warren, I was just thinking of you when you suddenly appeared."

Shocked by Carolyn's apparent daring, Warren felt compelled to match it. "Would I be shocked to know what you were thinking?"

"Watch out," Edward said.

Warren reacted as though he had touched a live wire.

"I know what's on her mind," the banker continued.

Carolyn, reddening slightly, turned away for a moment.

"Our conversation as you came into the lioness' den leads me to suspect she's seeing dollar signs before her eyes again." Edward's laugh filled the little room.

Betsy smiled politely.

"There *is* something rather urgent I want to discuss with you," Carolyn said.

"Remember," Edward interjected, "I warned you."

Warren knew he would feel so much freer to pursue Carolyn if he disliked the man. He wished, too, that he could stop reading subtle meanings into everything Emory said.

"Would tomorrow be convenient?" Carolyn asked.

"I'm sorry," Warren said, and meant it. "I'm leaving in the morning for a visit to the mines. I'll be in Montana and Idaho for three days."

"Oh, dear."

"Can it wait until I come back?"

"Of course, if it must." Carolyn turned to Betsy. "You must be bored with Jefferson Square by now."

The girl tried to register enthusiasm. "No, I'm thrilled by everything I hear about it."

"Look here," Warren said. "We're having an early evening." He remembered to smile at Betsy, and for her sake added, "I had some business scheduled for later tonight, but I can put it off." Everything was falling into place even better than he had anticipated, and his feeling of guilt was overwhelming.

Carolyn glanced at her husband before agreeing to the meeting.

"Governor Herder and a few others are coming back here with me, but we won't be in your way," Edward said.

"I wouldn't dream of inconveniencing you," she replied.

"If it wouldn't be too much trouble, we could talk at my place, and I'll drive you back," Warren said.

Edward unwittingly applied the finishing touch. "I'll keep David on duty after he drives me home, and he can take you there, Carolyn."

Betsy's insecurities welled up in her again. "This recording session isn't a matter of life or death. We could skip it, Warren."

Carolyn intervened before Warren could reply. "I wouldn't deprive you of your fun for anything in this world. Have a good time, and I'll talk Jefferson Square business with Warren later in the evening." How easy it is, she thought, to master the art of being a wife who cheats.

Jerry Solanz reclined in the deep padding of his seat in the first class passengers' compartment of the plane, his eyes closed, one hand gripping the thigh of Berenice Tolmey at the hem of her high-riding skirt. "This is how it is with me, sweetie," he said complacently, absently picking at the mesh of her black net stocking. "One minute we think we're staying in Europe for months, the next we're on our way home for a couple of days."

"I can't keep up with you." Berenice knew the man across the aisle was watching them, but didn't dare remove Jerry's hand for fear he'd create a scene. As always when she became flustered, she forgot to speak in the low, husky drawl he had taught her.

Jerry's mind, fortunately, was elsewhere. "The boys will keep everything rolling. That's what happens when a man builds a solid organization. Some directors are such egomaniacs everything grinds to a stop the minute they go to bed for a day with a cold or drop down to Acapulco to get some kinks out of the nervous system. Not the Solanz team, sweetie. An hour after we land in Dublin next week, we'll be on the set, shooting."

Berenice made the usual, semi-articulate sound of admiration he expected. She was bewildered, however, slightly annoyed and more than a little frightened at the prospect of her first serious encounter with the American press, so she dropped her fashion magazine onto the floor with the petulance of a child. "You still haven't told me why we're going home all of a sudden, Jerry. And you promised before we left that you'd explain."

"All right, all right." He opened his eyes, reassured himself that the seats in front of them were empty and that the two women behind them were too engrossed in their own conversation to eavesdrop. "This is strictly between us, and I'm letting you in on it to prove how much I trust you. Breathe one word to anybody, and I'll kick your teeth out." He lowered his voice to a confidential whisper. "One of my backers pulled out. Claimed he didn't like the shooting script. Imagine Solanz giving some idiot backer the right to censor a Solanz script! So we're going home to raise the rest of the capital. That's one of my reasons."

"You mean you're broke, Jerry?"

He was mortally offended. "The dividends from my stock portfolio and the return on my real estate properties would give me a comfortable income for the rest of my days. Worries I've got, but none of them are money."

Berenice became more confused. "Are you making double-talk?"

"You provide the sex, and let me do the thinking." He chuckled indulgently, and let his hand slide a little higher.

Berenice picked up the magazine and placed it as a screen over her lap.

"I don't invest in films, not even my own," Jerry said. "For this purpose I acquire backers. Usually banks. In this case I'll have no problem. The boys at Metropolitan-National have become my buddies ever since I signed to take over Jefferson Square."

"The whole thing?"

"The theater, for Christ's sake! Anyway," he added irritably, "they'll give me the million and a quarter. The film that's already in the can is the world's greatest collateral."

"A million and a quarter!"

Jerry snapped his fingers, his good humor instantly restored. "It'll net four dollars for every dollar invested. That's the record of my last three films. Any other questions, sweetie?"

"Yes." Her dark eyebrows drew together, and she raised a

79

hand to her very short and tousled platinum-colored hair. "I've been worried sick ever since you told me we've got to get off the plane separately so people won't know we're traveling together. What do I say to the reporters?"

"Show 'em plenty of leg, shove back your shoulders and press your arms against your sides so your boobs will stick out. You'll do fine."

"With photographers! I know what to do for photographers!" She always felt insulted when Jerry forgot she had been a successful model long before she had met him. Sometimes she thought he actually believed other people's lives began when they first came into contact with him. "What do I say to the reporters?"

"I'll go through the whole routine for you again. We land at Seaboard International Airport. I go down the ramp into the lounge. While I'm talking to the press, you wait. Take your time. It always takes a while to empty an airplane. I'll be the first off. You'll be the last. Okay, here you come, down the ramp. Plenty of ass wiggle—"

"I know how to walk. What do I *say*?"

"One. You have a part in Jerry Solanz' great new film. It's just a small part, but you hope it will bring you to the attention of the critics and the public. It's an honest part, and you've played it with conviction."

"I've played it with conviction," she repeated in a murmur.

"Two. You're thrilled by the challenge of the Jefferson Square Repertory Theater, and you hope you're a good enough actress to become a member of the company."

"You've told me that part over and over, too. I know both those things. What I mean is, they're certain to ask me about men, and love, and things like that."

"Shut your mouth, part your lips and give them the same smile you give the photographers. Tomorrow, at the hotel, the press agents will give you your lines before you have a meeting with the movie and theater page editors."

"I didn't even know there was going to be a whole press meeting." Berenice sounded frightened.

"Sweetie, you ought to know by now I always have more than one string to every bow, and plenty of bows. Solanz isn't going to waste this chance to present the future first lady of the theater to the press." Smiling, he closed his eyes again.

Suddenly Berenice squirmed. "Jerry!" She caught his forearm in a tight grip.

He withdrew, adjusting his cuff. "An actress," he said, "always controls her voice. She never lets it control her. Two. Except when she's playing for certain effects, and we haven't come to that yet in the lessons, her movements are always smooth. Effortless. You've got to make an audience believe you're the character, not somebody playing a part."

"This has nothing to do with acting, and you know it." She tugged in vain at the hem of her abbreviated skirt. "Just now, you—"

"Everything an actress does is the best of all possible practice for her future roles. Never, from the minute she wakes up until the minute she falls asleep, is she off stage. Believe me, sweetie, you've got great things ahead for you at Jefferson Square. You have a Solanz guarantee, and what more could you want? But for this you've to work. Tonight, after we catch Ritchie's performance at the Lyceum, we'll cut short our visit to Hector's. Maybe just a sandwich and a quick drink, so we'll be seen. Those job-hungry actors swarming around the table I don't need. Then, back to the hotel. You've got to be drilled in real-life-situation rehearsals until you react instinctively. So tonight we'll work."

Berenice caught her breath.

"Don't let it throw you, sweetie. You'll be in the best possible hands." He patted her thigh benevolently.

She was afraid that if she wept she would enrage him, so she closed her eyes and tried her best to fall asleep.

"Mama, I didn't take a taxi all the way to Fourth Street just to hear a blow-by-blow description of your pinochle game with Mrs. Elias this afternoon. Listen to me, for God's sake!" The charm bracelet on Sandra Masters' wrist jangled as she shook a finger under her mother's nose.

Maria Mascaroni neither blinked nor moved. "Stop shouting, you'll wake up Buddy."

"It'll serve the kid right, going to bed so early."

"You look like you need sleep, too. You have a blackness under the eyes. And the same bad temper like when you were a little girl and didn't get enough sleep."

"I don't know which is worse, your pinochle game or your lecture." Sandra flung herself into a chair, feet extended, the weight of her legs resting on the almost horizontal heels of her pumps.

"In those days," her mother said slowly, "you sleep alone."

"I've had a rough twenty-four hours, Mama, so knock it off."

Sandra's lips felt sore and puffy, and she touched them gingerly with the tip of her tongue. Even the thick coating of her favorite, creamy lipstick that she had applied just before coming here, immediately after Dougherty's departure from her apartment for his suburban home, had not soothed them. She had known for a long time that he drove a hard bargain in business, and should have realized he would be just as merciless in demanding his pound of flesh. From now on, she suspected, he would expect a daily liaison, and she was afraid that, whenever it was inconvenient for them to go to her apartment, he would take her in his office.

"I'm listening," Maria said, "for your wonderful news."

"Your baby girl is moving up in the world." Sandra brightened appreciably. "Mrs. Cavelli always buys the papers. Start looking for my name in the columns. I'll be there."

"When people talk about you, they will say only the bad."

"Jeez, you're cheerful. But you don't get it. Mama, I'm joining the jet set."

The old woman scarcely bothered to raise her shoulders a fraction of an inch, then let them droop wearily again.

"On Tuesday night, there's going to be a cocktail party of the in-crowd of Jefferson Square at the house of the Emorys. You know, he's the bank big wheel, and she's the broad who collects chips by the millions for worthy causes, as they say. I'm going to be there."

"You sleep with this man?"

"I never even met him. Her, either."

Maria looked at her scornfully. "You are invited to the fine home of the wealthy you have not met?"

"So help me, you don't know what happens anywhere outside this filthy old tenement—"

"This is where I live."

Sandra ignored the interruption. "All the top people go to a bash like this. The women you see in fashion magazines. The men who buy and sell whole towns when they feel like it. The idea is to get them to shell out more money for Jefferson

Square, only everybody is very polite about it. Even Warren Hopkins will be there. You know who he is?"

Maria's expression indicated that she neither knew nor cared.

"*The* Hopkins family, Mama!"

"You will become his mistress?"

Like a shot, if I could work the right angles, Sandra thought. "Mama, he's going to get engaged any day. You really should start reading the newspapers!"

"It is enough that I know what happens in the neighborhood."

There was nothing to be gained by renewing a fruitless argument that had never been resolved. "We just heard that Jerry Solanz will be there, too. He's going to be back in the country for a few days, so he'll be one of the star attractions. How do you like that?"

"What does it matter what I like? You do what Sandra wants."

"I guess you don't know who he is, either. He makes some of the movies that come to the Fifth Street Theater. And he's going to put on some shows at Jefferson Square. Mama, in Buddy's summer vacation, maybe I can get him a job as a walk-on."

Maria looked blank.

"In plays, sometimes, they have crowds. People who just walk on the stage. They don't say or do anything, but they get good pay for it. And it's fun for the kids. They get to meet other kids who come from rich families. There's no telling what kind of a break Buddy might get."

"Buddy," the old woman said, a metallic ring in her voice, "does not become the actor. This summer he starts to work as the apprentice. He will be like his father, and work as a cleaner in the Water Street Fish Market."

Sandra was outraged. "Haven't you got any ambition for Buddy? Hasn't he got any for himself? You want him to spend his whole life cleaning the scales off fish? That kind of a future stinks as much as he'll stink when he comes home every night!"

"From the day we come here from the old country to the day he died, your Papa worked in the Water Street Fish Market. Every day in the winter and in the summer except holy days. And every week he brought home his pay. Good pay, that gave you a home, and food, and the dresses you wore to school. Not one time did he look at other women. Not one time did he throw away his money on cards. With his friends, he drank only the beer and the wine. Your papa was a good man, and he had the respect of all the neighborhood."

"He was a fish cleaner without an ambitious bone in his body," Sandra said bitterly, "but he was a saint. Saint Angelo Mascaroni."

"All the neighborhood gave him respect!" Maria's voice rose. "All the neighborhood were his friends, and not one was his enemy. But his daughter has no respect for the dead."

"Okay, Papa was a great guy, just great. But Buddy has to make something of himself."

The old woman's jaw became set. "What does a man need? Money for food, and a home that will keep his family warm. The respect of his neighbors, and the love he shares with his friends. It is enough. Buddy will be like his father."

It was incredible, Sandra reflected, how many slum dwellers shared her mother's view. Even people of her own generation and Buddy's. Some of her former classmates were still living down the block, burdened by husbands who were content with minimal wages, and satisfied with rearing broods of dirty children who made their parents old before their time.

Sandra hoped the rumors she had read were true, that the Water Street Fish Market was coming down. If it vanished, Buddy, who was already too lazy for his own good, would be forced into the world, to become something more than an ignorant slob who gutted freshly caught fish.

Standing in her usual belligerent pose, Sandra shook her fist. "Mama, no matter how much you and the kid like decay and garbage in the streets, I'm going to help you. In spite of yourselves. What I'm doing is for your sakes as well as my own. Your trouble is, you don't know what you're missing. But I'm going to fix all that. Some day you're going to throw your arms around me and thank me for taking you out of all this crap. You'll be happier, and Buddy is going to amount to something!"

"Like you, Sandra?" Maria's voice was ominously, contemptuously quiet now. "Go back to your rich friends. It is too late for me, but God will punish you. Buddy will stay here, and be a good man. And I will stay here."

Sandra was sorry she had made the trip down to Fourth

84

Street. It was impossible, apparently, for her mother to realize that the grubby cocoon in which she had wrapped herself soon would be torn away by building wreckers. Even though other tenements and their inhabitants had disappeared, and the new marble buildings of Jefferson Square would soon rise, transforming the entire neighborhood, her mother was clinging to the only reality she had ever known in America. She was pathetic—and stupid—and disgusting.

Warren leaped to his feet when the door buzzer sounded, almost knocking over the ashtray at his elbow.

Carolyn stood in the door frame for a moment before she found her voice. "I hope I'm not too terribly late," she said. "I suppose I should have taken a taxi after you telephoned, but I thought it best to wait until Edward brought Governor Herder and the others home with him, as he'd said, and let myself be delivered by the chauffeur. Some of the speeches at their dinner were interminable, I gather, or they would have reached the house a half-hour earlier."

Her hands trembled slightly as she unfastened the clasp of her stone marten scarf. "I feel guilty, keeping you up when I know you have to leave early in the morning."

His own hand was far from steady as he took the scarf from her. "I can sleep on the plane," he said.

She walked straight into the living room, and carefully selected a chair rather than one of the divans where he could join her. "You're a dear to listen to my troubles."

"Between us we're learning about culture centers, I think. We ought to hire ourselves out as experts when some other town gets the bug, and puts up a culture center of its own."

Carolyn forced a laugh.

Suddenly he realized she had changed her clothes since he had seen her before dinner, and her snug dress, combined with the scent of her recently applied perfume, were not making the situation easier for him.

"May I get you a drink?" Warren asked. "A liqueur, perhaps?"

"I think not, thank you. I felt rather bad about dragging you away from the little Callison girl. I hope she didn't mind too much." Carolyn managed to be graceful even when she was patronizing.

"Not in the least. We were having an early evening in any

event, even if this conference with you hadn't developed. It all came up suddenly, and was quite impromptu."

"That's all right, then. I wouldn't want to upset her."

"Oh, Betsy is a big girl." That, he decided, was a ridiculous thing to say.

"She's very sweet," Carolyn said. "Although I suspect she's a bit naïve."

"I wouldn't know," Warren said with deliberation.

"This is none of my business," Carolyn said, "but we women are born with an insatiable curiosity—"

"There isn't a word of truth in anything the newspapers have been printing."

She took a deep breath. "Well. Back to Jefferson Square. You know about the enlarged budget, of course."

Warren nodded.

"I won't bore you with the details of the job I have ahead of me. But I do need your advice, if you can give it to me without betraying any confidences."

"I can't imagine that kind of a conflict of interests."

"Here's the acid test," Carolyn said. "How do I get a substantially larger commitment for the square from the Hopkins Fund?"

"Well, there are eleven of us on the board of trustees. Five are members of the family, and the other six hold a majority vote."

"That's no answer."

"I'm not finished. Only a couple are truly independent. The rest are either old friends of the family or are indebted to us in some way. Again, theoretically, my cousins and I are free to take any stand we please. In practice, everybody hedges until Uncle Ben tells us what he thinks. Sometimes his silence is enough. And then we vote."

"So the decision is up to him."

"You said it in so many words. I didn't."

"I'd also like to see him increase his own pledge."

"You have courage."

"I can see no practical alternatives."

"Then that's what you tell him. Have all your figures and facts ready. Compress all your arguments into something you can express in a very few minutes. He may try to trip you, as I'm sure you know from your previous experience with him, so be prepared for any curves he throws you."

"Would you pave the way for me?"

Warren shook his head. "I stepped in just enough to help you get your first interview with him, but it was like walking on the edge of a cliff. He can't tolerate intermediaries, and if he thought we were conspiring to use family influence, he wouldn't give the square another nickel. Our ancestors had extraordinary scruples, and Uncle Ben has inherited them."

"So have you, Warren."

"Some of them. Not all."

Their eyes met.

"Tell me about the recording tonight," Carolyn said hastily.

"I'm beginning to think Helsing is more of a romantic than he's willing to admit. His Chopin études and scherzos were just brilliant, and at the end, the musicians themselves applauded him. I'm no judge, but Ive never heard Chopin done with greater bravura and tenderness. It was strange, though. Betsy was talking to some of the men she knows—they took a quick coffee break at one point—and the concertmaster, I think it was, told her that every number they recorded tonight is on the program of Broussard's farewell performance."

"Obviously Helsing and Broussard couldn't care much for one another, but I wonder which of them scheduled his program first. It must have been Helsing. He has no reason to act vindictively."

"That's what we felt."

Carolyn suffered a quick, jealous stab when he spoke of himself and Betsy as "we."

Warren was aware of every change in her mood. "Have I said something to displease you?"

"Of course not." A clock chimed twelve times in an inner room, and Carolyn knew she could not stay indefinitely. She raised her head and again met Warren's gaze.

This time he rose from his chair, and when he took a single step toward her, she stood, too. When he put his hand on her shoulders gently, they kissed.

"I ought to apologize," Warren said, "but I'm damned if I will."

"I'd be insulted if you did," Carolyn replied.

Together they started toward the bedroom.

Carolyn stopped short at the threshold. "Please," she said in a small voice, "turn off the lights."

Warren obeyed. For a few moments they stood unmoving in the dark, then simultaneously began to undress at opposite sides of the bed.

They met on the bed, and for an instant the shock of nude body touching nude body was paralyzing. Then they embraced, fervently, lips seeking and finding, hands caressing, bodies straining.

The unfamiliar lean toughness of Warren made Carolyn's desire all the greater. Although she and Edward went to bed together infrequently, she had become accustomed to the puffiness of a middle-aged man who spent most of his waking hours at a desk. Warren's youthful, eager vigor was overwhelming, and she pressed still closer to him.

Carolyn seemed smaller, daintier than Warren had thought her, but her agility and the depth of her passion aroused him so thoroughly that his guilt was obliterated. Only their nearness, their intimacy seemed to matter.

She shivered when he first touched her breasts, and then nipped at his lips and tongue with her teeth in an ecstatic frenzy. Her excitement, in turn, caused him to redouble his efforts, and soon both were acting and responding instinctively. He was demanding, yet giving and gentle; she was yielding, yet seeking more and still more, and their mutual desire was boundless.

Then, gradually, they returned to other realities. Warren was spent. His love for her had been more ferocious, more all-encompassing than any emotion he had ever felt.

Carolyn, satiated, was restored to the full dignity of her womanhood. Clasping his head, she pressed it to her breasts and stroked it, whispering, "My lover. My baby."

"Too bad you can't keep these offices," Jerry Solanz said. "The view is great." He gestured toward the city spread out below, beyond the heights of Hopkins Tower.

"I always feel relieved when I remember these are just temporary quarters," Dan Robertson replied, smiling while studying his visitor. "It's a temptation, you know, to sit here all day doing nothing. In the new Administration Building I'll be on the second floor, with a view of nothing but the side of your Repertory Theater. Then maybe I can concentrate."

"That's the model over there, huh? The whole layout?" Jerry stood and walked to the far side of the office to look at Jefferson Square laid out in miniature. He was silent, peering through his thick-rimmed glasses and chewing on an unlighted cigar.

88

"This is the third set of dolls' houses they've made for me," Dan said, following him. "And the last. The architects have sworn they'll walk out on us if there are any more changes."

"Then they'll have to walk, and you'll have to get yourselves some new boys." Jerry used his cigar as a pointer. "This I just can't take." He jabbed at the front entrance of the model of the Jefferson Square Repertory Theater.

"I was told you'd seen and approved the design."

"Oh, the design, sure. Inside and out. But not the location. Nobody even mentioned the location, and I was a jerk not to ask." Jerry continued to frown.

Dan tried to conquer a feeling of dislike for a man with whom he had been acquainted for only a quarter of an hour. Most theatrical directors had firm ideas, and Solanz reputedly was a tyrant in a tyrannical profession. In any event, it would do no harm to allow him to let off steam; perhaps he was still jittery less than a day after making his unexpected and dramatic flight home from Europe.

"This is the main plaza, right? With the fountains, and the thirty-foot abstract statue of the nine Muses that Obermeier has been commissioned to make."

"In a sense it's the core of the square, yes. All of the units will fan out from the Fountain of the Muses. You'll note that the architects have made certain that there will be unimpeded sight lines to and from each of the units from the core. But the beauty of the architecture is that each unit will form its own entity."

"Good for them. But it won't do. Symphony Hall and the Grand Opera House are getting top billing, the way they've got it worked now. And the Repertory Theater is out in Sticksville. All that gets changed. I want my theater where the action is."

For a moment the man's audacity robbed Dan of his powers of speech. Work was already in progress on the Repertory Theater, and the mere thought of moving it to another location, like a toy, seemed an absurdity. "I'm afraid it's too late," he said at last, making a great effort to sound genial. "They're already pouring concrete, as you'll see when we ride out to the square, Mr. Solanz."

"I'm Jerry. You're Dan. And if you want to see a mountain mover, watch me."

The man's ego was insufferable, but Dan remained pleasant. "The present sites were chosen for both aesthetic and

89

practical reasons. There's a need for balance, you see, so the two largest units will be the anchors at the core. The Grand Opera House will have almost four thousand seats, and Symphony Hall will hold about twenty-eight hundred. The capacity of your Repertory Theater is only thirteen hundred. When you see the difference in the sizes of the excavations for it and Symphony Hall, you'll understand very quickly. The symphony will perform in a building with twice your capacity."

"The product we're selling is what will draw the crowds. The repertory will be the prime, A-1 attraction."

"Oh, you'll undoubtedly play to full houses. We're already being flooded with requests for seats for the Repertory Theater from individuals, schools, clubs—all sorts of organizations."

"That's what I mean," Jerry said, a note of finality in his voice.

Dan realized that something stronger than diplomacy was needed. "Of course, the symphony is almost completely sold out already, and seats for the opera are selling at a tremendous clip. The public response has been extraordinary."

"I'll get the headlines. They won't."

"The square's units aren't in competition. Each augments the others. That's the real significance of a culture center. Music, drama, the dance create a balance."

"Solanz productions don't need support. They stand on their own."

Dan was still hoping a quarrel could be avoided, and smiled in agreement.

"That's why there's nothing personal in my demand that the sites of the theaters be changed," Jerry went on. "It's just a matter of good show business sense."

Dan knew he had to lower the boom. "A few months ago the possibility could have been discussed. Even then it really would have been too late, but the door was still open a crack. Now it's too late. I'm trying to impress on you that actual construction has started, and that it would cost more millions than I could even guess to make the changes you'd like. The size of each parcel of land, as it becomes available, must be taken into account, too. There are more factors involved than I can tell you."

"We'll see about that. I know what I want, and what I'm

going to have, so I'm going straight to the man at the top."

"You're talking to him."

"You? I'm going to Benjamin Hopkins the Third, Esquire."

"I'm the final authority in all matters pertaining to the individual units." Dan spoke quietly.

"Sweetie," Jerry said, "I don't want to get into a fight with you. Get yourself a smaller hat-band, and we'll get along fine. I never do business with anybody except the man who sits at the very top of the pyramid."

"Help yourself to my telephone."

"I will. Is there a house number to get the Big Man?"

"No, you'll have to call Hopkins Enterprises." Dan turned a card-wheel. "There you are. Dial nine first to get an outside line."

Jerry spun the dial rapidly. "Mr. Benjamin Hopkins." He waited, then repeated his request and identified himself. "Wait a minute. How do you know he won't talk to me when you haven't even told him I'm on the wire?" He listened for a moment, then slammed down the telephone. "That's what I call a run-around."

"You might want to try him through Herbert Brookes, his executive assistant. That's how it's usually done."

"Why didn't you say so in the first place?"

"The same number." Dan walked to the windows and looked out. The view never tired or bored him, and he felt certain that, no matter how long he lived, the sight of the skyscrapers and river, the great ships at their wharves and the thousands of automobiles crawling on asphalt ribbons would always thrill him. He had become a part of the city, and the mere thought of abandoning what he had always wanted, and had now achieved, pained him.

Jerry was talking rapidly, becoming angrier with each breath he drew, and again he slapped the telephone into its cradle. "Shit. Brookes bounced the ball back to you."

"I wish you'd take my word for it. Not even Mr. Hopkins could change the location of the square's units."

"There are other ways I can get to him. I have friends on the board of directors."

"If you can get what you want, more power to you," Dan said, turning and facing his visitor. "I say you're wasting your time, but it's your privilege to kick up a storm. Just for the record, I don't care in the least which of the units are located on the center of the square. The architects are the experts, and I went along with them, as did everyone else. My real concern is the merchandise we sell to the public."

"That's where you're an expert."

"It's what I'm being paid to do," Dan said.

"You know all about the theater. All about music. All about opera. All about art. All about ballet. All about—"

"No, but apparently I know enough to have convinced the directors that I'm the man for the job they've given me."

"I've checked your background. Professor of the Humanities at a big university. Author of two textbooks—and I'll give you your due. Most of what you wrote about the theater made sense. And then that big book, *The Quandary*, that must have made a neat pile for you. I was thinking of buying the screen rights to it at one time, but I could tell right off from my reader's synopsis that I couldn't have used anything but the title." Jerry again became more belligerent. "Being a teacher doesn't mean you really know anything about plays."

"That's the old, old question, isn't it? Aristotle, who defined and explained the rules used in the drama for more than two thousand years—and still used in a great many plays today— never wrote a play, never acted in one and never directed one. Theater critics are observers, not participants." Dan realized he had been put on the defensive, and fell silent.

"Absolutely nobody interferes with a Solanz production, sweetie."

Dan knew it would be fatal to the future of Jefferson Square if he failed to clarify the issues Jerry Solanz was raising. "You and I are sensible, intelligent men who share a love for the theater. I have every confidence that we'll see eye to eye."

"Just so we both understand that the Repertory Theater is strictly my baby."

"I wouldn't presume to interfere in the selection of your acting company or staff. You'll choose your own set designers, costume designers, and so forth. I'll have to be informed of what you're doing, since you'll be working under a budget allocated by me."

"The professor is clever. I do what you want or you'll draw the purse strings good and tight."

Dan lost patience. "You seem determined to quarrel with me, Solanz, which is ridiculous." Dan completely lost patience. "We have the same goal, making the Jefferson Square Repertory Theater a success. I'll squeeze, bull and wheedle every penny I can get for you from the directors. And you'll spend the money as you see fit. You'll produce and direct your own plays. I don't know how to lay it on the line any more fairly than that."

Jerry was partly satisfied. "Now you're making a little more sense, sweetie. I'll also select the plays I'm going to give."

"After consultation with me." Here, Dan knew, was the spark that might set off the real explosion.

"I pick them. The right is spelled out in my contract!"

"Look at your contract again." Dan went to a file cabinet at one side of his office, and quickly found the document in a folder. "Here's a copy."

Jerry read it carefully. Then, finally lighting his cigar, he beamed. "You've done your homework well, sweetie. I'm obligated to consult with the Artistic Coordinator of Jefferson Square in the selection of my repertory. But that doesn't mean I can't pick any goddam play I want."

"It means we decide jointly, if you'll take the trouble to check with your attorney."

"Believe me, that's exactly what I'm going to do!"

"You're still borrowing trouble, you know. I find it very difficult to believe we'll disagree. Try me out. What do you have in mind for your first two or three plays?"

"My opener," Jerry said expansively, "is going to knock the whole world of show business off its feet. I'm coming up with the greatest. Can I trust you to keep your mouth shut?"

The man's boorishness was as intentional as it was offensive, and Dan did not deign to reply.

"Every critic in the country has been writing Sunday pieces, telling me the play to use for the opener. Their lack of originality slays me. *Oedipus. Hamlet,* yet. It's my contention that the theater must reflect the modern world if it hopes to survive as a medium of more than passing interest. Are you with me, sweetie?"

"I'm with you," Dan said.

Jerry looked as though he were dealing with an idiot. "What else?" he demanded loftily. "I'm talking specifics. The play that will open Jerry Solanz' Repertory Theater.

"In show business, you've got to have more than savvy. You need all the right connections, which is what I've got." Although the door was closed, Jerry lowered his voice. "What do you think of Jan Marek's work?"

"He's our best playwright," Dan replied promptly. "Or he

was. He hasn't done anything since *The Burning Bush,* and that was about six years ago."

"Seven. I directed it. I've done all eight of his plays, and he wouldn't trust another director in America to stage one. Guthrie, Kazan, Logan, even Mike Nichols who is so hot these days, they can all go fry. Only Solanz directs the plays of his protégé and friend."

Dan tried to winnow the torrent of self-praise.

"Marek," Jerry declared solemnly, looking owlish behind his thick glasses, "hasn't lost his touch. Solanz knows, nobody else. I've seen the first two acts of a new play he's doing, and it's great. The second act will need a little fixing, but I'm not saying anything to him until he wraps it all up. He has a new approach, really new, that combines symbolism and realism. First I thought he was using the technique Brecht tried in *Mother Courage,* but when I dug deeper, I saw this is unique. It's a challenge to the director, and the actors will be in heaven. Particularly the leading lady. I'm not privileged to go into the details at this point, but she'll play a half-dozen parts. It'll be a bravura tour de force that will guarantee top stardom to the actress who does the lead."

"I assume you'll want to sign someone of star caliber."

"Those plans I'm not ready to reveal yet, either. But you can bet your last dollar on the effect this play will have on the theater-going public. It'll be bigger than *The Burning Bush.* Or Miller's *Salesman* and Williams' *Streetcar* combined!"

A first-rate significant play by Jan Marek, directed by Solanz, would indeed be important, Dan thought, and worthy of the Jefferson Square ideals. But he tempered his enthusiasm, knowing that theatrical people often indulged in glowing dreams that did not materialize.

"How's that for an out-of-the-ball-park homerun?" Jerry demanded.

"It sounds wonderful. Naturally, I'd have to read the play."

"For now, you'll have to take my word for it." Suddenly Jerry had become curt again. "We open with Marek, and what a lift that will give all the rest of Jefferson Square. Two immigrant boys from Prague carrying the whole goddam culture center on their backs!"

Dan saw no reason to force a dispute at present. The prospect was exciting, to be sure, but there were possible pitfalls to avoid. The new play might be too commercial to meet the standards he was setting for all Jefferson Square productions.

And, although he was reluctant to think in such terms, it was possible that Marek, after a seven year absence, had lost his touch. Rather than become involved in a harangue with a man who appeared to be chronically hostile, however, Dan decided to wait until he read the play. Then, if he disapproved of it, he would fight.

"As for my second play," Jerry said, "I'm going back to the classics, but with a switch. You know the author, but I doubt if you've ever heard of the play. Ben Jonson's *Sad Shepherd*. The language has the roll of Elizabethan English that good actors love, there's a pastoral quality to the play that oozes charm, and there are chances for all kinds of honest tricks in the staging. There are elements of the supernatural in it, but you'll have to take my word for it that they aren't corny. It'll give me a chance to do what I intend to do with the Marek play, but with a different twist. In this case it'll be the combination of symbolism—that's the supernatural material—and romantic realism that's fresh and alive."

His patronization had become intolerable. "I wonder if you realize," Dan said, "that *The Sad Shepherd* isn't played because it's only a fragment. Jonson wrote just the prologue and three of the five acts. The play was never finished."

Jerry recovered at once from his surprise. "It should run two hours, which is plenty long enough, with one intermission after the prologue and first act."

"There was a strictly experimental production of it in Houston a few seasons ago," Dan said. "Unfortunately, I didn't see it, but I went through all the reviews, and they confirmed my own opinion. It reads well, as poetry, but there's too little action. Some of Robin Hood's lines are almost interminably long. So there's very little that can be done to give the play pace."

"A Solanz production is never dead-assed."

"I'm sure of that, but it might be wise to reconsider. Perhaps, after you form your company, you could have your actors walk through a reading. That might give us a better idea of how it would play."

"Actors don't show me. I show them."

Dan couldn't resist adding, "By the way, the playing time in the Houston experimental performance was an hour and thirty-six minutes."

Jerry became stubborn. "With the added stage business I have in mind, it'll go two hours."

"Well, we have no need to make a final decision now," Dan said quietly. "We have almost a year to make up our minds. I dare say you'll have a clearer picture of what you want to do after you've seen the completed theater and know what actors you can get for your resident company."

"*The Sad Shepherd* will be Solanz' second play." Jerry's voice had become thick and ugly. "That's definite and final."

"I'll pencil it in, subject to change."

"Godammit, I'll make the announcement today!"

"I can't stop you and won't try. But—much as I hate to embarrass you if it becomes necessary to make a change later—I refuse to commit myself now."

"I'm not asking you to do anything, Robertson. I'm telling you!"

"I've been hoping we could avoid a showdown this early in the game, but you give me no choice, Solanz. Now I'll talk and you'll listen. Nothing at Jefferson Square is going to be a one-man operation. There will be as many as a half-dozen different performances being given in the various units on a single night. That means they've got to be coordinated, knit together into a single whole. In a culture center—this culture center—we'll work together as a team, with all of us on the same side."

"Screw you!" Jerry said.

Dan found the urge to slug him almost irresistible. But that, he realized, was what Solanz wanted. If the Vice-President of the square could be goaded into losing his temper and making an exhibition of himself, he would be discharged and disappear from the scene, and Jerry Solanz would be free to do as he pleased. "All right," Dan said, "you want to play dirty. I had a call this morning, just a few minutes before you showed up here, from the Metropolitan-National. You've applied for a large sum of money to finish your new movie, and they wanted my opinion of you. I told them I'd call them back and give them my impression after I saw you."

Jerry chewed hard on his cigar, his eyes glittering behind the heavy glasses.

"Either we work together, or we fight, with no holds barred. Which shall it be?"

"Right now you've got me by the balls," Jerry said. "But I won't forget this, you bastard."

CHAPTER THREE

Sandra stretched out on the bed, too lazy to reach for a robe that would cover her naked body, and stared up at the ceiling of her little apartment. This was the second time that the old reprobate had surprised her by giving her satisfaction, and the unexpected bonus had upset her calculations. She would have been willing to bet damn near anything that he couldn't have aroused her, much less work her up to an orgasm, but she had been wrong. Live and learn, even though she still hated the crude bastard.

She turned on one side to watch him as he buttoned his shirt and reached for his trousers. "Francis."

Once Dougherty had been satiated, his mind turned to other things. "Mmm?"

Her tone became proprietary. "Francis!"

One piece of tail was like all the others. Lay them, and they began to think they owned you. He stuffed his shirt into his pants and glanced at her.

"What kind of dress do I wear to the Emorys' cocktail party?"

"How the hell would I know?" Dougherty couldn't remember where he'd left his necktie, and began to search for it.

"Please, Francis, I mean it. You know I've never traveled in that league, and I don't want to make myself look foolish."

The necktie, he saw, was at the foot of the bed, and he crossed the room to retrieve it. "When a broad has an ass and tits like yours, it doesn't matter what she wears." He reached out to stroke her buttocks as he bent down to pick up his necktie.

"Funny man. Thanks for being so helpful, you bastard."

Dougherty's temper flared, and he slapped her across the rump with all his strength.

Sandra squealed, twisted around and sat up. "Was that supposed to turn me on?"

"No, it was supposed to teach you to keep a civil tongue in your goddam head when you talk to me!"

She returned his glare. "That ape-man stuff isn't included in our deal."

He made no immediate reply. Instead he caught hold of her wrist, wrenched her arm and forced her back onto the pillow.

"You'll do anything I want, any time I want it. And you'll like it. If I decide to unzip my pants right now, you'll play those kinds of games, too. Right?" There was only one rule on Fourth Street. You made a woman knuckle under to you, and you belted her around until she jumped through hoops for you.

Sandra knew the rule as well as he did. A girl who didn't want a shiner, or worse, agreed to any demand and made the best of it. "If that's what you want, honey, okay. But don't leave any black and blue marks on me, please. I want to look right at that party."

Dougherty released her, proud that he hadn't lost the old touch. "Next time," he said, looking at his watch, "I'll dream up some stunts."

I can hardly wait, she thought bitterly. Neither next time, nor on any other occasion, would she come when they hit the sack together. No matter what he forced her to do before he laid her, she'd resist him, without his knowledge.

"You're lucky," he said, shrugging into his jacket, shooting his cuffs and then adjusting them so they showed no more than a quarter of an inch. "I'm keeping my part of our bargain, although I don't have to. If I welshed on you, there are only two things you could do. Walk out on me and get yourself another job—which wouldn't bring you any closer to the Jefferson Square crowd. Or call up my wife and tell her we've been playing house. You wouldn't be the first, and she doesn't listen to that kind of crap any more." Strutting slightly, he moved toward the door. "So you keep in good with me, and don't forget it."

The door slammed, and Sandra was alone. She examined her chafed wrist, then rose from the bed to look at her red buttock in the full-length mirror on the inside of the bathroom door. Francis was polite as all hell in bed with his wife, she felt sure. He was married to a daughter of one of his first big clients, and undoubtedly treated her like a lady. Like all Fourth Street punks, he slugged only those who couldn't fight back.

But he had chosen the wrong victim. Like everybody else, he was vulnerable, and once Sandra found his weakness, she would get her own back. She had a vague idea of a way to hurt him, but would have to check it out in greater detail. She'd never caught more than an occasional glimpse of the papers he kept in the confidential file, but she had her own key to it, and tomorrow, Saturday, she'd go into the office for a few hours to catch up on her homework while Francis was living it up out in the suburbs.

God, how she'd love to make him kiss her ass. That was funny. He had just done it. Gently rubbing the smarting buttock, she smiled.

The food served at the Indian Tea House, two doors from old Symphony Hall, was surprisingly good. The curry dishes were authentic, and the chef, who made his own Bombay Duck according to a drying process that had been a family secret for generations in Shahjahanpur, had won unstinting praise from the food editors of *Holiday* and other gourmets. But most of the patrons of the Indian Tea House either could not afford its specialties or were too engrossed in music to be aware of what they were eating. It was enough that the tea and coffee were strong, and that the management kept down the price of its sandwiches in order to prevent its student clientele from deserting to the antiseptic hamburger and waffle establishments that had sprung up nearby.

Bettina Callison sat in a booth in the dark interior of the Indian Tea House, and in her excitement did not realize that one arm had brushed against the set of brass Indian bells used to summon a waitress. "I envy you, Manuel," she said. "Your future is assured. You'll give your debut in old Symphony Hall within a year, and you'll be a guest soloist with Helsing and the orchestra no more than six months later!"

Manuel Rios raised a slender, long-fingered hand to his wavy black hair to make sure every strand was in place. It was a nervous gesture, so much a part of him that he no more realized he was indulging in it than he heard the pleasant tinkle of the thin gold identification bracelet on his wrist. "Soon, Betsy," he said with a light, high-pitched laugh, "you'll have me competing with Horowitz."

"That may have to wait until you've completed your two-year tour of Europe." She sipped her tea and smiled at the slender young man.

"You go too fast, dear friend," Manuel protested. "I am overwhelmed, it is true, to be accepted as a pupil by Anton Helsing after all these years of study and practice. But the world is full of promising pianists. It will be enough for me if I can afford—some day—to buy the hacienda I want outside Buenos Aires, and to give an occasional concert at which the critics will not laugh."

They were interrupted by an American waitress in the white, gold-edged sari that was the uniform of the place. "You rang for me," she said wearily, wondering why the attractive girl in the booth would bother with a queer. You really saw some odd sights in this place; maybe it was because fags were safe. She couldn't stand them herself, but the blonde looked old enough to add and subtract.

Betsy was puzzled for a moment, then had an idea. "Why don't we celebrate with champagne, Manuel?"

There was a trace of embarrassment in the young pianist's giggle as his hands fluttered in a self-deprecatory gesture. "If I could afford it, I would drink nothing but champagne."

"The treat's on me," Betsy said quickly, and nodded to the waitress.

The woman went off toward the bar, shaking her head and telling herself she would never understand the younger generation. Or maybe they were different because they were musicians, like all the other strange characters who inhabited the Indian Tea House.

"How was everything at the culture factory?" Phyllis asked as Dan came into the apartment.

"There was a guy who showed up today with a great idea," he said. "You package art like sausages. Can you get a sitter tonight, honey?"

"It isn't too late to try for one of the student nurses."

"Good. Ever hear of a movie called *Rain and Sun?*"

A strand of her loose, dark blonde hair fell forward as she shook her head.

"Neither had I, but this is once when we needn't be ashamed of our abysmal, provincial ignorance. It's a very little foreign film—one of those both-sides-of-the-Iron-Curtain products. An Italian producer, a Polish director, an international cast and shot in Austria, I believe. It won a couple of very arty prizes on the Continent, but apparently it never quite got off the ground, and there hasn't been even a whisper about it in this country. Somebody in the Comparative Lit. Department at Seaboard mortgaged his soul to borrow a copy that has to be flown back to Milan in the next day or two, and we've been invited to a private showing tonight."

"At the university?"

"Um-hum. We don't have to go if you don't want to."

"Let's. I know how much you enjoy visiting a university."

Now he was certain she was pampering him. "I'm game if you are, Phyllis. Call the sitter, honey. We ought to leave here at eight." Dan went to her and kissed the hollow at the base of her throat. "Use your phone, would you? I have a couple of business calls to make before I can settle down for the evening."

He went off into what they called their Catch-All Room, where overflow books were piled on newly installed shelves, and Phyllis' easel and canvases filled one corner. Waiting until he saw the light that indicated one of the phones was in use, he picked up the instrument on the work-table and quickly dialed a number.

"Harvey," he said in a low tone as a man answered at the other end of the wire, "I'm glad I caught you at home."

"Dan!" Harvey Simpson's heartiness poured through the line. "This is mental telepathy. Esther and I were just—"

"Give her our love. Harvey, I want to see you tomorrow."

"I'm sure I have a lunch date, but if you'll let me call you in the morning after I've looked at my appointment book, I'll put you down for the first free day, Dan."

"This is for talk, not food. I'll come up to Simpson and Smith whenever it's convenient for you."

"You sound distressed, Dan."

"I can't discuss it now, but there's something I want to hash out with you."

"I'll be available," Harvey said.

"What time do you get to the office?"

"Well, I—"

"Suppose I stop in at nine thirty, on my way downtown?"

"This does sound serious! I'll make a point of being there on time, Dan."

Edward Emory was the despair of secretaries who took dictation from him. He was maddeningly deliberate, often pausing for several minutes as he searched for precisely the right word to express precise thoughts, and, more frequently than not, making so many minor revisions in a letter that the typist knew it by heart before it suited him. This evening, however, he was not true to form. His normal day's work was done, he was anxious to leave the office and dictated rapidly, without hesitation.

"To all members of the Jefferson Square finance committee. Mr. Dougherty's warning has materialized. Enclosed is a photostat of a letter just received from the Jackson Drive Realty Company, owners of the property needed for the completion of Jefferson Square. You will note we are being asked six million dollars for this land.

"Were it possible to build elsewhere, I would recommend that we do so. In the opinion of the Metropolitan-National Bank's vice-president for real estate development, the property in question is worth no more than two million. It is obvious, however, that the directors of the Jackson Drive Realty Company realize we have no choice, and therefore have inflated the price.

"We must accept their offer. Mr Dougherty has tried, both in person and by telephone, to persuade these realtors to lower their price, but they refuse. Consequently this is the penalty we must pay for our failure to acquire this land for a reasonable sum when we were in a position to acquire it several years ago.

"Our overall budget estimates must be revised upward accordingly."

"The cuspidor, Eddie, is one of the last relics of the age of political bossism." Governor Herder sat with his feet on his desk, smoking. "My wife, being a lady, thinks the cuspidor is disgusting, but she isn't in politics, and her argument that you won't find one in the Oval Office of the President of the United States isn't valid. In the upper echelons of the federal bureaucracy one can get away with pretensions. But, if you took a survey, you'd find that the office of every governor and every big city mayor is equipped with at least one."

Taking a last drag on his cigarette, he flipped it into the

102

cuspidor at the far side of his office. "Good shot, huh, fella? Two points for Al."

"That was great, Governor," Eddie Brown said wearily. On the infrequent occasions when Herder unwound with a drink too many, it was even more important than ever to agree with everything he said. And cuspidors were non-controversial.

"Your enthusiasm is staggering. If I'd had the eye as a Princeton undergraduate that I've developed in the political arena, as we laughingly call it, I'd have made the varsity basketball team."

Eddie splashed more bonded rye into their paper cups. "Let's make sure your aim is as good when you throw your hat into the Presidential ring."

Governor Herder's hand-sewn English shoes hit the floor with a thump as he sat upright, and his flailing arm almost upset his drink. "What kind of a crack is that?"

"No crack." Eddie's disclaimer was weak.

"The hell it isn't."

"All right. The hell it isn't. You're leading with your chin by becoming too closely associated with Jefferson Square."

Al Herder laughed. "I've never known you to start seeing things after a couple of drinks, Eddie."

His assistant shrugged.

"There can be nothing less controversial than the world's finest, most glittering culture center. The square cuts across party lines—everywhere. People are no more against it than they are motherhood. It would be un-American these days."

"I'm not asking you to step out of the Jefferson Square picture, Governor. You're on the board, you've squeezed some handsome appropriations out of the Legislature and you're the champion of the arts. Good. That wins you the sympathy, if not the active support, of the college-educated and would-be cultured in every suburb from coast to coast. But you're laying it on too thick. You make too many public statements about the square. You're becoming one of their patron saints, and that's dangerous."

"I haven't heard such fascinating inanities since my friends at the Tennis and Badminton Club told me I'd be a traitor to my class if I ran for public office. What possible harm can intimate identification with the square do me?"

"I'll grant you that everything there has been running

smoothly. So far. But some explosions are inevitable. You don't want to be cut by flying debris, or have some of the shit stick to you."

A deep frown appeared on Governor Herder's ruggedly photogenic face. "What do you know that I don't?"

"Nothing, really."

"Let's not be coy, Eddie. If you've got something to say, out with it."

"Well, for one thing, I've heard that Dan Robertson had a terrible scrap with Jerry Solanz. I don't know any of the particulars, but there's a real feud building there."

Herder drained his paper cup, crumbled it and threw it into the Florentine wastebasket beside his desk. "Nothing but artistic temperament. That's part of the circus. I can always step in to reconcile the boys, and even if I fail, I get credit as a sensible peace-maker. You're seeing ghosts under the bed."

"Then there's the impossible financial deficit that's going to get worse now that the square will have to pay a fortune for the land that hasn't yet been acquired. You've been building a record as a prudent businessman who has stayed within his state budget—even though you've had to raise taxes twice. If the square gets into real financial difficulties, and I don't see how a crisis can be avoided, you know what the other Presidential candidates will do. You'll be nailed to a cross as the Pied Piper who led the culture crowd into bankruptcy. I hate to think of what Talbot of Idaho and Bosworth of Massachusetts can do to your image. You'll be the deadest duck in the Presidential primaries."

Herder's eyes narrowed. "How do you know about the land sale deal?"

"I'm paid a miserably inadequate salary to know everything that happens in the state. I'm not suggesting you pull out. But give yourself some maneuvering space. I've heard you preach the principle as Herder's number one law of political survival. Start practicing it!"

The photographers' flashbulbs popped repeatedly, and whenever there was a pause, Berenice Tolmey moistened her lips, smoothed her black net stockings and struck another pose. The press turnout had been wonderful, and she had every reason to be pleased, but she was tired, and longed for a stiff drink, a long night's sleep or both. But she knew Jerry

Solanz was lurking on the far side of the half-closed door of the hotel suite living room, so she let her skirt ride a little higher and pressed her elbows against her sides to make her breasts bulge still more.

"How about leaning forward for another shot?" one of the photographers called.

Berenice started to oblige.

The press agent for Jerry's film company immediately intervened. "Easy, you guys," he said, deftly stepping between the girl and the cameras. "Miss Tolmey doesn't object to a reasonable amount of cheesecake, but she has aspirations as an actress, not as a sex symbol. And she's no stripper."

The hell I'm not, Berenice thought. Jerry's instructions had been explicit. "I want every man who sees your picture in print to get a hard-on looking at you," he'd told her, "and I want every woman to envy the bejesus out of your figure. But do it with class, the way I've taught you."

She shifted her position slightly to reveal more of the cleavage between the swelling mounds of her unfettered breasts, and the photographers, grinning at her, were content. Everyone was paying lip service to her supposed talents as a budding actress, and there would be no problems if the flimsy façade was maintained.

At last the press agent called a halt. "That's enough," he called. "You've been working for more than two hours."

"I'll keep going if they want me to," Berenice said doggedly.

The photographers and some of the reporters surprised her by applauding.

The press agent started to shepherd them out of the suite, delighted the press conference had ended on such a positive note.

"Just one more question," a reporter from one of the news services said, anchoring himself firmly opposite the girl on the divan. "There have been all kinds of rumors about you and Jerry Solanz. Would you like to deny them?"

The press agent cut in. "There's nothing to them!"

But Berenice brightened at the opportunity to deliver an unrehearsed line. "I don't know what rumors you mean, but every actress has to contend with them, and—"

"You and Jerry have been seen together constantly ever since you got back to the States. And we hear you were mighty friendly on the Riviera, too."

"I have great respect for Mr. Solanz as a director," Berenice said with seeming innocence, "and he's a wonderful employer."

"No romance, huh?"

"I believe he's married."

The newspapermen, crowded together near the door, laughed loudly. "That's rich," one of them said.

Berenice was startled and hurt. "Did I say something wrong?" she asked the press agent.

"You've said enough," he told her grimly. "So long, gentlemen. And thanks."

The door closed behind the departing group, and Berenice stood. "What was my booboo?"

Before the press agent could reply, a livid Jerry Solanz stalked into the room. "Of all the goddam freak things to say, you walk off with the Oscar. Holy shit!" He turned to the press agent. "Get out!"

A moment later, alone with Jerry, Berenice felt a spasm of fear. Never had she seen him so angry.

"You dumb broad, you gave away everything!" he shouted. "Everybody knows I'm married to that bitch who lives like a princess in the Beverly Hills house. Everybody knows I worship my kids—which I do. You know it yourself. How could you miss knowing it? Every stinking day of every lousy week that bitch gets her name into print. She joins charity drives. She sponsors fashion shows for Vietnamese orphans. She— holy God!—she pays her own press agent two seventy-five a week of my dough to keep her name in the columns, and she does it just to annoy me! How could anybody who has ever read an American newspaper not know I'm married?"

Berenice cringed. "I didn't mean any harm, Jerry. I just thought that if I played it blank—"

"You thought! That was your trouble. You used that sorry excuse for a brain instead of leaving everything to people who know how to handle newspapers."

She was near tears. "I'm sorry, Jerry. But I still don't see what was so awful about—"

"Look, sweetie. There's an unspoken agreement. A gentlemen's agreement, like. Those guys aren't bird-brains. They know this is my suite. They know that even though you're registered in an adjoining room, you and I get together, maybe, by unlocking a door. But they're willing to play the

106

whole thing straight, at face value, as long as there aren't any goofs. But when a sexy blonde dish whose tits are hanging out of her dress sits on my sofa in my living room and bats her eyelashes while she says, 'I believe he's married,' it's too goddam funny for them to keep it quiet. Too funny for them. Not for me. And not for you." He removed his Harris tweed jacket and genuine gold nugget cufflinks, and methodically began to roll up the sleeves of his Paris-made silk shirt.

"No, Jerry! Please!" The girl was terrified, and looked in vain for an escape. "You're just upset because of that argument you had with Mr. Robertson of the square—"

"I'm going to teach you, once and for all, to keep your mouth shut except when I tell you to open it!" Jerry's mouth twisted into a smile as he started toward her.

Anton Helsing sprawled on the sagging divan in his office, his eyes closed as he listened intently to the playing of Liszt's concerto in E flat. He moved so seldom that, at times, he appeared to be asleep, but occasionally, when he opened his eyes, reached for a pad and pencil beside him and scribbled a few words, it was obvious that he was alert. At last the final notes died away.

Manuel Rios, hunching slightly on the piano stool, rested his forearms above the keyboard. "What do you think, Maestro?"

Anton neither replied nor moved.

"Maestro?" There was uncertainty in the young pianist's reedy voice.

"Your sense of the bravura is superb." Anton swung his feet to the floor and carefully smoothed the crease in his slacks. "But there's more than flashiness in the work of every composer worth playing."

"Not Liszt, certainly." When Manuel became scornful his Castilian lisp was more pronounced.

"Liszt above many," Anton said severely. "What do you think of the younger Johann Strauss?"

Manuel's dark, limpid eyes widened, but he saw that his instructor was not joking. "He was a—a popular composer who wrote only third-rate corn."

"You understand neither his aims nor his accomplishments. Wagner and Brahms envied his *Blue Danube,* and called it one of the most inspired masterpieces of the nineteenth century. And when Berlioz first heard the *Emperor Waltz,* he wept and said that he himself was a mere carpenter of music."

"I find it difficult to believe."

"That's why I'm telling you all this. If you hope to become a master of the piano, Manuel, you must concentrate on more than technique. Every great artist looks deeply into the soul of the composer whose work he's playing. One needn't be a great soloist to feel it, either. Toscanini had no rival because he instilled that sensitivity in the heart of every man in his orchestra. In a manner of speaking, it's an acquired genius. I'm using contradictory terms, but I hope you see what I mean."

Manuel was quiet for a few moments. "If I tell you the truth, Maestro, perhaps you will not want me as your pupil."

Anton raised an eyebrow, but made no comment.

"When one is an Anton Helsing, so gifted that in all the world there are no more musicians than one can count on one's fingers who are his equals, one can speak of finding rapport with the great composers. But I know myself. I have not the—what is the English word—the dedication to become immortal." Manuel's hand traced the waves in his hair.

"You think too little of yourself. You've already learned the most important dedication required of the artist, self-discipline."

Manuel's hand fluttered in a self-deprecatory gesture. "It is true that I practice long hours, Maestro, but the spending of time at the piano does not mean I enjoy it!"

Anton laughed. "I've never yet met an artist who finds any real pleasure in the grind of a ten-hour daily practice session. It's more difficult for the young than anyone else. You have so many distractions. Girls, liquor—"

"Girls mean nothing to me, Maestro. And I drink very little."

"I had a teacher who urged me to become celibate in order to achieve my potential." Anton grinned. "Since you've already put the most common temptations behind you, the rest should be easy."

"I have not yet told you what I want, Maestro. My ambitions are limited. There is a hacienda outside Buenos Aires that belongs to a cousin. She will sell it to me for a reasonable sum whenever I can raise the money. I would like to spend my days there. And because I am vain, I like applause. So I have concentrated on my technique. Audiences in many Latin American cities are not sophisticated. I do not speak now of the great cities like Buenos Aires and Rio and São Paulo, where the critical standards are European, higher than in this country. But I could make a tour each year to the lesser places where my technique would win me the admiration of those who know only a little music."

"You damned well ought to be ashamed of yourself." Anton rose to his feet.

"I am brazen, and I admit it." There was something feline in Manuel's slow smile.

"Your potential is too great to be wasted. I simply won't permit it!" Anton came to the piano. "I have some idea of your temperament, and I'm not asking you to do the impossible. But I'm sure you'll become more enthusiastic when you see how much you can improve in just a short time. Play anything. Anything."

Manuel giggled, sobered and devoted himself to a melange of Chopin preludes and scherzos; fingers flying, he became lost in the music.

Anton moved to a place behind him, and carefully watched his hands. Himself absorbed, he discovered that something was nagging at him, and, little by little, found he could not concentrate on the efforts of his pupil. Suddenly, with a sense of shock, it occurred to him that he was thinking of another time, two decades earlier, when he had been the boy sitting at the piano. History was repeating itself, with differences, of course. He had been desperately poor, while Manuel seemed in relatively comfortable circumstances; his tassled red suede shoes had cost at least thirty or forty dollars, and his custom-tailored shirt certainly wasn't cheap.

There was another, far more significant difference. Manuel's ambitions were lamentably limited. When Anton had been eighteen, several years younger than the boy now playing Chopin, he had been consumed by a desire to conquer the world that had mattered to him, the world of music. No one knew, no one would ever know, what he had gone through to achieve the place he now held, a place he was determined to protect with all his strength and cunning.

Talent simply wasn't enough when a musician was dissatisfied with the success he had achieved and yearned for even greater glory. A great many people claimed that Toscanini had been a temperamental bastard, and that dealing with him had been hell. But Anton could understand how the most renowned of all conductors had felt. Always eager to top his own triumphs, he had struggled incessantly, and when a man fought, someone was bound to get hurt.

Strangely, it was often the ambitious themselves who suffered the greatest pain, but in the long run, these experiences made one more resilient, craftier, better able to deal with the problems of avoiding the blows of those below, while at the same time pushing aside those who stood still higher on the mountain. It was odd, after all these years of hate, for Anton to realize he owed a debt of gratitude to Hans Erdler. . . .

. . . Hans Erdler immodestly called himself the greatest piano teacher on earth, and his former students, most music critics and virtually everyone who had known him in Europe agreed with him. They also called him eccentric, which he was in no position to deny.

The burly son of a burly Rhineland steel-maker, he had refused to take his place in the German industrial hierarchy and had enjoyed a notable career as a concert pianist before discovering that teaching was his true metier. But his Continental career had been cut short, soon after he had inherited the bulk of his father's fortune, when he had quarreled publicly with Josef Goebbels, propaganda director of the Nazi party that had just risen to power in Germany. After denouncing Goebbels as a liar, and indirectly criticizing Adolf Hitler, from a Berlin stage, he had decided to leave Germany quickly and discreetly. He had already transferred most of his fortune to American and Swiss banks.

Settling in the United States, he had lived in seclusion, refusing to give concerts, and accepting only an occasional, exceptionally gifted pupil. His town house was his fortress, and he rarely ventured into the open, even more rarely entertaining his few friends. He was content, he said, with his records, his books, the knowledge that the Nazis had been crushed—and the excitement of helping his few pupils.

Anton Helsing knew he was lucky to have been accepted by Dr. Erdler, but had to keep reminding himself of the fact. His widowed mother and his sisters had slaved enough years for his lessons at the conservatory, and it was a godsend to be getting free lessons from someone as proficient as Dr. Erdler. It was also a godsend that his mother, thanks to the easing of the financial burden, had been able to move to a middle-class neighborhood. A slum boy under the strictest of orders not to fight because he might hurt his hands spent most of his life running away; what Anton enjoyed most was that he didn't have to run any more.

But Erdler was a monster incarnate. He'd kept the boy at work for four solid hours, and Anton's fingers were so tired they were numb. His back ached, perspiration dripped into his eyes, blinding him, but the voice behind him was adamant.

"The elements of bravura in the music of Chopin reveal themselves. Play him delicately, with subtlety, or you play him not at all, Helsing!"

Anton called on his last reserves of energy, biting his lower lip so he wouldn't weep.

"*Das ist genug!* Enough!" the voice commanded.

The boy turned slowly on the stool, slumping, and found Erdler grinning at him.

"Today I have tested you," the instructor said. "Talent is not enough. Self-discipline is not enough. One must have also dedication."

"I'm bushed," Anton said, shaking his fingers, and taking a crumpled handkerchief from his pocket to mop his flushed face.

Dr. Erdler did not understand his slang, but his meaning was clear. "You are dedicated. *Wunderbar!* Also I find you have interpretations that are fresh, sometimes original. It will do you no harm to study for conducting as well as to continue to prepare as a soloist."

The boy forgot his fatigue and whistled under his breath.

Dr. Erdler nodded approvingly, running a thick hand over his short, bristling hair. "You are willing to work additional hours to learn the profession of the conductor, Helsing?"

"I'm willing to do anything that will help me get ahead," Anton replied.

"We will have much to discuss. But first you need to clear the mind, no?" Erdler rose and beckoned.

Anton followed him down a flight of polished oak stairs, and looked with unconcealed envy at the huge tapestry on the landing, the marble statuary in what appeared to be a greenhouse. It was wonderful to be rich as well as famous, to own great treasures and treat them as objects that made life more pleasant. Some day, he promised himself, as he had

111

long promised his mother and sisters, he'd have enough money to repay them a thousandfold for the sacrifices they had made for him.

Erdler opened a door that led to a tree-lined inner court.

Anton was surprised to see a small swimming pool set in the middle of the court, its blue water shimmering in the late spring sun. It had never crossed his mind that anyone might own such a pool in the city, surrounded by his own house, but why not? Money could buy anything, and he made up his mind to build himself precisely such a pool in the court-yard of his own town house some day.

Erdler smiled at his obvious delight. "Swim, if you wish. You have earned the right today."

Anton hesitated. "I don't have any trunks."

"We are alone. Enjoy yourself, and I shall bring you a towel."

Needing no further invitation, Anton stripped and plunged into the cool water. For the next quarter of an hour he forgot that he was a "dedicated" student of music. He was a boy relaxing after a grueling day's work, and the tensions that had knotted his muscles and wearied his mind vanished. By the time he climbed from the pool, his energy was restored.

"You swim well, Helsing." Erdler handed him a towel.

Never had Anton felt anything as luxuriously soft. "We lived near the river until I started studying with you, Dr. Erdler."

"You swam in the river?"

The boy was vaguely conscious of the fact that his instructor was looking him up and down, slowly. "It isn't very sanitary, but the poor have no choice. Besides," he added with a grin, "it was either swim or drown. One of the favorite pastimes of the neighborhood was to throw in some kid the others thought couldn't swim."

Erdler shook his head. "The young are barbarians."

Anton made no reply, and, depositing the towel on the back of a white-painted, wrought-iron chair, looked around for his clothes.

"I thought we might sit out here while we talk. It is pleasant, no? Your clothes I took inside, so you might wish to wear this."

Accepting a folded garment of brilliant blue, Anton realized it was made of rich silk. He struggled into it, then felt

112

his face growing hot. "Isn't this a—a lady's dressing gown?"

Erdler laughed. "It was all I had available. But you need not be self-conscious. You look most attractive in it."

The boy sat down hastily, wishing the silk robe weren't so short. It looked even more ludicrous on his husky frame.

Dr. Erdler reached for a pitcher and two glasses on a tray. "Now that the war is ended," he said, "I can again import from Germany the Rhine wine and gin I use in my punch."

"None for me, thanks." Anton had already discovered that music and liquor didn't mix.

"In moderation it will do you no harm. On special occasions."

"Is this a special occasion?" The boy was somewhat flustered by his instructor's insistent stare.

"This is the day when we put the seal of musical greatness on Anton Helsing."

"Then it's special, Dr. Erdler." The boy took a tall glass of punch and sipped it experimentally. The taste was too strong, but he didn't want to hurt his host's feelings. Erdler, who could teach him more about music than any man alive, who could open every door for him, was far too important to be offended, even in something minor.

"I want to know more about your family life. I have met only your mother—"

"She's terrific, isn't she?"

"A fine woman."

"So are my sisters."

"You have two?"

"Three, Dr. Erdler."

"And you are the only son."

"My sisters call it a sorority house at home." Anton smiled, then sobered. "You can't imagine how much they've done for me."

"I have a splendid imagination. You have also a girl?"

"Nobody special these days." Anton hadn't been laid in months, and his schedule was too rigorous to permit him to chase the more desirable girls, who demanded a great deal of attention. That left only the tramps in his old neighborhood, who'd roll over for anybody, and they offered him no challenge.

"So. You care only for music."

Anton took another sip of the gin and wine punch. "You want me to be honest with you."

"*Naturlich.*"

"Well, sir, I've been doing a lot of thinking ever since I started studying with you. I'm not like Mozart, for instance. All he cared about was music for its own sake. He didn't care if he had to work as a flunkey, and when I've read about him I've gotten the idea that music meant more to him than food."

"I believe it did." Erdler's eyes were hooded. "But Anton Helsing prefers food to music, *nicht?*"

Anton's face hardened, and he looked mature. "I've gone hungry, Dr. Erdler, and I don't like it."

The instructor nodded.

"I love music. I think I've got the stuff to be a pretty good concert artist. I'd like to compose—"

"Symphonies? Concertos?"

"Everything. There are always snatches of music in my head, and I want to learn how to develop them. Some day I want to be a top conductor, too."

Erdler was amused. "Another Toscanini, perhaps?"

"There's only one Toscanini, but I want to come as close to his level as I can get!"

"Your ambitions are boundless."

"I guess they are. But it isn't just for the sake of music itself. That's my point. You may throw me out of here after I tell you this, but I've got to be fair." Anton realized the potent drink was making him reckless, but his instructor was sympathetic, and this seemed the right moment for candor. "I want to be famous."

"Why not? There are few strong enough to agree with Goethe that the deed is everything, its repute nothing, and even he enjoyed his renown."

"I want to be rich, too," Anton said defiantly.

Erdler nodded, his face expressionless.

"When you live as we did in my family for a long time, you get hungry for expensive things. Big houses. Like this one. Grand furniture. Expensive clothes. The works. And I want music to buy all those things for me."

"So they shall," Erdler said calmly.

The boy could not curb his excitement. "You mean that!"

"Provided you do not lose your love for music itself, I can

114

see no harm in your desire for fame and money. They will goad you when your dedication sometimes falters."

"Then you approve, Dr. Erdler?"

"More. I will help you achieve your ambitions. For two years you will live here, and I will teach you all I know about music. You will learn composition and conducting as well as the piano. All."

The offer was so overwhelming that Anton was speechless.

"In all my life I had only one other pupil to whom I devoted my complete attention, and he became a Nazi. Now, after all these years, the hurt has gone, so I will do for you what I tried to do for him." Erdler leaned forward and patted the boy's bare knee.

"I've heard other students who are better than I am," Anton blurted.

"They lack your will to succeed. It is the driving force as well as the talent that wins one a triumph over one's competitors."

"Nobody wants it more than I do," Anton admitted.

"Then you agree." It was a flat statement.

"I—I guess so. But we ought to sign a contract, or something. You deserve a percentage of what I'll make when I get to be somebody."

"I live comfortably."

Uncertain what to reply, the boy reached for his glass of punch.

"I wonder if you know the background of Julius Caesar," Erdler said.

The sudden change of subject was bewildering. "I read the *Gallic Wars* when I was a sophomore in high school, like everybody else. And hated every minute of it."

"No, no. When Caesar was young, he had great ambitions, as you have. He was a junior officer in the Roman army, and there were many of his colleagues who had similar ambitions." Erdler spoke very quietly, but his eyes were bright.

Anton didn't know why he was reminded of a cat about to pounce on a rat or mouse.

"Caesar was stationed in an eastern part of the Roman empire, and there he met a powerful man, who ruled a vast province in the name of the Senate. The proconsul took a great fancy to Caesar, who accepted an invitation to spend his free time in the palace of his patron. In return, the proconsul used his influence, and Caesar won advancement ahead of his peers. His ambition and ability won him enduring fame, of course, but he might never have been given the opportunity had it not been for the proconsul."

Anton was stunned when he began to understand the full meaning of the story and its implications. Cursing his own naïve innocence, he wondered why it had never occurred to him that Erdler was a fag. The whole situation was so clear now, and he saw how cleverly he had been maneuvered into a corner. He hadn't gotten wise even when he'd put on the girl's robe, or negligee, or whatever it was.

The offer was simple. In return for the chance to fulfill his wildest ambitions, he'd be expected to live for two years as Hans Erdler's—mistress. The very word made him wince.

The alternative was equally plain. If he refused, he could find himself another music instructor. Someone of lesser caliber, who'd expect cash in return for his teaching services. The family would return to its slum tenement, his mother and sisters betting the long shot that he might achieve at least some of his goals. They had come to America from Uppsala, Sweden when Anton was two. Theirs was the familiar imigrant story, down to the death of Anton's father, a day laborer, in a construction accident.

Would the odds be better if he became Erdler's protégé? Undoubtedly. People in the music world either didn't know or didn't care that he was a homosexual, and the respect for his judgment and abilities was as universal as it was profound.

Erdler was waiting patiently while the boy wrestled with the problem. "I won't hurt you, Anton," he said quietly. "I shall be very kind, very gentle."

The need to reach an immediate decision was urgent, cruel. "I—guess it'll be—okay," Anton murmured.

Erdler moved swiftly, and lifted him to his feet.

In sudden panic Anton tried to escape, but the man, holding him firmly with one powerful hand, began to fondle and caress him with the other.

I'm nothing but a lousy whore, Anton thought, and closed his eyes. The very worst of his degradation, his humiliation, was the unexpected realization that he enjoyed love-making with a member of his own sex. . . .

. . . The music finally stopped, and Manuel Rios turned on the piano stool to look up at his instructor.

116

"I'm sorry," Anton said, "but you play Chopin with too heavy a hand."

The youth pouted. "Always I have been praised for my interpretations of Chopin."

"I'm not praising you. And you don't interpret. You roar through him like a rocket taking off. Chopin requires delicacy, restraint, great subtlety, and if you're going to work with me, you'll have to take criticism seriously."

Manuel looked hurt. "Show me, and I will try."

Anton thought that perhaps he was being too harsh. He had no right to strike out at someone innocent because he'd been wallowing in the memories of his own corruption. "You raced through the last thirty-two bars, but they require a very light touch. Keep your foot off the pedal." Reaching over Manuel's narrow shoulders to the keyboard, he began to play the piano.

"Ah, yes. I see." Manuel deliberately leaned back against him.

The gesture was no accident, Anton knew; the pressure was too firm. Familiar, overpowering urges gripped him, and his fingers faltered.

Manuel twisted his head upward to gaze at him, a knowing look in his wise, dark eyes.

The discussion in the lounge of the Faculty Club was spirited, as always, and several of the people sitting in the overstuffed leather chairs around a coffee table were talking simultaneously. Their eagerness to be heard, to make their opinions known, was pleasantly familiar, and Dan Robertson grinned as he held up a hand for silence.

"Wait a minute!" he commanded. "As the only non-academician here, I'd better act as referee."

"You're one of us," said Ray Bowning of the Classics Department. "You're just masquerading as an executive who carries an attaché case."

The comment was flattering, and Dan's grin broadened as he took a sip of his long bourbon and water. "Whatever I am, I know what we're talking about, I think. The motion picture as a serious art form."

Frank Levenstein, the white-haired chairman of the English Department, immediately demurred. "My whole point is that the film can't be a serious art form. Arty, yes, which is not the same. *Hiroshima* was arty, and so were dozens of other films. *The Umbrellas of Cherbourg, Juliet of the Spirits* —and *The Island,* to name the best of them."

"For my taste," Dan replied, "the best of them was this thing we saw tonight."

There was a chorus of agreement from the wives, who had learned through long experience not to let themselves become involved in such discussions.

"And I say," Professor Bowning declared, "that *Rain and Sun* is as pure a work of art, within its own self-imposed limitations, as any play by Sophocles or Shakespeare. I'm not comparing, mind you. I'm saying nothing of the film's literary quality, as such. It has great merit, but I'm not trying to claim it belongs in the same literary category—"

"You go too far, Ray," Levenstein said. "I understand and accept your distinction, but you fail to make your basic point."

"The problem," Dan said, "appears to be semantic, so I suggest we define our terms. If we accept Aristotle's definition of art—"

"Oh, no." Levenstein chuckled. "When I'm arguing with a classicist, I accept none of his fundamental tenets. Whose side are you taking, Dan? Let's use Alexander Pope's definition of art, to the extent that it differs from Aristotle's."

"Pope himself acknowledged his debt to Aristotle, to all the Greeks," Bowning declared.

"True as far as you go," Dan said, "but if you'll reread his *Essay on Criticism*—which he published in 1711, but had been preparing for several years—you'll see he strikes out on his own."

"Indeed he does!" Levenstein launched into a vigorous exposition of Pope's views.

Dan caught his wife's eye, and Phyllis smiled at him.

He knew, without the need for any other communication between them, what she was thinking. This was the life he loved, and she was pleased he was having the sort of evening he had once taken for granted, but now only cherished in memory.

All at once, however, her sympathetic understanding irked him. She was committed, as he was, to the new life they had chosen for themselves. She, too, liked the excitement of his association with Jefferson Square, as well as the ability to walk into a department store and buy what she needed and wanted without having to search for bargains.

Professor Levenstein was saying something, and Dan forced himself to listen.

"Unfortunately, ladies and gentlemen, I'm paying the penalty of a departmental chairmanship this semester. I couldn't persuade anyone to teach the eight A.M. class in Restoration drama, and had to take it myself. Which means it's far past my bedtime."

Dan realized he had missed the climax of the spirited discussion.

Professor Bowning signed the chit, and the party started out of the lounge, moving past the Faculty Club's library. As they did, someone bounded out of the inner room toward them.

"Ah, Chancellor Carl," Levenstein said. "We caught you. The next time we're told that the administrative heads of universities never read, we'll offer positive proof to the contrary."

"I was in the library, but that doesn't mean I was reading." Stephen Carl shook hands all around. "Mrs. Robertson, you're looking particularly lovely. Professor Robertson, I heard you were here this evening."

"I can't use that title these days, Dr. Carl," Dan said with a forced smile.

"Don't be too sure of that." Stephen Carl knew the advantages of a dramatic pause. "We must get together. Soon. Perhaps I could stop in to see you next time I'm in Hopkins Tower, if that wouldn't inconvenience you."

"I'm there most of the time," Dan said, his laugh genuine now, "and I'd be delighted to see you. But I warn you, I'll be uncomfortable. I'm not accustomed to calls from university chancellors. Perhaps I ought to come to your office."

To Dan's surprise, Carl remained serious. "I'd like nothing better. I'm flying to Boston for a conference tomorrow, but I'll be back the beginning of next week, and I'd very much like to hear from you."

They parted, the Robertsons and their friends walking down the stairs to the main entrance. The other couples lived within walking distance, so Dan hailed a taxi, and could scarcely wait until he and Phyllis were alone.

"What do you suppose is bugging Steve Carl?" he demanded.

"It was so obvious it reeked, darling. I thought Ray Bowning's eyebrows were going to disappear into his hair. I'm sure Chancellor Carl intends to offer you a job."

"Impossible!"

"I thought he was going to click his heels and kiss my hand," Phyllis said. "You know as well as I do that university presidents—or chancellors, if that's what they prefer to call themselves—never become effusive without a reason."

"But Carl had a hand in my appointment at the square. I know for an absolute fact that he sold Ben Hopkins on me. We heard about it at the farewell dinner for us at Great Lakes. You were right there, honey!"

"I remember. All the same, Dr. Carl wants you at Seaboard. I'll bet you—oh, dear, bets between husbands and wives are so meaningless—"

"I don't get it," Dan interrupted. "His Liberal Arts School is as strong as any in the country. He doesn't need a utility professor in the Humanities. What's more, there are men in the field far superior to me. There's Reichstadt at Chicago, Ross on the West Coast, and at least three top-notch men at Harvard, not to mention—"

"Then don't mention them, please." Phyllis reached for his hand. "One of your troubles, Professor Robertson, is your innate modesty."

Dan drew her to him and kissed her. "We haven't smooched in a taxi for a long time," he said as he released her.

"Ha! It was only last week, after that dinner party—"

"I retract everything." He became thoughtful. "There's something fishy in this Carl business."

"You'll find out eventually, Dan. If I know you, you'll worry away at it, like the children's puppy with that rubber-bone-that-has-the-taste-of-a-real-bone. And you'll come up with the right answers."

"Maybe."

"In the meantime," Phyllis said firmly, "I forbid you to stew over it. Don't waste your substance wondering whether you ought to leave the square in order to join the Seaboard faculty. Life is already complicated enough."

"Yeah," Dan said, and fell silent.

Dan remained lost in thought for the rest of the ride.

When they reached the apartment they dismissed the sitter, looked in at the sleeping children, and then went to the kitchen for milk and crackers, which they took with them to their bedroom. Dan was still lost in thought as they undressed.

Phyllis searched for a topic of conversation that would distract him, and was annoyed with herself when she realized she had been overlooking the most obvious. "That movie tonight was just marvelous."

"Mmm?"

She repeated her comment.

Dan found it relatively easy to put other matters out of his mind. "I don't remember seeing better. And no matter what anyone might say, it was real art."

"I cried for the last ten minutes or so. I don't remember any movie that ever stirred me up that much."

"It was a great job," Dan said. "I don't know how the script would stand up on its own. I spotted two places where author's convenience was a little glib and hard to accept. But the direction and photography were superb."

Phyllis knew she could relax now. When he became analytical in his discussion of a play or book or movie, he sometimes talked at great length, exploring every facet.

"Some of the acting was extraordinary. It seemed so effortless, which is always a sign it wasn't. What astonishes me is that the picture has never had the audiences it deserves. Did you hear some of the English Department people saying that it's only played a few obscure art theaters in Europe, and that no distributor in this country has even asked for it? That's a damned shame, and the public is the loser."

She searched under the bed for her slippers, found them, and then put away her dress and shoes.

"It would be the perfect film to open the little movie theater at the square. If no one else grabs it, I certainly will. It will set the right tone for the sort of films I want in that theater. The critics will go wild, and I'm positive it can play for at least six months. I'll do something about it immediately, so somebody else doesn't get hold of it first."

"I'm glad, darling. I'd like to see it again."

Dan grinned at her. "Just remember you'll have to pay. There will be no free seats at Jefferson Square for anyone except reviewers for major publications."

Phyllis laughed. "All right, policy-maker. Make rules that empty your own wallet."

He drained his glass of milk. "The two leads are becoming fairly well known, but even the actors who played the smaller parts were unusually good. The best were the Swedish boy and the American girl who did that scene in the chalet during the snowstorm. They were remarkable!"

"They were the first to make me cry."

"Who were they, anyway?"

"I have the program in my handbag." Phyllis went to her dressing table and took a folded, mimeographed sheet of paper from the bag. "The boy was Sven Bjornsen, and the girl was Berenice Tolmey." She smiled broadly.

"I'll try to remember those names. If I'm any judge, they're both going to be stars."

"One of them is well on the way." She giggled. "Doesn't the girl's name mean anything to you?"

"You know I never read the gossip columns, honey. You're probably thinking of someone else. She had some little quirks in her speech mannerisms, and is probably a Continental actress playing an American girl in *Rain and Sun.*"

"She's as American as apple pie or LSD, Dan. You honestly didn't recognize her?"

He ate the last of his crackers and started toward the bed. "No, and I wouldn't forget her."

"Men are incredible!" Phyllis laughed quietly.

"I'll grant you we're nature's noblemen, but what's so funny?"

"Berenice Tolmey is Jerry Solanz' girl, to put it rather politely. You've met her twice in the past few days."

"Nonsense. That little trollop he leads around on a leash is a super-blonde with short hair. The kid in the movie had long, dark hair and the most expressive, scrubbed face I've seen in years. The tootsie Solanz has in tow uses makeup an inch thick on her face."

"Hairdressers are magicians, would you believe it? They use a tool called a scissors to make long hair short, and they have potions that come in bottles to change the color of a woman's hair. As for makeup, it's available in every drugstore and five-and-ten. American women spend over two billion dollars a year on cosmetics, according to some figures my husband read to me a few mornings ago at breakfast, and—"

"I'd still bet anything it isn't the same girl."

"It was and is."

"I'll be damned."

"Probably, but that's something we've known for a long

122

time." Phyllis yawned as she moved to her side of the bed and kicked off her slippers. "What else is new?"

"I can't get over it. That girl can act!"

"The prosecution grants the point, Your Honor. Kiss me goodnight, darling. It's late."

He obliged her, then snapped off the light, and was silent for a few minutes. "Why do you suppose a girl like that—a real actress—would get mixed up with Jerry Solanz?"

"The usual reasons, I imagine."

"Such as?"

"Sex. They probably go for each other. Her career. He's a real power in show business, remember, even though you don't like him, and I imagine she can become a star much faster by doing things his way than by working in an obscure art film or two."

"It won't be obscure for long, and neither will Berenice Tolmey, honey. I'll see to that."

No lights were showing in the front of the house as Francis Dougherty backed his Cadillac into the two-car garage. But Ann's station wagon was in its usual place, so he guessed she was home. If so, it would be too much to hope she was asleep; she was probably waiting for him in the television room, killing time by watching one of those god-awful movies of the 1930's that she loved. He pulled down the overhead garage door and went into the house through the kitchen.

The place was far too big for two people, he thought. With both of the girls married and young Frank in medical school, he and Ann rattled around inside. He'd be smart to sell, as he'd been threatening to do for so long, and buy something smaller. For that matter, they could move into town. Their only reason for going out to the suburbs had been the children, and now that they were gone, an apartment in the city would be a great convenience. No more commuting. No more paying too much to some slob to cut the grass and do the odd jobs that he no longer had time to do. Or the desire. He was sick of the goddam suburbs.

But he'd have to test Ann's mood before he brought up the subject again. He'd seen her through enough of her crying jags, and he was too tired to listen to her bleating, "This is our home! Our roots are here!"

123

The television room was empty, and he debated whether to raid the refrigerator, but decided against it. He was hungry, as always after drinking, but he was putting on too goddam much weight and had to call a halt somewhere. He'd always hated paunches, and now he had one. He was a goddam kangaroo. But only female kangaroos had paunches. Or pouches. To hell with kangaroos, he thought, and wearily started up the carpeted stairs.

A light was burning in the master bedroom, and Ann Dougherty, propped up on pillows, put down her book when her husband came in. "You caught the last train."

"With a couple of minutes to spare. If I hadn't walked out of the goddam meeting, I'd have been stuck in town overnight again."

Ann knew from more than a quarter of a century of bitter experience that whenever he looked away while presenting her with some vague account of his evening's activities, he'd been with another woman. She no longer cared about his sluts—no, that wasn't true. The knowledge hurt, and she was haunted, more than ever, by the fear that one of them might be a lady. She'd refuse to give him a divorce, naturally, but he had enough political influence to sue her, and make it stick.

The children had reassured her that he couldn't, but she found it difficult to believe them. Whenever she knew he was interested in someone else, she was miserable for months. Five months, as a rule. To her knowledge, only one of his affairs, many years ago, had lasted longer.

It was easy enough for the girls and young Frank to tell her that Francis wouldn't stand a chance in court if he brought a divorce action against her. But they weren't dread-filled middle-aged women with graying hair and pudgy figures who would rather die than live alone. And they knew nothing of the fantastically clever stunts that Francis had pulled, in court and out, through the years. He had sworn her to secrecy when he'd told her of those cases, and she had never breathed a word, not even to the children. Francis was the most clever man she had ever known.

Ann admired that cleverness. The truth of the matter was that, in spite of his infidelities, she still loved him. And she supposed, or at least hoped, that in his own way he was still closely bound to her, too. They had gone through so much together, from the days he had refused an income from her father and they had lived on baked beans and canned soups.

"Are you hungry, Francis?" she asked. "I'll go down to the kitchen—"

"If I want something to eat, I'll get it myself. You're in bed, so stay there, for Christ's sake!"

"I wish you wouldn't take the name of the Lord in vain," she said automatically.

He did not bother to turn away from his dresser, onto which he was emptying the contents of his pockets, and his reply was equally automatic. "I'm going to fry anyway, so what's the goddam difference?"

"If you'd start coming to Mass with me, you wouldn't feel that way," Ann said. "Every time I see Father Grady—"

"Screw Father Grady."

"Francis!"

He had never broken himself of the habit of using the rough language he had learned in his boyhood, but he was careful in business and his court appearances, and it would be easy enough to tone himself down in front of her, too. He spoke as he did in her presence, he guessed, because she made such an issue of being shocked. It wasn't her fault she was a prude; all those years of convent schooling had left an ineradicable mark on her, and he was being goddam unfair to needle her. "I'm sorry, Annie."

Ann was instantly mollified. "I made meat-loaf tonight."

"You did, huh?" Francis brightened and forgot his diet. Ann's meat-loaf was one of the few dishes he really enjoyed eating.

"I left it under the cake pan in the pantry to cool. Put it on the second shelf of the icebox after you've taken what you want."

"You just bet!" He left the room immediately.

A short time later he was back, a large slab of the meat-loaf on a plate.

Ann thought of protesting, but desisted. It was useless to tell him not to eat in the bedroom. Francis never obeyed any rules except his own.

He perched on the edge of her dressing table, and his gaze wandered aimlessly around the room, pausing when he saw the tall glass on the night table beside her bed.

"I was thirsty," Ann said too quickly, "so I brought up some gingerale."

The contents of the glass were very dark, so she was really tanking up tonight. "I wish to God you'd lay off the booze."

"I've already told you," she said, looking straight at him, "that this is gingerale."

Francis nodded, too tired to call her bluff by taking the glass and proving that the gingerale was laced with a stiff shot of whisky. That kind of a scene sometimes lasted the better part of the night. He shoved the problem into a far corner of his mind and concentrated on the meat-loaf. "You did better than usual this time."

"I'm just sorry you weren't home to eat it when it was hot."

She always had to spoil things. "I like it just as much cold."

She sensed his anger beneath the surface, and decided not to start anything. She would let him finish eating, and when he took his plate back to the kitchen she would take the rest of her drink. She had been careless, and certainly didn't want to spend the rest of the night listening to him rant. His attitude was absurd, of course: he could drink himself glassy-eyed, but became livid when she took a few. A goose was entitled to her share of a gander's sauce.

Francis was frowning. "At the Emorys' cocktail party," he said, "go easy on the liquor. Don't drink anything stronger than sherry."

"That's insulting!"

"The hell it is! You—"

"Have you ever known me not to be in control of myself socially? Not just with your business friends. Anywhere!"

On a few occasions she had become half-bombed, but the consequences had been minor. It was wiser to agree than to start an endless round of charges and counter-recriminations.

"You've always been a credit," he said, "to the nuns at St. Margaret's and the whole goddam faculty of Miss Franklin's School."

Ann's sniff was disdainfully superior.

Francis felt an old, painfully familiar sense of inferiority. It was foolish, of course. They had lived together for one hell of a long time, gone to bed together more times than he could count, and, on top of everything else, Ann was the mother of his three grown children. All the same, he couldn't forget she had enjoyed the benefits and prerogatives of a girl who came from a moneyed family of class, while he'd been a punk ambulance chaser.

Yet he had enough sense to know he ought to climb to her level instead of hauling her down to his. "Forget I said anything," he muttered.

Ann savored the small victory; she won far too few of them.

"Get yourself gussied for that party," Francis said. "It'll be important."

"The society page photographers won't be interested in me when all those glamorous women will be there."

"The photographers can go hump themselves."

Her curiosity was stronger than her desire to rebuke him for his vulgarity. "Then what—"

"Goddammit, do what I tell you! Blow yourself to a new outfit."

"I've been planning to wear my mauve silk suit. Is there anything wrong with that?"

He could never remember any of her clothes. "Great, if it'll remind people you're your old man's daughter and not my wife."

"You mean there are times when my family standing is actually valuable to you."

Her amused condescension was intolerable, but he'd give himself a stinking headache if he started to shout at her. "If you've got something that's right, wear it," he said curtly. "If you don't, go out and buy it."

Ann gazed down at her husband from her invisible heights. "One never overdresses for a party at Carolyn Emory's."

"You've got to look on-the-nose right!"

She couldn't remember an occasion when he had made her appearance his concern. "I see. Your new mistress is going to be there, and you want to show me off to her."

Francis looked at her stonily. Sandra had seen her in the office many times, and Ann would feel really degraded if she found out he was laying his secretary. It was tempting to tell her the truth and watch her superior façade crumble. Instead, he merely said, "Ha-ha."

Ann was ashamed of her jealous outburst. She could keep her marriage together only by pretending to be ignorant of her husband's affairs, and although it was too late to retract what she had let slip, she would have to gloss over it. "Why is this cocktail party so much more important than all the other Jefferson Square functions? I've never known people so determined to entertain each other."

"Ben Hopkins and his wife are going to the Emorys' party."

Ann sat up.

"That's strictly between us. I heard it, off the record, from

127

Herbert Brookes in his office. Not even Ed Emory and his wife will know they're coming until they actually get there."

"Imagine meeting them!"

"Stick around me, Annie, and you'll get to know everybody in the upper crust." Francis smiled wryly.

"What could have impelled Mr. Hopkins—"

"He never does anything without a reason." Francis suddenly became irritable.

"I'm sure he doesn't, but why snap at me?" It was difficult to be dignified in an old nightgown, with her hair unpinned.

"Don't ever ask me questions about Ben Hopkins' motives," he said. "Everybody I ever dealt with before I got to his level was a no-good, third-rate nobody. He's the guy who makes all the wheels go round, and anybody who crosses him or gets in his way will be cut up into minced hamburger by those wheels. There are some things it's better that I don't talk about, not even to you. It's healthier, even, to tell myself I don't know a goddam thing about them. Get me?"

Ann saw that he was uneasy, perhaps a little frightened, which astonished her. She had never known him to become panicky. "Tell me what you please, hold back what you please. It doesn't matter."

"We're in the middle of a goddam sticky situation. I mean, I am. A guy in Ben Hopkins' league doesn't get his own shoes dirty. The mud spatters on other people."

She was sure now that he was frightened.

"You know that whatever may be wrong, Francis," she said, "I'll stand by you."

He put the plate of meat-loaf on her dressing table, started to wipe his mouth with the back of his hand, then reached instead for a tissue in a box on the table. He walked to the bed, bent down and kissed her cheek. "You may be a lady, Annie, but—goddam!—in the clutch you come through."

Without her false eyelashes, wiglet and corset, Helena Godoy looked like a somewhat overweight woman of middle years who would not warrant a second glance from anyone in a supermarket. When she spoke, however, her trained operatic voice was commanding, and when she was angry, the higher register of her mezzo-soprano made the glass in her living room chandelier tinkle in protest.

"You have no one but yourself to blame, Henri! What did you accomplish by slapping that—that fairy? Allow me to tell you. The very day you announced your program for the farewell concert, Helsing announced his new recording. Everyone knows he challenged you, and you look like the jackass you have become!"

Henri Broussard was accustomed to the temper tantrums of his mistress, and sat calmly in his favorite chair, sipping his coffee.

"You say nothing? You refuse to defend yourself?" The opera star looked around for something to throw.

"You still regret breaking that marble statuette they gave you at La Scala," Broussard reminded her.

"I do not! When I think of Max de Groot and that despicable Herder—and now Anton Helsing, too, I could tear down walls."

His placating gesture looked like the quieting of a symphony's woodwind section. "Gently, Helena. *Maggiore fretta, minore atto.*"

"More haste, less speed? That is why you become the has-been, Henri. Perhaps it is you, not Helsing, who needs the male hormone injections!"

"In bed I have never given you cause for complaint."

"You are also vulgar." She cursed him in Spanish, colorfully and at some length.

Broussard chuckled indulgently.

"What will you do, Henri?" The famous voice became piercing. "Sitting here, laughing, will not solve the problem."

"Neither will your screams, Helena."

"We must find some valid excuse to change the program for your concert!"

"Never," he said.

She stared at him, clasping her hands and pressing them to her ample bosom. "Then you have gone mad."

"What you fail to see is that Helsing has elected to challenge me on my own ground. I have spent thirty years conducting the works he is interpreting publicly for the first time. The critics will compare us. All who know music, hundreds of them who attend my concert, will compare us. The ignorant public, who accept what they are told, will compare us. Here is my opportunity to prove that I am superior to Helsing, that I was the victim of conspirators who took my post from me and gave it to a—musical parvenu!"

It was impossible for Helena Godoy to do anything in an ordinary manner. When she sat down, she chose to collapse dramatically into a low-slung chair. "My poor Henri," she murmured. "My poor lamb."

Broussard glared at her over the rim of his coffee cup. "I will not tolerate patronization, Helena!"

She was so aroused she was willing to risk quarreling with him. "My poor, poor Henri."

The cup and saucer clattered as he placed them on the table. "You are not now giving a performance of *Samson and Delilah*, Helena. You've never done the part well, and I think you should eliminate it from your repertoire."

Helena was stung. "Every critic who has heard my Delilah has called it incomparable. Who are you to dare—"

"I am the man who tells you the truth in all things. But I do not call you my poor Helena. Your voice is second to none. The thousands who sent that petition to de Groot will have to hear you sing at the Metropolitan or at the Lyric in Chicago. I applaud you in this. I support you. I praise you. I do not decry you."

"My sweet, angelic, adorable Henri," she said, gesturing extravagantly, "I fight at your side, my shield locked with yours. Your foes are mine, and I seek their annihilation!"

Broussard concealed his smile behind his hand. A serious conversation with Helena required patience, and he was short-tempered these days, but he knew if he could keep a grip on his own temper a little longer, she soon would say what she really had on her mind.

"You are a great maestro, Henri. You know I could not love or admire you if you were not."

He inclined his head slightly, accepting the compliment with reserve.

"I respect your courage. There are not many who would do battle with Anton Helsing in the way you choose."

"Helsing is an actor, not a conductor," Broussard said disgustedly.

Helena deliberately discarded her dramatic approach, and her calm was all the more effective. "Anton Helsing," she said, "is an accomplished musician. He is an exceptionally able conductor who understands the mood of the times, of his own generation. He is the musical spokesman for the young, and with Bernstein retiring, he stands alone and apart. If you accept his challenge, Henri, the critics will praise him. You they will also praise, but faintly. So you will lose the duel."

130

Broussard was outraged. "Do you suggest he is the better conductor?"

"Am I better than Callas? Was Pons better than Galli-Curci? Such comparisons are without meaning, Henri. You interpret in your way, Helsing in his."

"Answer me, Helena!" Veins bulged in Broussard's forehead, and his voice trembled.

"You will be called competent but old-fashioned," she said, and found it difficult to meet his gaze.

"So you agree I am a has-been."

"I do not. I enjoy your approach to music. I am comfortable with your interpretations. When I hear Helsing, I become restless. My skin itches."

"But he's not dull."

"No, Henri. Never."

Broussard seemed to shrivel in his chair, and sat for a long time, rubbing his hands together and staring at a portrait of Helena that dominated the room. "It might be best," he said at last, "if I cancel the farewell concert."

"I won't permit it!" she cried, leaping to her feet and striking a pose.

"What would you have me do?" He sounded old and lethargic.

"I have already told you. We will find some reasonable explanation for changing your program."

"No matter how reasonable it might seem, no one will accept such a flight. I will be accused of cowardice, and my future will be destroyed."

"It is because of your future that I insist you make the change, Henri."

Broussard squared his shoulders. "You and I know my position is tenuous, Helena. If I can create the right impression here—and on my tour—perhaps I will be offered a baton in another city. My agent tells me there will be three openings next season. None are orchestras with the distinction of my symphony here, but they are good. They are respectable, and no one could say, 'Broussard has been forced to step down a few pegs.' I have made my own hell, I know, but I cannot afford to run away."

Helena went to him, took his hand and pressed it to her bare throat.

"You see this decision is most critical."

"I see," she said, and then declared viciously. "How I wish there were some way to discredit Helsing!"

"He has already made his recording, Helena. Perhaps I should seek some new interpretations—"

"No, Henri. You have your own following, and must not lose it. Do what you have done all your life. It is the only way. Work hard, as you have always worked—and let us hope that Helsing is knocked down by a very large, very heavy truck."

The reception room of Simpson and Smith, Inc., was similar to that of many other publishers, with the firm's newest books displayed in one L-shaped, open-shelved case, and the best-selling perennials in another on the opposite side of the room. The receptionist seated at a white and gold desk was attractive but mature, and flowers stood in several vases, helping to brighten a chamber that depended exclusively on artificial light.

But there were several significant differences that distinguished the reception room of Simpson and Smith from that of its competitors. The desk and chair were genuine, two-hundred-year-old antiques rather than imitations, as were the couches and matching chairs for visitors. The flowers were real, and were changed daily. And when an author was expected to drop in, his most recent book was prominently displayed in a glass-enclosed case illuminated by a small but powerful spot-light.

The staff was exceptionally alert, too. When Dan Robertson walked in at precisely half-past nine in the morning and saw *The Quandary* in the display case, the new receptionist, who had never before seen him, instantly recognized him from his photograph on the back of the book's jacket, which she had studied. "Good morning, Mr. Robertson," she said. "Mr. Simpson is expecting you. Shall I ask his secretary to fetch you?"

"Don't bother, thanks," Dan said. "I know the way."

He made his way down a long, carpeted corridor, past open secretarial work areas and the closed doors of private offices. The ceilings and attractively papered walls had been sound-proofed, giving the establishment an aura of dignified quiet, and even the clicking of typewriters was muffled.

Harvey Simpson's private sanctum resembled a living room. His drapes and carpet were done in pastels, the only decorations on the walls were three water colors, two of them seascapes and the third a bucolic, pastoral scene. But the corner in which Harvey worked belied the otherwise gracious character of the office. Boxes filled with manuscripts were piled on a table, along with sheaves of inter-office memos, galley proofs and sketches of book jackets. His desk, the largest Dan had ever seen, was covered with papers, clippings of recent book reviews and sales department charts.

As usual, Harvey was talking into one of his telephones. He smiled brightly and waved his guest to a chair as he continued to talk for some minutes.

Dan lighted a cigarette, stared up at the ceiling and pretended not to hear anything being said.

At last Harvey put the instrument in its cradle, stood and grasped Dan's hand. "Forgive me," he said, "but we're buying a couple of television stations—that's confidential—and the details of the deal are driving me wild."

"Nature intended you to be a magnate, Harvey. Ben Hopkins would envy you this office."

"Hardly, my dear boy," Harvey protested, but looked pleased. "I'm sorry I couldn't make it for lunch today, but—"

"Neither could I."

"At least you'll let me get you some coffee. And a sweet roll, or some toast?"

"I've already had breakfast, thanks, and I'm trying to watch my weight."

"Aren't we all!" Harvey patted his paunch and reached for the phone. "Some coffee for Mr. Robertson, please. The usual for me. And I'll take no calls, unless Mr. Smith reports in from London. My partner," he explained to Dan after putting down the phone, "is gallivanting again." They were alone in the sound-proofed room, but he lowered his voice. "I think we're onto something big—this is confidential, of course. We're about to close a deal for the personal memoirs of a member of the Royal Family."

"That's wonderful, Harvey." Dan had come prepared to spend several minutes in meaningless chat, and tried to curb his impatience.

"Here are up-to-date sales figures for *The Quandary*. I'm sure you'll be as pleased as we are. And while you're looking at them, forgive me if I make just one essential call."

Dan took the chart, and while he was examining it, a secretary came in with two steaming mugs of coffee. The mugs, made of expensive chinaware, bore the seal of the company, and the girl was lovely. Dan thanked her and waited for the publisher to complete his call.

"Harvey," he said as his friend turned back to him, "do you hire showgirls to impress your authors?"

"You mean Miss Matthews. Charming, isn't she? And so bright. Unfortunately, she wants to be an editor, as so many of them do, so we'll lose her one of these days." He sighed, sipped his coffee and began the careful ritual of stuffing a pipe he took from an ivory rack.

This was the signal that the serious talk could begin. "I need your advice," Dan said.

"I'll do my best."

"I must ask you, though, to keep everything I say strictly between us."

"Of course, my dear boy!"

"I don't mean your usual confidential level, Harvey. I'm in earnest."

Harvey paused in the act of lighting his pipe. "You have my solemn word that no one will hear a word of what you and I say here this morning."

"Good, because not even Phyllis knows about this. I've dropped a few hints to her, but that's all. I have a problem that has me running in circles, and I've got to talk to someone."

"I'm flattered, Dan."

"You won't be when I've finished. It's a heavy burden, and just knowing it will make your own life more difficult, so you'll probably hate my guts."

"Tell me! You have me sitting on the edge of my seat." Harvey moved forward in his chair.'

Dan smiled fleetingly. "I'll have to do this in my own way. You may recall a recent conversation you and I had at lunch—"

"Every word of it. Something at Jefferson Square has upset you, and I believe I know what it is. You don't see eye to eye with that egomaniac, Jerry Solanz—"

"I don't, but no one could. That's minor, though. Harvey, I took my job at the square in good conscience and good faith, for several reasons. The most obvious is money."

"No one has ever been shot for wanting to make life better for his family and himself."

"I'm earning a very high salary, far more than I ever expected to make."

"You're worth it," Harvey said, puffing on his pipe.

Dan lighted another cigarette. "Yes, I am. I had other reasons, and I must be very candid with you. Phyllis and I like the kind of life we're leading. We enjoy the excitement of the city, spending our time with people whose names make newspaper headlines—I sound like a god-awful small-town hick, don't I?"

"I've known only two people in my life—both of them authors, by the way—who pretend they loathe the celebrity life. I think they're liars. So far you sound very normal to me, Dan."

"My biggest reason for accepting the job at the square was the opportunity it offered me to teach on a grand scale. There's an urgent need for culture centers, Harvey. More and more people are developing an unquenchable thirst for drama, music, art. I'm in a position to give them good drama, good music, good art. I can stimulate them, help them to enrich their lives, if you'll forgive the corny expression."

"I know what you mean, my dear boy, and I also know you, which is far more important. There's no need to explain your motives. I understand them."

Dan sucked on his cigarette, crushed it in the onyx ashtray at the edge of his chair and gripped the arms. "I can only do my job if I prostitute myself, Harvey."

"Isn't that a bit strong?"

"I've discovered one of the most mammoth swindles ever perpetrated on the public. Not just the people of this city. There are federal and state funds that have gone into the square, remember, so every taxpayer in the country has a stake in America's dream culture center."

Harvey was very quiet, neither speaking nor moving.

"The hell of it is that it's legal. No one has broken any laws or done anything underhanded. But it's a swindle, all the same." Dan stopped, perspiration glistening on his forehead.

"Drink your coffee," Harvey said.

"You'll have to excuse the dramatics." Dan sipped his coffee, then patted his face with a folded, clean handkerchief. "I stumbled onto this, Harvey. I wasn't looking for trouble, and I'm no detective—"

"You have an instinct for the newsworthy. You proved that in *The Quandary*."

"This is something that just revealed itself to me, you might say. Little by little. There was no sudden, overwhelming explosion. I guess I gradually put the pieces together, and one day there was the whole puzzle, completed, staring me in the face. You see, I read copies of all the top-echelon memos that go through the square. Edward Emory's finance committee stuff, even the notes that Ben Hopkins writes, some of them in his own hand. I sign my initials on the copy, and then pass it along—in person—to the next man on the confidential list."

"The usual executive procedure. We do something similar right here in our own little company."

"Jefferson Square is being built in a slum neighborhood, Harvey. Tenements have been torn down, and others will go soon—"

"Everyone knows that." There was an undercurrent of waspishness in Harvey Simpson's voice.

"The entire area will be changed. New apartment houses will go up, and I'm not speaking of the high-rise redevelopment project ghettos, although some of them are being planned, too. I mean expensive apartments. One hundred to one-fifty per room, with an extra hundred thrown in for balconies. Fancy food stores will replace the little groceries on Fourth Street. Restaurants where a couple can drop fifty dollars with ease for a simple dinner and a drink or two will move in. Some very impressive new skyscraper office buildings will go up. Acres and acres of what was once the worst part of town will be completely changed. Rehabilitated, some people call it."

"I see nothing strange in what you're describing, Dan. A project like Jefferson Square inevitably changes the whole character of an area. You don't want to stop progress?"

"I have no intention of arguing the pros and cons of urban redevelopment, although there's a great deal to be said on the side of leaving old neighborhoods alone, relatively speaking. Making the buildings habitable and decent and sanitary, and letting it go at that."

Harvey continued to wait, knowing he had to let Dan tell his story in his own way.

"The real estate of the district was virtually worthless," Dan said. "Now the prices are as high as the skyscrapers that will soon go up, and they're still climbing. One little section

136

for the square itself is costing millions more than the land is actually worth. I saw the memo on it just yesterday, and that's what convinced me I couldn't procrastinate any longer. But keep in mind that I'm not speaking of Jefferson Square alone. I'm talking of the real estate that fans out from it for a mile or so in every direction."

Harvey busied himself relighting his pipe.

"Who are the big donors to Jefferson Square?" Dan paused, then answered his own question. "Ben Hopkins and his relatives, above all. Edward Emory and his finance committee of high-powered bankers and corporation heads. Now, who owns the land on which Jefferson Square is being built? Who owns the real estate in the neighborhood?" Dan's voice was hoarse. "Ben Hopkins and his relatives. Edward Emory and the big wheels of finance who sit on the board of directors."

Harvey Simpson removed his glasses and, while polishing them, stared at his friend.

"It's the greatest racket of all time. Federal and state funds were used to buy the site of Jefferson Square, in the main. Although private money will be needed to buy the last lots from the Jackson Drive Realty Company—which happens to be owned virtually outright by Mr. Benjamin Hopkins. That's the least of it, and I can't stress this point too much. The Hopkins clan, Emory and the rest also control all the other real estate in the neighborhood. They're going to clean up!"

"Let me go over this slowly," Harvey said, suppressing his own excitement. "The men who are making the big contributions to Jefferson Square, excluding the foundations—"

"*Including* the foundations! The Hopkins Fund is the single biggest contributor, and is controlled by members of the Hopkins family. They pour out money from the fund, and it comes back in a much bigger flood—into their own pockets. I've done a little simple arithmetic, Harvey, and my figures are fairly accurate, even though they aren't precise. For each one hundred thousand that one of these benevolent philanthropists gives to Jefferson Square, either out of his own personal pocket or through one of the foundations he controls, he'll get five hundred thousand in return. A profit of four hundred thousand on each one hundred thousand he makes as a gift."

"This is fantastic," Harvey murmured.

"It's sickening," Dan said, and drained his mug, neither tasting the coffee nor realizing it had grown cold.

"Are you sure of your facts?"

"I certainly am!"

"You can substantiate them?"

"Of course. I wouldn't be in this sweat if I was basing deductions on guesswork, Harvey. What I've just told you is the solid, unvarnished, demonstrable truth."

Harvey decided to move slowly, very carefully, waiting to say what was foremost in his mind. "I can see why you're upset."

"The ironies," Dan said, "are like those in the plays of the ancient Greeks. The author of *The Quandary,* so concerned with moral and ethical dilemmas, finds himself in a quandary of his own that's excruciating."

"There's no doubt about it, Dan. It must be a nightmare for you."

"The worst of it is that people like Hopkins and Emory aren't crooks in the ordinary sense—"

"In high finance men are rarely criminals. They follow their own rules."

"But, damn it, Harvey, what they're doing isn't ethical! I've tried to tell myself that Jefferson Square will justify its own existence, no matter where the money comes from to build it and operate it! I can't reconcile the good with the bad, though. It drives me crazy to think of those rich bastards making fresh fortunes out of the public while offering them some brightly colored lollipops. I've been on the verge of resigning a dozen times."

"Don't do anything until you talk to Phyllis."

"Oh, I won't. But I can't lean on her in this mess. I've got to make up my own mind."

"You're still balancing both sides of the ledger, obviously."

"I'm whirling, Harvey. This is a situation that can't be reduced to the usual black and white terms. It would be ridiculous to accuse Ben Hopkins, one of the wealthiest men in the world, of trying to make a quick buck he doesn't need and probably wouldn't even know he had."

"The acquisitive habit becomes an instinct after just so many years."

"I wouldn't know about that," Dan said. "But Ben Hopkins has so much money I'm sure he doesn't know what he's worth from one year to the next. He's conscious of his social

138

responsibilities, as his contributions over a period of many years prove, and I find it impossible to believe that he's a member—much less a leader—of a deliberate conspiracy to hoodwink and fleece the public."

"Perhaps he doesn't look at the situation that way."

"I have no idea what he and his fellow property owners think."

"Why not ask them?"

"My, God, Harvey! I can't go to the head of the Metropolitan-National Bank—or whoever—and accuse him of pulling shady deals. And then ask him to justify what he's done."

"Yes, the more prominent the citizen, the more he'd resent you. I can see why you're whirling, Dan."

"It can be argued that no one suffers except the poor who are being displaced and relocated in new housing developments where there's a higher incidence of crime. Their situation is debatable, and only in the last few years have the experts started swinging toward the opinion that the razing of the old slums causes more problems than it cures. In every other respect, people benefit. A superb new culture center comes into being, and serves millions. A broken-down neighborhood is transformed. The restaurants and shops and specialty stores and all the rest that move in give jobs to thousands. Splendid new housing facilities are made available in a city where apartments are almost impossible to find. And if a few men happen to make a huge bundle out of real estate, what's wrong with that?"

"Are you trying to convince yourself, Dan, or me?"

"Me. The whole business sticks in my craw. I doubt if it would be possible to bring charges against them, on any grounds, that would stick!"

"Publicity," Harvey said cautiously, "could hurt them very badly."

"I don't want to hurt anybody. I have a personal dilemma to solve. If Ben Hopkins and Edward Emory sleep with clear consciences, good for them. I'm neither a reformer nor a trouble-maker. My worry is deciding what's right for me."

"I'd like to help you, Dan."

"That's why I've come to you, Harvey. I need a sounding-board, and if you have any advice to give me, I respect your judgment."

"A great many thoughts are going through my mind," Harvey said. "But I don't want to shoot from the hip. You have far too much at stake, and I dislike playing God and interfering in other people's lives."

"I'd appreciate the benefit of your thinking. You can be more objective than I can."

"How much time can you give me, Dan?"

"Oh, there's no great rush, I guess."

"Let me sleep on all this for a night or two," Harvey said. "I'll call you no later than the day after tomorrow, Dan, and we'll get together again."

"Thanks." Dan gripped his hand.

"Friends are meant to be called on when we need them." Harvey glanced at his watch, scarcely able to wait until Dan left so he could telephone his partner, in London, to tell him they had stumbled onto the hottest idea in publishing that had come their way in years.

CHAPTER FOUR

The smell of the wax used by the floor polisher mingled with the musty odors of papers and dust in the airless offices, where the windows remained closed on a Saturday. But Sandra Masters was too intent on searching through the files to be aware of her surroundings.

She had come to the office on a chance, a remote chance, of running into something that would give her a weapon to use over Francis, and she thought she might be on the right track. For the past half-hour she had been annoyed with herself for thinking in such melodramatic terms, but something fishy *had* been going on, by God!

She took pride, as a secretary, in knowing all of Francis' business, but he had been strangely secretive in a telephone conversation with Brookes of Benjamin Hopkins' office, and that had started her mind darting off in all directions. She hadn't heard much, Francis had seen to that, falling silent when she walked into his office with some papers and waiting until she had left before resuming his conversation. She had known his caller was Brookes, because she'd handled the call.

Her only clue was real estate. Something about property, that Francis had wanted to conceal from her. Why hide it? She was beginning to understand, she thought, and her excitement became unbearable. She was on the track of something big, far bigger than she had thought possible, and leafed quickly through the confidential memoranda and letters, pausing occasionally to make a shorthand note.

The ringing of the telephone on the desk behind her made her jump. She hesitated, deciding at first not to answer it, and then changed her mind. "Dougherty, Watson and Levine."

"Sandra? Thank the Lord I found you!" There was the sound of hysterical weeping at the other end of the line.

"Mama? What's wrong?"

"Three times I tried to find you at home, and finally I try your office. I thank the Lord—"

"Get hold of yourself, Mama, and tell me what's happened."

Maria Mascaroni made a supreme effort to compose herself. "Buddy and some other boys were playing this morning where they put up your fine buildings. Buddy means no harm. You know he is a good boy, Sandra—"

"What's happened to him?" In spite of her annoyance at being interrupted, Sandra was concerned.

"Officer Garrity called the police cars, and they took the boys to the station. Buddy is no thief. You know he is good—"

"What did he take?"

"They say the boys stole wooden planks. The others did it, maybe, but not Buddy. He is a—"

"Where is he now?" Sandra couldn't help grinning. Apparently Buddy wasn't as dead-assed as she had believed him.

"They hold him in the jail on Sixth Street." Maria was weeping again.

"Slow it down to a run, Mama. Whose phone are you using?"

"Mrs. Cavelli is my good friend. She—"

"You sit right there. I'll call you back." Sandra cradled the instrument, laughed and said aloud, "The little bastard." The files would have to wait, and she tapped a pencil against her teeth.

There was no choice, so she called Francis Dougherty's house in the suburbs.

"Hello."

"Good morning, Mrs. Dougherty. This is Sandra Masters. I'm so sorry to—"

"Why, hello, Miss Masters. It's nice to hear your voice. I should have recognized it right away."

Sandra felt a twinge of guilt. Damn the woman for being so pleasant to her. "I hate to disturb Mr. Dougherty on a Saturday, but I wonder if he's at home."

"Yes, he's out in the garden. He said he needed some fresh air. Let me get him."

Sandra tried to picture Francis working in a flower garden, but he just wasn't the type.

"Yes, Miss Masters?" Francis sounded brusque, so his wife probably was within earshot.

Sandra apologized for calling him, then explained her brother's plight.

He relaxed when he learned she had called about a minor matter. "Your whole family goes for Jefferson Square in a big way. How old is the kid?"

"Fourteen."

"Fine. I'll have no problems springing him. Where's he being held?"

"The Sixth Street lockup."

"That's the Fourteenth Precinct. Captain Mariano's."

"I didn't ask my mother the name of the magistrate. She wouldn't know—"

"It doesn't matter. I'll have Angie Mariano turn the boy loose, and if you'll remind me on Monday morning, I'll get the Presiding Magistrate's office to dismiss the charges. Shall I call you after I talk to Captain Mariano?"

"I'm—not home just now." Under no circumstances could Sandra reveal to him that she was calling from the office. "But I can phone you back."

"That won't be necessary. The boy will be home inside of a half-hour. Just tell him to keep his goddam mitts off our culture center."

"I will. And I'm very grateful to you, Mr. Dougherty."

Francis lowered his voice. "You'll have your chance to prove it. After work on Monday." He hung up quickly, before she could reply.

In spite of her relief, Sandra seethed as she relayed the good news to her mother, and was still angry when she had completed the task. When a man became powerful, he used other people, treating them as objects. Buddy's friends could rot in jail over the weekend, and would have to report to the juvenile board once weekly for the next year. But Buddy would go free because a man who knew all the right people and had sufficient influence over them snapped his fingers.

And I'll pay the price, she thought, on my back.

If Dougherty thinks I'm going to kiss his hairy can for doing me this favor, he's wrong. How I hate that bastard's guts. And all the other bastards who throw their weight around and make everybody else jump when they crack their whips.

She returned to the files with renewed energy.

Gradually she saw patterns emerging, with the same names

appearing again and again. Ben Hopkins and his nephew, of course. Edward Emory of the bank. Dougherty himself. And Governor Herder.

After another hour she had gleaned the information she needed. Huge parcels of real estate in and around Jefferson Square were owned by a handful of men, who were in the process of making a gigantic financial killing. The setup was so simple that she should have seen it all along.

Her mind working furiously, she replaced each folder she had removed, checked to make certain she had misplaced none, and then locked the file. Finally she went off to her own desk to repair her lipstick and put on some eye shadow. She'd been in such a hurry to get out of the apartment this morning she had scarcely bothered with makeup.

Now that she had the facts, how could she best use them to her own advantage? The mere thought of a confrontation with Benjamin Hopkins—or any member of the Hopkins family—made her shudder. Maybe David had killed Goliath, but maybe it was just a story, and Sandra Masters, girl secretary, had no intention of getting rough with the Hopkinses. Nor with Edward Everett Emory, who was out of her league, way out.

The idea of challenging Francis Dougherty outright didn't appeal to her, either. He played rough, her own Fourth Street brand, and was such a vindictive son of a bitch that he might become violent. And a lot of good an assault and battery suit would do if he broke her nose.

The others who were making a profit were just names to her, investment bankers and manufacturers. Instinctively Sandra shied away from them. She didn't speak their language, and unless she had certified photostats of the evidence she had unearthed in the files, she wouldn't get very far. Gentlemen had a way of getting nasty when their backs were shoved against a wall.

That left Governor Albert Herder. Granted that, like all the others, he was wealthy, his circumstances were nevertheless different. Every newspaper reader in the country knew he had his eye on the White House, and was already behaving like a candidate for the nation's highest office, even though the President had not yet indicated his own preference.

The mere hint of a juicy scandal would knock Herder out of the race, and his rivals wouldn't hesitate to use any weapon or lever. Therefore the Honorable Al was vulnerable. He would become her pigeon, Sandra decided, and snapped her compact shut.

Michele Helsing sat on the long drawing-room settee, beneath the twin portraits of herself and Anton, and opposite the grand piano. A friend once had said, in a frequently quoted remark, that she was the only woman of his acquaintance who could remain poised while entertaining a total stranger early in the morning, dressed in a negligee. She seemed to be living up to her billing. It was ten o'clock, of course, which wasn't really early, and only on the surface was she calm.

The dark-eyed Latin who sat opposite her, nervously fingering the ascot scarf he wore beneath his shirt collar, was such a screaming little flit he made her ill. She had numbered many homosexuals among her friends from her own days in show business, and didn't mind them if they were unobtrusive. But this one was just too much.

"When Mr. Helsing is in rehearsals," she said, "he always sleeps late. If you're his student, as you claim, you must know something of his routines."

"I do." Manuel Rios smirked. "But I have come to see you, Mrs. Helsing, not the Maestro."

"Oh?" The invisible barrier remained high.

A moccasin moved back and forth, its tassels swaying. "Now that I am here, I find it not easy to say."

Michele didn't believe a word. Rios' air of flustered innocence was a sham, and he knew precisely what he was doing. "I have a busy schedule today," she said crisply, glancing at the ruby and gold watch Anton had given her for her last birthday. "So could we come to the point of this visit, Mr. Rios?"

"Mr. Helsing," Manuel said, his eyes enormous, "seduced me."

The accusation neither surprised nor hurt Michele, but she deplored her husband's taste. He was slipping, badly, if this was the best he could find. "That is a matter entirely between you and Mr. Helsing." She was still icy, remote.

Manuel was astonished. He had expected her to react vehemently, denying the charge, but she had scarcely stirred. Obviously he had to change his approach, and his eyes narrowed.

Michele unblinkingly returned his gaze. "I hope you're planning to leave voluntarily and at once, Mr. Rios. I'd enjoy having you thrown out—but I doubt it will be necessary."

"You are not disturbed, *Senora?*"

"My feelings are my own, Mr. Rios. Be good enough to tell me why you've brought his information to me—and then get out!"

"Mr. Helsing has ruined my life!"

In spite of her suppressed anger and humiliation, she laughed. "You aren't claiming he was the first!"

"There have been no others, *Senora!*"

"Frankly, I think you're a liar."

"In Argentina my family is a good one! I am not one of the Maestro's cheap pick-ups he meets in men's washrooms!"

The shot struck home, and for the first time Michele's composure was shaken.

"I have friends here who can tell you I am a person of dignity. *Senorita* Callison—"

"You know Betsy?"

"She is my good friend!"

Then I deplore Betsy's tastes in her friendships, Michele thought. "Mr. Rios, you've come to the wrong person. If you believe my husband has harmed you, go to him. You and I have nothing to say to one another."

"It is well known that you are the directress of this ménage, *Senora.*"

Clever, Michele thought.

"So there is much I wish to say to you. And when I am done, I think you will wish also to speak with me. I have shown great promise as a pianist. The Maestro himself recognized my abilities, and took me as his student. But now I am shattered. I have no pride, no respect for myself. Oh, I fought him, *Senora!* But, as you can see, I am small and slender, and his strength was too great. Now I cannot eat, I cannot sleep, I cannot play the piano. I am destroyed."

"I still don't know why you've come to me."

"You have compassion, which the Maestro does not. You will wish me not to suffer."

"How can I help alleviate your suffering, Mr. Rios?" Anyone who knew Michele would have regarded her gentle tone as a warning signal.

"I must go back to Argentina, and retire to a house in the country outside Buenos Aires."

146

She nodded for him to continue.

"The house is not mine, but belongs to a relative. I must buy it from her."

They had fenced long enough, Michele decided. "What is the cost of this simple little place?"

"In dollars, *Senora,* one hundred thousand."

"Your psychic wounds would heal in an atmosphere of rustic comfort, I'm sure."

Manuel's eyes were hard. "I do not joke!"

"Oh, neither do I, Mr. Rios. Just so we have absolutely no misunderstanding between us, you're asking me for one hundred thousand dollars to keep your mouth shut and get you out of the United States!"

"It is my devout wish that you will take pity on me and—"

"Suppose I refuse? What then?"

"One who no longer has a career cannot be proud, *Senora.* If you turn me away, I must take the story of my plight to others who will befriend me."

"I'm glad you have influential friends."

"Maestro Broussard I do not know, personally, but he will hear me when he learns why I come to him."

That completed the picture. "I suppose you realize," Michele said, "that blackmail is dangerous as well as ugly."

"I must ask you not to insult me!" Manuel jumped to his feet and struck an indignant pose.

Michele wondered if he was a better pianist than he was an actor. "You have no proof of your charge."

"Maestro Helsing will not deny it!"

"But if he does?"

"I am not the first he has corrupted. There are many who will believe me. Even if they did not, I have enough proof to satisfy a justice of the courts."

Michele knew she could not dismiss the threat lightly. "You carry heavy ammunition, Mr. Rios."

Manuel tried to look naïvely pathetic. "This tragedy was not of my making, *Senora.* When honor has been lost, so little remains." He bowed stiffly from the waist. "You will wish time to ponder, so I shall call on you again in a few days."

The front door clicked shut and Michele was alone. She shuddered and wanted to retch. But this was no more the time for self-indulgence than it was for histrionics. Hurrying into Anton's study, she looked up Bettina Callison's telephone number in his address book, and a few moments later had the girl on the line.

"Betsy, do you know someone who calls himself Manuel Rios?"

The irony sailed over Betsy's head. "Of course. He's been a dear friend for a long time."

"Is he talented as a pianist?"

"I think so, but Anton is a far better judge than I am."

For the present, Michele had heard enough. "Would you be free for lunch with Anton and me today? Here?"

"Well, I had a date that—I'll break it."

"Thank you, Betsy. This is short notice, but it's rather important. Let's say twelve thirty, or as close to it as you can get here." Michele rang off, and went into the kitchen, where the cook was sitting at a table, reading the morning *Examiner*.

"Don't get up, Bertha. I'll take Mr. Helsing's coffee upstairs to him."

The cook raised an eyebrow, but continued to read the tabloid.

Michele filled a large pewter mug with coffee from a burner on the back of the stove, and went up to her husband's room. Placing the mug on his bedside table, she opened the drapes and looked at him. He looked so youthfully ingenuous when he was asleep that she was moved, and almost gave in to the impulse to go to him. "You bastard," she murmured, and then raised her voice. "Rise and shine, lover!"

Anton stirred.

She repeated the call, and at last he opened his eyes. "Very funny."

"I brought your coffee."

"*You* did? The millennium must be here." He saw her expression, and his wry smile vanished. "I belong to the old school of diplomacy," he continued, struggling out of bed. "I can't discuss the gold standard, the silver standard or the double standard until I brush my teeth." He staggered toward the bathroom, not bothering to put on his slippers, and the door closed.

Michele sat very quietly, her hands folded in her lap, resisting the desire to smoke. She supposed Anton was right when he accused her of harboring, even nurturing, a Puritan streak. There was no reason she shouldn't help herself to a cigarette from the package on his dresser, but her self-denial gave her a feeling akin to accomplishment. She actually enjoyed her abstinence.

That, perhaps, was where she had failed in her marriage. Instead of taking a firm stand and refusing to deviate from it whenever Anton had behaved outrageously, she had donned a hair shirt and liked wearing it. The fault, she felt, was completely her own. She had known when she had married him that, in spite of his mercurial brilliance, he was emotionally unstable and needed a wife who would act as his anchor. His genius in no way compensated for the lack of love in his life. His analyst had told her in so many words that he needed the affection denied him by a mother and three sisters who had driven and pushed him to the limits of his endurance.

But Michele had been ambivalent, giving him love one day, then withdrawing the next when she learned of his latest homosexual escapade. It was so easy for the analyst to tell her what he needed, but what of her own needs, her own pride? She felt so helpless when forced into sexual competition with his male lovers; she felt certain of her ability to offer him more than any other woman could give him, but floundered when he turned to other men.

Perhaps the problem was insoluble. She had been telling herself for a long time to fish or cut bait, but had been unable to do either. Now, however, in a moment of crisis, she couldn't allow herself to think beyond the immediate future. Anton wasn't the only one in jeopardy. She—and their child —had a tremendous stake in the outcome of the drama caused by his latest indiscretion.

Anton looked positively dashing as he emerged from the bathroom in his monogrammed black silk pajamas with a white silk handkerchief emerging from the breast pocket. He glanced at his wife, ran a hand through his hair and then went to the dresser to light two cigarettes. Often, when Michele had been on the verge of abandoning hope, he had demonstrated an almost psychic understanding of her own immediate needs. When a man was that sensitive, it was hard to give up.

Anton sat on the edge of the bed, took a large swallow of coffee and a long drag on his cigarette. "Now," he said.

Michele minced no words, and gave him a verbatim account of Manuel Rios' visit.

He spilled a long ash on the floor. He looked at it, apparently debating whether to continue smoking, and then stubbed out his cigarette.

"So much for Rios' fairytale," Michele said. "What's your version?"

Anton became defensive. "What do you want to know?"

"Everything!"

He stared down at his bare toes. "It's true we did some—playing around. On the couch in my office. Once. A couple of days ago."

"With that disgusting creature?"

"This is tough enough without the helpful editorial comments. May I go on—in my own way?"

"Sorry." Michele realized this was excruciatingly painful for Anton as well as for herself.

"As God is my witness," he said, "I thought of Manuel as a student. Just that, nothing more. I didn't start things. He did. If you want to be technical about it, he seduced me."

"Deliberately?"

"I—I guess so. I can't be quite objective in all this, Michele. Certainly Manuel knew I had a weakness, and exploited it."

"Then it was deliberate," she said, "and you were the patsy of all Creation."

"It looks that way."

She went to the dresser for two more cigarettes, and he looked so miserable she let a hand linger on his shoulder after giving him one.

"Thanks," Anton muttered. "I don't deserve that."

"Let's save the questionable joys of self-recriminations and breast-beating until later, after we work all this out."

He nodded, and was silent for a moment. "What really gets me is that the little son of a bitch has a genuine talent."

"I don't care if he can play the piano like a new Serkin! How do you think this should be handled?"

"I'd like to beat Manuel's ass off."

"There's been enough of that sort of thing already."

"Don't needle me, Michele!"

"A bad joke. For which I apologize."

"I didn't mean to flare up at you either. I'm not really awake yet, but I've got ice water running in my veins." Anton brushed off a cigarette ash that had fallen onto the bedclothes. "He actually mentioned going to Broussard?"

"In so many words."

"How Henri would love it! And I think Helena Godoy would start her own television and radio network to broadcast the story."

"People in music are always gossiping. What real harm could the story do you?"

Anton looked at her. "If the directors of Jefferson Square believe Manuel, it's the end of me. A few years from now, after the square is solidly established, it wouldn't matter so much. But right now, in the formative stage, it would be a death blow to the whole project. You can't create an image of a wonderful, wholesome culture center for the American family—and then let it leak out that the director of your symphony is a pervert. Dan Robertson is an able, decent guy, but he'd have absolutely no choice. He'd recommend that the board throw me out, and the vote would be unanimous."

The room was warm, but Michele rubbed her bare arms vigorously.

"I've handed you the opportunity you've wanted," he said. "You can take me to the cleaners when you walk out, and I don't think any court in the United States would grant me the right to visit little Anton as often as once a month."

"Who said I was walking out?" Michele demanded.

A note of anger crept into his voice. "One hundred thousand dollars is too much money!"

"Any blackmail is too much. Pay once, and we'll be paying forever. But we've got to be realistic."

"Meaning?"

"Rios has the power to create a scandal that will ruin your career."

"I'm not so damn sure of that," Anton said.

"He says he can prove you've had an affair with him. Can he?"

"Absolutely not! I've done some stupid things in my life, but I—" Anton stopped short and buried his face in his hands.

Michele was afraid to question him, and waited.

"He asked if he could wear my signet ring for a few days. I thought it an odd request, but I humored him. So he's got it. With the initials A. G. H. on it in heavy gold."

"That isn't conclusive evidence."

"It's enough." He began to shake.

"There's something that worries me even more." Michele steadied herself. "Is Rios of age?"

"My God!" Anton looked at her, horror in his eyes.

"Well, is he?"

"I believe he's over twenty-one, but I can't swear to it," he said.

"If he's under age, the state will have to prosecute you on the grounds that you contributed to the delinquency of a minor."

"I'm wallowing in dung, Michele. Don't rub my nose it, please."

"Couldn't you have thought of all this?" Her anxiety made her voice sharp.

"I've already told you. Manuel made a pass at me—he was so subtle about it that I didn't realize until we started talking just now that it really was a pass. So then I lost my head. I have no alibis, no excuses, no rationalizations. Now I'll be paying him off for the rest of my life—"

"We aren't paying him a penny, Anton."

"Wait. I started talking big and brave, too, but the deck is stacked against me. The least I can do is lose with grace."

"I won't permit it!"

"That lousy little whore! I could kill him!"

"If you should see him Anton, anywhere, you are not to speak one word to him, no matter what the provocation. Let's not add more fuel to the fire."

"You're serious about fighting this," he said, "even though it's a hopeless mess."

"I'm not at all convinced it's hopeless. First we'll see what Betsy has to say—"

"Who?"

"Betsy Callison. He boasted of his friendship with her, so I've invited her to have lunch with us today."

"No!" Anton jumped to his feet, knocking over the ash tray. "I don't care what I've got to pay him, but I—I can't admit to any of them—"

"Any of who?"

"The top crowd. Betsy goes with Warren Hopkins, and may be marrying him. I've spent all these years climbing and climbing, and finally I've made it. Anton Helsing, a poor immigrant Swede, a nobody, is accepted by the highest society people in the world. But do you realize what'll happen if they—find out? I'll be the leper of the century!"

152

Michele went to him, literally forced him to sit on the bed again and began to stroke his face. "We're not telling Betsy anything," she said, "We're going to learn what we can from her."

Anton allowed himself to be soothed, then glanced up at her. "Why are you doing this, Michele?"

"In God's name, why do you think? I wouldn't have thought I'd have to explain it to someone with your background."

He tried to pull away from her, but she held him firmly.

"Don't be petulant, Anton! You know I can stand anything but that sulky pout."

"Why are you having Betsy here? Spell it out, and maybe I'll find out that crack about my background isn't a crack after all."

"You're paranoid! I didn't mean your homosexual background—"

"Oh."

"When you were a boy, what did you do when you saw a gang waiting at the corner?"

"I ran away, naturally."

Michele sighed. "All right, then. What did you do when just one boy came up to you and tried to start a fight?"

Anton thought about the question. "Depending on how big he was, I guess I usually fought back."

"Exactly. We're fighting back. I want to find out what Betsy knows about Rios' past. Maybe we can dig our claws into something, somewhere. If he's doing this to you, maybe he's done it to others. Maybe he's been indiscreet in his relationships with other men—"

"You won't find out a damn thing from Betsy. She's too pure to know that fags even exist."

"Maybe so, maybe not. We'll find out. If we're going to fight, we'll need ammunition. Betsy is the start."

He was silent for a moment, and when he spoke there was a trace of huskiness in his voice. "I thought you'd walk out, but instead you're helping me. Why, Michele?"

She ignored the question. "I remember reading somewhere that one should never show fear when dealing with a blackmailer. I can see why."

"You'd have universal sympathy, but I suppose it's better to be the wife of a musical director who holds one of the most distinguished jobs in the country than to be demoted to the status of ex-wife of a fag who happens to be a musician."

She let her arms fall to her sides and moved away from him. "You have a genius for antagonizing me, Anton. I know that was intended as a slap at yourself, but don't you see you insult me, too?"

"I guess I don't trust anybody. After myself, you least of all." He stared morosely at the drapes of heavy silk.

"Stop feeling so sorry for yourself!" Michele said. "We'll have to reexamine our relationship, Anton, and decide whether staying together is worth the struggle. But, before we do, we've got to settle the hash of Manuel Rios. So we'll move one step at a time. Get dressed, stay out of trouble, and keep your mouth shut about this whole mess!"

Anton watched her sweep out of the room, and a familiar sensation of helplessness overcame him. People like Michele never knew the pains of uncertainty, the anxieties caused by indecision. He envied his wife's ability to exercise such strict control over her own life, just as he resented her attempts to direct his. No, that wasn't true, either. He needed her, desperately, and he wished to God he could fulfill her emotional needs, not merely her yearning for position and wealth.

"Why," he asked aloud, "do I even have to *try* to be a model of a middle-class American husband?"

The last barriers of self-restraint broke, and Anton stretched out on his bed, face down, and wept.

Dan Robertson, Jr. made an attempt to climb over the back of the dusty suburban train seat, but was stopped by a mother who, although engrossed in her book, seemed to have eyes in the back of her head. The thwarted boy, who had shown no interest in the coloring book and crayons his parents had brought along for the purpose of keeping him occupied, decided he wanted his sister's identical set. Dan, Jr. snatched. Margaret resisted. He jabbed her in the face and she began to cry.

The children were separated, and Dan put aside his newspaper. "Every time we take these monsters anywhere," he said, "I swear I'm not going to tolerate such bedlam again. Why don't I rent a car, as I keep threatening to do?"

"Hold still, Peggy, and let Mommy comb your hair. I don't know, Dan." Phyllis was thinking of the children rather than of his question. "Usually they don't become restless on a ride as short as this."

154

Dan rescued the crayons his son was on the verge of stuffing into the side of the seat. "Maybe they don't, but I do."

"Knowing how much your peaceful weekends mean to you, I was surprised that you accepted when Edith Simpson called this morning."

"I told you, honey. Harvey and I have been holding a dialogue, I guess you could call it, and he'd like to end it in the quiet of suburbia. No, Danny! Put that wrapper down!"

"No, Danny," his son echoed. "Put wrapper down."

"You've been advancing all sorts of mysterious hints for days," Phyllis said, "which isn't at all like you."

"I haven't been fair to you lately, I know, but I've had a problem to work out on my own. I imagine Harvey has some advice to give me, and that may be all I need. But, regardless of whether it is, I'll come clean with you this weekend."

"How about now? The single most potent force on earth is the curiosity of a woman."

"That ranks second. The strongest is the energy of a small child. I'd love to slap handcuffs on these two. Children, do you want to go for a ride in Aunt Edith's boat today?"

The little boy nodded solemnly, and his smaller sister, whose understanding of the question was dubious, followed his example.

"Then be good and sit still," their weary father told them, glancing at his watch. "We'll be there in a few minutes, but you'll go for no boat ride unless you behave yourselves right now."

"Aren't you sticking your neck out, Dan? You don't know whether Edith and Harvey have put their sailboat into the water yet."

"If I know Edith, she's been out in it every day for the past four to six weeks. If not, I'll have to take the kids out in a canoe or some damn thing from the Simpson boathouse. One way or another, Sailor Dan will come through."

Phyllis laughed. "I haven't heard you call yourself Sailor Dan for a long time."

"It just slipped out." He settled back against his seat, grinning at her.

She smiled at him, and they forgot the jolting, dirty train, their children and their worries. The mere mention of "Sailor Dan" brought back memories that remained fresh, even though almost a decade and a half had passed. . . .

. . . The Midwest was going through a boom unmatched even during the twenties. New skyscrapers were rising in Chicago, the home of the first of them, and in the other great cities of the lakes and prairies and rivers. The World War II veterans and their wives had filled the campuses of the mammoth universities, and after going out into the world had been replaced by a new breed, the "quiet veterans" of the Korean War, young men who were less cynical than their predecessors because they had been less passionately dedicated in their beliefs.

Everywhere there was change and prosperity. The Detroit automobile makers brought out bigger, shinier cars each year, each model more garish than the last. The well-to-do ladies of Milwaukee and Cleveland and St. Louis and Kansas City returned from trips abroad wearing fashions their mothers, back in the free and speakeasy twenties, would have found shocking. But the rich weren't alone in their enjoyment of travel. Everyone seemed to be going someplace, air fares were dropping, and with the arrival of jet planes promised within a few years, a new era in transportation was about to begin.

Only the ships of the Great Lakes Associated Passenger Steamship Lines and their sister companies remained unchanged, and seemed indifferent to the fading of the glories they had known since the days immediately following the First World War. The renowned and sophisticated of the Midwest no longer went abroad the S.S. *Prairie Schooner* and the other six-thousand-ton passenger giants of the inland waterways for voyages that lasted from one to ten days. But the *Prairie Schooner*, recently redecorated, was enjoying a new lease on her aged, honorable life.

Currently making her annual "grand voyage," she crisscrossed Lake Michigan, taking on and dropping short-haul passengers at South Haven and Racine. Muskegon and Sheboygan. Ludington and Manistee and Manistique before heading through the Straits of Mackinac into Lake Huron. Old-timers on the lakes swore the waters could be choppier, more vicious than the Atlantic at its worst, and there were ladies who became seasick at the mere thought of bad weather.

Most of the *Prairie Schooner's* passengers were enjoying every moment of the "grand voyage," however, and with good cause. There was enough activity to keep everyone busy. Most of the younger generation's social life centered on the Hall of Mirrors on Main Deck, where beer was sold, and two rock-and-roll combos, one of five pieces and the other of three, alternately maintained a steady flow of musical sounds. A few middle-aged adventurers and somewhat older secretaries or file clerks amenable to finding new companionship inevitably found their way to the Hall of Mirrors, too.

But the atmosphere there was too strenuous, too frantic for the couples posing as long-marrieds who rarely used the upper bunks in their narrow cabins lined with varnished oak bulkheads. Occasionally the men appeared in the Hall of Mirrors to buy cardboard containers of beer, but, in the main, these couples remained invisible except at mealtimes.

"I don't get it," Dan Robertson said to the other Great Lakes University undergraduates with whom he was making the trip. "They hide most of the day in their cabins. But when they come to the dining room—wow! Those gals do everything but the grinds in a spangled G-string to make sure you notice 'em."

"You're very naïve, darling," replied Phyllis Markham, who planned to marry him when he received his first payment under his graduate school fellowship. "You don't understand women."

"I'm only interested in understanding one."

"Please don't interrupt when I'm about to spout wisdom," she said severely. "They feel self-conscious. They feel we're noticing them."

"Which we are, of course, including what they're doing most of the time in those little cabins."

"Dan! That's vulgar."

"I'm being literal, Phyllis. If their cabins are as small as the one Jim and I squeeze into—never mind. Finish your wisdom-for-the-day."

"You always spoil my train of thought, and I think you do it deliberately. I think I intended to say they feel so self-conscious and ill at ease that they overcompensate by dressing up for dinner."

"In the first place, I have no intention of arguing with a psych major on the Dean's List. In the second place, I have no interest in the motives of those semi-tramps—"

"Oh, Dan," she said reproachfully. "They aren't. They're trying to find a little glamor—"

"On this tub?"

"The *Prairie Schooner* is the last word in glamor to them. If you had come from some dusty little plains town—"

"I'll take your word for it, Phyllis. My idea of real, dyed-in-the-mink, genuine glamor would be to cross the Atlantic in a suite on the *Queen Elizabeth*. Or on that gorgeous new superliner the French Line is planning to build—"

"I'm with you."

"You sure are, honey," he said, reaching for her.

"Dan! Everybody in 'the well' is looking!"

"Looking is free, but if they take snapshots, we'll charge 'em two bits," he said, and kissed her.

"The well" was a hollow, bench-lined square amidships on Veranda Deck. The benches offered the best outdoor sitting accommodations available to the short-haul passengers, so most of those taking the cruise avoided the section. Most of the short-haul people were not pleasure-seekers; many worked on assembly lines, a few were women in domestic service traveling with their children, and a handful of others were the wives of men in the Armed Services. All were primarily interested in the cheap transportation the *Prairie Schooner* afforded them, and the overwhelming majority brought their own lunches with them, usually hardboiled eggs, wedges of a heavy, rural Wisconsin cheese and dill pickles. Only the soft drink stand at one end of "the well" did business. The short-haul people rarely went into the dining room for a table d'hote lunch that would cost them two dollars per person, a price maintained because the chef wanted to discourage transients.

In the forward section of the Veranda Deck were the library and the parlor, twin public cabins used in the main by the bridge, poker and pinochle players.

The deck chairs of the cruise passengers were located in the aft section of the Veranda Deck, and a steward was on hand to provide them with blankets when cold mists settled over the lakes, or to fetch beer for them from the Hall of Mirrors. Those who preferred coffee could have a cup brewed by the steward in an ancient machine that looked as though it might explode at any time.

The old ladies and the few elderly couples making the cruise spent most of their waking hours in their deck chairs, in part because of the greater comfort they provided, in part because of the illusion that they were making a salt-water

158

voyage. Few of them ever appeared on the Sun-and-Sports Deck, where the shuffleboard and deck tennis courts were located, as were the Ping-Pong tables. Here the teen-agers, the younger married couples, the four collegians and a sprinkling of what the purser loftily called "singles" spent at least part of their time.

The heart of the *Prairie Schooner's* social life was the dining room, which could seat three hundred passengers. Actually it consisted of a series of large, connecting cabins, built around a central kitchen where stoves were lighted day and night. Breakfast was served from 6:00 to 8:15 in the morning, the relatively light midday repast, which was still called "dinner," was served from 11:30 A.M. to 1:00 P.M., and supper, the important meal of the day, began at 6:00 in the evening. Most diners were prompt, and only a few had to be reminded by the over-worked waitresses that anyone who showed up between 7:00 and 7:30 would be forced to eat cold left-overs.

The decor was simple, the owners of the vessel wisely having decided to rip out rather than replace the faded pre-World War II red plush banquettes and chandeliers of weather-stained glass. Servings were family style, with everyone helping himself from bowls passed around the room. Sauces were few, corn and tomatoes were fresh, as were whitefish, mackerel and lake perch, and only the best quality of fresh-killed beef was served. Those who traveled on the *Prairie Schooner* had simple tastes, but knew what they liked and could not be fooled.

Dan, who had consented to make the voyage because it was inexpensive, met Phyllis each morning at 7:45 outside the dining room. Their confrontation invariably produced a mild but distinct state of shock, a pleasant reaction, and neither wanted to break its spell.

"Hi," they said simultaneously, staring at each other, and he removed his horn-rimmed glasses to kiss her lightly.

She was wearing no makeup except a little lipstick, and, her eyes still heavy with sleep, undoubtedly looked much as they did when she first woke up in the morning. It felt wonderful to know that in three more months they would start seeing each other every morning for the rest of their lives.

"Jim's still asleep," he said, opening the door for her. "Karen?"

"Out cold." Phyllis made her way toward their usual table. "I've never had a roommate who could sleep so long in the mornings."

"Wait'll you get me for a roomie."

Two old ladies from downstate Illinois glared at them, and Phyllis reddened.

Dan tried in vain to stifle a chuckle.

"I'll fix you for that, my lad," she said, sliding into her chair.

He took the chair opposite her and reached for her hand.

She pretended to be indignant and snatched it away. "Ruining my good name."

"I'm changing it shortly." Dan leaned toward the next table to accept pitchers of apple and prune juice, then another of orange juice. He knew without being told that Phyllis wanted orange.

They fell silent as they began their breakfast, and Dan discovered, as he did every day on board the *Prairie Schooner*, that he was ravenous. He ate some corn flakes with fresh blueberries and cream, while Phyllis watched, and then he helped himself from a large platter of scrambled eggs and sausages. "You ought to have some of these eggs," he said. "You'll waste away, eating nothing but a couple of slices of toast every morning."

"I have a figure to watch."

"Let me watch it for you. I do, anyway—"

"I hope this isn't typical of your breakfast-time humor, Mr. Robertson."

"Considering the hour, I think I'm doing spectacularly well. We'll never be up this early, unless I get an eight o'clock class somewhere along the line."

"Do you always eat this much, Dan?" She watched him help himself to cottage fried potatoes.

"Well, no. But maybe that's because nobody ever offered me this much."

A mischievous smile lighted Phyllis' face. "I know how I'm going to get even with you for embarrassing me."

"Wait'll I brace myself. Okay, I'm braced."

"You'll have to eat my cooking, Dan."

"Ancient joke about brides. Nobody can spoil scrambled eggs and potatoes."

"Wanna bet?"

"Do you think I'd care?" he demanded fiercely.

"Not the first time, but you'd start feeling a little mean and snappy by about the sixth or seventh."

"Even if it's true that your mother never allowed you within arm's length of a stove, you couldn't help but become an expert egg and potato maker by the sixth or seventh try."

"If I do, that's what we'll live on."

"Among other things."

"Don't look at me like that, Dan!"

"Why not?"

"Because, well, it does things to me that are indecent at this time of day. And because all the farmers and their wives in this dining room stare at us and start whispering."

Dan saw she was truly uncomfortable, and looked down at his plate. "Some of these farmers might surprise you. That funny, little old guy who spends most of his time sleeping in his deck chair—the one who keeps shaking hands and saying, 'Hello, there, I'm Harry Allen,' gave me quite an earful on the modern farmer yesterday. In fact, I couldn't get away from him, and I now know all there is to know on the subject of modern farmers. What would you like to hear?"

"You're the professor." Phyllis poured their strong, black coffee.

"Well, the real farmer in this part of the country is basically a management expert these days. He owns a farm of from five thousand acres, which is small, to fifty or seventy-five thousand, which isn't nearly as big as you might believe. They may live in the old farmhouse, he and his family, during the spring and summer, but the whole place has been air-conditioned, and his son has probably put in a landing strip for his light plane behind the pasture. Mrs. Farmer does most of her shopping at Marshall Field, and the notorious daughter of the family runs up scandalous bills at Nieman-Marcus, which the old man has no trouble paying. Then, around about Thanksgiving time, they all take off to the new farmers' Valhalla, Fort Lauderdale and environs."

Phyllis watched him becoming increasingly engrossed as he spoke, and marveled. He was a born teacher, a man who literally loved imparting knowledge to others. She was making the right choice of a husband, she knew; there was no other man, anywhere, with Dan's qualities.

"The people we see on this oversized scow are the fellows who used to be known as the hired hands."

"Really, Dan?"

"Today, of course, they're chemists and technicians and mechanics. They use all kinds of sophisticated machinery, which has to be kept in good running order. They've got to know precisely how much nitrogen—other chemicals, too, depending on their crops, but chiefly nitrogen—they've got to spread. Most of these guys are the older generation, and go back to the old hired hands days, but they've survived in tough competition. They make around seven thousand a year, which is double what I'll have coming in the first year of my teaching fellowship."

Phyllis wanted to protest that she didn't care how much he made, but she knew from experience that he was too lost in his subject to hear her.

"The younger generation goes to agricultural colleges, and is concentrating on efficiency and controls systems, everything from scientific breeding and the prevention of livestock diseases to the curbing of soil exhaustion and reforestation. These new farmhands, and I use the word with a smirk, are farm managers. They'll take over the running of one absentee-owned property, then another, and so on. Either they do very nicely for themselves that way, or, if they develop the itch, they may buy a farm of their own."

She added hot coffee to his cup.

"What I'm trying to say, in essence, is that there's soon going to be very little difference between the hired farmer and the management consultant in business and the efficiency expert in industry. From my own standpoint, what's fascinating is that there's a parallel development in the arts. When our fathers were boys, the farmhand was a bumpkin, a hayseed, the butt of vaudeville stage humor. The new generation may appreciate Wagner as much as I do. More. I'm not particularly fond of Wagner." Dan smiled vaguely at his little, pedantic joke.

Phyllis was so pleased he had found his profession. He would be wasted in anything other than teaching.

"The odd part of all this," he said, "is that I had to make this trip in order to see the obvious. I was bribed by the low fares and prospect of spending all my waking time with you —not necessarily in that order of importance. I came very close to missing something of great significance." He paused to look at her.

Phyllis knew he needed her as an audience; besides, she wanted to hear his conclusion. "Tell me."

162

"There's a fellow from the Aggie School in my graduate seminar on Renaissance sculpture. I asked him one time, being funny, what he was doing there, and he was serious when he said, 'Because I like great sculpture.' Just like that, in so many words, and I missed the whole point."

"Which is what I seem to be doing right now."

"He's gone beyond the trade school approach to life. He enjoys sculpture, so he wants to learn more about it, even though it won't help him with corn planting schedules or crop rotation. And his case isn't unique. We're finally growing up as a nation, Phyllis. People are beginning to find fun and relaxation in the arts instead of looking only for vocational gain, which means we're becoming civilized, according to my definition."

"When I was little, I wondered why anyone ever wanted to become a teacher. Now I know."

"I'd like to do more than teach," Dan said.

Phyllis was surprised.

"Unfulfilled adolescent dreams. I want to be a playwright. Trouble is I can't put two natural-sounding lines of dialogue on paper."

"Maybe you're wrong."

"If I had any talent, it would begin to show somewhere by now."

Phyllis smiled at him across the table. Of course you can write, she wanted to tell him. You're articulate . . . and bright . . . and sensitive . . . and I love you. . . .

. . . Harvey Simpson met the Robertsons at the station with his eight-year-old Land Rover, which always looked as though it sat in the garage from one of their visits to the next. Three quarters of an hour later Phyllis and the children were leaving with Edith Simpson for a sail, taking a box lunch with them, and the men were alone. Harvey offered his guest a drink, which was refused because it was still too early in the day, but they each had a glass of sherry.

"Let's go out for a walk," Harvey said. "The woods are lovely at this time of the year."

Dan was amused. He had discovered within the past year or two that, like most authors, he tried to avoid physical exercise, while Harvey, a typical editor, always tried to prod him into becoming more active physically. "Why not?" It was easier to accept the inevitable without an accompanying lecture on health standards.

Harvey offered his guest appropriate attire, which Dan refused, and went off himself to change into heavy shoes made for him in London, a thick wool jacket with leather-patched elbows and a hunter's walking stick that opened into a seat. Two pipes, a freshly filled pouch of his privately blended tobacco and a supply of his oversized Swedish kitchen matches completed his equipment.

They entered the woods only a short distance down the road. "My neighbors and I," Harvey said, "have formed an association to preserve this whole area. About three years ago, old Dr. Sanford, who is an avid bird-watcher, discovered that a group of investors was trying to buy about fifty acres below the old waterfall. They were intending to put in one hundred homes—so-called 'luxury' homes—on that fifty acres. You can imagine what a housing development would have done to the whole area. Now, if anyone wants to sell his property for any reason, the other members of the association will buy him out and keep the property intact. No parcel amounts to less than ten to fifteen acres, and we intend to keep the neighborhood that way."

"You're a snob, Harvey."

"Of course I am, my dear boy! I've earned the right to live as I please, which happens to be a rather elegantly quiet way. Fortunately, my neighbors feel as I do. We deny no one else the privilege of living his way, but we ask him to do it elsewhere."

Dan had no desire to become involved in a long discussion of discrimination that would not change his host's views.

Harvey, who had been making small talk, was aware of his silence and let the subject drop. "I've been thinking about your problem, Dan," he said, brushing aside a creeping vine with his walking stick.

"So have I."

"You have several loyalties at stake. You don't want to be disloyal to Jefferson Square, which hired you in good faith. You don't want to force a financial sacrifice on your wife and children after giving them greater comforts and a higher standard of living. For your own sake you're reluctant to give up your new way of life, which we'll call big city celebrity living, for want of a more accurate description. And, in the final analysis, you feel a responsibility to the general public."

"That pretty well sums it up, Harvey." Dan stooped to pick up an acorn from the side of the path and throw it over the top of a young yellow maple that was just bursting into leaf. "But I'd like to make one thing clear. The end product at Jefferson Square won't be any less good because of the real estate shenanigans I told you about. Our art gallery is going to be superb. We'll have the best music and drama that talent and hard work and a generous budget—yes, and inspired imagination—can produce. I have confidence in the abilities of everyone associated with the square."

"All the same, land has been bought with taxpayers' money. The important thing is what you think of that. Now tell me, Dan. What do you really believe?"

"That the Hopkinses and their associates have pulled off something very slick and clever. That even though they've broken no laws, their ethics are questionable, to put it in polite language."

"Now you sound the way you did in my office."

"How else could I feel?"

"Knowing you, no other way. But I'd like a one-hundred-dollar bill for every man on the vocational make in this country who doesn't give a hang about ethics! Now, let's go back to my original premise. Am I right about your various loyalties?"

Dan pondered for a time. "I think so, basically, although you've over-simplified them somewhat."

"Dan, when Jefferson Square appeared to be the bright and shining concept you believed it, you could be true to all of your loyalties. But all that is changed now. Right?"

They came to a rustic bench, fashioned of a fallen log, a short distance from the top of a waterfall that made a smooth, murmuring sound. Nothing in the world of Harvey Simpson was harsh or abrasive.

"Let's sit here for a few minutes," Harvey said. "Your loyalties to your family, yourself and the general public are more important than those to your superiors at Jefferson Square. Is that correct?"

"I hadn't thought in those terms, but if it's possible to weigh loyalties—I dare say you're right."

"Then you have no real problem."

"I don't see—"

"You will. Resign from Jefferson Square. Write a book exposing this whole scheme. I can guarantee you it will be the

165

runaway best seller of the year. And you know how Simpson and Smith can promote a topical book, Dan."

"Wait, Harvey—"

"No, hear me out. The book will make you a very large sum of money, Dan. It would be foolish to predict the size of a trade sale or guess how much we might pick up on various subsidiary rights, but I can guarantee you'll earn far more than your salary at Jefferson Square pays you. Your family would lose nothing," Harvey said. "In fact, they'd gain."

"I've already understood that much," Dan replied.

"You'd enjoy even more of the celebrity life than you have now. Treble or quadruple the fuss that was made over you when *The Quandary* came out, and—"

"Dammit, Harvey, I'm not an actor who likes crowds collecting outside a stage door for my autograph. I enjoy the stimulation, intellectual as well as social, of city life. But I swear, I haven't the faintest desire to see my picture in the papers or to read about myself in the gossip column."

"Yes, yes," Harvey said impatiently. "We both know what you mean. To continue. You'd also be true to the public by giving people the unvarnished story behind Jefferson Square."

Dan reached for a cigarette and his battered lighter.

"I know you could write a book in eight months, and I'd hope you might do it in less. Let's say, in all, that it would be roughly a year from now until publication. You won't have to watch your pennies during that year. Your advance royalties will be equal to more than your present income from Jefferson Square."

Dan stared hard at the waterfall, watching the smooth sheet of water break up as it tumbled over jagged rocks.

"You'd be doing a public service of inestimable value, you'd be helping your family and advancing your own career in the way it should be advanced." Harvey knocked the ashes out of his pipe. "There you are, my boy. What do you think?"

"My first thought is that I'd be making a personal profit in both money and prestige at the expense of Jefferson Square."

"Dan, get back on the beam. You'd be making a profit at the expense of wealthy men who increase their wealth by posing as philanthropists."

"You're going too far, Harvey. That's the hell of this situation. They *are* philanthropists, not pretenders. From all I've seen, their devotion to the square has been as great as mine!"

"I'll concede you the point. It should make the book all the more fascinating."

"You don't think the square itself would be hurt?" Dan asked.

"In the long run, it should benefit. I've never yet known of any enterprise in which the general public has an interest at stake that hasn't been helped by the truth!"

Again Dan was silent for a time. "I'm not questioning your sincerity, Harvey, nor—for the moment—the validity of your arguments. But I do wonder whether you can be unbiased and impartial. If I take your suggestion and write that book, Simpson and Smith is going to make a few bucks, too."

"Simpson and Smith," Harvey replied instantly, "will of course not lose money. I don't pretend to be an altruist, Dan. Nonfiction that has the impact of newspaper banner headlines, written by a man of your proven literary talent, is difficult to find. Frankly, I'm already thinking in terms of sales promotion and publicity campaigns."

Dan had to grin at him. Harvey, for all his airs and his fraudulent love of playing the role of an English country gentleman, was honest.

"Judging your position from where I sit, Dan, I believe I'm being impartial and fair. As for my own position, I really don't know. Every publisher in the industry would love to get his hands on a book like this. Every man tries to find the answers to the dilemmas of modern living in his own past experience. A clergyman probably would tell you to pray for guidance. One of your educator friends might urge you to go back to teaching. I think in terms of publishing, which is fortunate, because a book—the right book, of course—will solve most of your problems."

Dan flipped his cigarette into the waterfall, and stood. "You weren't expecting an immediate decision, I hope."

"Knowing your caution, I didn't dare." Harvey laughed, then sobered. "Seriously, Dan, I wouldn't want to rush you. This is one of those crossroads crises that a man sometimes faces, and whatever you do, it'll have a major influence on the rest of your life. You'd be unwise to make up your mind too quickly. Think about all this. Take as much time as you like, and then tack on some extra. Discuss it with Phyllis, and give her time to mull it over. It's important that you and she see eye to eye in this."

167

"You're being generous, Harvey."

"Pragmatic, Dan. If I put the heat on you, you'll resent me. Then if you write the best seller of the decade for me, you'll start looking for another publisher."

"You're quite a guy."

"Publishing has its own code of ethics. My partner and I lay our cards on the table, and our authors stay with Simpson and Smith. In your case, there is also a personal friendship that I value. Just one thing, Dan—if you take a very long time, you may give me an ulcer."

Dan's tensions eased still more, and he laughed.

"If the decision were up to me," Harvey continued, "I'd have a contract back at the house right now, waiting for your signature. But, remember, I want you to go through with this only if you can give me something that has the depth and solidity that made *The Quandary* a real work of art."

"I don't think any man can consciously create art. I think it was Michelangelo who said that every man starts a new piece of work with a block of marble in front of him and a chisel in his hand. But not until he's finished—if then—does he know if what he's making has any meaning."

"You've already thought of turning this financial scheme into a book," Harvey said shrewdly.

"Maybe so, but it wasn't conscious until you mentioned it. I'll tell you what tempts me, Harvey, and it isn't what you think. I've developed a great respect for Ben Hopkins and Edward Emory and some of the other principal backers of the square. And it isn't that I'm impressed by their money or their authority. It's the intelligence and personality drives of the men who earn that money and wield that authority that tempts me—I'd like to analyze it, to explore it."

Harvey was afraid his elation would show, and averted his face while stuffing his second pipe.

"These men could retire this minute, every last one of them, and live in super-comfort for the rest of their days, never worrying for a minute about stinting their heirs. Instead they work harder than any men I've ever seen, and the more they're worth, the harder they seem to work. Ben Hopkins is fantastic. He must put in a sixty-hour week at his office, and then spend most of his nights reading books and papers that relate to his work. He already has more money and power and status than practically anybody on earth, so why does he work so hard? That's one of the questions I'd like explored in a book like this.

"I'd also want to examine his philanthropy—and that of the others, of course—as a sort of philosophy of life. These men don't give because they have to give. Oh, it makes sense for tax purposes if they make large endowments and the like, but I'm speaking now in the real sense of giving. They aren't throwing around money on Jefferson Square. They care what happens. Every dime that is spent is important to them, but they're generous and patient, far more than I'd be. I've seen them settle a silly argument between two architects by digging into their own pockets for enough to incorporate both architects' ideas into the plans."

"Aren't you going a trifle overboard?" Harvey asked. "If they're coining money on the rise in real estate values in the neighborhood of the square, why shouldn't they be generous? What's a few hundred thousand here or there?"

"You miss my whole point! Their time is all-important to them, far more than money. If they have the time, they can make the money. It's that simple. Well, they sit down for hours and hours, chewing the smallest details of the square's plans. Just the other day Ben Hopkins kept me in his office half the afternoon talking about the acoustics for Symphony Hall. He's never cared much for music, you understand, and by his own admission something that his nephew said triggered him on acoustics. Probably a budgetary question, initially.

"Anyway, Harvey, no matter what it was that started him, Ben Hopkins has made himself an expert on acoustical problems in theaters and auditoriums. I'm fairly well informed on the subject because I've had to keep up to date, although I'm admittedly no acoustical engineer. But Mr. Hopkins left me at the starting post while he ran the mile and seven-eighths in record time. He's read book after book on the subject, and in a short time, too. He has one of those incisive minds that cuts to the heart of a problem. He wasn't just interested in the engineering aspects—and I know what you're thinking —the budget. He spent most of the afternoon talking in purely human terms. He has the interest in people that was typical of the great patrons of the Renaissance. An almost abstract interest, because he's so shy.

"Yet—at the same time he has all these other qualities,

he cold-bloodedly initiates this tremendous cultural project smack in the middle of a neighborhood where he and his friends own most of the property. Is this cynicism? Is it an unwillingness—hell, a refusal—to accept the standards of the rest of us, that is, middle-class moral and ethical standards?

"Here's what I'm really asking, Harvey—what makes Ben Hopkins tick? What makes Edward Emory and the rest of them tick? I've been pretty severely disillusioned, and if I knew the answer I'd be inclined to quit my job and write the book for you. But I don't, which means that anything I'd write now would be nothing more than muckraking."

"Rather spectacular muckraking, Dan."

"Sure, but lacking the depth and solidity you mentioned a little while ago. So it's just as well that I don't give in to a sudden impulse. Before I can really make up my mind, Harvey, I've got to know two things. First, what I really want. Second, what these financier-philanthropist-robbers are really like. I'm not going to procrastinate, I can promise you, chiefly for my own sake. But I can't write a book unless I convince myself that I really understand these men.

"And even more important is the square itself. I've believed in it, Harvey, and even though I'm on the sour side right now, I still have faith in it. So—if the unscrupulous financial tactics of the principal backers is going to force me into the opposition, I've got to have the satisfaction of knowing the whole story, of understanding why they're behaving as they are."

"At the risk of losing a book, Dan, has it occurred to you that these men may not be aware of the real estate hijinks? I mean, they have a great many, varied interests, and—"

"Not a chance in this world," Dan said. "I've thought of that angle, but it won't wash. One or two of the directors may be remote from their own companies' operations. But not Ben Hopkins—above all men. He can tell you without even glancing at a piece of paper how many tons of copper were hauled out of the Hopkins mines in the Rockies yesterday. And where the geological teams doing investigative work for the Hopkins interests in South America made their camps in the Andes last night. He knows everything. And Emory is a close second. As for Al Herder—"

Harvey grasped his arm and leaped to his feet. "My God, Dan, you didn't tell me Governor Herder is mixed up in this!"

"Well, he is. I can't tell you offhand how many acres in the slums he owns, but I have the figures at home. The property all comes from the same sources, you know. Emory and Herder are very distant cousins, I believe, and it was their mutual ancestor who first settled the district."

"This is even bigger than I imagined." Harvey could no longer control his excitement. "This book can have a direct bearing on the next Presidential election. You can kill Herder's chances to reach the White House."

Dan tried to calm him. "I have nothing against him personally. At directors' meetings, I say, 'Good morning, Governor.' And he says, 'Hiya, fella.'"

Harvey did not laugh. "You have a story so hot that somebody else will latch onto it and write it if you don't."

"I've already given you my word I don't intend to stall," Dan said. "But from here in I'll have to work this thing out for myself."

It was late in the evening, long after the children had been put to bed and the Simpsons had provided a good dinner and convivial conversation, before Dan and Phyllis had a chance to talk privately. Then, because they were guests in the house of others, they instinctively lowered their voices.

Dan did most of the talking, with his wife asking questions occasionally, and finally he brought her up to date. "I certainly didn't mean to complicate the whole mess with an offer from Harvey to write a book," he said. "That just happened today. All I'd wanted was his advice. You see, honey, I was hoping I could come to you with the whole problem solved. Instead, it's more confused than ever."

"We really don't have to whisper," she said in a subdued tone. "The walls here are very thick."

Dan grinned at her. "But they have ears," he declared in a stage-whisper.

Phyllis rose from the foot of the bed, went to his chair and, standing behind him, put her arms around him and rubbed her face against his. "We Robertsons have a special genius for creating our own problems."

"That's a polite way of saying we're masochists."

"It's no such thing," she said. "You've been living with all this for some time, Dan. Let me become accustomed to it before we start to probe and analyze."

"I'd rather not do either. What I mean is that I don't want

to burden you. If you have any strong feelings one way or the other—"

"I think I'm too numb to feel, Dan. It isn't just our own personal situation. I'm thinking of all the other people who are working at Jefferson Square—the architects and the builders, and all the artists who are being hired, and—"

"I know. I've been thinking about them for a long time."

"I'll be satisfied with whatever you decide."

"Since when have you been a rubber-stamp? I'll expect you to tell me what you honestly think. I'm just reserving the right to disagree, that's all."

Phyllis realized he was tired and irritable. "No more talking tonight," she said firmly, "or we'll have one of our stupendously inane fights about nothing at all. Drink that nightcap you brought upstairs with you, and let's go to bed."

He was unwilling to end the discussion, but realized she was right, and made the effort. "Are you drinking that glass of milk?"

"Did you want it, Dan?"

"Good Lord, no!"

"I didn't think so. Of course I'm drinking it. I happen to like milk." She went through the familiar routine as though it were the first time.

He did his part, too. "I'm married to the only grown woman in the world who drinks milk when she isn't pregnant."

"There must be others."

"Well, yes. I suppose. But I don't know them."

They continued their exchange of small talk while they undressed. They embraced and kissed before climbing into bed, and Phyllis murmured, "Go to sleep, darling. You're weaving on your feet."

"I guess I am, at that." He settled himself for the night, then reached across the intervening space to her bed for her hand.

Phyllis remained wide awake, thinking of all Dan had told her. At times she felt at home in their new way of life, but occasionally she considered herself an impostor. Certainly she didn't feel like an executive's wife, nor the wife of a distinguished and very successful author.

That was ridiculous, she told herself angrily. She was Dan's wife.

"Almost without exception," Harvey Simpson said as he helped himself to the hot dishes on the dining-room sideboard, "finnan haddie is creamed when you find it on American menus. Why, do you suppose?"

Phyllis, who sat at the table facing the lawn, where she could watch Danny and Peggy at play, was finding it difficult to concentrate. "I don't know," she said.

"Neither does anyone else." Harvey sounded triumphant. "There's the tragedy of finnan haddie. Smoked haddock that's broiled with a little butter and lemon juice is delicious. The dish was invented to be eaten that way, not smothered in cream sauce. And I can assure you, it's the only way we ever serve it in this house. Let me help you to some."

"I've already eaten more breakfast than I should," Phyllis said. "I'm strictly a one-slice-of-dry-toast girl."

"But not when you're visiting us!" He brought his heavily laden plate to the table, and beamed at her.

"I've already eaten some eggs and kippers, thank you."

"Aha! We're weaning you away from your Midwestern tastes at last. Kippers are delightful, aren't they?"

"I like them better each time," she said politely.

Harvey was eating with relish. "Wonderful. To Edith and me, Sunday morning breakfast is the most civilized meal of the entire week. I'm always up early—the habits of a lifetime, unfortunately—but not Edith. And not Dan, either, I take it?"

"He was dead to the world the last time I looked in at him."

"I'm not surprised. But I *am* pleased you and I have an opportunity for a private chat."

"I'm wondering," Phyllis said hurriedly, "whether I ought to bring the children inside."

He looked surprised. "Country air and sunshine, my dear girl! On every pediatrician's prescription for good health!"

"You have no idea what two little monsters can do to your lovely lawn, Harvey!"

"This lawn is indestructible. It was seeded with the very finest blue grass," Harvey said with pride. "The owner of one of the big stud farms in Lexington, Kentucky, wrote a book for us several years ago, and we've become friendly, so he sent me enough seed for a much larger piece of property than I own."

"Well, knowing my children, don't be too surprised if you have to do some new seeding on your side lawn."

"I gladly take the risk." Harvey had mastered the art of seeming to devote his full attention to his companion and his meal, simultaneously. "I'm afraid you didn't sleep well."

"If I didn't, it's no reflection on your hospitality and Edith's."

"I'm sure Dan had a talk with you last night." He went to the sideboard again for a cup of steaming coffee and, without being asked, brought another for Phyllis. "You know, I can't help wishing that you youngsters would regard this situation as the golden chance of a lifetime. You shouldn't be depressed by it!"

"Jefferson Square has meant a great deal to Dan. It still does." She felt herself being pulled into a discussion against her will.

"Never having been an optimist, I've never felt as he does. But I know how disappointed he must be."

"But he isn't, Harvey! When he was talking last night it was obvious that he doesn't feel the potential of the square has been hurt in any way! It's just that he himself feels uncertain about the men who are the principal sponsors of the square."

"I don't pretend to know your husband as well as you do, but I'm certain that he'll become disillusioned with the whole idea of Jefferson Square. It's an almost inevitable outgrowth of his discovery that the men behind the project are using it as a front for their own money-making real estate schemes."

"You may be right, but I've learned never to predict how Dan's feelings will crystallize."

"It's obvious that I stand to gain if he writes this book for me." Harvey looked at her, waiting for confirmation.

Not knowing what he expected her to say, Phyllis nodded.

"But you and Dan can gain far more. I realize he saw Jefferson Square as an extension, so to speak, of his role as an educator. But Dan is primarily an author. *The Quandary* established him as a writer of stature, and his standing will be far greater after he does this new book."

Phyllis could feel Harvey bearing down, and felt uncomfortable. She was certain he wanted to enlist her aid, and didn't know how to put him off without becoming rude.

"The advantages are self-evident. The Robertsons will

174

achieve financially independent status. They'll have prestige —real prestige, my dear girl. Dan will be studied in the very courses in modern American literature he once taught! In fact—"

"Please, Harvey, I'd rather we didn't go into all this."

"I know you're tired, and it's plain you had a poor night's rest, so I must apologize to you for my insistence. But you and I don't often have the chance to talk frankly and alone. If Dan were just one of fifty or so Simpson and Smith authors, it wouldn't matter to me. But you and he have become our good friends. Edith and I feel very close to both of you. And we don't want to see Dan muff this chance—perhaps his only chance—to achieve what most men would give almost anything to attain."

"I'm grateful for your friendship, and I know Dan is, too," she said wearily, making an effort to sound gracious.

"I'm not seeking gratitude. All I want is recognition of Dan's worth!" He peered at her. "I'm sure that's what you want for him, too."

"I wouldn't have put it that way, but I suppose it is." Phyllis added sugar to her coffee and stirred it.

"Then you'll help?"

She tried in vain to think of a diplomatic reply.

Harvey repeated his question.

There was no choice; he was forcing her to be blunt. "I'll help Dan to do whatever he believes right," she said.

"You're very persistent, Mrs. Emory." Benjamin Hopkins, leaning back in the chair behind his desk, sounded amused but looked stern. "Anyone but you would have given up after being told I was making no appointments this month."

"Well, I suppose I have a reputation to maintain," Carolyn said, smiling.

"I was tempted to have Brookes tell you that Mrs. Hopkins and I are planning to stop in at your cocktail party for a few minutes on Tuesday."

"How nice!" It was more than nice. She would win the prize as the season's most successful hostess, since everyone knew that Ben and Frances Hopkins never went anywhere.

"That would have done no good, however, as we couldn't —and can't—discuss culture center finances at a social event. So I decided it would take more time to fend you off than to see you today, hear your reasons why I should give additional sums to Jefferson Square, and then tell you I can't do it at present."

The secret of Carolyn's record as a fund raiser was her persistence, larded with charm. Ben Hopkins was impervious to both, and therefore represented the greatest challenge she had yet faced. "There's hardly a need for me to tell you the square's problems, Mr. Hopkins. What little I know I've heard from Edward, but I'm sure I could learn far more from you."

It was his conviction that women had no legitimate place in finance. He had to admit, however, that this one was infernally clever. But he said nothing; as one of his grandfather's biographers had written, "The traditional Hopkins defense is tight silence."

Carolyn was undismayed by his failure to respond. "I can think of only one thing to ask you, Mr. Hopkins. As chairman of the general Jefferson Square Board, you know your deficit is growing rapidly, and soon will become unmanageable unless steps are taken to reduce it—"

"Who says it will become unmanageable?"

"The chairman of the finance committee."

"I never quarrel with anything a man tells his wife."

She hated being patronized, but forcibly reminded herself that he wasn't one of Edward's run-of-the-mill colleagues, and forced a smile. "In this case, neither do I. What do you intend to do about the problem, Mr. Hopkins?"

"I've already turned it over to my finance committee chairman." The subordinates who rarely saw Ben Hopkins smile would have been surprised by his hearty chuckle.

"Edward is expecting me to raise a good many of the millions, and so I will. I think you'll be interested in the new pledges that have been given to me in the past forty-eight hours." She reached into her handbag for a folded sheet of paper containing a neatly typed list of names and figures.

He scanned the sheet so quickly he scarcely seemed to glance at it, but Carolyn knew from experience that he missed no detail.

"You'll note," she said, "that every member of the board is increasing his personal pledge."

By going to his associates, including the men he had persuaded to join him in sponsoring the square, she was subtly increasing the pressure on him.

176

"Before I give this list to the public relations department to release to the press, I thought you'd want your name included, Mr. Hopkins."

He had thought her worthy of a less obvious ruse, and was disappointed.

"I'm sure you don't care what people say about you, but I know you'll agree that the public image of Jefferson Square is terribly important."

Advertising and publicity men were very fond of that word. "I don't know what you mean by image, and I doubt if you know it yourself."

His sharp tone startled her.

"Talk like that is especially effective with the young. I see my nephew fell for it."

She hoped he would never learn the very personal reasons that Warren had increased his donation. "We're all working together for the same purpose, Mr. Hopkins."

Her earnest intensity was unusual, and he was enjoying this respite from more serious concerns, but his schedule was crowded. "Mrs. Emory, I'm always being told I'm difficult, and I am. You would be, too, if people saw dollar signs in front of their eyes every time they looked at you. At the little meeting at which I first brought up the idea of creating a culture center—and Edward will bear me out in this—I said we'd need a broad base of financial support."

"We've taken your advice literally, Mr. Hopkins." Carolyn met brusqueness with brusqueness. "So far we have more than fifty donors who have each given contributions of more than one hundred thousand dollars. More than twenty-five thousand small contributors will have their names engraved on seat plaques. Dozens of industrial corporations are making substantial contributions. A friend of Warren's is doing some discreet missionary work at the embassies in Washington, and I believe we'll be getting checks from several foreign nations. The labor unions are surprising us with their generosity. Everyone is giving to the hilt. But we still don't have enough."

"Your argument is cogent." He was silent for a moment, then stood and walked around his desk. "I wonder if you've ever considered the unique position I'm in. Most people of substance are applauded if they give an extra one hundred thousand, as I see you and Edward are doing. I'd be severely criticized if I gave less than an extra million. Very well, Mrs.

Emory, you may put me down for one million more."

Carolyn started to thank him.

He held up a hand, chuckling. "Don't say it. You were hoping it would be several times that much, and you're disappointed."

"I am, a little. I thought that between you and the Hopkins Fund—"

"If I have any voice in the matter," he said, "the fund will allocate no additional sums to Jefferson Square at the present time."

"May I ask why?"

"The demands on foundations are increasing far faster than their financial reserves accumulate. The fund staff must reject fifteen out of every sixteen legitimate requests for help, and I'm told the situation at the Ford and Rockefeller Foundations is even more critical. I have every reasonable expectation that the fund will make another contribution to Jefferson Square before your campaign ends. But there are other projects, all of them equally significant, that are also being studied. One or more of them may have a higher priority call on the fund's investment powers." He moved to the door, one hand on the latch.

Carolyn knew the interview was at an end, and felt crushed. Never before had she felt such an abject sense of failure after obtaining one million dollars.

On Monday morning Francis Dougherty awoke with a cough, a blistering headache and a fever. He dragged himself out of bed and made his usual preparations for the day, but, never one to hide his miseries, complained bitterly about them at the breakfast table.

"Why don't you stay home?" Ann asked. "Be sensible for once. Your colds always get worse when you don't take care of them, and you'll be miserable at the Emorys' party tomorrow night."

"To hell with the party."

She knew he didn't mean it, but a challenge, particularly when he was feeling out of sorts, inevitably produced a battle royal.

"I'll kill the goddam cold with a couple of drinks at lunch."

"Let me get some of those pills the doctor prescribed last winter. They're in the medicine chest in our bathroom, I think. Anyway, I'll find them. Take two with your coffee right now, and——"

"Sit down, Annie, and stop your goddam nagging!"

She was too accustomed to his raging to be intimidated.

But he caught her arm, and forced her back into her chair at the kitchen table. "I mean it. Those pills make me too groggy."

"No groggier than a couple of drinks at lunch, I'm sure."

He grinned at her. "You ought to know, huh? Now, wait. Don't get huffy. I've got to be on my toes this morning, that's all."

Ann allowed herself to be mollified. "Are you going into court today?"

"That would be a relaxation, even though I'm losing my voice. I've got a meeting—a private meeting—with God J. Almighty himself."

"I wish you'd stop——"

"Okay! With Ben Hopkins, then. Pass the cream."

She was silent, wanting to know more but not daring to ask. "I'm impressed," she said at last.

"You ought to be," Francis replied. "Even though he's going to hate my guts before we're through."

"Mr. Hopkins could be a dangerous enemy."

He coughed, then sipped his coffee before glancing at her.

"Run your own department, why don't you? Hire yourself a new maid so you don't have to cook so much——"

"I've been trying! There simply isn't anyone these days."

"Okay, so go off to your society lunches at the Sheraton-Plaza, and make like grandma when you visit the kids. But leave business to the old man." He looked at her with amused affection. "Jeez, you worry about everything."

"Only about you, Francis," she replied truthfully.

"Sure, sure." He leaned toward her, then stopped himself. "I don't want to give you this cold. Anyway, you let me take care of my business with the great Ben. I'm on his side, and he knows it. Maybe I'll have to remind him of it a couple of times, but it'll all work out. It has to."

"Jerry Solanz has been calling you every five minutes for the past half-hour," Dan Robertson's secretary said as he walked into his office on Monday morning.

"From London?" He was genuinely surprised.

"He's still in town."

"Oh, I thought he was flying out before the weekend." Dan picked up a slip of paper. "Is that the number?"

"Yes, Mr. Robertson. Shall I—"

"No, he's so touchy, I'll do it myself. In his kind of work a man's rating is determined by how many secretaries a caller has to go through." Dan smiled and started toward his inner office.

At that moment the telephone rang; the secretary answered, and then called out, "He's beaten you to it. On line two."

Dan reached for his telephone and punched a button as he sat down at his desk. "Hello, Solanz. I just this minute walked in and heard you've been trying to reach me this morning."

"This morning!" Even on the wire Jerry sounded wildly disturbed. "Ever since Saturday morning I've been chasing you all to hell and back."

"I'm sorry. We went out to the country on Saturday, and were driven back just now. Has something—"

"Sweetie, I've got to see you. Now. *Right* now!"

Dan's dislike for the man had in no way lessened, but he thought that, if they were going to be working together, it would do him no harm to make a conciliatory gesture. "Would you like me to come over to the hotel?"

Jerry was caught off guard, and was silent for a moment, but recovered swiftly. "Yeah, that's the best," he said.

"I won't even take time to look at my mail. I'll be there in no time."

"It can't be quick enough. Come straight up. Suite 1800." The line disconnected.

Dan flipped through his mail, stuffing the more important pieces into his attaché case to read in the taxi. "I've got to hold a genius' hand," he told his secretary, "and I'll be back as soon as I can. If I'm not here by ten forty-five, call me. Anton Helsing is coming in at eleven, and I don't want to keep him waiting."

The mail was routine, but it absorbed his attention until he reached the hotel. The Sheraton-Plaza was one of the oldest hotels on the eastern seaboard, and care had been taken in its many face-liftings to preserve its exorbitantly expensive old-fashioned charm. The Oriental-carpeted lobbies were high-ceilinged, with crystal chandeliers placed at stately intervals, and the aura was that of dignified spaciousness in a city where space was at a premium.

There was a quiet bustle in the Victorian room, where breakfast was being served to those who preferred eating in public to room service, and a concierge, resplendent in his morning coat and striped trousers, looked efficient behind a desk mounted on a dais that enabled him to observe the be-behavior of lesser mortals. From the outside the gilded elevator looked a trifle rickety, but the interiors were carpeted, lined with satin wallpaper and equipped with useless little benches and a pair of excellent mirrors.

The floor clerk's desk was unoccupied, and Dan hurried down the corridor to 1800, where he halted to tap at the door.

It opened almost immediately, and Jerry, looking rumpled in a dressing gown of maroon and green silk, glared at him. "So you got here."

"I dawdled all the way," Dan said pleasantly.

"I never knew a guy so hard to reach." Jerry led him into the living room, where cablegrams and letters, stacks of play and movie scripts, and newspapers opened to the entertainment pages were piled on every sofa, overstuffed chair and table. In the center of the room was a table laden with a silver coffee server, cups and several covered silver dishes. At the table stood two straight-backed chairs, and Jerry waved his guest to one of them. "I had some coffee sent up," he said gruffly, embarrassed to be playing host to a man he disliked. "You want something to eat?"

"I've already had breakfast, thanks."

"A little low-calorie toast won't hurt you."

"My favorite kind." At least they had something in common.

"Sweetie, you ought to let somebody know where you've gone when you pull that vanishing stunt," Jerry said.

"I certainly would have, if I'd known you were trying to locate me."

"That's the least of it! I postponed my flight because of you." Jerry sounded deeply offended.

Dan neither could nor would apologize again. "What is so terribly important?" He was determined not to let himself be maneuvered into making a final decision on the Ben Jonson play. It was absurd to worry about such matters so many months before the theater was built.

"You saw a movie the other night," Jerry said.

So much had been happening that Dan's mind was a blank. "I did?"

Rain and Sun. There was a private showing at Seaboard University."

"Of course! It was first-rate."

"Hardly that, but it wasn't half-bad. A professional director would have brought out all sorts of dramatic values that the amateur misses. But everything considered, the kids who made it did a creditable job. The boy who directed it—I can't for the life of me remember his name—will go places in the industry when he learns not to use arty symbolism for its own sake."

Dan nodded discreetly, as though in agreement. He saw no reason to start a controversy when it was obvious that he and Solanz would never be in agreement on the film.

"I've been informed," Jerry said very quietly, "that you've asked for the movie. You want to open the new house with it."

"Yes, it seems just right for Jefferson Square." Dan sipped his coffee and helped himself to a slice of low-calorie toast.

Jerry carefully spread a thick layer of butter on another slice of the toast. *"Rain and Sun,"* he said in the same carefully controlled voice, "isn't available for distribution anywhere in the United States and Canada."

"So I hear, but I'd think the producers would jump at the chance to have it shown at the square. They could follow an appearance there with showings at art theaters all over the country."

"The reason it isn't available," Jerry said, "is because I've seen to it that no distributor will touch it. Anybody who does will lose all my films—and those directed by at least a dozen of my good friends. The lid has been clamped tight. Don't try to pry it open, sweetie."

Dan was taken by surprise, and thought rapidly. He decided to meet the issue squarely. "Berenice Tolmey gave a very touching performance. The part wasn't big, but she made it memorable. I didn't realize it was the same girl as your protégé until my wife mentioned something to me later in the evening." Now he had thrown down the gage of battle.

Jerry unhesitatingly picked it up. "The reason I signed Berenice to a personal contract is because of the potential as an actress she showed in that film. She wasn't very good, mind you. In her little scenes, when she should have been setting character in the minds of the audience, she underplayed. And in her big scenes she chewed the scenery. But the camera doesn't lie about potential, not even an amateur's camera. I saw the possibility of making her into a real actress."

Dan realized he was on dangerous ground. Ordinarily he'd have told Solanz off, since the girl's performance had been sensitive and charming. But one simply didn't argue with a man about his wife or mistress. So it was best to say nothing and wait.

"I'm handling her very carefully," Jerry said. "She has a solid supporting part in my new film that will make her reputation. Then she'll be ready for the big things I've planned for her. The time-table is all worked out, and I don't want anything to screw it up."

"Forgive me for being dense," Dan said, "but I don't see how a showing of *Rain and Sun* at the square—"

"It would ruin her! Look, sweetie. For the sake of keeping the peace between us, let's say you're the great expert on drama that you like to think you are. Okay? I still know more about the building of a box-office personality. It's tricky. One mistake, and that's the end of a potential star who otherwise would be a major draw for many years. It'll do Berenice harm, not good, if *Rain and Sun* is ever seen by audiences in this country!"

The entire picture was clear now. Solanz wanted to portray himself as her discoverer, and was eager to take credit for her development as an actress. It was a rotten stunt to play on an actress who had already demonstrated her worth.

"Let me tell you something confidential, and you'll see why it's so important." Jerry hitched his chair closer to the table, and glanced in the direction of a closed bedroom door.

Dan inadvertently followed that glance.

"I know what you're thinking, and you're wrong. If all I wanted was nookie, I could get fifty girls—a hundred—by snapping my fingers." Jerry illustrated his finger snap. "But this girl is going to become one of the biggest properties in the business. She'll be tremendous, as big as anybody who has ever worked for me."

She would become a star, Dan thought, completely on her own, if she never set eyes on Solanz again.

"I told you my first play is going to be Jan Marek's new

'one. Right, sweetie? If I could, I'd let you read what's already on paper. In fact, I'll put in a call today to Jan. I think he's resting for a few weeks at Acapulco or Palm Springs, but I know his hangouts, and I'll find him. I'm sure he'll give his permission for you to read the first part of the play. Then you'll understand why I'm so concerned."

I understand already, you egomaniacal bastard, Dan thought.

"This I don't want breathed to a soul. Nobody knows it except Jan, who has complete, absolute faith in my casting, because he knows I've never once let down one of his plays, and I never will. Not even Berenice suspects what I have in mind for her. The kid would panic, you see. Anyway, here it is, straight. The lead in this play is fantastic. It will give an actress the opportunity to run the entire gamut of human emotions on a stage, to shoot fireworks. I tell you, fantastic! There isn't a leading lady in the business who wouldn't give her soul for that part. It's so good there are stars who'd beg to do it for Equity scale pay, that's how good it is. And who will play the part? Berenice! If I told her now, before she's ready, she'd panic. That's why I'm going to such lengths to protect her."

"You're assuming, of course, that she can do this part."

"I never assume, sweetie. I know."

Dan had seen unscrupulousness, but Solanz' gall was outrageous, and he felt slightly ill.

"You and I have a big stake, together, in the Jefferson Square Repertory Theater. So now you can see why you've got to cancel your request for *Rain and Sun*." Jerry sat back in his chair, removed his heavy-rimmed glasses and polished them with his napkin.

Dan saw a great deal. Solanz obviously had power in the motion picture industry, but not even he had the strength to block a billing order from an organization with the prestige of Jefferson Square. So, on the surface, the issue was a simple one, whether to give in to the man's unfair demand, or insist on booking the film as a matter of principle.

But the question was not as simple as it seemed. Solanz had already indicated he would be the most difficult of colleagues. If crossed in something that so closely touched his vanity and was so important in his romantic life, he would become a permanent, unrelenting enemy. Balancing the factors, Dan finally told himself it was not his place to act as the protector of a maiden who apparently didn't realize she was in distress. In fact, the very idea of calling the young woman behind that closed bedroom door a maiden was ludicrous.

She was a platinum blond tart who had no inhibitions about posing half-naked in publicity pictures, and who was happily selling herself to Solanz in return for the stardom she craved. Neither she nor a sensitive little film was worth the disruption of the already strained relations at the Jefferson Square Repertory Theater. And dilemmas in real life were far more painful and complex than the author of *The Quandary* had led his readers to believe.

"I'll have to go along with you," Dan said.

"I knew you'd see it once you heard the whole pitch!" Jerry was ecstatic, and, reaching across the table, pumped his visitor's hand so vigorously that he almost knocked over the pot of coffee. "Tomorrow night, after the Emory's party, let's have a drink together."

"You're staying over for the party?" Dan felt ashamed of his weakness, and wanted to escape.

"Usually I see bankers in their offices. How often does anybody get to see them in their own homes? Don't go yet, sweetie. Let me get Berenice out here so you can meet her. Just don't mention *Rain and Sun* to her. She doesn't like to talk about it."

"Another time, thanks." Dan was wrestling with enough problems of his own.

"Any time." Patting him on the shoulder, Jerry walked him to the door. He had been wrong in his first estimate of Robertson; the man could be handled by making him privy to what he believed were significant confidences.

Francis Dougherty tried to overcome the sense of diffidence he felt in Benjamin Hopkins' office by speaking more loudly and aggressively than usual. "I couldn't get to you before we made the asking price on that property semi-public. Your watch-dogs keep you sealed off."

"I assumed that was why you were trying to get in touch with me." Ben Hopkins was unruffled.

"You seem to be missing something in this situation, Mr. Hopkins. I'm worried, and if I were you, I wouldn't be any too happy."

The financier sat wooden-faced—and serene.

"Anybody who wants to can find out the ownership of the

185

Jackson Drive Realty Company. All it takes is a couple of minutes at the city's real estate licensing office. I wanted to set up a dummy front for the company."

"I make no secret of my interests, Mr. Dougherty."

"This is one time you should have." Francis realized he was pushing his luck, speaking so bluntly to one of the richest and most powerful men on earth, but he believed he had no choice. "There are people who don't like you—or your associates."

"I understand I'm regarded as an unpleasant symbol in some quarters, but I've never been interested in winning popularity contests."

"This goes beyond popularity. Some crusading young punk of a newspaper reporter out to make a reputation for himself could get wind of the Jefferson Square sale and crucify you."

"Crusading young reporters have been trying just that for several generations. We don't crucify easily in my family, Mr. Dougherty."

"I'm sure you've had to develop a tough hide, but all the same, I'd be happier if the sale to the square wasn't too apparent. Your partners are vulnerable, too, and some of them may have thinner skins."

"Including you, Mr. Dougherty?"

Francis bristled, but controlled his annoyance. "Including me, Mr. Hopkins, even though my percentage is very small. One suggestion leads to another, and what bothers me is that somebody may start printing the whole story."

A clock chimed, and Benjamin Hopkins took a tiny gold pill box from his vest pocket, removed a pill and swallowed it with some water. "What do you consider the whole story?"

"That you and Governor Herder and a few others are making a mint on real estate from the square itself and the whole neighborhood. My little cut is peanuts, but it'll be the biggest profit I'll have ever made!"

"I can't say the same. I view this as an ordinary business venture in which I've taken ordinary risks and will now be assured a modest return."

"That isn't how it'll look to the public," Francis said. "People are going to think you backed the square with one hand so you could rake in money with the other."

"My philosophy is not complicated," Ben Hopkins declared. "I never announce my personal philanthropies. The Hopkins Fund sometimes makes its grants known, although many of its gifts remain unpublicized. I also consider my financial ventures my own business. My corporations that issue stock to the public keep shareholders informed in the usual manner. But the Jackson Drive Realty Company and its associated enterprises has no such obligations to anyone."

Francis had to admire him. He had never seen anyone so cool under fire. But he was afraid he had not established his basic point. "I wish you'd clear all this with your public relations office—"

"Sims and Sims keeps check on all of my activities. You and I apparently differ on fundamental grounds, Mr. Dougherty. I appreciate your attempt to help me—as well as yourself—and the conscientiousness of your approach is impressive. I'm sure my legal department will have reason to consult you on a variety of subjects hereafter."

Francis was pleased. To have earned himself Benjamin Hopkins' good will would be enormously valuable, assuring him greater income and status. All the same, he was troubled. "How do we differ?"

"I gather you think there's something shady in our real estate transactions—"

"Hell, no! They're legal!"

"I was speaking on ethical rather than legal grounds."

"I'm not concerned with ethics, Mr. Hopkins. It's public opinion that bothers me. For you, for Ed Emory, for Governor Herder—for all of us."

"I can see nothing wrong in what we're doing," Ben Hopkins said coldly. "The public will enjoy the many benefits of a superb new culture center. And, since there is general support for Jefferson Square, any of its business can and should be made public, should there be a demand for an airing. What a few associates and I choose to do privately, however, is strictly our own affair, and I will use all of my influence to prevent the publicizing of our business dealings. I'm grateful for your vigilance, but you're unnecessarily disturbed."

"Whatever you say." Francis buttoned his jacket and stood. "I won't take up any more of your time this morning."

"That's very considerate of you. If and when we should be attacked, we'll know what to do. Until then, let me urge you to remember a truism that has helped my family for several generations: 'There is no sentiment in business transactions.' "

CHAPTER FIVE

The rites performed at the cocktail party were as rigid as the rituals of long-established, orthodox religions, Dan Robertson thought, trying to make himself an inconspicuous observer as he leaned against a wall of the huge living room in the Emory house. The only difference between a wealthy Eastern banker's shindig and that given by a young academician at a Midwestern university was one of degree. Here a professional bartender stood behind a long table, mixing and dispensing drinks with mechanical efficiency; there the host, and sometimes the guests, made their own. Here waiters hired for the occasion, augmented by the household staff, circulated with trays of liquor and food; there the hostess did what she could, but guests were expected to fend for themselves.

Here the bourbon cost ten dollars per quart, and Scotch twenty-five, double what professors could afford. Here the caviar for canapes was the finest gray Iranian or Russian, at eight to ten dollars for a tiny jar, while there the sticky red salmon caviar from the local supermarket was a staple. Here there were fewer cocktail frankfurters and tiny meatballs on toothpicks, and many more angels-on-horseback, oysters wrapped in small strips of bacon and broiled. Here the women wore French imports or dresses from the most expensive shops in town that cost anywhere from four hundred to one thousand dollars; there the faculty wives did their best to change the appearance of their thirty and forty dollar dresses so no one would recognize them from the last party.

Aside from these trifling variations, all dictated by a couple's financial standing, the fundamentals were the same. The reckless, the adventurous and the few who actually liked the taste of gin drank martinis almost devoid of vermouth. The in-crowd, including most of the Easterners, touched nothing but bourbon-on-the-rocks; by next week they might switch to rum and water. The majority whose drinking habits had been formed west of the Hudson took only Scotch, principally because it had taken them years to acquire a taste for the stuff. A few young people like Bettina Callison, who had never really cared much for liquor, confined themselves to sherry, and those with a sweet tooth took old-fashioneds and manhattans.

The air was thick with smoke, of course, but no thicker than at an academician's house. The babble of conversation was incessant, sometimes rising to a sustained roar, and since it was mandatory that a house should be filled with twice the number of people it could hold, it was impossible to cross the room without bumping into other guests and spilling their drinks.

It was astonishing how, after three or four cocktails, so many seemingly restrained men and women openly sought the private goals that had impelled them to attend in the first place. Surprisingly few of the advances were blatantly sexual, however. Even the flamboyant redhead, whom Dan vaguely recognized as Francis Dougherty's secretary, seemed to have something other than an assignation on her mind as she trailed Governor Herder, who was at best polite to her. Whatever her motives, she was making Dougherty unhappy, perhaps because she was embarrassing him.

Dougherty was typical of the cocktail party goer of another sort. On several occasions Dan had seen him slug down liquor, but today he was nursing one drink, and was obviously on his good behavior. It was amusing, and a little disturbing, to see Mrs. Dougherty, a rather sweet-faced patrician, taking another glass from a waiter, then another, whenever her husband's back was turned.

The most obvious fish-fryers were Carl of Seaboard University and Max de Groot of the Grand Opera Company. They had cornered a retired retail merchant who was devoting his last years to philanthropy, and were competing rather urgently with each other in their attempts to charm him and gain his full attention. That was fair enough: universities and opera companies always needed money.

The hostess, Dan had to admit, was good at her job. Carolyn Emory was everywhere, unobtrusively making certain the trays were refilled, disappearing occasionally into the kitchen, circulating constantly. Perhaps it was just his imagination, but Dan thought that her steady smile was a touch warmer whenever she paused for a brief word with Warren

Hopkins. Carolyn, he knew, was angling for another big chunk of Hopkins money, and was playing it very cool indeed. She was casually polite to Benjamin Hopkins, the fount of all seven figure donations, and made no attempt to break through the phalanx of investment bankers and corporation chairmen who formed an almost solid wall around him, protecting him from lesser mortals.

It was interesting that Frances Hopkins, Ben's wife, seemed the most relaxed person present. Her dress was understated, although it had probably cost a fortune, and she chatted pleasantly with anyone who approached her. Since relatively few people knew her, thanks to her husband's insistence that they live the lives of semi-hermits, she spoke mainly with her own friends, which made it easier for her. Besides, she had so much power, so much standing, so much money that she could afford to relax.

Dan took another bourbon and water from a waiter's tray and glowered. He didn't belong here, he told himself bitterly, and felt out of place. His salary of thirty-five thousand a year was pin money to most of these people, even to a member of his own generation like Anton Helsing. Anton had it made, and although Dan envied him, he certainly didn't resent him. Helsing was a genius, and was entitled to the crowd of ardent music lovers and celebrity worshippers who encircled him. He was one of the few who deserved his eccentricities, and if he occasionally came out with a word or made a gesture typical of the third sex, that was his own business.

It was his wife's too, presumably, but she seemed very busy at the moment herself. She was deep in conversation with Bettina Callison's father, whom Dan remembered as a one-time, distinguished American ambassador and Assistant Secretary of State. The combination was intriguing, and it would have been fun to watch them if Dan's mood hadn't been so sour. Michele Helsing was almost literally clutching Callison's lapel, but he was only mildly polite to her, his attention wandering around the room. It was impossible to imagine what she was trying to sell him.

"Dan." Phyllis had made her way to him.

Dan raised his glass to his wife. "The only normal person here. I salute you, honey."

"Are you all right?"

"Sure, fine."

"You look as though your lunch disagreed with you."

"It's the company. I'm up to my ears in pseudo-culture, and how wonderful it is of me to devote my life to the little people. Of all the patronizing—"

"Not so loud."

He smiled an apology.

Phyllis studied him, and knew that, although he had consumed several drinks, this was not one of the very rare occasions when he allowed himself to become stoned. Relieved, she said, "You ought to be circulating."

"I've had enough for one night."

"That girl of Jerry Solanz' is very pleasant and quite bright. Not at all the way she looks—or you'd think."

Dan felt a flush of anger as he looked at Solanz, who was talking rapidly to two industrialists who were apparently impressed either by his reputation or by his sales pitch. Why someone who had socked away a fortune didn't devote himself exclusively to plays and motion pictures of substance instead of swinging from the extreme of the cheapest commercialism to that of the arty—and back—was incomprehensible, but Dan supposed he wasn't being fair. Disliking Solanz so intensely, he probably would find nothing right in what the man did.

"You go ahead, Phyl. Have fun. I'm thinking."

Phyllis knew it was useless to try persuasion when he was in one of these unusual moods, but she hesitated.

"If you really want to know—"

"I do."

"I'm thinking about Harvey Simpson's offer."

"*Now?*"

"This crowd is giving me a perspective. Honey, I see Solanz' girl looking at you. She needs rescuing. Go help her, and we'll clear out of here in another half-hour."

Obviously reluctant, Phyllis drifted away.

Dan took still another drink from a passing waiter, then braced himself when he caught a glimpse of Helena Godoy and Henri Broussard bearing down on him, the diva looking like an aircraft carrier heaving in rough seas. At that moment, however, Governor Herder materialized beside him, and the couple turned away. Dan had no desire to make small talk with a millionaire politician, but Herder's company was better than that of a temperamental opera star who would explain to him, for the hundredth time, why her feud with de Groot made it impossible for her to sing at Jefferson Square.

"Hiya, fella. Sitting this one out?"

"Something like that, Governor."

Al Herder clapped Dan heartily on the back. "I know how you feel. I thought this would be one party where I could unwind, but I should have known better. That damn secretary of Dougherty's has been tailing me ever since I walked in. I don't know what the hell she wants, if anything, but she won't get it from me. I'm damned if I know why Carolyn and Edward invited her."

Dan wondered how much the Governor would make from his share in the real estate deals in the Jefferson Square vicinity, and a hard knot formed in his stomach.

"One of these days, when you've worked out your program for the first year of the Repertory Theater, the Symphony and the Opera, you and I ought to sit down together and go over it. Not that I'm going to interfere. I'd just like to familiarize myself with your plans. You see, I'd enjoy sitting in on the press conference when you announce your opening schedules."

Dan tried to wrench his mind away from real estate. "Sorry, Governor, but there's such an infernal racket I didn't hear you."

Herder repeated what he had said.

Dan forced himself to smile. "Of course," he said. "I'll be glad to give you an advance briefing." The Governor's request was, when reduced to plain English, very simple. Herder wanted to horn in on any session with the press in order to maintain his own posture as champion of public culture.

Again the Governor slapped him on the back, and worked back into the crowd.

Suddenly Dan felt physically ill. The basic concept of Jefferson Square, that of providing the general public with the best in the performing and visual arts, was magnificent, but virtually everyone connected with the project had axes of his own to grind. The wealthy sponsors were making more money than they donated. Politicians wanted to improve their image so they would gain more votes when they next ran for office. Artistic supervisors like Solanz wanted to use the contacts they made to obtain financial support for their commercial ventures, which were their primary sources of income. No one, it seemed, had any real faith in Jefferson Square itself, for its own sake.

Dan drained his drink, crushed out a cigarette and fought his way through the throng to Phyllis' side.

She opened her mouth to make some wifely pleasantry, saw his expression and abruptly changed her mind. She liked parties of this sort no better than he did, but, once here, would have preferred to remain somewhat longer. When he was seething, however, as he was doing now, it was far better to offer no objection, and she allowed him to pilot her first to Edward Emory then to Carolyn, for a quick word of thanks.

When they reached the street Dan breathed more deeply, but remained grimly silent as they walked to the corner and stood there, trying to hail a taxi. At last one stopped, and after they settled into their seats he came alive. "A bunch of goddam hypocrites. You and I aren't perfect, but at least we wouldn't feel at home in Gibbon's *Decline and Fall of the Roman Empire.*"

"Did you have a quarrel with someone?"

"No. If I had, I'd be able to keep my feelings under control."

"You need something to eat, Dan."

"I'm not drunk."

"No, but you've had several drinks, and you're annoyed—"

"Since the baby-sitter isn't expecting us until we get there," Dan said, "I'll be happy to take you to dinner somewhere, if you want to go."

"I think I'd rather go home," Phyllis said.

"Honey, I refuse to hassle with you simply because I'm disgusted with a pack of greedy slobs. Maybe I really made up my mind before tonight, or maybe seeing all of them gathered under one roof is what did it to me. Whatever the reasons, and I'm too tired for soul-searching, I've decided to accept Harvey Simpson's offer and write that book."

Phyllis weighed her reply carefully. "As you say, you're tired. You've drunk just enough to make you want to thumb your nose at everybody connected with the square—"

"There's a principle involved. I want to do more than expose them. I want to show how a pack of sophisticated, wealthy vultures can prostitute a grand idea."

"Harvey can't do anything about it tonight," Phyllis said. "Wait until morning, and you may change your mind. If not, you've lost nothing."

Dan fought an inner battle. "All right," he said at last. "Are you sure you don't want to stop off at a restaurant?"

"Very sure. I've seen enough people to last me for the evening, too."

He reached for her hand, and they rode home in silence.

The telephone was ringing as they walked into the apartment. "Dan, this is Stephen Carl," the Chancellor of Seaboard University said. "I'm still at the party. I was hoping we could have a little chat, but you ducked out before I knew you were gone."

"If I'd realized you wanted to see me," Dan lied, "I'd have stayed."

There was a brief pause. "I don't believe in discussing matters of real significance on the telephone," Carl said, "but I don't want to create a mystery, either. I'm thinking of establishing a new Humanities division, and I've already been given the green light by my administrative and business departments. I still need the approval of the University Senate, but that's a formality."

Dan grinned quietly. It was probably true that Seaboard professors would cause no difficulties, but they would become furious if they learned that the Chancellor regarded their sanction as automatic.

"I'd like to sound you out on the possibility of making you chairman of the division. I might be able to get you a distinguished service chair that would pay more than the usual full professorship, but I can't promise. However, I'd get the full story for you before asking you to make up your mind. Naturally you'd have tenure and all the other prerogatives, and you'd have complete freedom to set up your own curriculum. And, within budget limits, to hire any new people you might want."

"This is very flattering," Dan said.

Carl sounded smug. "I realize this is a little touchy for both of us, particularly since I initially recommended you to Ben Hopkins for your job at the square. But the university must be my primary concern. If we should be able to work out something, I'll take full responsibility for tamping down Ben Hopkins."

"That would be generous."

194

Carl missed the irony. "I'm very anxious to explore the possibilities with you. I'll be out of town, speaking to several of our alumni clubs the early part of this coming week, but I'd very much like to sit down with you when I come back."

"This next week is going to be rather full," Dan said, stalling.

"We'll suit your convenience. Call me whenever you're free."

When Dan wandered out to the kitchen he found Phyllis, who had dismissed the baby-sitter, heating a can of soup and making tuna-fish sandwiches. "You're the only cook I know who works at her trade in a white brocade dress."

"I was hoping you'd find it madly glamorous."

"I admit I like it. All those women's magazines have the right idea after all." Dan sat down at the kitchen table and searched his pockets for a cigarette. He told her about the call.

She halted in her work, a jar of mayonnaise in one hand, a long-handled spoon in the other. "If you're really intending to write the book, this is a wonderful break."

Dan shook his head firmly. "No matter what salary or other inducements he offers me, I can't accept. Stephen Carl is as much of an operator as all the rest of them, but I've been able to see through him all along. He cooperated in setting up Jefferson Square, partly because so many of his own trustees are involved, most of all Ben Hopkins. And partly because he didn't realize, any more than anyone else did, that the square's budget would shoot up more than fifty percent, with no end in sight. He's afraid—with good cause —that contributions to Seaboard are going to suffer. So he'd like to slow down the square's development. Subtly, of course. If he can hire me, it would take months to find a replacement for me, and by then he can pick up a lot of loose change in his endowment fund drive."

"I think he wants you," Phyllis said, stirring the soup vigorously, "because he knows you can put together a first-rate Humanities division."

"Oh, sure, he's familiar with my record, and he knows I won't disgrace him. But I'm not vital to him. He could take good men from any one of a dozen universities without making the wheels of Jefferson Square grind to a halt. Don't look so shocked, Phyl."

"I can't help it!"

"Both of us realize that—in theory—everyone serves his own self-interest. That's what we did, remember, when I came to Jefferson Square."

"We saw more than a personal opportunity. You recognized the chance to educate people on a grand scale—"

"Of course. I could salve my conscience while doubling my income."

"Please don't be cynical, darling. It isn't like you."

"I recognize the world's imperfections. And I recognize my own. But I also know something magnificent when I see it. The good that Jefferson Square can do—and the joy it can give—are beyond measure. I'm not interested in tearing down people like Ben Hopkins and Governor Herder. Maybe my book will sting them, but I'm not out to hurt them. My motives are—"

"Egocentric! My God, Dan. Listen to yourself. If you're not drunk, then . . . then what's happening?" She was crying. And she left him, then, alone in the kitchen.

Michele Helsing had dressed with unusual care in her subdued two-piece suit of beige linen, and although she hated hats, had worn one with a big brim that made her look attractively matronly. One didn't barge into the office of Charles F. Callison without looking one's appropriate best for the occasion, and one was careful to have planned every phase of one's approach in advance.

When Callison had retired from the State Department to clip investment coupons, write an occasional article for *Foreign Affairs* and hold himself available for advice to Presidents of the United States who wanted the benefit of his experience, a news magazine had commented that he was one of the few American diplomats who belonged in the British Foreign Office. It was true, Michele thought. He was urbane, his suits and shirts had been made for him by craftsmen who specialized in the handsomely unobtrusive, and his bland, smiling manner was that of a man who never allowed himself to lose his temper, raise his voice or seem to become deeply involved in any problem, including his own.

In brief, he was a very cold fish, but a woman in desperate circumstances had to seek help anywhere she could find it. "You're very kind to give me your time, Mr. Callison," she said.

The lean, white-haired man behind the polished desk

196

pressed his fingertips together. "Not at all. I've admired your husband's work for years, particularly his Concerto in E. Brilliant work."

"It is my favorite, too. Did you enjoy the party last night?"

"A fine party, wasn't it?" His tone indicated that he had found it identical to scores of others. "Carolyn and Edward are two of my favorite people."

"I like them very much, but we don't know them well."

Callison smiled bloodlessly, and, leaning back in his chair, assumed an attitude somewhat similar to that of a physician. "Now, Mrs. Helsing, what's this about my daughter?"

"We're very fond of Betsy—"

"So am I."

"—and Anton says she has an unusual sensitivity to music."

"She should, you know. Her education has cost me a fortune." Callison chuckled politely.

Michele's laugh matched his. "I invited her to lunch with us a few days ago—for a special reason. She's been associating with a very obnoxious person—someone who may actually be quite dangerous. I tried to question her—delicately, of course—and I'm convinced she doesn't recognize the man's seamy side."

"Bettina has led a sheltered life, Mrs. Helsing."

"So I gathered. Manuel Rios is a music student, Mr. Callison, an Argentinian, I believe. He's been in this country for several years on a student's visa."

"Your husband is the only musician she discusses at home."

"I'm afraid she sees him only as a fellow lover of music. She doesn't recognize—well, scum. Don't think I'm criticizing her. It's just that she's naïve."

"That she is." Callison waited patiently.

"Rios has been a part-time pupil of Anton's so we've happened to learn something about him. Bettina knows nothing of this, but Rios is involved in a mess that may burst into a public scandal at any time. He and Bettina have lunch together frequently at the Indian Tea House, and I'm afraid her name might be dragged in. Anton and I couldn't speak to her about it, you understand. She'd be too shocked, and I'm afraid she's so loyal she wouldn't believe us. But I felt certain you'd want to know."

"I certainly do." Callison selected a cigar from a humidor at one side of the desk. "You don't mind?" He waited until she shook her head before he unwrapped the cigar. "As you were saying."

Michele made an effort to sound impersonal. "Rios is a sexual pervert."

"Surely our society has become sophisticated enough to take that sort of thing in its stride."

"In most instances, yes. But Rios blackmails the men with whom he has his affairs, and one of them—a person of some consequence—is going to the police."

Callison averted his face momentarily so she couldn't see the amusement and sympathy in his eyes. "All of us are entitled to be a little indiscreet when we're young."

Was he saying what she thought he was saying? She wasn't quite sure.

"Have you ever read the Kinsey Report?" he asked lightly. "It's astonishing how many men have had at least one homosexual experience. We're a curious breed, you know, and more often than not, after one taste, we come back for more."

So her long shot was paying off. What she had heard about Callison was true.

"Our society places the homosexual—regardless of whether he's a dabbler or an addict—in an untenable position. Almost everywhere there are old, Puritanical laws that have never been repealed."

Michele knew everything he was saying, and wanted to come to the point of her visit, but she realized she had to listen to his lecture, which, it appeared, was turning into something of a rationalization for his own ambivalent youth.

"We make a problem of something the ancient Greeks took for granted, and I don't think we can claim that our civilization is superior to theirs. The Athenian wife knew her husband indulged in relations with other men once in a while, but she thought none the less of him for it."

"I'm not condemning Anton. I—"

"But our social code is still one of complete disapproval." Callison chose to ignore her interruption. He knew without being told that she was discussing Anton. "So blackmail inevitably flourishes in such an atmosphere."

"I can hardly be expected to condone the blackmailer's schemes when my marriage, my husband's reputation and the future of our child are at stake!"

"Hardly." His indulgent smile faded, and he looked stern,

uncompromising. "Even if our moral climate makes black-mail inevitable, the blackmailer is no less culpable. He's a criminal, and he must be treated accordingly."

Michele breathed an inaudible sigh of relief.

"Has this person been warned that he's breaking very serious laws?"

"I made it plain to him, Mr. Callison, but he—well, I've never seen anyone quite so brazen."

He nodded. "The homosexual who can't fall back on masculinity often displays a rather shocking bravado. It's his only defense, and his only form of attack."

She had no desire to probe into the psyche of the gay boy, but she tempered her impatience.

"Some people claim that the so-called feminine homosexual thinks, acts—and reacts—like a woman, and that this is particularly true when his own security is threatened. I believe otherwise."

He made the statement so flatly that Michele felt certain he had been in a not dissimilar situation at one time.

"He reacts in his own way, which is erratic. It's almost impossible to predict, because it's neither masculine nor feminine. In short, he creates a very dangerous problem."

"I've come to you, Mr. Callison, because I recognize the severity of the problem, and I don't know what to do about it."

Callison's eyes hardened. "Why come to me?"

"I came to you," she said bluntly, "because you held an important position in the State Department for a long time, and it's general knowledge that you still have influence there."

"Oh?"

"I've had very little experience in this sort of thing, so please forgive my ignorance. But I can't help wondering if it wouldn't save embarrassment for a great many people if this Rios person were deported as an undesirable alien." She watched carefully as the urbane man across the desk considered her suggestion before replying.

"That might be the best solution. But you realize that the Immigration and Naturalization people will have to conduct an investigation first. They work very quietly, and they don't talk to the press, Mrs. Helsing. But they couldn't deport him on just your word—or mine."

"No, I quite understand." Michele struggled to maintain her façade of calm.

"Naturally, if a scandal is threatening, they'll have to act quickly. I think I have enough of the right connections in Washington to guarantee fast action. After all, I do want to protect—ah—Betsy."

Her smile became real.

Callison rose and extended his hand. "Thank you for coming to me, Mrs. Helsing. I'll look forward to seeing you at your husband's next concert."

After Michele left, he returned to his desk and sat for a moment, staring into space. "The poor devil," he said, picking up his telephone and dialing a number in Washington, D.C.

"What was the big idea of following Al Herder around for two and a half hours like a puppy at the party last night?" Francis Dougherty scouled across his desk.

Sandra tugged at the hem of her skirt, and wished she had worn a longer one. She was finished with Dougherty, she hoped, having made the contacts she wanted at the Emory's party, but once he began ogling her legs, he'd get his usual ideas. "I didn't know that there are any laws that say a girl can't talk to a man over a drink."

"Very funny."

"I wasn't keeping tabs on you."

Her evasiveness did nothing to reassure Dougherty that her pursuit of the Governor had not been sexual. "I got you to the party—"

"But you're not responsible for what I do," Sandra interrupted. "I'm a big girl. Do you want to finish dictation now, or shall I get started on a rough of this brief?"

"What are you up to?"

"I was having fun!" she flared. "What I do on my own time is my business. Until last night I never had a drink with anybody as important as Governor Herder, and I kept wishing the kids I knew back on Fourth Street could see me. Is that so awful?"

He knew the feeling well, and sympathized with it, but was still not satisfied. "What's the game?"

"It was called after four innings because of rain. You pay me a reasonably good salary, Francis, and I earn it. Any time you don't want me here, let me know, and I'll find a job

200

somewhere else. There isn't a better legal secretary in town."

He stared at her.

She felt a sudden, unusual urge to cover her breasts with her hands. He had been easy enough to ignite, too easy, but now he was going to be difficult about turning off the current. Perhaps she should have waited until she could catch him in a better mood, but she was impatient. No girl with any guts, she told herself, wanted a lover who always slapped her around.

Dougherty continued to eye her. He could insist, of course, that she continue to sleep with him, and he knew he could apply enough pressure to force her acquiescence. On the other hand, there was no worse lay than a reluctant, dead-assed broad, and he had just met a hot little sketch through one of his clients, so he wouldn't be hurting. For the moment, at least, it might be wiser to go along with Sandra, while keeping a close watch on her. She was too ambitious for her own good, and perhaps for his. He decided he'd learn more by pretending to back off.

"Send in somebody else for the dictation, Miss Masters," he said calmly. "That brief is enough to keep you busy for the rest of the day, and I don't want to pile too heavy a load on you."

Sandra wondered, as she gathered her papers and returned to her own desk, why her victory gave her no sense of triumph.

Jan Marek had been called "the gloomy Bohemian" for so many years that he automatically played the part. Scowling perpetually behind his thick, horn-rimmed glasses, he rarely smiled, his long, lanky body was bent in a permanent, hunch-shouldered stoop that made him appear to be carrying the burdens of the world, and when he raised his hand to his head in a frequently repeated nervous gesture, he seemed to be tearing out his short, black, curly hair.

He had been acclaimed as one of the world's great living playwrights for enough years to enable him to dress as he pleased. His hand-tailored slacks were unpressed, his eighty-dollar English moccasins hadn't known a shine in months, and the elbows of his cardigan were threadbare.

But now, as he roamed the living room of Jerry Solanz' hotel suite, there was a graceful distinction to his movements. No matter what his personal feelings of inadequacy, his professional self-confidence was solid. "When I got your long telegram, Jerry, I had to fly here before you went back to Europe."

"There's nobody I'd rather see, sweetie. Nobody." Jerry, lounging on the base of his spine in a deep-cushioned chair, beamed at him. "How is the play coming?"

"I've finished a complete draft. But I'm not sure I'm going to let you see it." Jan gazed morosely out the window, then resumed his pacing.

"It's that bad, huh? Don't worry. We'll whip it into shape."

"It's the best work I've ever done in my life. It'll win me another Pulitzer, and maybe the Nobel Committee will begin to realize I can write. Maybe it'll occur to them that although I'm not Ibsen and I'm not O'Neill, I'm Marek, who is worth something in his own right."

"You're great, sweetie. That's what I told you when I first discovered you, and I've never stopped beating the tom-toms. Screw Arthur Miller and Tennessee Williams. Screw Pinter and Osborne and the rest of the English crowd. Marek is it. I'm your best press agent." Jerry spoke warmly, but his eyes were wary.

"Yeh," Jan said flatly. "Hooray for me."

"Now, no coyness, sweetie. I've been dying to get my hands on your completed script—"

"I know. You haven't been able to eat. Or sleep. You haven't even had your mind on what you were doing in the hay with that little blonde you've got. I know the whole routine, Jerry."

"Are you sore at me, or something?"

"And just for the record," Jan continued, "you didn't discover me. Kazan directed my first play, and it was a smash hit. You and I didn't start working together until almost two years later."

Jerry did not shift his position, but assumed a new mantle of dignity. "The record has been set straight. Is that why you flew three thousand miles on a plane that left Los Angeles before dawn?"

"I'm very upset, Jerry."

"So it appears."

Jan stopped short and pointed a long, bony finger at his old associate. "This play is different."

"So I've gathered from what I've read of it. If you've kept

202

up your first act pace and characterization, it'll become a classic."

"I wish you'd stop trying to sound like a quote from a critic's opening night notice."

"All right, Jan. There are cigarettes on the table. I'll get you a cigar from the bedroom, or a drink from room service. Or a bottle of tranquilizers from the bathroom, if that's what you want to make you happy."

"This play is my confessional, Jerry, but it's more than a personal document. I've managed to achieve a universality of theme—you might even call it an Everyman quality. I'm not quite sure how I did it, but even that isn't too important. It's there."

"I'm already convinced," Jerry said, "even before I read the script."

"Every author is supposed to think his newest work is his best, but this play really has it. I'm thinking of calling it *Confessional.*"

"Offhand, I don't like the title, but I can't give you an objective opinion until I've gone over the script."

"I'll name my own play, thanks."

Jerry spread his arms wide in a gesture intended to indicate that he was the most reasonable of men. "Naturally, Jan. It's your baby. I'm available to help you, to give you a sounding board, if that's what you want."

Jan removed his glasses, blinked myopically as he polished them and then shoved them on again. "Thanks," he said dryly.

Jerry hauled himself upright. "Look. You and I have been friends for a long, long time. More than friends. It's no accident we're called the Bohemian Twins. For the past twelve years every review of every play you've written has said Solanz is the perfect interpreter of Marek—"

"Sure. We go together like pork and beans. But it so happens I don't eat pork."

"If you enjoy being cryptic at my expense, that's your prerogative, sweetie."

"Jerry, you know what Paula did to me. Before we were married. While we were married. My God, she crucified me—"

"Who saw you through those days and saved your sanity? I remember, if you don't. Solanz."

"I've forgotten nothing, Jerry." Jan tugged at his hair. "You did more than anybody else to keep me from going insane—as insane as Paula. But was she insane? That's the question I had to keep asking myself, and I kept asking it while I was writing *Confessional*. I contend that the Paulas of this world are psychiatrically well-adjusted—in their own morbid way, although you may say I'm contradicting myself. They need male conquests to satisfy their narcissistic appetites. They've got to have scalps—and balls. They're Lilith incarnate. It's their Lilith-identification that gives the play its Everyman quality, you see—"

"I'm following you, I hope. But not completely, sweetie. You've had all this in your head for a long time, and now you've put it onto paper." Jerry was gentle now, soothing. "The next step is to bring these concepts to life on a stage. That's our system, yours and mine. Together. And we've never failed. When you put a play into my hands, I mold the images that you've seen in your mind. I bring your creation to life. That's the wonder of the marriage of a dramatist and his director."

"Until now it's worked, Jerry. But this time it can't, unless you're reasonable." Jan searched in vain for a cigarette.

Jerry handed him a pack, then struck a match for him. "You and I have never had a major misunderstanding, which is probably a record for show business."

In spite of his agitation and belligerence, Jan was forced to nod grudgingly.

"Until you tell me what's bugging you, there's not much we can do about it, sweetie."

"It's this girl of yours, Jerry."

"I should have guessed! Listen, Jan—"

"No, you listen. I'm not making any secret of my past, Jerry. I kept thinking of Paula while I was writing the play, and I've actually called the girl Paula. I don't want to change that unless my lawyer insists—"

"It would be marvelous if you could get Paula herself to play the part, wouldn't it?"

"She'd lap it up. But she's off in India with her damn ex-maharajah, living like a princess—and screwing with every male on the household staff every time her maharajah goes off to Calcutta or Delhi or somewhere on business."

"Exactly. So you've got to have someone else to play the part. Paula herself wouldn't be right for it. Do you know why? Because she *is* Lilith. She lacks the sensitivity of the great actress to communicate with her audience."

"Now," Jan said grimly, "you've made the point I've been trying to get across to you. The part needs a great actress. A star. Someone who has glamor and talent and experience and sympathy for humanity. Someone who knows how the Paulas of the world feel, and can understand them, be sorry for them, without actually being one of them herself."

"You've just described Berenice Tolmey."

"Jerry, for Christ's sake. I've met the kid. She's pretty. She's got sex. And she's scared half out of her panties all the time. But she isn't Paula. I warn you, if you insist on casting her in the part, I'll hold you to the Dramatists Guild rules. The author has veto power over all casting. Rather than wind up with that kind of a *schlemozzle,* it'll be better if I have the play done somewhere else, with another director!"

The weariness of martyrs who had given their blood and their lives through the ages weighing him down, Jerry hauled himself to his feet. "Have I tried to cram her down your throat? No. Have I said, even, that in my own mind she's positively set for the part? No. Have I told you to take my word that she—"

"I'm willing to believe she's the new Bernhardt, Jerry. But I don't see her as Paula."

"Could it be because you haven't looked?" Jerry paused, then said forcibly, "It could."

Jan reached into a pocket of his cardigan, drew out a crumpled slip of paper and unfolded it. "I've made out a list of actresses—"

"Don't show it to me!" Jerry extended a hand in the manner of a policeman halting traffic. "If it will make you happy, I'll draw up a list, too, and the chances are ten to one it'll be the same. Let some other directors read your script— Nichols, Kazan, Logan, anybody you like. Then ask them to make out lists, and you'll find the identical names. In today's theater there are three or four women—let's be generous and say six or seven—who could do the part of Paula as you've written her."

"How in hell do you know what I've written?"

"I've read your first act. Also I know you. Also I know Paula. So be good enough to let me finish. Every last one of us will give you the same names. Nobody new. No surprises.

The critics, the first-night crowd will know exactly what to expect."

"I was taught by a director named Jerry Solanz," Jan said, "to forget the critics and the opening night audiences. He taught me to ignore them and write for my real audience."

"Of course. But they're the pacesetters. They're the in-crowd who'll bring all the sheep flocking to see *Confessional*, or whatever we decide to call it."

Jan cursed, sharply.

The inspired martyr could not hear him. "Suppose, and you have an imagination greater than mine, that somebody new did the part. Suppose she was breath-taking. Suppose she brought down the house with an avalanche of applause like no actress has had since Jessica Tandy did Blanche in Williams' *Streetcar*. Suppose—"

"I have an almost unlimited imagination. I can suppose almost anything except that this gifted super-star is a girl named Berenice Tolmey. Jerry, let's call it quits. No hard feelings, no unpleasantness, no spitting at each other."

Like Napoleon reviewing the Imperial Guard before riding into battle at Austerlitz, Jerry struck a pose that lost none of its drama because it was obviously intentional. "The Jefferson Square Repertory Theater will open in about nine months from now with the new play by our finest playwright, Jan Marek. Every member of the cast, every actor and actress who appears on the stage of the most beautiful, modern theater in America, will be approved by Jan Marek. Not one member of the cast will be up there without his enthusiastic endorsement. It doesn't matter that knowing actors, understanding how to bring out all of the nuances of their talent, is Solanz' business. Solanz will do absolutely no casting without his friend's permission, and is willing to put that in writing. Your lawyer can draw it up, if that will give you peace of mind."

In spite of his skepticism, Jan was impressed and removed his glasses again, cleaning them to give himself time to think.

Jerry waited, showing surprising patience. "Is that fair?" he asked at last.

A liberal found such an appeal overwhelming, and Jan often said he was a spokesman for old-fashioned, fundamental liberalism. "I can't quarrel with a word."

"You admit Solanz is being honorable and decent. That's

all I ask." The review of his Guards completed, the Emperor was about to mount his horse and give the order of battle to his staff. "In return I ask only one small favor. When the time comes to start casting—not now, but when the play is in final shape and we're making specific production plans, I'll appreciate it if you'll listen to Berenice read the play for you. Today she couldn't do it justice. But give me a copy of the script, and I guarantee you that by then she'll be ready. Is it a deal?"

Jan peered at him through the thick glasses, and it was his turn to become gentle. "After what I went through with Paula, I know what you're feeling. So this girl happens to be your *schtik*. So, all right, Jerry. You'll have a copy of *Confessional* before you board your plane."

"A city park," Dan Robertson said, scuffing his shoes on the gravel walk, "isn't the right place for a business conference. I apologize, Harvey. But I couldn't talk in my office, and for reasons purely paranoic, I preferred not to come to yours. Okay?"

Harvey Simpson was both tolerant and amused. "In my business," he said, "one becomes accustomed to dealing with authors. So the preposterous becomes the mundane. I must admit, however, that I have never conferred in the park before."

"I know how much you like walks, and I thought you'd appreciate a morning constitutional before you buckle down to a day at your desk." Dan grinned, but could not hide his tension.

Harvey glanced at him, then decided to let him take charge in his own way. "I have a meeting scheduled at eleven this morning with an author, a literary agent and two lawyers on a controversial nonfiction book dealing with sex in the city versus sex in the suburbs. There's nothing that will put me in the right mood for it quite so much as watching the nursery school set romping around."

"I'm being overly sensitive, I know, which isn't like me, Harvey, and I'm really sorry to do this to you. But I spent a sleepless night, and when I picked up the phone to call you this morning, I felt a sudden aversion to your office."

"I'll have it done over for you in a pastoral theme."

They walked in silence for a time, and Dan flipped his

cigarette butt onto a pile of dirt where excavators had been digging a hole in the road, but, for some inexplicable reason, had abandoned it. "I've decided to do the book."

Harvey waited a moment or two before replying. "You won't regret it, Dan."

"I'm not so sure of that, but I'm going to take the plunge. And before you start rubbing your greedy paws together, I want you to listen to some provisions."

"You'll be writing it, Dan, not I."

"Listen anyway, because you may not want to publish the book I intend to write."

They halted at a traffic light, and watched automobiles roar down the asphalt road that cut through the park. Neither spoke again until they reached the path at the far side.

"I can't write an exposé on Jefferson Square," Dan said. "Sure, I'll have some damned unpleasant truths to tell about some people who won't appear quite as benignly angelic when I'm finished with them as they do now. But I want to be certain that I don't injure or destroy the basic concept of the square itself. The good it can do and the pleasure it can give millions of people is beyond measure, Harvey, and I couldn't live with myself if I hurt their faith in the square itself."

"It seems to me that you aren't quite ready to write this book."

"I'm as ready as I'll ever be," Dan said. "I planned to call you last night after the Emorys' party—"

"A rough time?"

"Only because I made it rough for myself. Phyllis urged me to wait, and she was right. I was browned off at all the right people for all the wrong reasons. What they're doing is immoral and unethical, regardless of whether it's legal, and I've got to show them up. But I want to do a great deal more. I want to dig into the psyche of Jefferson Square in depth. The square as it's developing, not the ideal."

Harvey paused to pick up an acorn, and turned it over in his hand. "These things rarely take root in the city. Odd, isn't it? Dan, you sound impressive, but I must admit I don't know what you mean."

"I sounded pretentious, didn't I? That's what a few whiffs of relatively fresh air do to a rube who isn't really accustomed to living in a city this big or this complicated. I can't tell you in detail what I mean, but I can give you one example that'll be illuminating, I think. Have you met the actress Jerry Solanz has in tow?"

"They were sitting a couple of tables from me at lunch in the Victoria and Albert Room a few days ago. Blonde sex-pot."

"We saw her do a bit in a foreign film the other evening. She's a remarkably good actress, Harvey. But Solanz plans to give her the lead in the opening play—the new Marek work —and by the time he's done with her, she'll be literally nothing but a sex symbol. Solanz is no better than the philanthropists who are making a mint out of the square, or Carolyn Emory, who is building her own image as Lady Bountiful. Solanz is just milking the square for his own purposes, and it burns me."

"That's fine. Now you're talking."

"And I'd like to tell this Tolmey girl's story. I want to devote one section to her—to what she was, what she is, what she feels, how she's being destroyed."

"Fine. What else?"

"Well, there's one thing else that didn't occur to me until almost dawn this morning." Dan moved toward an empty bench at one side of the path. "I accepted an obligation when I took the job at the square. And it seems to me I'll be as derelict in my duty, as guilty as the people I'm criticizing, if I walk out now. I'd also be unfair to my family—and myself."

"I'm in no position to say whether you'd be unfair to Jefferson Square." Harvey wiped off the bench with a handkerchief before sitting down. "But I certainly recognize your responsibilities to your family. Forgive my bluntness, Dan, but how much are they paying you?"

"Thirty-five thousand."

"And how long will it take you to write the book?"

"If I devoted full time to it, I could do it in about ten months, Harvey. But that's what I'm trying to tell you. I'm going to keep my job at the square—and write the book at the same time. So I'll need approximately eighteen months."

"If you're worried about money, I think I can promise you an advance payment of forty thousand. So you can leave the square immediately, and not lower your standard of living while you're doing the book. Once you've finished it, the money will come pouring in from various rights."

Dan shook his head. "I'd rather you hold the money for me, Harvey. Whatever deal we work out, I don't want any actual income from the book while I'm still on the square payroll. That would make me feel like a traitor, a spy and a louse."

"Dan, you're one hell of a mixed up fellow. You want to be faithful to the square, keep your job going, and write the book all at the same time. Well, I tell you it won't work. But I'm willing to bet on the writer. It's the book I care about. Nothing more. I say you're crazy. But I say go right ahead. I'm willing to do it your way."

Dan picked up a small, smooth rock and rubbed it against the palms of his hands. "I'm serious about staying at the square until it starts rolling. The Repertory Theater and Symphony Hall will be open in less than a year. With luck, the Museum of Fine Arts will be ready for the public by a year from now. I want to see all three of them through their labor pains, and I don't intend to leave until they've established their own public identities."

Harvey watched a small boy chasing a big, multicolored ball while a nursemaid hovered nearby. "Have you told this idea to Phyllis?"

"Sure. She says it's up to me."

"She would."

Dan turned to him. "What's that supposed to mean?"

"One of the questionable joys of being a publisher is that my vocation forces me to offer gratuitous advice to my authors. In plain language, what bothers me is that you'll be carrying two conflicting emotional burdens. You could tear yourself to shreds before you finish the book and bring Jefferson Square to life."

"I don't see it that way, obviously, but it's a risk I'll have to take." Dan threw away the stone and brushed his hands. "Remember I'm primarily an educator, Harvey. That's where my first sympathies invariably lie. You think of me as an author, and you attribute authors' qualities to me, whatever they are, but writing is strictly a second string to my bow. I did *The Quandary* because it had to be written—"

Harvey stifled a soft chuckle.

"—and I'm going to do this new book because there's a story that must be told."

Harvey glanced at his watch, and they stood, then headed

toward the street at the edge of the park, where they could hail a taxi. "Dan, suppose you were faced with a choice, that of staying on at Jefferson Square or writing the book. Which would you do?"

"I have enough real problems, so I refuse to worry about something that won't happen."

"Here's a taxi. Can I drop you somewhere?"

"No, thanks, Harvey. I feel like walking."

The aged, linoleum-covered stairs creaked in protest beneath Michele Helsing's feet, and she hurried past the second-floor landing, where chunks of tomato, eggshells and other refuse she did not pause to identify overflowed two large metal garbage cans. Surprisingly, the linoleum was fairly clean, although old, and a coat of bilious green paint, thick because it had been laid over previous applications, was fairly new on the walls and heating pipes.

She had forgotten the odors, inconveniences and aura of the brownstone walk-ups inhabited by the young and ambitious, but her own first years in the city came back to her as she climbed on to the top floor. She had been an ingenuous young dancer then, with no thought of the career as a choreographer that awaited her. In those days she had been consumed by a burning desire to be another Markova, and only experience, most of it bitter and frustrating, had taught her that her only real professional talent was that of plotting and charting the dances of others.

Certainly it had never occurred to her that she would become the wife of one of the most renowned musician-composers of his generation, the mother of his child, wealthy beyond her most avaricious dreams—and a miserable woman. Recalling the flavor of those early days, she told herself they had been far more carefree and exciting than they had seemed at the time. Nostalgia was always tricky, of course; the anxieties of the past were forgotten, the problems that had caused them having been long solved.

Michele shivered slightly, then clutched the handle of her alligator hand bag more firmly. She had taken enough beatings through the years, even though the stripes didn't show, and today she intended to enjoy herself.

Pausing for breath when she reached the door of Apartment 4-B, she lifted the imitation antique metal knocker that, when examined closely, proved to be a rather crudely made Persian phallic symbol. The sound of her rapping echoed down the stairwell.

After a long wait she heard a faint sound inside the apartment. Then a chain was removed, and the door opened a few inches.

"You're expecting me, I believe," Michele said.

Manuel Rios opened the door. He was barefooted, and clad only in a very short Japanese "happy coat," which belied his appearance. The smudges beneath his eyes were almost as dark as his pupils, his face was pale from lack of sleep, and his cheeks looked suspiciously streaked. He stood uncertainly for a moment, then admitted her.

Michele swept into the one-room flat, and looked around critically. The walls were filled with posters, photographs and newspaper clippings of male ballet dancers, athletes and actors, arranged in some semblance of artistic order. The daybed that dominated the room was rumpled, its canary-yellow spread in a heap on the floor and several plush pillows of other shades of yellow thrown into a corner. A movie director's chair with a canvas seat and back, an inexpensive radiophonograph and a sagging wicker chair were the only other items of consequential furniture, and the kitchen corner was an indescribable mess. A single glance at a partly consumed loaf of bread, several stubs of Italian sausage, a small, dripping can of olive oil and several empty wine bottles was enough, and Michele looked away.

Rios made an effort to compose himself. "You have brought me the money?"

Michele looked him up and down very slowly. "Are you kidding?"

He made a desperate attempt to save face. "I warned you—"

"You don't give up, I've got to say that for you, sister." Michele's contempt was brutal, and when she lighted a cigarette, she deliberately threw the match onto the floor. "I know you've been given the word, so let's not pretend you're still in the driver's seat."

A flush momentarily restored Rios' skin to a semblance of its normal, swarthy appearance. "Late in the afternoon yesterday," he said, tugging nervously at the tie of his happy coat, "two officials of the United States came to see me. At four o'clock this afternoon they are coming to take me to the

bar

212

airport. And out there," he added, pointing with a slender, trembling finger toward the window, "is a man who stands and watches. I guessed that you did this to me."

"We have laws to protect us from undesirable aliens." She hoped she sounded calmly disinterested rather than vindictive; the effort would be much greater.

"*¡A cada puerco su San Martín!*"

Michele's Spanish was limited, but she realized he had told her, in slang, that every dog had its day.

"I go to my own home, *Senora*, because I have no choice. You and your Fascist friends have seen to it."

It became impossible for her to curb her temper. "Fascist be damned. You're being thrown out on your slutty behind because you're a damned fag."

"One who is married to a queen should not be so free in her choice of language."

The last of her self-control deserting her, Michele started toward him.

Rios shrank against the wall, holding both hands before him in a futile gesture of self-protection.

Michele's anger suddenly evaporated; he looked so ludicrous that she laughed.

Her amusement was even more insulting than her threat of physical violence, and he looked as though he would become ill. "You are fortunate," he said, his lisp disappearing and his voice deepening, "that you suffer from no affliction. It is good that you are such a healthy woman."

It occurred to her that he might be baiting her, and she knew it would be unwise to fall into a trap, yet couldn't resist asking, "Just what's that supposed to mean?"

"I am younger than you, but my eyes are open much wider. Every woman I have met who is married to someone . . . like me is a heavy."

Michele looked at him blankly.

"Before you became a respectable matron—in the days when you were making love with other women—they called you a butch, no?"

"No." She recognized the tendency of the homosexual to tar everyone else with his brush, and was sorry she had come here. She had been wrong to seek satisfaction at his expense; he was too warped to see life in any form except his own distorted version of it. "I'm interested only in men, thanks."

"Ah, you call Anton Helsing a man, then?" Although he

realized he was running the risk of angering her again, he giggled.

Michele had asked for the slap, and forced herself to refrain from defending her husband, from explaining that he was capable of leading a happily adjusted heterosexual life when he wasn't tempted beyond endurance. She walked quickly toward the door, then paused with a hand on the knob. But she could think of nothing to say. His squalid depravity was beyond endurance, and she fled down the stairs.

Rios' high-pitched, mocking laugh followed her. In his own way he was achieving the last word, even though defeated.

When she reached the street Michele stopped running, smoothed her dress and headed toward the nearest taxi stand. There were times, she thought, when the price of protecting Anton's genius was too high, the humiliation too great to bear. It was not his fault that she had gone to Rios today, yet she couldn't help blaming him for robbing her of the cheap victory she had tried to achieve. All that would matter to him was that he was safe from the threat of a blackmailer.

Eddie Brown removed two of the chalk-like pills from their glassine wrapping, chewed them, and poured himself some water from the carafe on his desk. This was one of those days when even a man with a healthy stomach would feel shooting pains, and Eddie's ulcer had been acting up ever since Al Herder had started bellowing orders through the squawk-box early in the morning. His Excellency was having one of his days, and, as a result, so was Eddie, who in turn had spent hours communicating his displeasure to the staff.

Glaring through the open door of his office as he gulped down the water and resisted the desire to reach for still another cigarette, Eddie noted that, for once, the state's damned civil service employees were models of efficiency. No one loitered near the water cooler, inviting companionship; secretaries remained at their desks, typists clicked away steadily and even the cool crew who operated the computers stayed in their own sound-proofed world, far from the temptations of girls and inter-office gossip.

If Al Herder weren't such a mean son of a bitch when the White House rebuffed him, the order-loving Eddie would have been happy to run up flags and beat drums. But, unfortunately, one man was really paying for the President's refusal to back a Herder-inspired request for an increased Congressional appropriation for culture centers. It was Al's own goddam fault, of course, but at times he was inclined to forget the ways of professional politicians and lapse into his amateur ways.

He should have known better than to push the button for the introduction of a new bill, jointly sponsored by the state's Congressional delegation, without having cleared it with the White House. Not only was the President miffed, as he had every right to be, but Representative Harry Wycnski, the dean of the state's Congressmen, had chewed Al out on the phone for a half-hour. Wycnski had a valid point, too, having assumed that the White House had given its okay before he allowed his name to be put on the measure. For his own self-protection he had undoubtedly called the President to protest his own innocence, so Herder was doubly damned.

The buzzer on the squawk-box sounded, and Eddie wearily flipped a key. "Yes, sir?" he asked carefully.

"Where in holy hell are the school construction estimates I want?"

"You just requested them a half-hour ago, Governor. The Finance Department people are working them up for you, and I'll have them on your desk the minute I get them."

"They shouldn't have to work up anything that basic! Finance and Education should have them at their fingertips!" Al sounded as though he'd have a coronary any time.

"I'll chew them out, Governor." Eddie automatically shook a cigarette from the pack at his elbow.

"Don't bother! I'm working on a memo to all department and bureau heads that will be self-explanatory!" The machine clicked off.

Eddie flipped the switch back to neutral, and sighed when his secretary appeared at the entrance to his office. "Rosemary," he said, "you're irresistibly glamorous, and I love you dearly. Now get the hell out of here. One more problem today, just one, and I'll puke."

"I'm sorry, Mr. Brown," the girl said, "but that young lady from Mr. Dougherty's office is still waiting to see the Governor."

"Shit. You know he'd make God Almighty sweat today. Can't you get rid of her?"

"I tried, Mr. Brown."

Eddie yanked his necktie an inch or two lower and ran a hand across his bare throat. "Well, he won't see anybody, that's sure. Did you find out what she wants?"

"I've been girly-girly confidential, brisk and plain rude, but she won't open up."

Eddie stubbed out his cigarette. "Send her in, then. Enough people are sore at us today, and we don't want to get Dougherty's wind up, too."

The secretary turned at the entrance, and smiled fleetingly. "Be careful, Mr. Brown, she's your type."

Eddie laughed hollowly and took two more of his chalk tablets. He was still chewing them when Sandra Masters appeared and introduced herself.

She was everybody's type, and knew it. Her sleek dress that looked like silk, but wasn't, defied fashion, and was neither close-fitting nor loose, but hid no detail of her figure. Her spike-heeled shoes helped show off her long legs, which were encased in net stockings, and the scent of her perfume immediately filled the office.

"As you've gathered," Eddie said, swallowing the half-chewed tablets, "my name is Brown and I'm Governor Herder's executive assistant. What can I do for you?"

Sandra accepted the chair he offered her, and smiled pleasantly. "Nothing, I'm afraid. My business is with the Governor."

Eddie was expert at studying people unobtrusively. "If Francis Dougherty wants to call the Governor, maybe he can get through, but I can't guarantee it. This is one of those days."

The buzzer sounded again, and the mellow voice that had placed the name of the President in nomination at two national conventions was rasping. "Eddie, I'm surrounded exclusively by idiots, nincompoops and jackasses! This highway extension map isn't accurate!"

"If you'll look at my note attached to it, you'll see it's last year's, Governor. The new one won't be ready until September, but the Highway Commissioner's office is preparing a special one for you. They'll have it in the morning."

"They goddam well better have."

Eddie flipped off the switch and turned back to his visitor. "I see what you mean." Sandra's smile was warmly sympathetic.

Eddie felt himself thaw slightly.

"Mr. Dougherty," she said, "doesn't know I'm here. My business with Governor Herder is personal."

"I see."

"I don't believe you do. It isn't what you think it is."

Eddie was too tired to laugh, and grinned weakly. "How do you know what I'm thinking, Miss Masters?"

"If I read your mind too quickly, Mr. Brown, accept my apologies."

Still studying her, Eddie conceded that any man—except one in Al's position, who had to be careful of every move— would leap at the chance to roll in bed with this broad. She was built, and unless every sign of an experienced eye proved false, she knew the score.

Sandra was aware of his subtle scrutiny, but pretended not to notice it. If Eddie Brown wanted to ogle her and day-dream, she had no objection.

"Maybe," Eddie said, "I can help you."

"I'm afraid this is confidential."

"I'm not being nosey, Miss Masters, but it's *my* business to pry. I see literally everything that goes across Governor Herder's desk."

"I hate to sound coy, but I'm sure Governor Herder will agree with me that this is personal."

Eddie had no desire to press the matter after a harrowing day. "As you will, Miss Masters, but I don't know how soon you'll be able to see him."

"I'm prepared to wait. I know he's a lot busier than I am." She was undismayed by the prospect of an indefinite delay.

"I'd suggest that you send him a letter," Eddie said. "Tell him who you are—"

"Oh, we've met. Socially." She couldn't resist putting on a few airs.

Eddie raised a mental eyebrow. To the best of his knowl-edge Al Herder had never played around, even before he'd gone into politics and had started walking on eggs. But it was impossible to tell what any man would do when a tempting piece of tail was waved in front of him. "Then, by all means, write him a note and try to set up an appointment. I wish I could be more helpful to you."

"You've been very sweet. Thanks." Sandra stood and held out her hand.

Eddie took it and immediately noted that she was in no hurry to withdraw it. He was willing to bet she could be laid,

217

and some day, when Al was in a better mood, he'd find out more about their relationship. Eddie wasn't in the habit of throwing away gifts presented on a platter.

Sandra was just as glad that her heels and tight skirt made her walk with an ass-wiggle. Eddie Brown might be useful somewhere along the line, and it never did a girl any harm to make a man remember her. She had promised herself she would see this business through with Governor Herder on a high, impersonal level, but even if she had clamped on a chastity belt, it did no harm to let a man look—and hope.

The Italian restaurant was located in the theatrical district, and had been a national institution for almost a half-century. Somehow the Corsini family that had owned it for three generations managed to keep the red brick walls that lined the interior looking new, the high ceilings always appeared freshly plastered and painted, and the brass pots and kettles hanging from pegs were always shined. The red-and-white checked tablecloths, the candles stuck in empty Chianti bottles on every table had been copied by countless other Italian eating places, but none of them had Corsini's atmosphere. Perhaps the signed photographs of grand opera singers and composers that filled the entire wall behind the long, old-fashioned oak bar were responsible for the aura, perhaps it was the knowledge, inherent in the attitude of every insolent waiter that this was the most renowned restaurant of its kind on the Eastern seaboard.

Dan Robertson didn't particularly appreciate Italian food, drink or attitudes. And since his approach to grand opera was basically intellectual rather than emotional, Corsini's made him slightly uncomfortable. During the evening hours the waiters often revealed they had talents other than that of serving food gracelessly, and broke into arias, in which they were joined by patrons who were prominent in both the opera and concert fields.

At night there was a sense of semi-repressed excitement that made the place interesting, but at noon Corsini's was dull. The food was too rich and heavy for Dan's taste, and whenever he ate there he always felt distressed for the better part of the afternoon. The crowd was different, too, and most patrons were either businessmen from the immediate area, attracted by the relatively moderate noon prices, or out-of-town tourists unable to obtain tables during the seven to ten P.M. glamor rush hour.

I'm turning into a city snob, Dan thought, absently eating a breadstick. It's a sure sign of patronization when I start turning up my nose at the tourists. It wasn't so long ago that I was one myself, and although Phyllis and I didn't happen to have come here, it's accidental that we didn't.

Refusing to let himself dwell on the change he seemed to be undergoing, he glanced impatiently at his watch. Helena Godoy and Henri Broussard were late, which he had more or less anticipated, but he nevertheless felt an increasing sense of irritation. It was at their suggestion that he was meeting them. He was not looking forward to the lunch, but had believed it his duty to accept their invitation.

He had no idea why they wanted to meet him, since Helena had been rather deliberately vague and mysterious on the phone. But there was a chance, he hoped, that she might be reconsidering her refusal to sing with the Jefferson Square Grand Opera Company, and, unwilling to lower her pride sufficiently to make peace with Max de Groot face to face, was choosing to deal instead with the square's operating cultural head.

It was possible, of course, they planned to appeal to him for help in obtaining Broussard's restoration to the directorship of the Symphony Orchestra, but he was prepared for such a maneuver. Dan quickly ran through the main points of the little speech he intended to make if the subject was raised. Then, satisfied that he could cope with it, he sat back in his slightly rickety chair, and, rather than smoke another cigarette, reached for a second breadstick. It was no wonder that most men developed ulcers, contracted cancer or became victims of an expanding waistline in city living. Tensions were ever-present, the pace was relentless and opportunities for physical exercise had to be created and utilized in the face of great odds. Everybody, it seemed, smoked, drank or ate too much.

Idly glancing around the room, Dan suddenly froze, looked a second time and then shifted in his seat so he was turned in another direction. Seated on a banquette at a table for two in a far corner were Carolyn Emory and Warren Hopkins, and their intimate involvement with each other was obvious. Unaware of anyone else in the restaurant, they were holding hands, whispering and gazing at one another like a pair of adolescents parked in an open convertible under a new moon.

It was always a shock to discover friends and acquaintances tangled in the grubby mesh of illicit love, and Dan realized he was naïve. It was taken for granted, in the Midwest as well as in this part of the country, that supposedly contented wives frequently cheated on their husbands, sometimes with bachelors, more frequently with men who were themselves allegedly enjoying happy marriages. The practice was as common in academic circles as in any other, and people whom Dan and Phyllis knew in every professional and business realm often strayed. In fact, they sometimes joked and called themselves unusual because they were devoted monogamists.

All the same, hearing rumors of a couple's affair and seeing evidence of it were far different, and in spite of the sophistication that Dan liked to think was one of his endowments, he was embarrassed.

Analyzing the couple across the room, he told himself he shouldn't feel surprise. A desire to appear in the public eye as the financial guardian angel of causes that needed money apparently wasn't Carolyn's only reason for throwing herself into fund-raising drives with such vigor. A man didn't need to be a psychiatrist to realize she was bored with a marriage that had turned sour.

Warren's involvement with her was more disturbing than her own infidelity. As a bachelor he was relatively blameless in a society that condoned the philandering of the unmarried man. Perhaps he seemed despicable because of his public attachment and devotion to Betsy Callison, who was as sweetly innocent as the undergraduate virgins who had once been Dan's students. But equally unsettling was his lip-service to principles and the frequent stand he took on behalf of higher morality. Like most people, he didn't practice what he preached, and was a charlatan.

On reflection, it occurred to Dan that Warren's affair with Carolyn was, in all likelihood, typical of the man. His devotion to Jefferson Square, his generosity with his money and time, had won him universal public praise, but he, like his uncle and all the others involved in the under-cover real estate deals, was making a new fortune posing as a philanthropist. Anyone capable of such duplicity probably suffered no qualms of conscience about making a cuckold of an older man who happened to be a close family friend and business associate.

Disgusted in spite of his attempts to tell himself that he had no right to judge others and was becoming a prude, Dan stared fixedly at the autographed photos behind the bar. With luck, Carolyn and Warren would see him, and would either have the decency to leave or would move apart on the banquette.

Dan was so lost in his thoughts that the arrival of Helena Godoy and Broussard startled him, and he greeted them with a joviality somewhat greater than his slight acquaintanceship with them justified. The younger of the Corsini brothers came to the table for a prolonged chat in Italian, and after gossiping with them for ten minutes about various personalities in grand opera, helped them in their selection of dishes. He and they considered the ordering of their meal a solemn matter, and every suggestion was weighed, balanced and discussed in detail.

Knowing only a smattering of Italian and not caring what he ate, Dan sat, only occasionally rousing himself enough to make half-hearted attempts to follow the conversation. Finally, when Corsini went off and a waiter came to the table with a half-bottle of slightly chilled aperitif wine, he stole a glance at the banquette across the room. Carolyn and Warren were gone, and he wasn't quite sure whether he was relieved for their sake or his own.

Helena dominated the small talk, with an occasional assist from Broussard and less frequent responses from Dan, until the remains of the first course, stuffed clams served with a fiery sauce, had been cleared away. Then, suddenly, she launched into the subject that was the reason for the meeting.

"Mr. Robertson," she said dramatically, "your precious Jefferson Square is going to be destroyed by a terrible scandal!" Not pausing for breath, she gave him a lurid version of Anton Helsing's encounter with Manuel Rios.

Dan's mouth was burning from the sauce, and he tried a sip of the white Orvieto wine that had just been brought to the table, then asked for a glass of water, much to the horror of the waiter.

Occasionally Helena paused in her narrative to glance at Broussard, who nodded in grave agreement. When she was finished she leaned forward and clutched Dan's arm. "We have not enjoyed being the bearers of tales, Mr. Robertson. But we know you will want to hear the truth."

Dan squirmed slightly in his seat, and, ignoring his resolution to smoke less, took a cigarette. Aside from his distaste for the subject in general and the details in particular, he felt sympathy for Helsing. The flashing of Godoy's and Broussard's knives were so obvious that he felt angered as well as a little embarrassed. "You present this story as fact," he said, not realizing how belligerently he was speaking. "May I ask you how you know they're true?"

"You must take our word for it!" Helena, it appeared, spoke exclusively in exclamations. "In something of this consequence, we would not lie. We could not!"

They were making this difficult, and Dan remained silent.

Broussard took charge. "I see no reason why we should not reveal our source to Mr. Robertson."

Helena started to protest.

The conductor ended the passage of the woodwinds with a sweeping gesture. "A practical man does not act on the basis of mere gossip," he said. "Mr. Robertson, the poor boy seduced and damaged by Helsing came to us."

"For financial help?"

"I gladly would have given it to him, but he showed no need for money. No, Mr. Robertson, he had been crushed in a depraved experience, and wanted sympathy."

"Ah. He's a pianist, you say, so I assume you had known him previously." Dan was very calm.

"Neither of us set eyes on him until he came to us—out of the blue." Helena had difficulty with her clichés.

Dan absently swept some crumbs of Italian bread from the red-and-white checked tablecloth and said nothing.

Helena looked uncertainly at Broussard. She had expected Dan to react with the scorn of the middle class, and she thought he had failed to understand what she had told him.

"I don't quite see," Dan said, "why there should be a public scandal. Let's assume that everything you've told me is a fact. Helsing will say nothing. The boy won't want his own reputation hurt, and will keep quiet. And you—since the matter doesn't concern you—won't betray the boy's confidence."

Broussard, who had checked carefully, had heard nothing to make him believe Dan was a Helsing supporter, and therefore concluded he was slow-witted. "Scandal," he said, his manner that which older Europeans still use in their dealings with Americans, "does not necessarily mean there will be articles printed in the tabloid newspapers. Even the Roman Emperor, Caligula, could not conceal his depravity or that of his wife and sisters. People talk, and their gossip has been known to uproot the foundations of kingdoms, to say nothing of culture centers."

Dan could tolerate no more nonsense. "Western society may be more licentious than it was a half-century ago, but the general public has become more tolerant. There are many people still alive who can remember that Lily Langtry and King Edward VII had to use countless subterfuges to conceal their affair. Today, no one cares if a famous, talented woman goes to bed with a man who has an international reputation."

Helena reddened, and Broussard bit his lower lip.

"I'll grant you that most people continue to condemn the homosexual," Dan said, "but we don't tar and feather him unless he tries to force the rest of us to adopt his code. On behalf of the square I appreciate your concern, but I think—and hope—that your alarm may be unfounded."

Helena Godoy exploded. "My dear sir, the boy who was raped by Helsing intends to bring action against him in the courts! The director of your symphony will go to prison for the ruin of a minor!"

Dan felt his first twinge of real uneasiness. "The—victim—is under twenty-one?"

"Of course!" Helena was triumphant.

"No, not a minor," Broussard said, in almost the same breath, "he is of legal age."

Loathing the singer, but feeling pity for her lover, who was trying within his own limits to be honest, Dan knew he had to end the ordeal. "I'll have to use my own judgment," he said. "Perhaps I won't have to do anything, perhaps I can handle the matter myself, and only if I have no choice will I refer the case to the Jefferson Square Board. But, no matter what the outcome, I'll always remember that you called it to my attention."

He was denying them the satisfaction of knowing what, if anything, he intended to do, and he was damned if he would tell them. Until he had a chance to think the problem through, of course, he didn't know himself. He was certain, however, that even if it became necessary to drop Helsing, he'd fight the rehiring of Broussard. Until someone proved him conclusively wrong, he was convinced that the private sex life of Anton Helsing would have no influence on the future of Jefferson Square.

Carolyn Emory kicked off her shoes, stretched out her legs on the living-room rug in Warren Hopkins' apartment and looked ruefully at a long run in her stocking. "I should have known this is one of those days when nothing goes right."

Warren stood near the windows, hands clasped behind his back, and tried to look unperturbed. "You're making a fuss over nothing," he said. "I'm sure Robertson didn't see us."

"And I'm positive he did."

"For the sake of argument only, suppose he did. It's quite natural and normal that you and I would have lunch together. He'd think nothing of it."

"Then he would have spoken to us!" Carolyn unfastened the offending stocking and savagely hauled it off.

"He's a gentleman."

"You contradict yourself, Warren. If there had been any need for him to pretend everything was normal, then he'd have known it wasn't!"

They had been going in circles for several hours, and he was weary. "You just did something foolish. Unless you're carrying a spare stocking, you'll be wearing only one."

Deliberately, she removed the other. "At this time of year a lady doesn't have to wear stockings. Satisfied?"

Their bickering tired Warren. "If you are."

"And I nearly died, seeing Godoy and Broussard. I'm sure he knows I voted in favor of terminating his contract, and he'd get even if he could. He'd love it!"

"I watched them the entire time we were waiting for our check and as we were leaving. And I swear to you they didn't glance once in our direction."

"All the more reason to be afraid they—"

"This is absurd! I don't pretend an affair like this is idyllic. The disadvantages intrude too frequently. But I say we forget them, if we can."

"I don't mean to spoil the day, Warren. I need this time together more than you do."

His voice softened. "I know of no device to measure our

224

needs. All I can tell you is that I need you, too. And want you."

Carolyn felt the sudden desire to lose herself in a realm beyond thought. "Do you?"

"Shall I show you?"

"Yes." She backed away as he approached her, erotic anticipation struggling with a sense of propriety. "But not in here."

Paying no attention to her feeble protests, he pulled her down onto the living-room rug.

Anton Helsing sat at his living-room piano, idly playing a few strains of Schumann, subtly shifting to Bach and then, without a break, sliding into jazz improvisations. Under ordinary circumstances his noodling would have made fascinating listening, but Dan Robertson was too intent on their conversation to listen.

"I'm sorry I had to come to you, Anton," he said, "but I figured you'd want to know. And it'll help if you can tell me what this is all about."

"It isn't easy." Anton's right hand slid up an octave.

"I realize that."

"On the other hand, it's absurdly simple."

"These things usually are."

"I needn't tell you that Broussard and that old bag who should have given up singing and bought a newsstand concession years ago are insanely jealous of me. Broussard actually tried to slug me in my office."

"I heard rumors."

"They and a little gay boy who had been a part-time piano pupil of mine got rather chummy recently. I don't know the details, and don't want to know them.

"The next thing I knew, the gay boy came to me with threats of exposure if I didn't pay him off."

"Blackmail."

"That's what it's called."

"Were Broussard and Madame Godoy involved in all this?"

Anton's shrug was a masterpiece. "I refuse to condemn anyone unless I know the facts. Actually—and this may have been weak—I wouldn't bring charges against poor little Manuel. The boy is sick, and you can imagine what some of those life-termers would have done to him in prison. There wouldn't have been any improvement in his condition by the time he was released." The monologue seemed to call for a more somber background, so he switched to snatches of Sibelius' incidental music for *The Tempest*.

The living-room door opened, and Michele, overly casual, looked in. "Sure you won't have a drink, Dan?" she called.

"Positive, thanks. Phyllis is expecting me home right now, and if I start to relax after the kind of day I've had, you won't be able to get rid of me for hours."

"We'd enjoy that, but I won't insist. Let me know if you change your mind." The door closed again.

Dan hoped she wasn't listening on the far side, and waited a few moments before asking, "You didn't let the whole business drop?"

"No, that would have been criminal negligence on my part." Anton looked sorrowful. "Manuel is an alien, and I guess mine wasn't the only report to the Immigration and Naturalization Bureau. He's been deported. Very quietly, very discreetly. And that's the end of the matter."

"I see."

Anton stood and wiped his hands on a silk handkerchief which he removed from the breast pocket of his embroidered smoking jacket. "I can only guess at this, but it seems clear that my good friends, the bright stars of yesteryear, don't know he's no longer in the United States and that his claws have been clipped."

From the way Helena Godoy had talked, Dan agreed with his analysis. "Then that's that," he said, relieved. "I hope you'll forgive a rude intrusion, but I wanted to be armed in case any of the square trustees came to me. Trouble-makers often keep a pot boiling, but in this instance they'll only hurt themselves if they repeat their story elsewhere."

"Let them," Anton said. "I certainly didn't enjoy having Manuel deported, but I have no objection to telling any member of the board what I've just told you."

"I can spare you that embarrassment," Dan said as they started toward the door.

"All this is damn decent of you."

"It's my job. There isn't much that a Dan Robertson can do for an Anton Helsing, you know, but I can try to earn my salary by stopping irresponsible talk that will hurt you—and the square."

"The harder I work and the bigger the name I'm able to

make for myself," Anton said, "the more people there are who climb out of the woodwork to carve me up. Any time I can return the favor, Dan, please let me know."

They shook hands at the front door, and Dan took his leave.

Michele appeared behind her husband almost as soon as the door closed. "Bravo!" She clapped her hands lightly. "That was one of your best performances, Maestro."

"I heard you skulking in the dining room, and I'm sure he did, too." Anton's charm had vanished, and he became petulant. "No matter how I banged the piano, I couldn't drown out those thumps and clatters."

"If he did hear, it doesn't matter. He's sure to understand I was concerned for the spotless reputation of my shining knight."

"Your shining knight can use a stiff drink. That was an ordeal."

Michele tried to dismiss the thought that he had been spared all but the peripheral discomfort, and moved closer to him. "The drink," she said, "can wait."

For a moment he was puzzled, then held up a hand. "No!"

"Why not?" She tried to slide her arms around his neck.

"I refuse to wrestle with you in the front hall. Where's your dignity?"

"I'll show you where I've stored it. In the same place you can leave yours."

Anton continued to hold her off. "I'm indebted to you for all you've done, Michele—"

"Your gratitude is the last thing on this earth I want!"

"You also have my affection, my loyalty—and the unqualified promise I gave you that I won't be—naughty—again."

She refused to move away. "We've got to start again some time," she said.

"I know, and I'm willing. But I need a breathing spell. I've got to have time to readjust my feelings and my thinking."

Michele couldn't decide whether he meant what he said or was merely trying to avoid her.

"You have my pledge that I'll come to you as soon as I'm ready."

She had to admit defeat. "If ever."

"If sex with you meant nothing to me," Anton said, "it would be very easy to go to bed right now. But we've had a very special relationship—that I've bruised. And I've got to repair the damage in my own way and my own time. I can't do more than promise you that. I want to wait until the pain —and the shame are gone."

Michele looked at him for a long moment, her face expressionless. "Do you want your drink in the living room or in your study?"

CHAPTER SIX

The extra layers of insulation added to the ceiling, walls and floor of the rehearsal hall muffled the sounds of the incessant pounding of the workmen in the main auditorium of the Repertory Theater, and everyone connected with the production of *Confessional* had become so accustomed to the remote noise that it was no longer a distraction. The actors, taking their cue from Jerry Solanz, regarded the less than ideal conditions as a challenge, and were meeting it.

Dan, sitting at the rear of the hall that itself would become a small, experimental theater in the repertory complex, had to admit to himself that the Jerry Solanz who worked with an acting company bore little resemblance to the grasping, egomaniacal poseur he had known. Infinitely patient, always in command yet surprisingly gentle and sensitive, Jerry was a master puppeteer who suggested rather than ordered, pointing the way instead of actively leading.

"Julian," he called suddenly from his seat in the third row, where, surrounded by the members of his staff, he was directing the rehearsal, "I like that new piece of business you've put in with the alarm clock. But don't make too much of it, or you'll upstage Berenice. Want to try it again?"

Julian Adams, the star of *Confessional*, ran a finger inside the turtle neck of his black sweater, and began the scene once more.

All was well for a few minutes, and then Jerry groaned. "Hold it! Sorry, ladies and gentlemen. Berenice, sweetie, do you understand the significance of the alarm clock bit?"

There was a moment's silence. Then Berenice, in slacks and a black turtle-neck sweater similar to that which Adams wore, shaded her eyes against the glare of the naked work light that stood near the apron of the stage. "I—I think so," she said uncertainly.

Jerry beckoned, and she came to the lip of the stage.

Dan felt distinctly uncomfortable. Only with Berenice was Jerry a slave driver, hounding her ceaselessly, humiliating her in front of the other actors, constantly finding fault with everything she did or failed to do.

"You're Paula, remember?" Jerry was scathing. "Paula has decided she wants to marry this guy, to hook him permanently. They've just spent their first night together, and her mind is full of ideas. But she's less sure of herself than anyone else knows. Do you follow me, so far?"

"We went into all this yesterday. And the day before." Berenice's voice sounded high and thin, almost childish when she addressed Jerry.

Dan saw that Jan Marek, lounging in a seat off to his right, was unhappy, too. The playwright, no matter how great his desire to see his new work succeed and no matter how close his association with Jerry, had a compassion for Berenice that was completely lacking in her lord and master.

"When Julian becomes interested in the alarm clock, you think it's just an excuse. You try subtly—very subtly—to attract his attention. You don't just stand there like a useless telephone pole. Since you haven't yet worked out any useful stage business for yourself, I'll do it for you. Later."

Dan felt her mortification, and cringed.

"Be patient, Julian," Jerry called. "Trust me, sweetie, and this whole thing will straighten itself out just fine."

Adams was obviously embarrassed. "Berenice is going to be great in the part," he said, but his voice lacked conviction.

Jan Marek unlimbered his long legs and stood. "The fault isn't in the playing, Jerry," he called. "There are a couple of basic flaws in the scene."

"You think so?"

"I know it. I can fix them in a half-day of rewriting, but I'd like to go over them with you first." The playwright moved down the aisle.

"I haven't seen the holes myself," Jerry said, "but I've been concentrating on other things."

"We'll have to go over it line by line."

Jerry glanced at his watch, then reached for his sports jacket of Harris tweed. "All right, everybody! Lunch break! Be back in an hour!"

"Make it an hour and a half," Jan suggested. "I don't want to be rushed."

"Okay. Report back here at two o'clock!" Jerry started

toward the rear of the theater, the dramatist fell in beside him, and they immediately became absorbed in their conversation.

Members of the cast and staff streamed up the aisle, some heading for nearby restaurants and lunchrooms, others going to the lobby telephones to order something sent in.

Dan reached for his overcoat and stood.

Berenice Tolmey was the last to move up the aisle, her camel's hair polo coat thrown over her shoulders. She was alone and looked like a crushed, bewildered child.

Dan was quick to seize the opportunity for another talk with her, and hailed her. He had filled the better part of a looseleaf notebook with his own observations and the comments she had made in the score of interviews, but as yet had obtained no more than a fraction of what he wanted for the chapter he intended to write about her. "Can I interest you in trying that new place that's just opened across the street?" he asked.

There was an elfin quality in Berenice's smile, but the look of pain remained in her eyes. "You're sweet, but I don't know. Another session of Twenty Questions, Dan?"

"I promise you I'll confine myself to ten."

They headed out into the raw cold, where a biting wind blew across the open spaces of recently demolished tenements.

Berenice had to raise her voice to make herself heard above the drills of workmen who were putting up the marble façade of the Museum of Fine Arts. "Is your family back?"

"Last week," Dan replied, and anticipated the next question. "Phyllis is just fine, and the kids are so full of energy they're impossible." He couldn't help envying his wife the vacation of ten weeks she had spent in the Midwest.

The restaurant was one of a score that had been opening in the new buildings that were mushrooming in the area. Jefferson Square was changing the entire neighborhood, and only the two tenements that continued to stand beyond the new Symphony Hall, a few grocery and shoe repair shops, and two tiny candy stores continued to hold out against the tide. Ben Hopkins and his associates were raking in pure gold, Dan thought.

The restaurant was designed to cater to the matinee trade, and undoubtedly would do a tremendous business, regardless of the quality of its food and service, once the square was operating in full swing. The wallpaper bore a resemblance to gray satin, the chandeliers of imitation crystal and the Louis XV chairs gave the place a vaguely "Continental look," and the ladies from the suburbs would love it.

A head-waitress in the inevitable uniform of black dress and pumps, pearls and an overly bright smile led them to a booth in the far corner. Some of the lawyers and doctors who were moving into the area occupied other tables, and Julian Adams was sitting with his agent in a booth on the far side of the room.

"Would you like a drink?" Dan asked.

"I'd love one, but Jerry would have a screaming fit if he smelled liquor on my breath."

"There's always a Bloody Mary."

"He'd find out—he always manages to worm everything out of me—and then he'd insist you were on the make. You know Jerry."

"Yes." Dan ordered her a glass of tomato juice, and, for himself, a bourbon-on-the-rocks. "Do you always tell him everything?"

"Just about." Frown lines that were incongruous in a face so young appeared on Berenice's forehead, but gave way to a quick smile. "Except about us."

She couldn't be as naïve as she appeared, Dan thought; no one could. "Will you please stop worrying. It's perfectly all right. He knows we have lunch together occasionally, or a drink."

"Yeah. I guess so." Her quick nod was almost bird-like.

He tried to speak patiently and slowly. "Why does he think we get together?"

"For the same reasons you sometimes have lunch with Julian Adams or Anton Helsing? Because it's part of your job?"

He could reassure Berenice up to a point, he supposed, but the time would come when Solanz would be sure to protest strenuously.

Berenice's eyes were very wide as she looked at him across the table. "You've been everything you told me you'd be that first time you took me to lunch. A safety valve. And I sure do need one."

"I hope I'm helping," he said.

She reached across the table and, for an instant, placed her hand over his. "You'll never know how much our friendship means to me."

Dan made an effort to smile at her, hoping he looked like a fond uncle. For the most part, he had been truthful with Berenice. She not only knew he was a married man with children, but that he loved his wife. He had made that clear to her. Nevertheless, the girl was taking it for granted that their meetings were inspired by his attraction to her. Certainly she was flattered, but in Berenice's case there was another factor that added to Dan's sense of uneasiness.

Like so many other members of her generation, she was indifferent to the old-fashioned middle-class virtues and standards. She knew Jerry was married, yet lived with him more or less openly because he could advance her career. Similarly, Dan thought, she had no compunction about going out with him because he had a wife, even though they saw each other more frequently than did mere friends, and her only concern was to prevent Jerry from becoming jealous.

But there was little choice. It was essential that the book contain a section on Berenice. Harvey had agreed that it would be valuable, and would put the "human element" of Jefferson Square in its right perspective. Therefore Dan could not change what he was doing, which, in essence, was taking advantage of a girl who trusted him.

It annoyed him that Phyllis had so little sympathy for his predicament. When he'd told her how his dishonest relationship with Berenice made him writhe, she had laughed at him. "My heart really bleeds for you darling," she'd said. "You go out to a bar or a restaurant with a girl who's going to be tomorrow's universal sex symbol, and you can even give me a blow-by-blow account because it all comes under the heading of necessary research for your book. In my next incarnation I think I want to be an author."

Berenice was talking. Dan had missed the beginning of what she was saying.

"It was an adorable dress, but Jerry wouldn't let me buy it. He said it didn't have enough pizzaz. Does absolutely everything I buy have to ooze sex?"

He was afraid that if he agreed with her she might quote him to Solanz the next time they argued. "You're out of my league."

"But you like me just as much when I'm completely dressed as when I'm half-naked," she persisted.

"Maybe I'm odd that way," Dan said.

"I don't think so!" Berenice's sulky pout gave her something of a sexual quality that Solanz was trying to create in her. "Sometimes I hate Jerry. Would you believe it?"

"I believe it," Dan said as the waitress appeared to take their order.

Like so many actresses, Berenice had a ravenous appetite, and ordered steak, potatoes, two vegetables and a salad with cheese dressing.

Knowing she would want a rich dessert as well, and watching her eat a honey roll on which she spread a thick layer of butter, Dan quietly marveled at her ability to remain slender. Her youth was partly responsible, of course, as was her devotion to an exacting profession. But he suspected that an even more important factor was the ever-present tension of her relationship with her lord and master.

"Do you always do what Jerry wants?" he asked.

Berenice's slender shoulders rose and fell. "I don't have much choice."

"I'm speaking of you as an actress and of him as a director," he said hurriedly, afraid she misunderstood. "Specifically, I was thinking of the scene you were rehearsing just before lunch."

She raised a hand to her hair for a moment, then reached for another roll. "Julian Adams just put in the stage business with the alarm clock today. If I had enough time to think—and to feel my way—I—I guess I could come up with something to do that would be in character. But Jerry," she added, striving for loyalty, "is used to working with more experienced actors. They think of stage business right off. So he gets impatient with me, naturally, when I'm a little slow."

It was astonishing, Dan thought, that Solanz could inspire such fidelity after mistreating her so consistently. "The last time I sat in on part of a rehearsal was about a week ago. You were working on your big scene at the climax of the second act."

Berenice nodded, her eyes darkening. "That scene scares me half to death. And your being there didn't help. When you showed up at rehearsals, Jerry had real fits. But I guess that, by now, he's getting used to seeing you around occasionally."

Dan saw no point in mentioning to her that Solanz assiduously ignored him whenever he appeared at rehearsals.

"Here's what I'm trying to find out. You were doing something that looked effective to me. You moved upstage—stage left, I think it was—turned your back to the audience and buried your face in your hands. But Jerry changed everything you were doing."

"I was being myself. When I'm upset and truly feel awful, I don't want to be near anybody. I just want to be left alone and bury my head to have a cry until I get rid of all the whirling around inside me."

She made sense, and Dan nodded.

"But Jerry said that Paula isn't that way. He said she's the kind who has to have an audience, no matter how awful she feels. That's why he changed everything I was doing."

Dan had become thoroughly familiar with *Confessional*, and knew one of the strongest points Marek was trying to make was that his character, Paula, suffered periods of intense self-doubts as well as narcissistic exhibitionism. Unless both those aspects of her personality were made evident to an audience, the play itself would be drained of much of its impact. However, he could not interfere with what Solanz was doing; it wasn't his place to defend the integrity of the play, which was Jan Marek's responsibility.

"Jerry worked out all the new business for me. I'm doing the scene the way he wants, even though I still don't feel right. Jerry says I'll work my way into it."

Dan summoned the waitress and asked for another basket of rolls.

"I keep telling myself I'll do exactly what he wants. After all, he's the greatest director there is, and I'm nobody."

Dan was fidgeting with a cigarette and matches. If *Confessional* should be a success, which he was inclined to doubt, Berenice would acquire a considerable reputation, provided, of course, that Solanz didn't stifle her so completely that she gave a mechanically wooden performance.

"I'm still not positive what I'll do when there's an audience out front." The girl took still another roll. "I just mentioned this to Jerry once, and I thought he'd flip, so I haven't said anything since. But when I was working in stock, and in London—"

"You didn't tell me you'd acted in London."

"Oh, sure. I spent two seasons in the West End. I was in four big flops and in the one play that ran at all, I had a part

235

nobody noticed. Anyway, something crazy has always happened to me when there's an audience in the house. I feel waves coming out of the audience at me, and I'm not myself any more. Is that wild?"

"What does Jerry say?" Dan asked.

"Oh, he's in favor of the Stanislavsky approach, up to a point. He thinks an actor has to feel the character, and maybe even become the character. But he keeps insisting it has to be restrained by discipline. I wish I had the guts to tell him that it has to be one way or the other. Either an actress —me, anyway—approaches a part intellectually, or else she feels it and puts herself into the character. I'm not the intellectual type."

Dan smiled warmly.

"You want to know the real trouble?" Berenice leaned forward. Beneath her thick coating of makeup and false eyelashes, she looked—at this moment, anyway—like a disturbed adolescent.

"I'd give anything to get out of playing Paula," she said.

"It's a big break," Dan said lamely. "A star part."

"Except it isn't for me." She glanced at her reflection in a long, antiqued mirror set into a wall. "I suppose I look like her, with my hair this way, and all. At least I look like Jan Marek's ex-wife, and I guess it isn't any secret that's who the play is about. But I can't see me marrying an Indian factory owner who used to be a prince, or something. In Des Moines, where I went to high school, I went with a boy who couldn't even get to play regularly on the varsity football team."

Dan laughed.

"No, I mean it," Berenice said. "I've been jazzing up the way I look, and all, even the way I walk, ever since I've been with Jerry, because that's the way he likes it. But I can't see me being the sex queen of the universe. I'm not the type!"

"Maybe Paula doesn't feel that way, either. The Paula in the play, anyway," Dan said. Then, before he could stop himself, he added, "I saw you in *Rain and Sun.*"

"Really? In Europe somewhere?"

"No, there was a private showing for a few people at Seaboard University last year. And although I don't claim to be an expert critic of either acting or films, I thought you were wonderful. So did everyone else who was there."

Berenice nodded her thanks. "Making that flick was just great. We had a ball, all of us. It wasn't at all like work."

236

"It was obvious that you were enjoying yourself."

She closed her eyes, so that he could see only the shiny black eyeliner and the platinum-blue shadow. "I don't like to think about those days any more."

The waitress brought their lunch, and Berenice immediately brightened. "I'm famished!" She ate rapidly, for several minutes. Then, suddenly, she put down her fork and knife. "God," she said, "I never knew I could be this tired."

It was a unique sensation, a real thrill to be riding in the long, black limousine bearing license plate number 1, with the state flag fluttering above the radiator cap and an armed, uniformed state trooper sitting in the front seat beside the chauffeur. Sandra was relishing the experience, savoring every moment so she could live it again later.

"I'm sorry it's taken all these months for us to get together," Governor Herder said. "You must have thought I was trying to avoid you, Miss Masters."

"No, I know you're busy, Governor." She was conscious of the dignity of his position, and made a futile attempt to haul her skirt down an inch. There hadn't been time for her to dash home from the office to change when she'd received the long-awaited telephone call summoning her to his office.

"I really thought we could have a quiet little chat, but my staff forgot I was scheduled to make a speech this afternoon. So I hope you don't mind riding with me and talking in the car."

"I love it!"

Her explosive candor was refreshing, and Herder laughed, then sobered. "In your last note, you made a vague reference to real estate in the vicinity of Jefferson Square. I didn't quite know what you meant, and frankly, I'm a little curious."

Sandra cast a nervous glance at the trooper's broad back. Her note had been deliberately vague, of course. A girl in her right mind didn't threaten one of the most popular and powerful politicians in the country, a governor who, in the next few years, might be living in the White House. But now, after all the long months of waiting, she found it difficult to speak coherently, and completely forgot the few lines she had rehearsed.

"You own a lot of property around Jefferson Square. So does Mr. Hopkins." She was breathless, and hated herself for sounding inane.

Herder nodded, frowning slightly. "Yes, I inherited several parcels, along with Ben Hopkins. Our grandfathers were partners at one time."

Sandra was stunned by his easy admission of the truth. In all the times she had imagined this scene, he had either lied or had been trickily evasive.

"Is there something with regard to the property you want to discuss with me, Miss Masters?"

The chauffeur touched a button, a siren moaned briefly and softly, and the limousine slid through a traffic light while all other cars halted. This was the way to travel, she thought. "I've been fascinated by all the new buildings that are going up." Sandra realized she was talking too quickly now, but could not slow herself down. "Just about the only old places still standing are the one my mother lives in, and the one next door. I guess you might say that you're my mother's landlord, Governor."

Herder gave her the benefit of his bland public smile; he had always been a little touchy about his participation in the ownership of slum tenements. "Someone looks after all those things for me. A corporation. And since I hold public office, I have no voice in their handling. I dare say your mother isn't too comfortable—"

"She just loves her home! She can't stand the idea of moving!"

"—so it's a good thing, for everyone, that the last of those old places are finally coming down. As you know if you've studied my record, Miss Masters, I've fought a long and highly successful battle for slum clearance."

"You bet," Sandra said, feeling increasingly gauche, "and I voted for you both times. You have my vote any time you run. For any office."

"Thank you." He was puzzled, still unaware of what she was seeking. A student of human nature long before he had gone into politics, he had sharpened his analytical powers during his years as governor, and found, as a rule, that his snap judgments were fairly accurate. This young woman was flashily attractive, but wasn't trying to use her sex appeal on him, which was a relief. One of the oldest of the opposition's tricks was that of hiring a high-priced call girl, and Al Herder knew of at least two men in high office who had been forced to retire to private life because their enemies had confronted them with highly embarrassing photographs.

238

Certainly the Masters woman was no fresh-eyed innocent. Her mouth was hard, her eyes calculating, and there was a trace of a slum accent in her voice, although she made careful efforts to eliminate it. Virtually everyone who came to him had an ax to grind, particularly someone as persistent as she had been, but he couldn't, for the moment, imagine the significance of her disclosure that she knew of his real estate holdings. He had owned property in the city from the day of his birth, when his grandfather had put a number of parcels in his name, and it was no secret to any voter that he was a wealthy man. In fact, not until half-way through his first term had he lived down the name of "the playboy Governor."

"Dougherty didn't send you to me?" The lawyer would telephone him, not send a secretary with a message if he wanted to discuss something, so the question was inane, but Herder was feeling his way, cautiously playing for time.

"Oh, no. He has no idea I'm seeing you."

The Governor sensed rather than heard her contempt for her employer, and wondered, briefly, whether she might be seeking a new job. Perhaps she was hoping he'd put in a word on her behalf with the state Civil Service Commission that would eliminate the usual bureaucratic red tape, and, although he thought it unlikely, had mentioned his property holdings to show that she knew something of his private business affairs.

Sandra found his calm unsettling. According to her logic he should have been disturbed by her revelation that she knew so much about him. Perhaps he was putting up a bold and clever front, and she decided to turn the screw a little tighter. "Since I'm one of your admirers, Governor, I've been bothered thinking how awful it would be if the people who don't like you started saying that Jefferson Square was a good thing for your bank account."

"I don't believe the newspapers or anybody else will find out—unless you tell them, Miss Masters."

She could feel him staring hard at her. "I don't plan to say one word to anybody," she assured him, took a deep breath and added boldly, "I want to help you, Governor, not blackmail you."

The girl had courage, Herder thought, but was still convinced she had not told him her motive. "I'm grateful to you."

Apparently he thought it unlikely that there would be a public scandal over the property in the Jefferson Square area, and Sandra suspected he had his own flanks covered. But his smile was warm, and it was possible she had accomplished her purpose.

"There's nothing you want for yourself, Miss Masters?"

The sudden question surprised her, but she remained consistent and shook her head. "Not really."

"If I can return the compliment in some way, let me know." There was always the possibility that she might be sincere, but he could take no chances, and made a mental note to tell Eddie to run a check on her.

For the moment Sandra was satisfied. She had been trying, ever since the Emorys' cocktail party, to start moving in higher circles, and now that the Governor was indebted to her, he would be obligated to give her a boost.

The limousine began to slow to a halt as it approached a hotel canopy, where several city policemen and a state trooper were waiting, their mere presence having caused a small crowd to gather. "Would you like the car to take you on somewhere?" Herder asked.

Sandra caught a glimpse of a news photographer standing a few feet from the policemen and the doorman, and had a sudden inspiration. "No, this will be just fine, thanks. I'm staying downtown, anyway." With luck, the photographer would snap her picture as the Governor helped her to the curb, and the photo, in newsprint, would be a major step in helping her escape the anonymity she hated.

The sounds of Anton at work at his piano filtered into Michele Helsing's sitting room, but she paid no attention, and neither did her guest. Betsy Callison came from a family that really did drink tea in the late afternoon, which always amused Michele, but the girl was too upset to accept the cup Michele offered her. Michele couldn't help feeling sorry for the girl. Betsy was having a rough time.

"Anton says he'll have the *Jefferson Square Concerto* finished in another week to ten days, at the most," Michele said, making polite conversation. "And if you'd like, I'll be delighted to see to it that you're invited to the private preview, when he plays it for a few friends."

"I'd more than like it, I'd love it." Betsy meant it. "Forgive my ignorance, but I thought it was done last month, before I went off with Mother and Daddy to Palm Beach."

"It was. But Anton is a perfectionist, and he'll keep gnawing at it until he has to sit down with the arrangers and his concert-master. Now that the opening of Symphony Hall is really in sight, he'll soon be forced to stop. Thank God. I wonder if you can imagine what it's like never to be able to play a single bar of music on a phonograph or radio while he's in the house—and he rarely goes out when he's composing. No, of course you can't. He's even forbidden our son to watch Saturday morning children's cartoons on television, you know. He claims the music distracts him, although I honestly can't hear anything at the opposite end of the apartment. Anton insists he can."

Betsy murmured something sympathetic.

"It's the price of living with a genius," Michele said lightly. "But I don't want to impose our domestic problems on you. I gathered, when you phoned this noon, that there's something special you want to talk about."

Betsy nodded, fussing with the trim on her Chanel suit. "I—well, I hardly know where to begin."

"Try me. I haven't had much practice giving advice as an older woman, if it's advice you want. But I can be a good listener."

Straightening and brushing back her long hair, Betsy was unable to look at the other woman. "I suppose you know," she said in a small voice, "that I've been seeing something of Warren Hopkins for quite a while."

"If I didn't know it, the society pages would call it to my attention three or four days out of every seven," Michele replied dryly.

"I've always assumed—I mean, not that he's said anything specific—but you, well—you know how it is."

"I can guess."

Betsy carefully toyed with a jade figurine on the table in front of her. "While I was in Palm Beach, I had a letter from a friend of mine. She's been married for a couple of years, so she has no reason to be bitchy or anything. If you see what I mean."

"I get the drift."

"She told me to forget Warren. That he's running around with somebody else. A married woman."

Michele remained silent.

"Last week, when Mother and I came home after dropping Daddy off in Washington, someone else told me the same thing."

"Do you know who this woman is?"

"I know who they say she is, but—"

"Carolyn Emory," Michele said quietly.

Betsy was stunned. "Then it's true!"

"I only know what I hear. I've never hidden under a bed while they were in it."

"But if everybody knows—"

"I'm never sure just how many people it takes to include everybody, Betsy. The world's biggest cities are little villages. I'll correct that. Medium-sized villages. It was only ten years ago that there were a number of separate worlds here. Music and show business. The Social Register crowd. The literary. The climbers with money. Now they're all thrown together into a part-time melting pot. Sometimes each world whirls in its own orbit. Sometimes the worlds merge. But one thing is common to all of them. Gossip. It spills over from one world into the next. A prominent actress takes a new lover, and the news spreads instantly, if she's prominent enough. Within a few hours the word has become gospel in London, Paris, Los Angeles, Rome—you name it. But there's a catch. The story may or may not be true."

"I can't believe so many people would know about Warren and Mrs. Emory if it weren't!"

Michele shrugged. "I learned a long time ago to reserve judgment. The reputation killers drink blood, and if a story is dripping with enough of it, they don't bother to check on whether it may be accurate."

Betsy made a futile attempt to regain her dignity. "So many little things fit—that I'm sure—this story is true."

"What do your parents say?"

"I wouldn't dare mention it to them. They'd make a terrible fuss about my seeing Warren again, and they'd go straight to Mr. Emory. I wouldn't want to be responsible for causing a major scandal—and a divorce."

"It would hardly be your doing, you know." Michele thought of the help that Betsy's father had given her in a moment of crisis. "Besides, your parents may not be as old-fashioned as you think."

"I couldn't take the chance."

"Your real reason is that they'd try to stop you from seeing Warren. It isn't the scandal and divorce that bothers you."

Reddening, the girl could only nod.

"How much do you want him?"

"I'm in love with him. But I can't compete with—Mrs. Emory—or any other woman—on those terms." Betsy folded her hands in her lap.

Michele went to the small bar at the far side of the room, and took several minutes selecting a bottle of sherry before pouring herself a glass. Then, still playing for time, she made a long search for a cigarette before returning to her place on the divan beside her guest. "You have two possible approaches, as I see it."

"One is to play it cool. And wait until they break up."

"That's the hard way, but it would be the most effective, I imagine. You'd need infinite patience and self-control."

"I could try," Betsy said. "I don't guarantee the results, though. In a situation like this, I don't know that I'm as cool as the rest of my generation."

"Would it be easier for you to go to Warren—and have it out with him?"

"I'd die, Michele!"

"Not quite. But let's assume the rumor is true. You'd put Warren in a spot if you forced him to choose. She's going to bed with him. You aren't. So it isn't too difficult to figure who'd win."

"I don't think," Betsy said faintly, "I could compete that way."

"I'm not suggesting you change your standards, and even if you did, you'd lose."

Betsy became indignant. "Whatever you do, please don't start sounding like my mother. I don't think I could take one of those, 'He-won't-respect-you-if-you-sleep-with-him' lectures."

She had a backbone after all, and Michele approved. "You'd lose because you have too much at stake. Maybe you've had an affair or two yourself, and maybe you haven't. It doesn't matter. You have a virgin's attitude, so you couldn't win."

Betsy was still aroused. "I'm at least twelve years younger than she is. And I'm honest. So I'm not at all sure he'd want to drop me."

"Maybe not. But would he want to marry you?"

Betsy became less angry as she considered the question. "I don't know."

They were silent, and the sound of Anton at his piano, reworking a four-bar variation of a theme, seemed to become louder, more insistent.

"When a woman gambles for high stakes," Michele said, "she should know her man. That way she can reduce the odds. And she's got to decide for herself whether the risks she runs, and the integrity she may lose, are worth the victory she hopes to win. I can't tell you what to do, Betsy, and wouldn't if I could. You're the only one who knows how much Warren Hopkins may mean to you, and how much you're willing to sacrifice in order to get him—and keep him."

Dan Robertson roamed the apartment restlessly, looking in on the sleeping children, leafing through a magazine in the living room but finding himself unable to concentrate, wandering into the kitchen for a snack only to find he wasn't hungry. The clock that had belonged to his parents chimed twelve times, and, unable to tolerate the suspense any longer, he walked into the bedroom.

Phyllis, snug under the covers, was propped on several pillows, the bottom half of a box of typewriter paper on her left, the top on her right. She was reading, taking manuscript pages from one side and, after finishing them, dropping them face down in the other. If she heard her husband come into the room she gave no sign, and seemed completely engrossed.

Dan went back to the kitchen, and reached for the bottle of bourbon at the rear of the counter. But it occurred to him that he didn't really want liquor, so he poured himself a glass of tomato juice instead, and with it ate several soda crackers, spewing a few crumbs onto the floor.

Phyllis called out to him from the bedroom.

He deliberately took his time, finishing the juice and washing the glass before returning to the bedroom.

The two halves of the box were still resting beside Phyllis, who smiled up at him.

The first words had to come from her, he decided, sitting down in the small easy chair next to his dresser.

"I've never been a good judge of your work," she said.

244

His reaction was immediate and emphatic. "You don't like the book!"

"But I do! I think it's fascinating!"

He thought she was straining. "Don't be polite, Phyl. I want a candid opinion."

"I already knew so much of what you wrote that none of it was a surprise. Really, darling, I can't criticize any of this. I've been living with Jefferson Square, too."

"How much have you read?"

"I stopped on page seventy-five, at the end of the third chapter."

"Then you're getting your feet wet." He reached for a cigarette and his lighter.

She knew he wanted her to volunteer comments, that he hated digging for her reactions. "Your style is always good. And your wit is sharper than it was in *The Quandary*."

"What about the substance?" Dan demanded. "Never mind the window dressing."

"I like what I've read. Very much." Phyllis was afraid her voice lacked conviction. "I'm just getting started, remember, and you've told me nearly everything that's in these chapters. I'm anxious to read some of the other things, like the part on Berenice Tolmey."

"That section isn't written yet." Dan tugged at his bathrobe sash and leaned forward, his elbows on his knees. "If you think the book is no damn good, honey, say so. You won't be hurting my feelings."

She could think of nothing that would hurt him more. "If I didn't care for it," she said honestly, "I wouldn't hold back. But I have no perspective. I was shocked when you first told me about Mr. Hopkins and the others making money on real estate in the neighborhood of the square, so I'm not shocked all over again when I read what you've written about it—"

"That part isn't complete, you may have noticed. I need to fill in more details, and I don't have them yet. As soon as I can spare the time, I've got to do some detective work and get more actual facts."

"You picture a complete manuscript in your mind, but I've been reading a fragment, so I become confused. Don't forget I'm just an amateur, Dan."

He put the two parts of the typewriter-paper box together. "I want to read the rest of it tomorrow!"

"I'll just put it on my dresser overnight."

Phyllis watched him as he turned down the thermostat and removed his robe. "You're not upset, darling?"

He managed a grin and shook his head.

"I wish you'd let Harvey Simpson read what you've written so far."

"He's been pestering me enough for a look. I'd rather wait until the whole manuscript is finished, but maybe I'm being short-sighted. I don't know. I'll sleep on it for a night or two—assuming I can start getting some sleep. The opening of the repertory and the symphony is like giving birth to twins—except that I suspect the labor pains are lasting longer."

The poor bastard, Francis Dougherty thought. The whole town knows his wife is screwing with Warren Hopkins, but nobody has the guts to tell him. Including me. If it was my wife and I found out, I'd break her goddam neck. But a gentleman is different. He'll pack her off to Nevada or Alabama or Mexico, and he'll even pay her plenty of cash. How I'd like to represent him when the time comes. I'd cut her off without a nickel and send her out into the streets, where she belongs.

"Ed," he said aloud, "we've got to make a choice in a hurry. "Either we up the ante on the square again and start raising more money, or we hold the boys to their budgets. The architects, the decorators, Robertson, everybody."

"The more I deal with a culture center, the more I realize it isn't a business enterprise." Edward Emory hated being called Ed by any but his oldest friends, but his urbanity remained unruffled. "The acoustical engineers say their new walls for Symphony Hall will cost one hundred and thirty-five thousand, which is a total waste of the last quarter of a million. But Helsing is supporting them, and there's nothing Dan Robertson can do about it. Solanz is demanding an extra turntable on the Repertory Theater stage for his first production, and we don't even have the estimates yet on what that will cost."

"Suppose he doesn't get it?" Dougherty became belligerent.

"Dan tried to talk him out of it, and they almost came to blows." Edward Emory leafed through the papers before him. "The answer, I'm afraid, is that artistic people can't be kept within the bounds of financial absolutes."

"The hell they can't. If the money isn't there, they can't spend it."

"That would be true in the commercial theater, of course. But symphonies and opera companies are always subsidized. It's paradoxical, you know, that in spite of the culture boom from Lincoln Center to Los Angeles County, few centers show operating profits."

The two-timing bitch has him brainwashed, Dougherty thought, and took a sheet of paper from the sheaf. "Look at this. Three hundred grand for the free-floating sculptures that will line the central plaza. They don't make any sense, and even when you look at them, you don't know what you're seeing! For three hundred thousand bucks, I think maybe I'll become a sculptor myself."

"You and I may not understand and appreciate modern art, but Carolyn was chairman of the sub-committee that selected those sculptures. She's very enthusiastic about them, and so are Warren Hopkins and the rest of the committee."

Dougherty concealed his disgust. It was bad enough to hear Emory talking about his wife and young Hopkins in the same breath, and he didn't want to rub salt in the unsuspecting cuckold's wounds. "Ed," he said, "I'm just a lawyer. I know what I'm doing when I swing a deal for a ninety-nine-year lease on a new apartment house to be built three blocks from the square. You and Ben Hopkins and everybody else in the syndicate will clean up on that one. Good. But some of the problems of the square are out of my league. We're going to need an additional two to three million, but if you won't worry, I'll be damned if I will."

"Now that the first units are nearing completion, the members of the finance committee are showing much greater enthusiasm. I wouldn't be surprised if I can get the pledges to cover this deficit at the next meeting of the group. We may not even need an outside appeal."

"Just so you know where we stand." Emory and his friends were showing such a huge profit on their property sales and leases in the rejuvenated square neighborhood, Dougherty told himself, that they wouldn't feel the pinch if they made a new contribution far greater than two to three million. He wished, not for the first time, that he were working on a percentage rather than a retainer.

"The only thing that could hurt us would be a financial or

247

personal scandal," Emory said, "and I anticipate neither."

A man didn't become head of the Metropolitan-National Bank by closing his eyes to trouble, so maybe the guy was just covering up, Dougherty thought. Of all men connected with the square, Edward Emory was the most vulnerable, and it was difficult to believe he didn't know it.

"Mama," Sandra said, speaking slowly and carefully into the telephone, "the evacuation notice is an order. It can be enforced by the courts. You have four months to get out of that firetrap. I've taken options on two new apartments for you, and both times I've lost my money, but the next place I find—"

"Save your money," Maria Mascaroni cut in. "This is my home, and I stay here."

Sandra had warned herself not to blow up, but it wasn't easy. "They're going to tear down the building in four months. Don't you understand?"

"Mrs. Cavelli will stay, too. And Mrs. Elias. All the neighbors."

"Holy God, Mama! Do you want them to heave you and Buddy into the street?"

"God will punish you if you take His name in vain," the old woman said sharply.

"Never mind about me!" Sandra felt her temper rising. "There are laws—"

"In America there is no law that makes me give up my home." Maria was obdurate.

"You'll leave if I have to drag you out of that dump myself!"

"Buddy is big now, and will protect me."

Sandra could picture the incredibly ludicrous tabloid photo, with Buddy at the door of the tenement apartment, a piece of lead pipe or a switchblade in his hand, their mother sitting stubbornly at her usual place near the window behind him. Even if no one discovered they were related to her, the prospect was insufferable. But it was a waste of breath to press any harder now; the more she argued, the more her mother would dig in her heels. "I'll come to see you tomorrow or the next day, Mama, and we'll talk again." She placed the telephone in its cradle quickly, so she wouldn't hear the reply.

248

Trying to soothe herself, she looked at the newspaper spread out on her daybed. There she was, just as she had anticipated, getting out of that big car, lots of leg showing, smiling straight into the camera, with Governor Herder standing beside her. She was really getting somewhere in the world, and she would be goddamned if Mama was going to spoil her future by becoming a squatter in one of the two condemned tenements still standing on Fourth Street.

Benjamin Hopkins lined the ball across the net, and it landed just inside the back court, beyond his nephew's frantic reach. "Forty-thirty!" he called.

"Nice shot." Warren retrieved the ball and lobbed it back.

The older man stretched, served and then bounded forward a few paces as the tennis ball whistled toward Warren.

Expecting a driving serve, Warren was prepared, and managed to return it with a backhand chop.

His uncle waited, timed the ball on its hop and sent it into the far corner.

Warren managed to catch it with a forehand stroke, and the ball cleared the net, but had no force behind it.

Grinning, the older man drove it viciously beyond his nephew's reach. "Game, set and match," he said calmly.

They met at the net, shook hands and went to pick up their sweaters. "I thought you said you hadn't done much playing on indoor courts this winter, Uncle Ben."

"I don't believe I've come over here to the club more than once every couple of weeks." Ben sat down in a canvas chair, and a waiter appeared as soon as he signaled. "Two glasses of lemonade," he said, not bothering to ask what his nephew wanted.

"Well, whatever it is you're doing, you haven't lost your touch. I thought, before you took me, seven-five, in the first set, that I was actually going to beat you."

"I always play to win."

"As if I didn't know."

"Also, I keep in condition." Ben busied himself signing the chit the waiter presented him. "I get to bed at reasonable hours, and I try to live temperately."

Warren stole a glance at him, but his uncle's face was expressionless.

"I try not to take on extra burdens, particularly emotional

burdens." The older man sipped his lemonade, and nodded. "They've finally learned to make this the way I like it. Not too sweet."

"It's good lemonade," Warren said awkwardly.

"Unnecessary tensions ruin a man, you know."

"Yes. I suppose they do." The conviction grew in Warren that his uncle knew of his affair and was telling him, in a typically oblique way, to terminate it.

"You played well in the first set, but I shouldn't have beaten you six-two in the second. Have you been coming over here much?"

"No, very seldom, Uncle Ben."

"You need more exercise."

"Between work and Jefferson Square business, I haven't had too much time lately," Warren said lamely.

"I think you'll find the square is beginning to gather its own momentum. Let it. Our function—yours, mine, the whole board—should be strictly supervisory now. Robertson and his people must have the freedom to work as they see fit."

"I wouldn't think of interfering with Dan, Uncle Ben. I stopped in at just one of Jerry Solanz' rehearsals—out of curiosity, really—and I don't think he appreciated it. I'm on friendlier terms with Anton Helsing, but he's been out of circulation lately, and I—"

"Drop the square. Leave it to its own devices," Ben cut in, his voice cold.

Warren, angry with himself for babbling, knew positively now that his uncle was ordering him to terminate his relationship with Carolyn. How anyone had learned of the affair was not important; what did matter was that Benjamin Hopkins had given a command, and automatically expected it to be obeyed. But there were areas in the lives of others that were beyond his control, and Warren resented his interference.

"I always try to live up to my obligations, Uncle Ben," he said stiffly.

Harvey Simpson paced the length of the Robertson living room, his pipe emitting clouds of blue, aromatic smoke. "You want me to be honest with you, Dan. And you know I'd be unfair to both of us if I weren't."

"The manuscript is that bad?" Dan was mixing drinks at

250

the portable bar Phyllis had given him as an anniversary present.

"No. I didn't say that. There are good things in these two hundred pages. Very good. Your description of the problems with the square's architects and builders is fascinating. And in spots it's very funny."

"I know. But I'm not writing a joke book."

"Where you fall down is in your exposure of the real estate deals in the square neighborhood."

"That section isn't finished." Dan felt irritated. It hadn't occurred to him that he'd be forced to spell out the obvious to his editor.

"I realize you need more facts. And specifics. But there won't be anything worth publishing unless you take a completely different approach."

Dan thrust a drink at him. "I don't know what the hell you're talking about."

"Don't snap at me until you hear me out. Your moral indignation was infectious the day you told me that Hopkins and the others were making a fortune because of Jefferson Square. Between then and the time you wrote about them, you lost your spark."

"How do you mean?"

Harvey relighted his pipe, and ignored his drink for the moment. "I don't know whether you think they're wrong for buying and selling property in the vicinity of the square, or whether you admire them for it."

"Don't be funny, Harvey," Dan said. "They're getting away with something reprehensible, and I'm sure there are millions of people who will agree with me."

"That attitude doesn't come across." Harvey was inflexible. "You present them as men of intellect and charm and personal integrity. I'm amazed at the sympathy you show for Benjamin Hopkins."

"I'm writing about three-dimensional human beings, dammit! Hopkins is an exceptionally complicated man. So are Edward Emory and Blackwell—who may be an investment banker, but who privately writes poetry, I discovered. So is Governor Herder. Sure he wants to be President. But that doesn't make him any less dedicated a governor, any less devoted a public servant. Look at the two Roosevelts. And Adlai Stevenson. They were wealthy men who caught the White House disease, but they were great governors."

"You miss the whole point."

"I can't lie about them. I can't picture them as dirty villains when they're not!"

"I'm not asking you to distort—"

"My book is going to be an accurate report on a major culture center, not a propaganda tract!"

Harvey unconsciously raised his voice, too. "Either you're writing a crusading book demanding ethical justice, or you're writing trash. Presently Hopkins and Herder and the rest are men of intelligence and charm. So much the better. But then you've got to show—as strongly and clearly as you can, with as much punch as you can pack into every page—how inconceivably shocking it is that men of that caliber should be fleecing the public. Legally, perhaps, but nevertheless lining their own pockets while acting as champions of culture."

"They're not acting or posing. They honestly believe in the square!"

"Wonderful! Then they deserve to be awarded medals and beaten over the head—all at the same time. You do neither. You walk a middle path. You do a genteel tightrope balance that leaves the reader wondering why you bother!"

The door opened, and Phyllis looked in. "Is everything all right in here?" she asked, trying to hide her concern.

"It's just dandy," her husband said sourly.

"We haven't yet chosen either rapiers or pistols at twenty paces, but we may." Harvey grinned at her. "But we'll give you fair warning, so you aren't startled by the shots."

"You're sweet, Harvey." She made a mute appeal to Dan, asking him to control his temper. "Let me know when you're ready for sandwiches." She closed the door, and the two men were alone.

"I'm sorry to be saying all this to you, Dan—"

"Sure. I can see your heart bleeding."

"We'll get nowhere if you take my editorial critique as a personal insult. Either you'll accept my observations as a professional, in the same spirit I'm making them, or we're not speaking the same language." The vestiges of Harvey's joviality vanished.

Dan struggled hard. "I'm trying, but please remember I've been living with this book for a long time."

"Of course you have, which is one reason you can't see your objectives in focus any longer. I'm not enjoying this, Dan, and I know how painful it is for you. But the result both of us want is a book that will be significant, not drivel that will be ignored by the reviewers—and the reading public."

Dan took a long swallow of his bourbon and water, sat in his favorite easy chair and planted his elbows on its arms. "All right," he said, "I'm listening."

"It's my feeling, a purely subjective reaction, that you ought to leave the section on financial chicanery until the end. Write everything else first, and once you catch the right mood, the real estate skulduggery portion will almost write itself. Just change your sight-lines, and you'll turn out the book both of us want."

"How do I accomplish this latter-day miracle?"

Harvey pretended not to hear his bitterness, took another pipe from his pocket and spent a long time stuffing it. "Let's talk about the section you want to devote to the Tolmey girl."

"I haven't written it yet."

"So much the better. I found your extensive outline on the section very revealing."

"I'm off base there, too, I suppose."

"That's what I'm trying to find out, if you'll be a little patient with me. What do you think of her?"

"I can't answer that in a phrase or a sentence."

"I didn't ask you to. Tell me in your own way."

"All right. Officially, first." Dan took a deep breath. "As Vice-President of Jefferson Square, I'm afraid *Confessional* isn't Marek's best play. He can't be objective about his ties to his own past, and the Repertory Theater may have a terrible failure with its opening play. That's why I'm not pressing the issue of the second play with Solanz. Once he's been clobbered, he'll become more reasonable."

"The girl," Harvey prompted. "Berenice Tolmey."

"I'm coming to her, and I'm doing this in my own way, as you so generously suggested. Officially, I'm scared to death she'll fall flat on her face. She has a concept of the character she's playing, and although it isn't fully developed, because she's been given no chance to work it out in her own way, it is an interpretation. Unfortunately, neither Solanz nor Marek seems to agree with her. They're trying to cram her into another mold—one that doesn't fit her, in my opinion—and the results well may be god-awful. She's got to carry the play. We can't rely on Julian Adams, in spite of his star billing—and the fact that he's really a first-rate actor. And if Berenice doesn't come alive in the role of Paula, we may as well close the box-office and confine ourselves to giving away free seats to colleges and drama schools for the run of the play."

Harvey took a small sip of his drink, but said nothing.

"Unofficially, as someone who has always loved the theater and enjoys good acting, I think she has a tremendous potential," Dan continued. "I told you about that European-made movie she did. Her impact was tremendous. She seemed to leap right out of the screen at her audience. Properly guided, she could become a star in her own right, in her own way. She has a quality of her own, or whatever it is—that makes a Helen Hayes or a Judith Anderson. Not the Hayes quality or the Anderson quality, you understand. The Berenice Tolmey quality. Jerry Solanz has given her the complete sexpot image, of course. Short skirts, bikini panties, plunging necklines with no brassiere, that platinum hair always in disarray, a full, wet mouth—every trick. She doesn't register that kind of sexual abandon, at least not on me. When she's being herself, she has a very different kind of sex appeal. She's more the warm, helpless, stray cat type of girl."

"Why is she letting Solanz change her whole personality?"

"Ambition, naturally. Who else would cast her in a star part at this stage of her career?" Dan rose and took their glasses to the bar, where he began to mix fresh drinks. "That's where the balance becomes so delicate. Berenice has the dedication and drive of the actress. But she's sensitive enough—to feel that what she's being made to do in the part of Paula is all wrong. She's frightened out of her wits that she's going to make a fool of herself on the stage—and ruin her career."

"But she can't convince Solanz that she thinks his approach to the role is wrong?"

Dan grimaced. "Your ignorance shows, Harvey. It's very obvious you've never tried to work with Jerry Solanz. He isn't reasonable with anyone. When he pretends to go along with you on a point, it's only because he's twisting and juggling and conniving, so that, in the long run, he'll get precisely what he wants. He's the Oracle speaking in the temple at Delphi, and once he's laid down the law, there's no appeal. I've had my scraps with him, and haven't yet won a real victory. I've watched Jan Marek get slapped down repeatedly.

What do you suppose a girl who is sleeping with him, and who depends on his good will, could do to change him?"

Harvey rattled the ice cubes in his glass. "This may seem irrelevant, but it isn't. Suppose Solanz was directing *Confessional* for the commercial theater, and had invested a chunk of his own money in the production. Would he have given the Tolmey girl the lead?"

"Absolutely not!"

"How can you be so sure?"

"You may have read that he completed a big film in Europe before he came back here to set up his repertory company and put *Confessional* into production. It's going to open shortly, before the Repertory Theater opens, actually. Well, I don't know whether he sunk any of his own money into the film or not. I'm inclined to doubt it. But I do know that he gets a percentage of the profits—which will be tremendous. I saw a preview recently, just before Phyllis came home—"

"How was it?"

"Pretty good, I'm forced to admit. The louse does have talent. But my point is this. There were four juicy women's parts, all of them of the type he's trying to change Berenice into, that she might have done. I'm not talking about the starring role, that Helga Borg did; he needed a box-office name, which is fair enough. But he could have used Berenice in any one of the other three important women's roles—and didn't. Instead he gave her a token, a bit part. She isn't on the screen for more than two or three minutes. I have an idea that the only reason he put her into the film at all was to keep her relatively quiet in bed."

Harvey slapped the arm of his chair. "Now go put that into your book and you've got it made."

"Put what into my book?"

"How human greed, lust, ambition and stupidity are making a mess of an ideal."

"I thought that's what I was writing."

"The guts are missing, Dan. You're walking on eggs on every page. I'm not asking you to be evangelical, much less attack culture centers. The reader would have no respect for you if you tried to make Jefferson Square look shabby. All the same, you're hedging. You were honest with yourself in *The Quandary*, which made it a first-rate book. Your integrity came through to the reader. In this one you're trying to jump back and forth from one side of the see-saw to the other, and it doesn't work. I've made some marginal notes for you. They may help."

"Thanks." Dan stared into his glass.

"I hope I'm right," Harvey said, "in feeling that we're good enough friends for me to throw in some personal advice."

"Why not? You've already ripped apart what I've written. Why stop there? Anyway, I think Phyllis agrees with you." Dan raised his head and forced a smile.

"You're a professional, Dan," the publisher assured him. "Even when your writing misses, your style is always good. I think the basic problem is being caused by your own ambivalence."

"Meaning what?"

"I didn't think it was my place to interfere when you told me you intended to keep your job at the square while writing this book. But I felt it was a mistake. And I'm convinced of it now. You're trying to carry water on both shoulders—forgive the cliché—and it won't work. Either resign now, or let the book wait. Unfortunately, if you wait, Jefferson Square won't be that newsworthy two years from now. This book has significance only if the reader believes it to be topical."

"I can't walk out now," Dan said. "The Repertory Theater is in an uproar. Anton Helsing is making so many innovations in the symphony that it would be unrecognizable unless somebody exercises a restraining influence on him. The opera people are having so many feuds I can't keep them straight. I'd hoped that Max de Groot would be able to keep order in his own house, but he thrives on squabbles as much as his singers do. And the newest headache is the fine arts commission that's buying paintings and sculpture for the museum. The people who want old masters and the modern art crowd are barely on speaking terms. We've been given a collection worth more than three million dollars—it hasn't been announced yet—and some members of the commission are actually opposed to accepting it. What a comedy it would be —if it weren't so serious. I can't leave the square now. If I go, there will be guaranteed chaos."

"If you're capable of being a fireman at the same time you're a reporter who writes about the fire, more power to you," Harvey said. "But so far you haven't shown me that you can do it."

Sandra's three attempts to reach Governor Herder by telephone had failed, and she finally realized that, in spite of the ride with him in his limousine, she would have to deal through Eddie Brown if she was to keep in touch with him. Eddie, as she had anticipated, immediately asked her for a date when she gave him an opening.

Her social experience with newspapermen—in his case a former reporter on a long leave of absence—was limited, and it dawned on her before they ate dinner that she was incapable of matching him drink for drink. His capacity seemed unlimited; he ordered steins of ale for both of them throughout the meal without bothering to find out if that was what she wanted, and now, in a smoky bar with dark wood-paneled walls that was inhabited almost exclusively by working members of the press, both male and female, he ordered a new round every time she consumed about half of what was in her glass.

Sandra knew she was feeling the drink, and repeatedly warned herself to be cautious, but she had lost count of how much she had consumed, and it no longer mattered as much as it had earlier in the evening. Eddie didn't care whether she was a regal lady or not, so there was no need to put on a false front with him. In fact, it pleased her that he introduced her to the friends who drifted past their booth, and by no stretch of her sensitive imagination was he embarrassed or condescending toward her.

He accepted her as an equal, so she could relax, even when she realized he was trying to pump her for information.

"You know," he said, "Al Herder is a strange guy."

"I don't know him at all well, of course, but I like him." She made no attempt to move away when his leg touched hers beneath the narrow table.

"If I were Al, I suppose I'd feel as he does. People on the make have been trying to get to him all his life. Partly because he's loaded with dough, and now because he's governor. It's a hell of a way to live, having to keep your guard up."

Sandra knew he was fishing, and answered politely, "I guess it must be."

Eddie waited until it became obvious that she wasn't biting at the bait. "You really threw him, or maybe I shouldn't tell you that."

"I did?" She shifted her position slightly so his leg could press against a longer section of hers. She was assuming he had been ordered to find out what he could about her, and she knew of one sure-fire way to distract him.

"Yeah. You mentioned the slum property he owns, but you didn't seem to want a thing from him."

"That's right." Sandra leaned forward, her elbows on the table, so her face was no more than two feet from his.

Eddie brought his other leg into play, proving he could concentrate on two things simultaneously. She was playing it coy, so he decided to try the candid approach. "What the hell do you want from him?"

"Nothing."

"Two more, Phil!" he shouted, and turned back to Sandra. "Don't try to fool Eddie, the faithful watch-dog. You've tried three times in the last few days to get Al on the phone."

"What does that prove?"

"That you want something. When a gorgeous doll starts burning up the wires, the Governor gets a big question-mark in his mind. And so does the faithful watch-dog."

Sandra laughed. "So that's it. You have me pegged wrong, Eddie." She moved her legs away. "I don't know whether he's happily married, and care less. It's good enough for me that he's been married for a long time, and I realize that somebody with his ambitions can't afford to play around. If he were single, that might be something else. He could really send a girl."

Eddie's legs followed hers. "Get rid of that drink, will you? This table is too small to be cluttered up with them."

"I'll be stoned."

"Me, too, but what of it? All you dolls go for Al—"

"Not me." She allowed him to play his below-the-table game.

"Maybe it's his money that gives him glamor, or maybe it's being governor. But what's wrong with me? I'm single. Divorced, actually. And I think I'm one hell of a guy."

"I agree," Sandra said, and immediately regretted it when he dropped a hand under the table.

"You aren't trying to buy or sell some land from him, are you?"

The idea was so preposterous she giggled. "I can barely pay my rent."

He had learned literally nothing from her, and came to the conclusion there were other ways to soften her up. "Let's get out of here." He gulped his drink and called for the check.

She took only a few sips, but discovered, when she stood, that she was dizzy. This was one time she had more than met her match. "Hang on to me going out," she murmured, "or I may stagger all over the place."

Eddie put an arm around her and successfully guided her to the door. "Are you okay?"

"For the moment, but what this air will do to me, I don't know."

"It's my fault. Sorry about that. Come on. We'll get you sober in no time." He took her arm and began to walk.

They were in a part of the city unfamiliar to Sandra. Once an aristocratic district, it had started going to seed, but had been rescued from degeneration by the construction of new apartment buildings and restaurants. There were no tenements here; the brownstones were in good repair, air conditioners could be seen in virtually every window, and the young executives on their way up the ladder and their wives saw to it that the neighborhood remained respectable. A successful campaign put on by several advertising men had resulted in the planting of trees, dusty young maples protected by iron grills, and there was an aura of gentility to the area that, somehow, escaped being midle-class.

"Where are we going?" Sandra asked.

"Leave everything to the faithful watch-dog. Step number one to sober up. A little walk in the smog-filled air. Now comes step number two." He led her up the stoop of a brownstone, unlocked the inner door and headed toward one of the two ground-floor apartments.

She knew he had ideas and was taking her home with him, but she was curious about the way people lived in this part of town. Besides, she was confident of her ability to look after herself.

The interior of the apartment was impressively, solidly masculine. There were signed photographs of the President, Governor Herder and a number of other high office-holders in the entrance foyer, and the leather-upholstered furniture in the living room was heavy and conservative. It was expensive, too, so maybe a governor's executive assistant made more than Sandra had imagined.

Eddie took her coat, hanging it with his own in the front closet, and led her to a large, immaculate kitchen, where pans and pots with copper bottoms were hanging in neat rows. He became busy with an electric percolator, and although he wasn't sober, either, he worked quickly and efficiently. "Step number two," he said. "Strong coffee guaranteed to clear the head. That leaves us with time on our hands until it's ready, so let's take advantage of being smashed. We deserve it."

Before Sandra quite realized what was happening, he turned, swiftly took her in his arms and kissed her. Had he used strong-man tactics she would have resisted, but he was as gentle as he was expert, and she found herself responding before she could stop herself.

By then it was too late. In spite of her intentions she found herself becoming aroused, and Eddie gave her no chance to recover her balance. In what seemed like a single motion he unzipped her dress, unhooked her bra, and bent to kiss her bare breasts.

"There's a place for everything," Eddie said, "and the kitchen is for cooking."

She was surprised when he picked her up with apparent ease, and although neither tall nor particularly muscular, carried her through the apartment. It was difficult for her to focus, and she knew only that she was being deposited on a bed, then undressed by skilled hands that stroked and patted and explored while they worked. Her plan to maintain a dignified reserve had been shattered, and her craving for sexual satisfaction became more intense, driving everything else from her mind.

Eddie's hands and mouth ran up and down the length of Sandra's body, inflaming her, and she writhed involuntarily. Groping for him, she felt warm flesh, and it was a surprise to discover that, somewhere along the line, he had removed his own clothes. Perhaps her sense of time was inaccurate, but she didn't care, and her long nails dug into him as she clutched him, hauling him closer.

He was in no hurry, however, and continued to caress and play, tease and arouse until, in her frenzy, she began to moan. Then, with great force, he took her.

At last they separated, and Sandra, exhausted but satiated, lay back on the bed, her eyes still closed.

"You're as good as I knew you'd be," Eddie said.

"You're not so bad yourself," she murmured, half asleep.

He laughed. "Now that delayed step number two. Coffee."

She wrenched herself into a sitting position as he left the room. She was completely nude in a strange bedroom, her

260

clothes and his scattered on the bed, chairs and floor. She had no way of knowing whether Eddie would tell his boss he had screwed her, but she remembered he had called himself a faithful watch-dog. She began to think that this bedroom was the closest she would ever get to the Honorable Albert Herder himself.

There had been a time when the conference room at the Metropolitan-National Bank had made Dan a trifle uneasy, but he had grown accustomed to the Renoir and the Matisse on opposite walls, the luxurious Oriental rug on the floor, the highly polished table and the padded chairs that looked as though they belonged in an exclusive gentlemen's club. He had also become accustomed to Edward Emory's habitual banker's caution.

"I know I submitted a set of supplemental figures to you only a short time ago, Edward," he said, "and I hate to add another million and half to the total, but it can't be helped."

Edward Emory sat stiff-backed, looking at the papers spread out before him.

"As you know from your previous association with the symphony, the key members of the orchestra have always held long-term contracts. Anton Helsing insists that if he's to build and hold together the best unit in the country, an orchestra that achieves a stature greater than that of the Philharmonic, Boston, Philadelphia and the rest, he wants to treble the number of contracts he offers. He also says it's essential to add another twelve men to the orchestra, and he wants three additional arrangers. That's item number two."

Emory studied the paper, then made a small check mark on it.

"The turntable for the Repertory Theater is going to cost twice what we thought it would. Item number one, with the estimate breakdown attached."

Again the gold pen made a small, neat mark.

"Item three is my own idea, and for once Jerry Solanz and I are in agreement. If he's to create a permanent acting company in the next year or two, a company that will achieve the stature of the Comedie Française, he'll need to establish a school for actors."

The pen remained poised in the air. "It's an outrageous

sum," Emory said. "That's more than a half-million—just for an actors' school."

Dan felt himself growing angry. "There's nothing outrageous about it. If anything, it's modest."

"These other items are self-explanatory." Three more check marks were placed on the paper, and Emory sat back in his chair. "It was just a day or two ago that I defended the supplemental appropriations you wanted. I believed then—and still believe—that I can persuade the members of the finance committee to make up a deficit of an additional two million dollars, perhaps two and a half million. But I can't agree to still another million and a half. I'm afraid I must disapprove all of these requests."

The check marks, then, indicated a negative reaction, and Dan's temper rose still higher. "You're being damn shortsighted!"

Few people had ever spoken to Edward Emory in such a tone, and he blinked in surprise. "In my opinion, none of these requests are essential to Jefferson Square's operation."

"They are in mine! We could put the Repertory Theater in a tent and hire a bunch of semi-professional actors, of course. And we could tell the symphony to play in the open. In the central plaza, maybe, surrounded by those atrocious sculptures!" Dan well knew that Carolyn Emory had been instrumental in selecting the plaza's art works, and that he was being gratuitously, deliberately insulting, but didn't care. His long meeting the previous night with Harvey Simpson had been tiring, he had felt frustrated all day, and the lack of understanding being shown by someone who was using the square to increase his own fortune was infuriating.

"I see no need to become unpleasant." Had any of Emory's employees been present, his expression would have made them wince.

"Well, I do! I've heard all of you money people, and I'm including you, Edward, making graceful little speeches about the square. It mustn't be regarded as a commercial venture, you've said. We've got to do what's right artistically, you've said." Dan was slightly surprised by his own scathingly mocking tone. "The chips are down now. So put up or shut up. Sure, we'll get along on less, if we have to. We'll tug our caps, say, 'Thank you, sir,' and make do with whatever you choose to dole out to us. But don't expect the finest culture center in the world. Not with that attitude!"

Emory had never seen him lose his temper, and wondered if he might be working too hard, or, perhaps, had domestic problems. This wasn't the Dan Robertson with whom he had worked so congenially. "Take a day or two to think over my suggestion," he said, "and you may agree I'm being more reasonable than you appear to feel right now."

"Like hell I will!" Dan gathered the papers and rammed them into his attaché case. "I'm protesting—in writing—to Mr. Hopkins with copies to the full board. And I'd better write my opinions on asbestos!"

Phyllis saw her irate husband off to work, dressed the children and gave them their breakfast, and was relieved to send them off to the park with the part-time nursemaid. Her own nerves were far too jumpy for more coffee, but she poured herself another cup and took it to the bedroom. Dan had been utterly impossible for days, ever since his evening with Harvey, but she couldn't—and wouldn't—complain. She had a job to do as a wife. With a smile.

She sipped her coffee, and was just lighting a cigarette when the telephone rang.

"Michele Helsing, Phyllis. I hope I didn't wake you up."

"How I wish you had. We get up with the birds around here, I'm afraid. The children haven't learned to tell time yet."

"My son is an angel," Michele said, "but everyone tells me it's easier with one."

"In some ways, I suppose it is."

There was a slight pause, then Michele said, "This isn't a social call, and I hope you'll forgive me. But I'm terribly upset, and I've just forced Anton to take a sedative."

Phyllis was embarrassed by the confidences of someone she knew only casually, and murmured something sympathetic.

"I wonder if you happen to know why Dan is making such a fuss."

Phyllis stiffened at the mention of her husband's name. "I'm afraid I don't know anything about—"

"He's been calling Anton for several days. Three or four times a day. I haven't let him through, and neither have the servants. When Anton is composing, as he's doing, he takes the veil. He won't see anyone, speak to anyone—you just can't imagine how he retires from the world. I'm lucky if he eats an occasional meal with me. Well, Dan called him again this morning—about a half hour ago, and he was in such a stew that I made the mistake of telling Anton to talk to him."

Dan must have made the call as soon as he reached his office, but Phyllis knew nothing about the matter. He hadn't said a word to her about Anton Helsing.

"I'm sorry I did. As nearly as I could make out—Anton is inclined to become a little hysterical when someone rips into him, so he wasn't too coherent—Dan insisted he come to Symphony Hall today and run through his new *Concerto*. Anton tried to tell him it isn't in final shape yet, but Dan kept saying it makes no difference."

Phyllis groped unsuccessfully for the right word or phrase.

"As nearly as I could tell, only Dan and one or two others are going to be there. He told Anton that with rehearsals so near, someone has a right to hear the *Concerto*."

"I wouldn't think Dan intends to criticize it. He doesn't know that much about music, and he always defers to Anton's judgment."

"Yes, he made all that quite clear. I wouldn't blame him for being curious, or even wanting to know if the *Concerto* has actually been written—if he were dealing with anyone but Anton, that is. Dan does have the ultimate responsibility, I know, so it's his job, and all that."

Phyllis said, reaching for her coffee and discovering it had grown cold, "All I can tell you is that Dan is one of Anton's greatest admirers. And it was just a few days ago that he put up a tremendous fight with the finance committee people for some appropriations Anton wants. I wasn't told any of the details," she added hastily, afraid she had said too much. "I just mention it to show you that I'm positive Dan feels a great loyalty to Anton."

Michele sighed. "Maybe I can convince Anton of that."

"Is he going?"

"Oh, yes. Dan gave him no choice." Michele forced a little laugh. "I wouldn't have bothered you about it if it weren't for the problems I have trying to handle a temperamental husband."

"If this is any comfort to you," Phyllis said, "you aren't the only one whose husband is temperamental."

They chatted about inconsequentials and then terminated the conversation.

For the moment Phyllis felt too weary to heat more coffee. Obviously Dan was making life miserable for everyone.

"I don't know what you think you're doing," Francis Dougherty said acidly, "but you've been acting like some kind of nut."

Sandra had been expecting a showdown for months, knowing their coldly formal office relationship could not continue indefinitely without the injection of a personal note. But she remained silent, waiting to see what was bothering him, and feeling her turtle-neck sweater coming loose at one side of her waist, casually tucked it under her wide belt of red leather.

"I kept quiet when I saw your picture in the paper, hobnobbing with the Governor. I told myself that was none of my business. But when Al Herder calls me up to tell me you've been pestering him on the telephone, that's too much!"

Sandra wondered whether Eddie Brown had been responsible for the Governor's call to Francis. It would be typical of a man, any man, to turn on her after getting what he wanted. Regardless of whether he had pulled the switch, she was ready to murder the bastard, who had called her repeatedly since their night together. She had ducked another date with him, knowing he was after just one thing, so maybe this was his idea of revenge.

"What's got into you?" Francis was thoroughly aroused.

"I do my job here," she replied sullenly. "I earn my salary. So anything I do on my own time is my business."

"Except when it boomerangs on me. I've been handling some of Al Herder's law business for a lot of years, and I was one of the original group that urged him to get into politics. He's not just a client. He's damn valuable to me!"

Sandra knew it had been the Governor's influence that had won Francis the position of general counsel for Jefferson Square, and, according to office gossip, a number of state court justices were inclined to favor his cause in court because of his known friendship with the Governor. That, however, was his worry.

"Well?" he demanded, his face reddening.

"I'll be glad to tell the Governor anything he wants to know," Sandra said loftily.

"He doesn't want anything to do with you!" Francis was

shouting. "He wouldn't touch you with a ten-foot pole, much less his own!"

"That's not what I'm after."

"What the hell else are you good for?"

Sandra started toward the door. "I don't have to listen to that kind of garbage."

Francis reached the door first and blocked it. "You'll tell me. Now. Or I'll break your neck."

In his present mood he would make the threat good, even if some of the office staff heard her screams, and she knew the information he demanded was more important to him than the flurry of a minor office scandal. "Keep away from me!" She backed off, bumped into a table and retreated behind it.

"Then stop wasting my time, goddammit!"

"What do you want to know?" Sandra tried to stall.

"The Governor says you mentioned his real estate holdings." His eyes were narrowed.

"Is that a crime? I just wanted him to understand that I know about it. It was a friendly gesture."

"Friendly, my ass. If you ever say one word, to anybody, about anything you've learned in this office, I give you a solid gold guarantee you'll never hold another job in this town!"

He was frightened, Sandra thought, and took courage. "Is he doing something with his property that he shouldn't?" she asked, wide-eyed.

Francis stared at her for a moment. "No," he said. "But I think I see your game."

"You don't." She lost patience. "If you believe I'd try to blackmail somebody who could send me to prison for twenty years, you're as crazy as you must think I am!"

"But you've admitted there's a game. What is it?"

She could see why he had earned a reputation as a trial lawyer, and, weary of fending him off, saw no reason to conceal the truth, particularly since the Governor would be of no help to her. "I was hoping," she said, "that he'd get me in the swim. He was so nice to me at the Emory's cocktail party last year, and—"

"I remember how you chased him at that party." Francis became incredulous. "The swim, huh? You want to be a queen of the Jefferson Square society-arty crowd. Is that it?"

Sandra's sudden flush told him more than anything she might have admitted in words.

Francis laughed raucously. "Christ, that's funny! You? A pal of the Emorys and Hopkinses? A chum of people like Anton Helsing and Julian Adams? The only one of them you've got anything in common with is Max de Groot's wife. She was an Italian gutter-rat, too, but she made something of herself. She was a star at the La Scala Opera when Max married her. What's your talent?"

"Go to hell," Sandra muttered.

He roared again. "Now I've heard everything. Don't you know they laugh at you, every last one of them?"

"That's not true!"

"It isn't, huh? Take a good look at yourself in the mirror, sister. You look like a slut. Not even a high-class call girl. You wear too much makeup, and you wear it all wrong. Everything about you is a tip-off. The way you wiggle your rear when you walk. The way you bat your eyes at every guy you meet. Those clothes—"

"I always dress in style!"

"Like right now, with your boobs practically busting out of your sweater. Your skirt so tight in the can that it'll come apart at the seams when you sit down. You may think you look like a stylish lady, sister, but there isn't one man or woman in the Jefferson Square crowd who doesn't recognize you for what you are. A tramp."

"Damn you—"

"You talk like Fourth Street. You think like Fourth Street. You act like Fourth Street. You've got it written all over you. Can you talk about theater and music and art—the things they're interested in? Big joke. Do you know anything about international affairs or literature or domestic politics? Get in the Jefferson Square crowd, huh? Holy God!"

Sandra wanted to stuff something into his mouth to silence him.

"You can get to know some of the guys, of course. When a broad is giving it away, they'll take what they can get."

Unable to tolerate any more insults, Sandra sprang at him, filled with an overwhelming desire to claw his face.

Francis caught her wrists and forced them to her sides, where he held them tightly.

She struggled in vain to free herself.

He continued to laugh at her. "But not even the horniest of them will hang around you very long. Because they'll find out what I did. That you're not even a very good lay." Suddenly he became hard. "Pick up your terminal pay—yeah, and your vacation pay—from the auditor. And then get to hell out of here." He released her and shoved her toward the door.

Her degradation complete, Sandra faced him for a moment, rubbing her chafed wrists with trembling hands. "Screw you," she said, "and screw Jefferson Square." She had the ammunition to destroy the square, and with it all the people who had been laughing at her. She'd fight now as she had been taught on Fourth Street, with nothing barred.

The rehearsal had been halted while Jerry Solanz and Jan Marek conferred in the third row, arguing in low, intense voices. Members of the production staff made a pretense of being busy, and bustled about the auditorium and on the stage, calling to one another occasionally as they consulted clipboards that had become almost permanently attached to them. Most cast members, discreetly staying away from the quarreling director and author, retreated to backstage areas to smoke. Julian Adams, leaning against the proscenium, was engaged in a spirited discussion with the costume designer, and was demonstrating his ability to utilize his celebrated charm in handling people.

At the rear of the rehearsal hall, in the half-dark, Dan sat with a tired Berenice Tolmey, whose disposition matched his. "No cross-examinations today, Dan. Please. I think I'll scream!"

"There are a few things I need to know," he said firmly, "and by tomorrow you'll have forgotten them."

"Oh, God. All right."

"Dan!" Jan Marek was standing, peering toward the back of the little theater through his thick-lensed glasses. "Could you join us for a minute?"

Dan groaned. "I shouldn't come to any of these rehearsals. Those two keep wanting me to referee their fights, and I'm sick of it!" Deliberately, just to be contrary when he knew Marek and Solanz were waiting for him, he took his time moving down the aisle.

"We hate to interrupt your intimate little chat," Jerry said. "Tell me, what the hell are you and Berenice always whispering about?"

"In the first place, we don't whisper. In the second place, I enjoy talking to her when there's nothing else to do around here. She's a bright girl."

"Yeah, sure. And she tells me how interesting you are." Jerry glowered. "There's a pitch here I don't get. But I will."

Marek was impatient. "Where can we talk privately for a little while?"

Aware that some of the actors had drifted back onto the stage and were straining to hear what was being said, Dan recovered his aplomb. "There's my office, if you don't mind some sawdust."

They left the theater and made their way across the central plaza to the new Symphony Hall, where the administrative headquarters were located, temporarily, until the permanent executive offices were ready in a wing of the Museum of Fine Arts. Railings of antiqued stainless steel were being imbedded in the marble steps of the two buildings that were virtually finished, riveters were at work on the skeleton superstructure of another, and a huge crane was scooping dirt out of a hole in the earth.

Prolonged silences made Jan Marek jittery. "Those two tenements over there look like orphans," he said.

Dan wasn't in a conversational mood, but tried to observe the basic amenities. "Demolition was supposed to begin a month or two ago, but some old immigrant women are making a hash of the construction schedules. They won't move out —God knows why—and have to be evicted, which takes time."

Marek continued to look at the dilapidated structures. In spite of the cold, wash had been hung to dry on lines strung between them, several small boys were playing stickball in a field of rubble perilously close to the pit the excavators were digging, and a choice variety of four-letter words and other graffiti littered the walls of the tenements. "That's what my old lady would have done. She was scared purple of this country, and the old dump where we lived was the only security she knew. They'd have had to blast her out." His face mellowed and softened.

"It's a rotten situation all around," Dan replied gruffly.

They went in the rear entrance of Symphony Hall, climbed two flights of bare concrete stairs and made their way over a tangle of insulated telephone and power lines that littered the floor. The most that could be said for the dusty offices was that they were warm and spacious. Partitions of sheet rock had been raised to make a series of separate cubicles, the sounds of clicking typewriters and ringing telephones bounced off the concrete walls and ceilings, and the heels of secretaries and file clerks clattered as they walked back and forth.

Dan's office occupied a corner, so he had windows on both the north and west sides, but only his desk and swivel chair were in good condition. The rest of his furniture looked as though it had been rescued from a junk pile, and was in danger of collapse, and even the dirty venetian blinds had seen better days. Until lately he had not minded the unpleasant surroundings, but recently had become sensitive to them.

"Sit down," he said, "if you dare. The square carries full employee insurance, so you're covered if your chairs fall apart."

Jerry took the nearest chair, but Marek preferred to lean against a wall.

Dan moved behind his desk. "All right, gentlemen, what's today's quibble?"

"A gag writer," Jerry muttered.

Marek slouched despondently. "This is no quibble. I want you to tell me something, Dan, with no interruptions from the great genius. What would happen if the opening of *Confessional* had to be postponed?"

Dan glanced at Jerry, who had averted his face. "That would depend on how long."

"Six weeks, maybe two months."

"At least two months," Jerry interjected. "An indefinite postponement that might run as long as four months."

"We couldn't do it," Dan said flatly. "We've sold out thirty-four performances to schools, and more than two hundred groups have already bought other blocks of seats. I doubt if we could make even a one-day postponement. The television networks have scheduled live shows on opening night, and the President is going to push a button in the White House that will raise the opening night curtain."

Jerry looked triumphant. "I've been trying to hammer it into his thick Bohemian head. I'd have to junk *Confessional*, and then put in calls to agents for actors who can play the classics."

"Then start looking for your Hamlet or Lady Macbeth right now," Jan said.

270

Dan looked at him without sympathy. "Why?"

"Berenice stinks. I want somebody else to do the part."

"Who?" Dan asked, his manner still severe.

The playwright shrugged. "Well, I've sounded out a few agents I can trust, and nobody happens to be available at the moment. It might take a few weeks to find a replacement and rehearse her."

"Or it might take months," Jerry said.

"I prefer a postponement of several months to a miserable failure," Marek said.

Dan shook his head. "It wouldn't be a postponement. We'd have to reschedule the play completely for next year—or whenever."

"You see, Jan?" Jerry polished his glasses with the tail of his silk shirt. "Even Mr. No Brains here admits we couldn't juggle everything just for you."

Dan curbed his temper and ignored the slur. "Are you formally withdrawing your play?"

Marek hesitated. "I've been hoping we could work out something reasonable."

"In my whole career I've never had a flop," Jerry said, "and my best friend doesn't trust me. Not once since I've been a director—"

"That isn't true, and all of us know it," Dan interrupted curtly. "Two and a half years ago the critics tore you apart when you brought in *A Horn of Plenty*. And two years before that you didn't exactly distinguish yourself with *The Ferris Wheel*. It closed after twenty-one performances, and should have shut up shop the second night. You kept it running for a movie sale, but didn't get one."

Marek brightened slightly. "What a memory!"

"The professor," Jerry said, "had nothing better to do in his classes than remember statistics. Do you also know how many hits I've had, sweetie, and how many Oscars I've won?"

"I'd need an adding machine for those figures, I'm sure," Dan said sourly. "The playwright is the pilot of his own airplane," he added, turning his back to Jerry.

"Like hell he is!" Jerry jumped to his feet. "He approved the casting of Berenice, and we even got Equity to grant us an extra rehearsal period. He can't close us down now, with the opening just a little over three weeks away. If he does, I'll file a formal complaint with the Dramatists Guild. I'll go into the courts. I'll—"

"I'm sure," Dan interjected, "that threats don't frighten him. Jan, you've already said you're willing to be reasonable. All of us want to open on time. And since you yourself say no one else is available for the part, what other suggestions do you have?"

"Find somebody who'll teach Berenice Tolmey how to act!"

"She's already a fine actress," Dan said.

Both men stared at him, and Jerry chuckled. "How do you like that? The professor isn't as stupid as he looks."

Dan continued to address only Marek. "My interpretation of the part of Paula when I read it may not be what you had in mind when you wrote it. And I'm not sure the few re-hearsals I've seen have given me a clear idea of what Bere-nice can or can't do. But I do believe that if she's allowed to develop the role as she feels it, she'll be good, damn good."

Jerry leaned across the desk. "Are you insinuating that Berenice shouldn't follow my direction? Is that what you've been plotting with her when you get together with her and whisper?"

Dan stood and faced him. "Solanz, you're paranoid. No, I haven't been plotting with her, as you call it, and I haven't encouraged her to strike out on her own—although you'll never know how tempted I've been. I've kept my opinion to myself until the playwright asked it. Which he has. So I'm telling him—and the director, if he cares to listen—that Berenice Tolmey is a sensitive, intelligent actress, and that if you'll give her a chance, she'll come through for you. For all of us."

Marek had stirred up a greater storm than he had antici-pated, and became somewhat apprehensive.

Jerry was so indignant that he could scarcely speak. "In all my years in show business, from the time I broke in as a hoofer in vaudeville, I've never seen such *chutzpa*."

"I stand by my opinion," Dan said.

"I ought to shove your goddam teeth down your throat!"

"Want to try it?"

Marek came between them, and pushed them apart. "Look, I started this, and I don't want to fight anybody. Let's cool it!"

Jerry grasped his lapel. "Either you have faith in me as a director, or you don't! You accepted my casting. You recog-nized the girl's potential. But now, before she's had a chance to jell, before the concept of the character is really formed, what do you do? You panic. And you give this dimwitted oaf a chance to put in his nickel's worth of amateur advice."

"Solanz," Dan said, "I'm not one of your actors who can be insulted and patronized—and made to like it."

"So lump it."

Marek remained between them. "If you two don't cut it, there'll be a real fight."

"Professor Robertson," Jerry said, "doesn't realize that professionals always have disagreements during rehearsals. It's the tension, naturally, and it builds. But we always work out our problems and satisfy everybody. Jan, you're a pro, sweetie, and so am I. Look. I'll turn the rest of today's rehearsal over to Milt Nusbaum. You and I will go back to the hotel, where it's quiet. You show me every line, every piece of business Berenice does that you don't like. Tell me how you want her to play them. And I give you my sacred word that's how she'll do it, right down to the last nuance. Fair enough?"

For a long, tense moment Marek was silent. Then he sighed and wilted. "Fair enough," he said.

Jerry walked back to his chair, shrugged into his overcoat and jammed his hat onto his head. "Let's go." Dan no longer existed for him as he went out into the cavernous general office.

Marek was embarrassed as he struggled into his coat. "I'm sorry."

"What's between Solanz and me," Dan said, "has been growing for a long time. It has nothing to do with you. Or with *Confessional*. I hope the play is a hit, but I'm afraid it won't be unless Solanz turns her loose."

"Maybe you're right, and maybe you're not," the tortured Marek said. "I don't know. All I can tell you is that Jerry has done great things with two other plays of mine when they were in trouble."

"Then pay no attention to me. You're professionals, and I'm just an outsider."

"Are you coming, sweetie?" Jerry called.

Marek stopped at the door. "He doesn't mean all that name-calling, Dan. If you pay no attention, and look behind that big, gabby front he puts up, he's really a very decent fellow." There was no response, and he walked out.

Dan picked up a pencil and broke it.

"Maybe you can afford to be smug, Francis, but I can't."
Governor Herder's voice sounded rasping and tired over the
telephone line.

Francis Dougherty glanced into the living room, where
Ann was reading, or least pretending to read. "Al, you're in
an uproar over nothing."

"Maybe it's nothing to you that a woman in your employ
saw our confidential correspondence—"

"I fired her."

"She still saw it!"

"You can take my word for it, Sandra is too damn stupid
to realize the significance of anything she read. Anything."
Again Francis looked in his wife's direction, and knew from
the way she held her head that she was listening.

"She's pestered me, and she's been after my staff. If she's
so damn stupid, what does she want?"

More concerned than he was willing to admit, Francis
forced a laugh. "Maybe she thinks you're pretty."

"I'm in an exceptionally vulnerable position, as you and I
well know!" the Governor snapped. "If she talks, she could
do me a lot of harm."

"But she can't prove anything." Francis' soothing techniques were awkward. "It would be the word of a cheap little
tramp—who was thrown out of her job, remember—against
that of the state's first citizen. Who'd believe her?"

"Too many people. What you fail to realize, Francis—"

"What I do know is that you're in an uproar without legitimate cause. Have her tailed, if you're nervous. Put a tap on
her phone—"

"I'm reluctant to play detective. If she's gone to any one of
a dozen or more people who hate me, and they found out I
was trying to check on her, it would be a tacit admission of
guilt. I've got to play this carefully, so I'll hold off on the
rough stuff."

Francis sighed quietly.

"What's more, I'm depending on you to put out any fires."

"At the first sign of a fire, I'll douse it," Francis promised.
"Okay? I know broads who could give you or me a real headache, but not this one. She's a social climber, and her mind is
too small to grasp more than one concept at a time."

"I hope you're right—for all our sakes." The Governor was
so weary he ignored the amenities as he rang off.

Francis was tempted to retreat upstairs, but thought it

better to face Ann now, before she had additional time to ponder. "That was Al Herder," he announced.

"I know." Ann had a knack for the casual approach. "You hadn't told me Sandra Masters wasn't working for you any longer."

"I guess it slipped my mind."

"Why should a secretary matter to Governor Herder?"

"You know how Al gets. He's always nervous."

She had no interest in the Governor's nerves. "What did Sandra do?"

"It's a long story, and not very important. Al is afraid she was snooping in some confidential files."

"Was she?"

"I believe so."

"But she had the right to go into any of your files, didn't she?"

"The right, maybe, but no valid reason." Francis hated to encourage his wife's drinking, but poured her a stiff Scotch, hoping the liquor would choke off her interminable questions.

The expression in Ann's eyes indicated she knew why he handed her the drink. "I always liked Sandra," she said.

"Me, too."

"I know."

Francis wanted to challenge her, but thought better of it.

"I've always thought her very attractive."

"For her type," Francis muttered.

"She's the type men always like." Ann's voice was almost too gentle, her manner too tranquil.

Irritated and apprehensive, he decided to mix himself a drink, too.

"Do you have another secretary yet?"

"I've moved up a girl from the office of one of the junior partners. On a temporary basis. If she works out, I'll hang on to her. If not I'll find somebody else." Francis turned toward his wife, and became rigid.

It was obvious that Ann knew of his past relationship with Sandra, and was relieved that she was no longer employed by him. She met her husband's gaze briefly, then returned to her reading.

Francis' panic subsided. Had Ann intended to make an issue of his affair, she'd have done it before now. The subject wouldn't be mentioned again, but he had been warned not to stray, so he'd have to watch his step for six months, maybe longer.

What really mattered was that Ann had forgiven him, or at least didn't intend to leave him, which was virtually the same thing. It was odd how upset he became—frightened, actually —when he thought she might walk out on him. He always claimed she needed him, but it occurred to him that his own need for her was just as great. The idea didn't appeal to him, and he downed his drink too quickly, knowing but not caring that he would suffer heartburn for the rest of the night.

On all four sides the garden was surrounded by the balconied walks, five stories high, of the Oscar Donnheimer Museum of Art. Only a few tables were occupied now, mostly by out-of-town tourists who were resting after walking through the endless galleries of the museum. In the summer, of course, when the plastic dome that covered the garden was removed and umbrellas shielded each table from the sun and city soot, the atmosphere was far livelier.

But even now the place was exotic, thanks to the banks of heavy foliage that edged the garden. Anyone looking at the camellias, gardenia bushes and palms would find it difficult to believe that the temperature outdoors was only twenty degrees above zero.

"I just love it here," Berenice Tolmey said, sipping her vodka gimlet.

Dan grinned at her. "You should. They use real hot-house flooring and heating. I saw the plans when we were thinking of doing something like it at the square, and it's fantastic."

"With all the pictures they have here—by Rembrandt and Hals and all the other great painters, I'm surprised there was enough money left for a hot-house garden."

Dan realized the tourists were staring at her, and small wonder. She had shrugged off the coat that had been resting on her shoulders, and the tourists could see, just as he could, that she was wearing no bra beneath her turtle-necked sweater of white silk. "Money," he said, trying to concentrate on their conversation, "meant very little to Oscar Donnheimer."

Berenice became aware of the attention she was creating.

It amused Dan that she reached into her shoulder-bag for her dark glasses instead of draping her coat around her again. "I'll take that back. Oscar Donnheimer was one of America's greediest industrial barons. He collected coal mines, steel

276

companies and railroads the way other men collect stamps. He made so much and had so much power that the money itself didn't mean anything to him. What he enjoyed was hauling it in."

"I'm such an ignoramus that I never even heard of him," Berenice murmured.

"Well, he died about twenty years before you were born, so it's no wonder." Dan took a swallow of his own drink and couldn't help wishing she'd take off the sunglasses. Her eyes were such an expressive mirror of her feelings that he hated talking to a blank wall. "Eventually old Donnheimer retired, and a London art dealer persuaded him to start collecting paintings, which he did. With the same enthusiasm he'd shown for accumulating big corporations. His mansion—which stood over there where the north wing is—was loaded from top to bottom with Old Masters."

The girl listened with rapt attention, her glossy pink lips slightly parted.

It occurred to Dan that she was no older than many of the students he had taught. "When Donnheimer died, the house was turned into a museum. And he left it such a huge amount of money that his heirs eventually tore down the old mansion and built this place. While acquiring more paintings, of course, in accordance with the instructions he left in his will." He reached for his cigarettes and lighter.

"Me, too."

He absently lighted two cigarettes, as he often did when he and Phyllis were out somewhere.

"Aren't you nice!" Berenice removed the glasses as she took the lighted cigarette he handed her, and he saw her eyes were shining.

"For telling you a little about Oscar Donnheimer?"

"No, for lighting this for me. I'm around Jerry so much that I'm not accustomed to being treated with consideration."

"Finish your drink," Dan said gruffly, "and we'll have another."

"Do you think we dare have three?"

"Well, you know your capacity better than I do."

Berenice was lost in thought, then defiantly ran a hand through her short hair. "Oh, why not? It'll be hours before Jerry finishes rehearsing that big scene of Julian's, and if I get a little tight, I can always sleep it off."

Dan signaled to the waiter, who stood discreetly nearby.

"Did Mr. Donnheimer really like his pictures?"

"I don't believe they meant any more to him than a railroad or two. But the way he earned his money and the way he used it pose some fascinating questions." If he hadn't been so conscious of the girl's disturbing proximity, of her nylon-clad knees touching his beneath the tiny table, he could have imagined himself speaking from a classroom podium. "Donnheimer was a robber baron. He used every trick in the book to earn his pile. But he's more than repaid his debt to the public with this legacy. Millions of people have enjoyed his collections of Old Masters, which is one of the finest anywhere. So—are the ultimate results worth the piracy, would you say?"

"I get all confused when you ask me things like that!"

Dan's smile was reassuring. "Think about it. Slowly. But let's get rid of these drinks, because our new ones are here."

Berenice's laugh indicated that she was having a thoroughly good time.

Dan knew he was behaving somewhat foolishly, but justified this little interlude at the Donnheimer Museum by telling himself that this was the first time in weeks he'd been free of a sense of pressure. He owed himself a two-hour holiday that did no one any harm.

"Ethically," he said, "the methods Donnheimer used to build his fortune were wrong. Today some of them would be considered criminal. But judged only on aesthetic grounds, he did mankind a great service."

Berenice took a large swallow of her new drink. "All I know is that I'm having fun."

"That's why we're here. Today's rehearsal was so hard on you that I thought seeing some of the paintings here would help you relax."

"Being with you is what's done it," she said candidly. "I tried for a while to remember all the things you were telling me about all those pictures, but I couldn't keep it all straight. How can you possibly roll out all those facts and interpretations. Do you memorize them, or something?"

He tried to reply in terms she would understand. "Art, along with drama and literature and sculpture, were my business before I came to the square."

"Well, you snowed me, darling."

He was accustomed to the way show business people used

terms of endearment carelessly, but he had the feeling that Berenice's "darling" wasn't casual.

She placed her bare elbows on the little table and leaned forward. "If I don't fall flat on my face in *Confessional*, it'll be your doing!"

"That's hooey," he said. "You're going to be a success because you have a very real talent." He wanted to add that her director would be at least partly responsible, but could not force himself to speak the words.

Tiny bells on her huge, chandelier earrings tinkled when she shook her head vehemently, causing the tourists to stare at her all the harder. "If it weren't for you, I'd have flipped my lid by now."

Warring sensations of pleasure and guilt made Dan confused. As a teacher—hell, as a male—he was flattered by the thought that he might be contributing to the success of an attractive and talented girl. But he hoped she wasn't becoming emotionally involved with him. He had been using her for his book, so he was devoting attention to her under false pretenses. All he felt toward her was sympathy tinged with pity.

No, that wasn't completely accurate. She was young, and fresh, she had an erotic appeal he could hardly ignore, and she obviously admired him.

"I'll make you a bet that you're the theatrical sensation of the year," he said.

Berenice giggled. "What do you want to bet?"

It was evident that she was feeling her drinks, so he took an immediate, firm stand. "Let's think about it," he said, and summoned the waiter.

Berenice drained her drink. Then she stood and, without self-consciousness, leaned back against Dan for a moment as he picked up her coat. "Just throw it over my shoulders, honey," she said.

He followed her out of the garden, aware of the gaping tourists, equally aware of the wiggle that had become second nature to her. Perhaps he felt his liquor slightly, too, but she certainly wasn't making the situation any easier for him.

He struggled into his own coat before they reached the main entrance and kept a firm grip on his hat. In spite of the heavy rush-hour traffic they were in luck, and the doorman got them a taxi almost immediately.

An icy blast of air struck them as they moved across the

sidewalk to the waiting taxi, and Berenice gasped.

Ordinarily this was Dan's favorite time of day. He had endowed the early evening hours in the city with a magic that, he often thought, existed only in his own mind. The haze of darkness erased the sharp outlines of office buildings and softened the strained faces of hurrying pedestrians. Even the gleaming headlights of the countless automobiles contributed to the mystique. But his tensions of the moment were too great for him to be conscious of anything or anyone but the girl who settled into the seat and made a token tug at her high-riding skirt.

"I'm frozen," Berenice murmured, shivering, and snuggled close as the car door slammed shut.

Her proximity was irresistible, and, in spite of his intentions to the contrary, Dan found himself putting an arm around her, which prompted her to close the little remaining space between them.

A single glance into the rear-view mirror was enough for the driver. "Where to, mister?" he asked, looking straight ahead.

"I don't want to go back to the hotel yet." Berenice's voice was scarcely audible.

Dan was torn by anxiety, embarrassment and desire. The last thing on his mind had been an involvement with the girl, but her warm accessibility swept away all other considerations. "Take a few turns around the park," he directed. Then, remembering all the old jokes he had heard on the subject, his embarrassment increased.

They were lost in the anonymity of heavy city traffic.

Berenice stirred slightly, and Dan saw she was looking up at him, her eyes shining, her lips slightly parted. Unable to resist the lure, he could no longer stop to think of the consequences, and bent down to kiss her.

His first reaction was one of shock. For more years than he could remember he had kissed no woman but Phyllis, and had grown so accustomed to her he had forgotten that no two women were alike. The girl's lips were fuller than Phyllis', she was smaller boned and even her scent was different. In spite of her youth, she was far more knowledgeable, too, and her lips, tongue and teeth worked busily, expertly.

The very act of cheating was erotic, and Dan was unable to cling to the last vestiges of caution. He placed a hand over one of her breasts, which he had been wanting to do ever

280

since she had removed her coat in the Donnheimer Museum garden.

She shivered again, and pressed closer to him.

His kissing became more prolonged, more intense, and their embrace became still tighter. Only vaguely aware of what he was doing, Dan could not hold his hand still. He caressed her breast, his own desire mounting as he felt her respond, and then dropped his hand on her knee. From there it began to move up her thigh.

The taxi drew to a halt.

They wrenched themselves apart, breathing hard and blinking, and Dan saw they had halted in heavy traffic, somewhere in the park. This heavy petting was insane, he told himself, drawing back a little, and could lead nowhere.

Berenice continued to cling to him. "It's awful for people like us, isn't it, honey?" she asked in a low tone.

Dan was uncertain what she meant, but agreed, his discomfort as great as his physical need.

"I don't dare take you back with me," she said. "What a scene Jerry would make if he walked in. But I'd better get back now. Please, Dan. Tell the driver."

They left the park. The lights of the hotel were directly ahead.

Berenice covered Dan's hand with her own. "You were a real life saver today, honey, and I won't forget it. Not ever. Don't get out of the cab. It doesn't take much to start gossip."

The door opened, and she was gone, turning for an instant with a half-shy, half-wise smile.

Still aroused, still conscious of the taste of her lips, the feel of her slender body, even of her lingering scent, Dan knew he could not go home to face Phyllis. He needed time to compose himself, to work things out in his own mind, and craved solitude as well as another drink. "Take me to Jefferson Square," he told the driver.

The city was quiet at four o'clock on a cold winter morning. Only a few cars sped through the streets, here and there merry-makers hurried into buildings, and few pedestrians who went to work early were yet abroad. At this hour a metropolis showed her age; her skyscrapers and brownstones and town houses looked as dirty as her littered pavements, and she seemed shabby and dispirited.

Dan let himself into the apartment house and slumped against the paneled wall of the self-service elevator. His head ached, he was too exhausted to think any more, and his legs were so weary they threatened to collapse under him. He had fought a long battle with himself—and had lost.

It was a fortuitous, technical accident that he hadn't taken Berenice to bed; the only reason was that no bed had been available. So he, who had always prized fidelity and his own moral strength, was as weak as all the men he had long despised. He loved Phyllis, more now than ever before, but deserved neither her love in return nor her respect. He had stopped dramatizing what had happened early in the evening, aware that it could not be undone, and he wasn't overemphasizing its importance, either. But it wasn't easy to admit that he hadn't known himself as well as he had always believed, that when tempted he was as vulnerable as the men he had always condemned for playing around.

Perhaps, after he exorcised his guilt, he could become a better husband. But nothing could compensate for the harm he had done to Berenice. A relationship that had been inspired solely by his desire to obtain material for his book had been complicated beyond measure because the girl trusted him.

The apartment was very quiet. Dan put his hat and coat in the front hall closet, and it suddenly occurred to him that he was hungry.

He walked into the kitchen, closed the door behind him and then snapped on the light. After rummaging through left-overs in the refrigerator, he cut himself a slice of roast beef, poured a glass of milk and sat down at the enamel-topped table. He was just starting to eat when the door opened.

Phyllis stood in the frame, her eyes puffy with sleep, her hair tousled as she clutched her robe of fluffy wool. "I thought I heard you come in," she said.

"Go back to bed," Dan told her gruffly, his guilt becoming more aggravated as he glanced at her.

"I wasn't really sleeping. I just dozed on and off. I was worried about you, honey."

He cringed, wishing she had used any other term of endearment. "I told you when I called that I'd be at the office for a long evening."

Blinking, she peered at the kitchen clock. "Some evening! It's after four!"

"I know." He tried to direct his full attention to the food on his plate.

"Didn't you have any dinner?"

"I forgot about eating." That much, at least, was the truth.

"Oh, dear. What was tonight's crisis?"

"It's too late to talk now. Go back to bed, Phyl."

"I'm wide awake now. Give me a cigarette."

He took a pack and his lighter from his pocket, and, still unwilling to look at her, shoved them across the table.

She sat down opposite him, and made herself comfortable. "Tell me."

"For God's sake, Phyl!" His voice was savage. "I'm beat!"

"Well. Excuse me."

"I didn't mean to chop off your head," Dan said lamely, "but I'm really out on my feet."

She made an effort to accept the half-apology. "Of course. I understand."

Dan wished she wouldn't be so damned sweet. Looking down at his plate, he ate rapidly.

Phyllis took a drag on her cigarette. "Can you sleep a little later in the morning?"

"No." He was curt again without realizing it. "There's a meeting in my office at nine thirty."

"Postpone it."

"Let me run my business, will you?"

"I'm just thinking of you, Dan. You're so touchy."

He gulped the milk, wanting to get away from the table as soon as he could.

Phyllis fell silent.

The growing tension made him still more uncomfortable, and he felt he had to say something. "It wasn't any one thing that kept me tonight. A lot of papers were piling up on my desk faster than I could handle them, so I wanted to get caught up."

She hesitated for an instant. "You aren't carrying too heavy a load, trying to write the book, too?"

"There are times," he said, "when I'm sick of the damn book."

Phyllis stood. "Leave the dishes when you're finished. I'll do them in the morning." She walked out of the kitchen.

Dan was torn. He was relieved that she had gone, yet wanted to call her back. Miserable and bewildered, he slumped in his chair, his hands covering his face.

"I am not God," Benjamin Hopkins said, "nor have I been appointed His archangel. That sort of story usually starts on the level of corporation vice-presidents and seeps downward. Frankly, the moral standards of the people who work for me are their own business. I have my own ideas of heaven and hell for me and mine. They'll have to settle with their Maker for their own licentiousness."

Dan, sitting across the table in the private dining room high in Hopkins Tower, tried to appear relaxed, but remained wary. He still didn't know why he had been summoned to lunch, but the whole tenor of the conversation made him apprehensive. He had no idea how Hopkins might have learned of his abortive relationship with Berenice Tolmey, but the man had an uncanny knack for ferreting out the secrets of other people.

"I'm a monogamist because of my scruples, and because I had the good sense to marry the right woman. Mrs. Hopkins and I have spent thirty-two happy years together. I don't condone today's standards, but I can't set myself up as the judge of others."

The last of Dan's doubts faded, and he knew why he had been asked to a private lunch meeting.

"On the other hand," Hopkins continued, "I have responsibilities to my family. If they can't guard their own morals, I must do what I can to help them. You needn't look blank, Robertson. I'm sure you've heard rumors about my nephew."

Dan wanted to laugh. His own guilt had caused him to jump to false conclusions, and he was relieved rather than embarrassed to find that Hopkins wasn't accusing him, but instead was discussing Warren.

"You've heard the stories?" the older man persisted.

"I suppose I have."

Hopkins leaned back in his leather-padded chair. "I'm afraid they're true." He paused. "You don't seem surprised, Robertson."

"I've lost most of my ideals," Dan said dryly.

"I could have ignored the problem," Hopkins said, "but that would have been contrary to my scruples and my trust. On the other hand, the cure is delicate. I thought of appealing to the lady, but she'd have condemned me as a meddler, and might have insisted on marrying the boy, just to spite me."

Now that Dan could think clearly, impersonally again, he was impressed anew by Hopkins' talent for understanding others.

"I had a friendly little chat with my nephew, but he refused to listen to me."

Dan, sipping his coffee, hoped he would never find himself on the receiving end of a similar "friendly" discussion.

"I thought of still another approach, perhaps the most obvious. I could have gone to the lady's husband with the whole story. But I was afraid to take the risk. As well as I've known him for many years, we've had a relationship rooted in our mutual business interests. I can't predict how he might react to something so personal. I couldn't blame him for creating a scandal, but that's the one thing I've wanted to avoid."

Dan couldn't help wondering how Hopkins would react to his book. If Warren's illicit romance worried him, he would be far more concerned about an exposé of his own financial opportunism, which would be even more harmful to the Hopkins name.

"My nephew is the one member of the triangle who can be approached. Only through him can this situation be alleviated." Hopkins poured fresh coffee for his guest and himself. "But he sees me as the symbol of authority, financial and vocational as well as personal, so he rebels against me. I warned him to break off his affair, but he hasn't taken my advice. Now I'm hoping he'll listen to you, if I can persuade you to intervene."

I'm a great guy to give advice to a poor slob trapped in a romance he probably didn't want, Dan thought.

Hopkins was watching him. "I have no right to ask for your help, and I won't press you if you turn me down."

"Why would Warren listen to me, Mr. Hopkins?"

"You're more or less a member of his own generation. You're a professional in the arts, and he's an amateur. He respects you."

Dan sipped his steaming coffee.

"I'm not saying he'll pay any more heed to you than he did to me, but it would be worth the attempt."

"What's the alternative, Mr. Hopkins?"

"I'd have to apply other methods."

It wasn't difficult to imagine himself in Warren's shoes, and Dan felt queasy for a moment. "I wouldn't blame him for slugging me and telling me to stay out of his yard, Mr. Hopkins. But an affair that can't end in marriage can only cause unhappiness for all the parties involved, I believe." Dan wondered whether he was merely trying to salve his own battered conscience. "So, whatever the outcome, I'll do what I can."

The odors of fresh paint had given most members of Jefferson Square's administrative staff headaches, but it was too chilly outdoors to keep the windows open in order to get rid of the smell. Some were indifferent to the inconvenience, but a few, knowing they would be forced to endure it all over again when they moved into their permanent quarters in the Museum of Fine Arts, resented it.

Dan had been irritated for several days. He looked across his desk at the flashily dressed redhead, and although she looked vaguely familiar, disliked her because she was taking his valuable time.

"I was Francis Dougherty's secretary until last week," Sandra Masters said, "and I met you at a few parties and places, too."

She was a job hunter, Dan thought, and wished she had gone to the personnel department. He would try to be polite for a minute or two, and then would get rid of her by referring her to the right place.

Sandra seemed to read his mind. "I'm looking into several job offers," she said. "That's not why I'm here."

Dan relaxed slightly.

"You and Mrs. Robertson have been decent to me whenever we've met," she continued. "You didn't try to freeze me, and you treated me like a human being. So I want you to know there's nothing personal in what I'm going to do. For your sake, I'm sorry I have to do it."

Slightly mystified, he was relieved that there was a break in the day's routine, and offered her a cigarette.

Sandra leaned forward for a light.

"I guess you don't know it, Mr. Robertson, but you're working for a gang of crooks."

"Really?"

"All these rich people who have been giving money to Jefferson Square are earning back a helluva lot more than

286

they're handing out. They own all the property around here, and the prices they're getting for it are just fantastic."

Dan kept a poker face, but felt himself growing taut.

"You don't believe me."

"I've just heard an interesting accusation, Miss Masters—"

"But you want proof." She reached into the large shoulder bag she had been carrying, and drew out several folded papers, which she handed to him.

They were photo copies of correspondence between Dougherty and Benjamin Hopkins, Governor Herder and Edward Emory, and Dan found it almost impossible to contain his own excitement. A cursory reading was enough to indicate that these letters contained the kind of facts and figures Harvey Simpson had told him were essential, but that he had been unable to obtain for his book.

"These are just samples," Sandra said, watching him closely. "I've got plenty of others."

"Mr. Dougherty doesn't know you have these documents, I assume."

"I don't care what he knows!" There was venom in her voice. "He can sue me."

"Why have you come to me with this information, Miss Masters?" Dan was being very cautious.

"Like I said, you and your wife didn't treat me like dirt. You're the only ones at this—this mausoleum." She jabbed a forefinger in the direction of the window overlooking the other units of the square that were in one or another stage of construction.

Her nail polish, Dan thought irrelevantly, was garish.

"I try to be decent. When people are nice to me, I'm nice to them. So I wanted to give you a chance to climb into your shelter before I set off my H-bomb. And don't try to talk me out of it."

"Since you've confided this much in me, I wonder if you'd mind telling me what you plan to do."

Sandra took the papers from him, carefully refolded them and tucked them away in her handbag. "I have an appointment with somebody. Today. Tomorrow the whole story about these rich hoods will be in print."

In spite of her desire to keep her precise scheme of action secret, she could not resist the temptation to show off a little. "I happen to know a columnist. Don't ask me which one."

Dan stalled by leafing through the copies of the letters

again. The appearance of Sandra's information in a newspaper, even in a gossip column, would diminish the impact of his book, perhaps make it meaningless. He desperately needed this data for his own, exclusive use.

Suddenly a sentence in a letter from Governor Herder to Dougherty leaped out at him: *"My partnership in Harrison, MacFee is irrelevant to the realty sales."*

The implications were stunning. Harrison, MacFee and Company was the general contracting firm erecting the buildings that would comprise Jefferson Square. So the Governor was not only making a fortune out of the property sales and leases involved, but, if his statement was to be taken at face value, was also lining his pocket with building profits.

"If I understand you correctly," Dan said, concealing his excitement, "the various members of the Jefferson Square Board who are mentioned in this correspondence have been making money out of the land on which we've built, and on other property in the neighborhood."

"You're fast on the uptake," Sandra said.

"Is there any other data of value in the papers you've collected?"

"Haven't I got enough?" she retorted.

She stirred, restlessly.

He had to obtain this information for himself. "Why are you doing this, Miss Masters?"

Sandra's dark eyes were angry. "Because I hate the guts of those hypocrites."

Dan reached for another cigarette. "I have a rather important use for the information myself."

"It isn't for sale, and if you think you can either bribe me or scare me into shutting up, you're dead wrong!"

"I don't make it a practice to frighten anyone, and I wouldn't demean you by offering you a bribe." Dan stood and crossed the room, where he picked up his attaché case, then returned with it to his desk. He had brought his manuscript with him, hoping he could find the time during the day for some minor editing, and he leafed through it until he came to the opening of the section dealing with the real estate operations of the square's sponsors. "You might want to look at this, Miss Masters," he said, handing her a few pages.

Sandra scanned them, stiffened, and then read them more carefully. "Who wrote this stuff?"

"I did."

"God almighty! Then I'm not telling you anything you don't know already!" She laughed. "What's this for? A magazine article?"

Dan was reluctant to reveal too much to her. "Something like that."

She fell silent, and her smile faded. "With a guy in your job writing it, that'll really cut their— That'll really fix them."

He wanted to protest that she misunderstood his motives, that he had no desire to "fix" anyone. But it didn't matter whether she understood his reasons for writing the book. All that counted now was the protection of his investment in time, effort and emotion. If she walked out before striking a bargain with him, his entire enterprise would be ruined.

Sandra peered into the attaché case and saw the thick pile of manuscript pages in the typewriter-paper box. "You've written all that—about this place?"

"That's only part of it. The work isn't finished yet."

She whistled under her breath. "I knew you were okay." Her admiration gave way to a long reflection, and she would have been shocked had anyone told her that at this moment her expression resembled that of her shrewd peasant mother. "You want me to give the letters to you instead of to my newspaper friend."

"I certainly do! And I think you'll agree that a book will serve your interests better than a gossip column. My book will be hundreds of pages long. A column couldn't devote more than a paragraph or two to the subject. The book will be a permanent document that will be read by a great many influential people—"

"Okay. Let's say I'm sold," Sandra declared. "Then what?"

"That depends on what you want." Dan was reflective, too. Obviously she was untrustworthy, having taken and copied correspondence from Francis Dougherty's files while in his employ. For reasons of her own she seemed to be seeking revenge rather than money, which made her all the more unreliable.

"You've mentioned that you've had several offers of jobs," he said, ignoring the nudges of conscience telling him he was compounding his disloyalty to Jefferson Square. "We might be able to find something here that you'd like. We'd have to put the application through the personnel department, of course, so they could check you out, and I'd have to see what's open."

Sandra laughed. "What a gasser that would be, working at Jefferson Square. I'd be right here to watch the fireworks pop." But she, too, had reservations. "I'm the best executive secretary in town, Mr. Robertson, and I don't work for peanuts."

"I'd try to match other offers." If necessary, he thought, he would pay part of her salary out of his own pocket in order to obtain exclusive use of the information she had obtained.

"That sounds pretty good. But I'd like to think about it for a couple of days. Okay?"

"Fair enough." He was afraid that too much pressure might send her straight to the newspaper office.

"That'll give me a chance to think about your book, too."

"Didn't you have an appointment this afternoon?"

"Sure, but I can put him on ice. He'll keep until I can make up my mind."

"I ask only one thing of you. Please let me know before you show these letters to anyone else."

Never had Sandra been treated as an important person by someone of stature, and she beamed at him as she stood and held out her hand. "Why not? It looks like we're on the same team, Mr. Robertson." She glanced out of the window at the solid structures being erected on all sides of the central plaza. "Between us, we can drop a real H-bomb on Jefferson Square! How about that?"

They quarreled in the taxi all the way to the Sapphire Room, where one of the first dinner parties celebrating the forthcoming opening of Jefferson Square was being held.

Dan was in a whirl. His guilt over Berenice was unalleviated, he found the prospect of talking with Warren Hopkins distasteful, and now, until he heard Sandra Masters' decision about her explosive material, he'd be even more on edge. But he mentioned none of these things.

Instead he complained because he had forgotten the party and resented the need to wear evening clothes. The cold he had caught after spending the better part of a night at his office still bothered him. And the stiff bourbon he had downed while dressing had brought all his hostilities to the surface.

Phyllis was equally unhappy. The children had come down with their father's cold and had been utterly impossible all day, their incessant whining driving her to distraction. And to make matters still worse, Dan was finding fault with literally everything she said and did.

"If you're so miserable," she demanded, "why didn't you say so before we left? Nobody is forcing us to go to this party."

"Ha! You told me in so many words you've been looking forward to it."

"So I have, but—"

"I'd rather go than listen to you moaning and wailing for weeks. This is the lesser evil."

Phyllis started to retort, changed her mind and carefully smoothed her long chiffon skirt. "Is that what I do?" she asked quietly. "Moan and wail?"

"No, not really," he admitted grudgingly.

"Apology accepted."

"Don't start all over again, Phyl!"

Again she was silent for a time. "You've changed, Dan."

"So have you. Nobody stands still."

"I realize you're taking a beating on all sides—"

"I'm not complaining!"

"Let me finish a sentence, please," she said. "Just this once. I keep telling myself your temper will improve, but it gets worse."

"Do you want me to move out?"

She was deeply shocked, and gasped.

Dan realized he had gone too far. "I'm sorry."

"Forget it," Phyllis said with an effort, afraid she would weep unless they changed the subject. "Let's be careful tonight. The pace of city living is beginning to show."

"You and I," Dan said, "aren't made for this mad, mad party whirl. I think one reason we've been squabbling is because we've seen so little of each other lately."

The real reason, she knew, was the incessant pressure on him.

"I wish," he said, sounding unexpectedly boyish and wistful, "that we were staying home tonight."

"So do I."

"I can remember when we were a couple of hicks from the corn belt who would have thrilled at the prospect of going to a party being given by people who are taking over the whole Sapphire Room for it. But that was before we knew the Blackwells."

"They're a charming old couple."

"He has the charm of a boa constrictor. His wife is related to Ben Hopkins, you know, so you can be sure he's getting his cut on these big property deals. No matter how much this party is costing him, there won't be any draughts in his pocket."

"Don't get all worked up again, or you'll have a miserable evening." Phyllis drew her mink more closely around her as the taxi pulled to a halt.

Dan paid the driver, climbed out and helped Phyllis to the pavement. "I haven't been drunk, really drunk, in more years than I can remember. Maybe I'll feel better—or stop feeling altogether—if I take on a load."

She couldn't imagine him drinking too much, and smiled serenely.

They took the express elevator, and found several hundred people milling around the two bars that had been set up in the cocktail lounge of the Sapphire Room. Dan fought through the throng to the checkroom, where he left their coats, then had difficulty in finding Phyllis. After he located her it was another battle to pay their respects to the Blackwells, and by the time they pushed and wormed their way to the nearer bar he was once again in a foul mood.

He ordered a bourbon-and-water for Phyllis and a double bourbon-on-the-rocks for himself, thinking it would be too much of an effort to go through another such struggle just for the sake of a refill. But they found themselves pinned to the wall near the bar, where actors from the Repertory Theater, symphony musicians and Jefferson Square staff employees came up to greet them. There had been a time when Dan would have been pleased by so much attention, but he had grown accustomed to the obeisances made to executives. His legs ached, he was anxious to find their table inside the Sapphire Room itself and sit down, so he gulped his drink. One of the new arrangers recently hired by the symphony handed him another.

The pressure of Phyllis' hand on his arm was a discreet warning to drink more slowly, and Dan realized she was right, but rebelled. He had been handling liquor for a great many years, and knew how to drink.

Anton and Michele Helsing were standing a short distance away, making their first public appearance in weeks, and Dan, aware of his rudeness to the conductor a few days earlier, tried to make up for it by being jovial now. Both couples were constrained at first, and Dan nervously sipped his drink. But the embarrassment passed when they were told they would be sitting at the same table, and although the conviviality was somewhat forced, the tensions eased.

The Blackwells started toward the inner room, and a general movement started in that direction.

"Anton," Dan said, "take the girls to the table, will you? I'll join you in a couple of minutes."

Helsing was agreeable.

Dan drained his glass, set it on the bar and started toward the washroom, making his way against the main flow in the opposite direction. He was feeling the liquor, he knew, but wasn't too concerned; some bread and butter and the first of the dinner's many courses would sop it up.

Suddenly he and Jerry Solanz came face to face. Both stopped short, and Dan felt a sudden urge to hold his ground. He realized he was being infantile, but saw no reason why he should be the one to step aside.

Jerry stiffened and blinked. "Professor No Brain," he said. "It's my bad luck to run into you everywhere. Get out of my way." His voice was thick, he slurred his words, and it was evident that he, too, had been drinking.

Dan said, with surprising calm. "Take off your glasses."

Jerry blinked again, laughed and, removing his glasses, dropped them into the breast pocket of his dinner jacket. Then, in almost the same movement, he lunged.

Dan side-stepped, warding off the blow with his left arm. Then he struck, putting all of his weight and force behind his right fist, which smashed into Jerry's cheekbone.

A woman shrieked, Jerry Solanz crumpled to the floor, and the photographers from the newspapers, who were present to make society page pictures of the event, climbed onto the bar and chairs to record the unexpected clash.

CHAPTER SEVEN

Dan sipped coffee from his breakfast mug and stared ruefully at the open newspapers spread on the kitchen table. "You've got to admit," he said, "that when I do something, I go whole hog. Pictures splashed over all three morning papers. In this one I look as though I'm ready to leap at Solanz again. And in this one I look as though I'm smirking."

"You were smirking," the haggard Phyllis replied. "I saw your expression myself."

"Well, I can't say it caused me any heartache to slug Solanz. But what a place to do it. I'm just thankful not many people at the party knew what happened."

"They knew, Dan. I've never heard word travel so fast."

"At least," he said lamely, "we got what we wanted, an evening at home. You hustled me out of there so fast I hardly had time to apologize to the Blackwells."

"If it's any consolation to you, I think they were pleased. Not that you and Jerry behaved like a pair of ten-year-old boys. But they loved all the excitement."

"I'm glad somebody got something out of it." He put his empty mug on the sink, glanced at his watch and sighed. "Here goes. Round one."

"I still think you're silly to resign."

"I have no real choice. A man in my position loses his usefulness when he embarrasses the square as I did." His smile thin, he went into their bedroom, picked up the telephone and dialed rapidly.

Perhaps it was just his imagination, but he was sure he heard amusement in the voice of Benjamin Hopkins' secretary as she asked him to wait.

"Good morning, Robertson." Ben Hopkins, as always sounded cool, almost remote.

"Good morning, Mr. Hopkins." Dan had rehearsed his

speech carefully. "I suppose you've seen this morning's newspapers—"

"Yes. I was particularly interested in the text of the President's press conference. If I interpreted him correctly, some additional funds will be made available to culture centers."

Dan was surprised by his reaction, and floundered. "That isn't what I meant. I was referring to last night's—"

"I also glanced through an interesting review of a book on the effect of hostilities on accidents. You might enjoy reading it."

"Mr. Hopkins, I—"

"When men are under tension, unfortunate incidents sometimes occur. This one is closed." Hopkins rang off.

Dan stood for a moment, then replaced the telephone in the cradle and turned to Phyllis, who had come into the room. "He wouldn't listen to me. He didn't even give me a chance to offer my resignation."

"Mr. Hopkins has perspective, even if you don't."

Dan took his suit jacket from its hanger. "All right. I'm still on the square payroll. As of this morning. Now, round two."

"Wait," Phyllis said. "I know we spent most of the night talking ourselves hoarse, but I honestly don't see what you can gain by going to see Jerry Solanz. There'll be another fight. I just know it."

"I promise you, Phyl, I'll keep my temper under control, no matter what. But I've got to do it. With the opening of the Repertory Theater only a couple of weeks away, we'll have complete chaos if he walks out. And he just might. We'd have to postpone the opening of *Confessional*. We might even have to cancel it."

"Would that be so awful? You've said all along that it isn't a very good play."

"It would be a catastrophe, and my opinion of the play doesn't matter. More than sixty groups have bought seats for various performances, many of them taking over the whole theater. We can't change our schedule."

She followed him to the front-hall closet. "Then be careful. Please."

"Don't worry. I've had enough newspaper coverage to last the rest of my life."

The immediate problem was tactical, whether to announce

himself from the lobby or go straight to Solanz' suite, and Dan decided the latter would be wiser since it would give Solanz less chance to turn him away. In the elevator he thought people were looking at him, but told himself that he was being ultra-sensitive, or paranoid, or both. Then, at the entrance to the suite, he braced himself.

Jerry, attired in slacks and sports jacket, opened the door and blinked in astonishment. "Of all the two hundred million people in the United States," he said, "you're the last one I expected to see standing here."

Dan had to admit he had a sense of humor. "May I come in for a minute? I'm carrying no concealed weapons, and no boxing gloves."

Jerry shrugged. "Why not?" he muttered, and led the way into the living room.

Berenice was sitting at the room-service breakfast table, and an expression of genuine pleasure appeared in her eyes when she saw Dan.

He had hoped she wouldn't be present, and her appearance increased his embarrassment. She was wearing a two-piece sleeping outfit, nothing more than a bra and a bikini, and over it had thrown a flimsy negligee that was semi-transparent. Huge gold hoops dangled from her ears, and he wondered if she wore earrings to bed.

"Hi!" she called, her enthusiasm greater than her discretion.

"Sweetie," Jerry told her, "make yourself scarce."

"I have no objection to having her hear what I have to say," Dan said, and hoped his smile of greeting was impersonal.

Again Jerry shrugged. "I'm listening."

Dan looked around the room, and saw that Jerry, too, had opened all the newspapers to the photo of their fight. "I hope *Confessional* gets as good a press."

Jerry made no reply.

The delight in Berenice's eyes was so obvious that Dan felt certain there would be an explosion if Solanz happened to glance in her direction. "Solanz," he said, "I'm here to apologize. Not for our little scrap. Both of us had been building up to it. I'm just sorry we let it happen where it did."

"You caught me by surprise, or the results would have been different, Robertson!"

Dan felt a twinge of disappointment when he saw that the

296

other man's face was unmarked. Perhaps, he thought, his own prowess wasn't as great as the immediate consequences of the exchange had led him to assume. But, in any event, he could afford to be generous. "I'm willing to concede that you're the better boxer."

Berenice stifled a giggle, and her admiration for Dan became still more evident.

"I'm even willing to concede that you could probably knock me down if we went at it again."

Jerry ran a hand around the inside of his open-throated shirt. "I've never earned my money in the ring, and neither have you. So why all this crap?"

Berenice could keep quiet no longer. "Don't you see, Jerry? He wants to be friends."

"Either shut your goddam mouth or get out." Jerry did not bother to look at her.

She reacted as though she had been slapped.

Dan fought to control his temper. "Up to a point," he said, "Berenice is right. You and I will never be buddies—"

"What an astute observation!"

"—but we've got to work together—"

"Who says?"

"Your contract with the square. And mine. And if we carry on a feud, it's the square that will suffer. If you want to hate me, there's nothing I can or would do to stop you. And my private opinion of you is my own business. But we'd be smart to bury the knives in public."

"I've already spent a half-hour on the phone with my lawyer this morning," Jerry said coldly. "He says there's no way I can bar you from my rehearsals or from the Repertory Theater."

"He's right."

"He also says I have no grounds for a lawsuit. There were witnesses—and he happened to be one of them—who think I was as much of a horse's ass as you were."

"I'll keep my own views on that," Dan said. "But I am proposing we act like big boys. Gentlemen, if we can."

"I don't go for this Boy Scout shit. But I agree because it's better for my own public image. I intend to be around show business for a long time. Long after you've been shipped back to Podunk College."

"You're trying to start something again," Berenice murmured.

"There's one condition," Jerry said, seething. "Keep the hell away from my girl!"

Dan looked at Berenice, then turned back to Jerry when he felt himself beginning to waver. "I don't want your girl," he said, and hoped his voice sounded level and calm.

"Want her, don't want her, it's all the same to me. But stay away from her!"

They glowered at each other. Only Berenice enjoyed the confrontation. She curled her bare legs under her and leaned forward, elbows on the breakfast table.

Dan realized that the bra of her sleeping outfit was loose-fitting, and that she was revealing her small but lovely breasts. A sudden surge of desire for her was a warning to leave before the situation became even more complicated. "I'm too busy to come to your rehearsals today, Solanz, and it's just as well. I don't want to be a distracting influence."

"You're so considerate I think I'll puke."

Dan nodded to Berenice, then walked straight to the door.

"If I were a prize-fight manager instead of a publisher," Harvey Simpson said expansively, "I'd sign you to a long-term personal contract. I'd—"

"I haven't come here to listen to jokes," Dan snapped.

Harvey sat back behind his desk, still grinning. "You'll have to develop a tough hide for the next few days. Everybody who knows you is going to—"

"Never mind. I'm here because I think I'm going to get all the factual material I need to substantiate my charges of a real estate swindle at the square," Dan said. "And a great deal more." He launched into a detailed explanation of Sandra Masters' visit to his office.

Harvey's smile faded, and he listened intently. "Do you really believe Governor Herder is a partner in Harrison, MacFee?"

"So it appears. I'll want corroboration, which is simple enough to get. There's a list of the stockholders of every company incorporated in the state that's on record somewhere in the official archives. I'm going to the Capitol library this morning, and if I can't find what I want there, I'll keep looking."

"This book keeps getting bigger." Harvey's geniality was non-existent when he was on the scent of a project that would create a sensation. "We'll be in print long before the political conventions, and it will completely knock Herder out of the running for President. What a scramble that will cause!"

"I've been trying to imagine his motives," Dan said. "He's already a rich man, and—"

"His motives don't matter. He's doing it. He's coining money on Jefferson Square from every angle. His grandfather was a pirate, and so was his father, so I suppose the appetite runs in his bloodstream. Deal with the facts, Dan, and leave his motives to the psychiatrists. The most important thing right now," Harvey said emphatically, "is nailing down this Masters woman. We can forget the book if she goes to one of the newspapers."

"I'm reasonably confident she won't."

"When are you seeing her again?"

"I expect her to get in touch with me before the end of the week."

Harvey chewed on the stem of an unlighted pipe, his own plans forming rapidly in his mind. "We're going to have an even bigger book than we thought, Dan. Stick to your typewriter—and keep out of fights."

Symphony Hall's acoustical problems had been solved at last. Men carrying sound meters and sophisticated electronic equipment had been roaming the auditorium for weeks, especially during the orchestra's daily rehearsals, and others, relying on their own hearing and experience, had been even more critical. New, inner walls had been installed, and all that remained of the original plans were the crystal chandeliers that descended from a ceiling that had been rebuilt three times.

The results, Anton Helsing said, were well worth the efforts. Of all auditoriums used in the twentieth century, only the Vienna Opera and Chicago's old Orchestra Hall had better acoustics. Even the carpeting had been replaced, and the railings on the mezzanine and balcony had been covered in thick velvet. "Not only can you hear a pin drop," Anton said after listening to a three-hour rehearsal of the orchestra, "but it makes a musical sound."

For all practical purposes the auditorium itself was finished, and the decorators confined their activities to the glass and marble lobbies, the padded elevators and the sweeping staircases where free-form metal art works were being erected, many of them suspended from the high dome of double glass that would enable music lovers to see the stars in the heavens on clear nights.

Gradually the musicians were taking possession of their future home. The assistant director and the concertmaster, no longer obliged to play for the benefit of the acoustical engineers, concentrated on their own activities. Members of the orchestra arrived early for rehearsals and lingered late, seldom venturing into the twin Green Rooms where they would relax, play cards and drink coffee. Even the arrangers, already at work in their tiny cubicles, left their upright pianos and sound-proofed walls to venture repeatedly into the main hall.

Maxwell de Groot claimed that the Jefferson Square Opera Company would be the real beneficiary of the symphony's early mistakes. His own building still in the early stages of construction, the director of the opera spent hours each day in Symphony Hall, an unlighted cigar clenched between his teeth as he and his many assistants read the gauges of the engineers, listened to the arguments, watched the rebuilding, and took notes.

Opera Company singers were drawn to Symphony Hall too, as were music students, virtuosos of piano, violin and cello, and, inevitably, the celebrity-hungry wives of Jefferson Square Board members. One afternoon Dan Robertson counted an audience of more than four hundred and fifty in the hall.

Anton, who did not mount the podium during this hectic period, seemed unaware of the excitement. His own composition, the *Jefferson Square Concerto,* still occupied most of his time and energies, and only after the last of the acoustical problems had been settled did he begin to immerse himself in preparations for the gala openings and the programs to follow.

Dan, sitting with Michele Helsing in the main auditorium of Symphony Hall late one morning, was dazed by Anton's seemingly inexhaustible energies. The lethargy that had seemed to possess him for so long had vanished, and he was everywhere, on the stage in animated conversation with his concertmaster and the members of his string sections, in the front of the hall arguing with the arrangers, sitting in the rear with the orchestra's business manager and checking subscription lists.

"He's been up and down that stage at least twenty times

in the last hour," Dan said, watching him as he flourished a sheaf of sheet music and spoke animatedly with three of the arrangers. "What do you feed him—raw meat?"

"He doesn't eat, and his sleep is a joke," Michele replied. "He'll lose at least ten pounds between now and opening night."

Dan stared at the dapper Anton, towering and trim in a matching outfit of jacket, turtle-neck sweater and slacks.

"Oh, he'll be fine." She patted the bulge at the hips of her tweed Chanel suit. "I'm sorry to say I won't lose a single pound. In fact, I'll gain weight, and go through hell having it pounded off."

Anton was becoming increasingly angry. "Very well," he shouted. "I'll prove you have tin ears. Rudi!"

The assistant director appeared from the wings.

"Full orchestra on stage, please!" Anton turned back to the arrangers, gesticulating furiously.

"I feel sorrier for them than I do for myself," Michele said. "He's a demon about his arrangements. I've seen him throw a tantrum over nothing more than two or three bars that he doesn't like."

The members of the orchestra began to drift onto the stage, took their places and started tuning their instruments.

Anton jabbed so hard at a sheet of music to illustrate a point that he poked a hole through it. But none of the arrangers laughed, and the youngest of them, a slender man in his late twenties with curly, black hair, looked as though he might burst into tears.

"I knew he was going to be a bastard today," Michele said. "I gave him a new Jaguar convertible for his birthday, and he insisted I drive him here this morning—he hasn't been behind the wheel yet. And all he did was criticize my driving from the moment we left the house. I know how that arranger feels. I was ready to do some screaming of my own."

"Is it the interview with *Look* tomorrow afternoon that's bothering him?" Dan asked.

"It's everything."

"We could postpone it a day or two, if that would help."

"Don't. He'll go from impossible to absolutely unbearable in the next month." Michele spoke calmly, and was actually smiling.

At last the full orchestra was assembled, and Anton mounted the podium. When he picked up the baton on the stand there was a murmur of appreciation in the audience, and he turned, his manner icy. "I must ask all unauthorized persons to leave at once," he called. "All of you!"

People rose reluctantly from their seats, and Dan started from his seat, too.

"He doesn't mean us," Michele said.

Max de Groot paused beside them for a moment, and removed his cigar from his mouth. "I don't blame Anton," he said. "Visitors can be a damned nuisance. But I want you to remember this, Dan—you're my witness. He'll have a fit when I throw him out of one of my opera rehearsals, but I'll do it." Chuckling, he wandered up the aisle.

At last Anton was satisfied that the hall had been cleared. Tapping with the baton for attention, he addressed his musicians. "Gentlemen," he said, "your impartial assistance is needed to settle a friendly dispute."

Someone in the woodwinds laughed.

Anton glared at him, and he subsided abruptly. "Now, gentlemen. We'll do Number Fourteen, the first movement, from the top. Take care to play your parts precisely as they're written."

Pages rustled, and the musicians poised themselves.

Anton tapped twice on the side of his music stand, and raised the baton.

The selection was unfamiliar to Dan, but he was impressed by the authority of the conductor, the professionalism of the musicians. To the best of his knowledge Anton Helsing and the orchestra had not worked together on the number, but their efforts blended flawlessly, the men responding instantly to the nuances their director demanded, their teamwork a blend of harmonious perfection.

The music soared, its tempo diminishing, and then the strings played alone, more rapidly.

The arrangers, sitting in the seventh or eighth row, were making scribbled notations on their sheet music.

Michele was listening critically, her back arched, her head cocked. "He's right, of course," she whispered.

Dan could hear nothing wrong, nothing that jarred him. He enjoyed music, and by the standards of the ordinary layman was something of an expert, especially in the history of music, but the subtleties of the dispute were beyond his grasp.

There was a brief silence when, after a quarter of an hour,

the movement ended. Anton tucked the baton under his arm and bowed slightly. "Thank you, gentlemen," he said. "What time do you want them this afternoon, Rudi?"

"At two," the assistant called.

"Your slave driver expects you at two o'clock. Enjoy a long and leisurely lunch, gentlemen."

The musicians began to move off.

Anton, taking his time, placed his baton on the rack, then fussed with the loose sheets of his score, which he finally settled to his satisfaction in a folder. At last he turned to the arrangers, his expression arrogantly scornful. "Well?"

"It was obvious after the first five minutes that you were right," the principal arranger replied.

"And what does Teddy Howard say?"

"Very little, Mr. Helsing." The young arranger looked crestfallen.

Anton bounded down the steps from the stage, hurled himself into a seat beside the upset Teddy Howard and, opening his score, began to speak rapidly.

"Chalk up a point for the home team," Michele said. "After a victory like this he may even become human for a few hours."

"I couldn't hear a thing wrong," Dan confessed.

"You haven't been married for years to a musician who won't settle for less than one hundred percent." She spoke dryly, but without bitterness.

"I'm anxious to hear his *Concerto*."

"It's the best he's ever done. And it'll silence old fossils like Henri Broussard forever. Even when it becomes maddening to live with Anton, I remind myself that he's a genius and needs special treatment. He's doing work that will live long after all of us are gone."

Her loyalty was so fierce, so protective that Dan smiled. "Are the Helsings having lunch with me today?"

"I reminded Anton as we were driving up here that you have an agenda of a dozen or two items to take up with him. He groaned, but he knows it's necessary, so I don't think he'll balk."

"I'm just sorry to subject you to a lot of business."

Michele shrugged. "I'm used to it. Whenever Anton is in one of his crisis states, he needs me on tap twenty-four hours a day as a nursemaid." Suddenly she stiffened. "I also have my own reasons for wanting to be near him," she added.

Dan followed the direction of her glance and saw that Anton, still talking to the arrangers, had draped an arm around the chair of Teddy Howard. Although ostensibly concentrating on work, he was absently toying with the short, black curls at the nape of the young arranger's neck.

Michele stared at the scene, her body rigid.

Dan felt as sorry for her as he did for Anton.

"You've seen what I see," Michele said, speaking in a very low, controlled tone.

"Yes."

"When he's under great tension," she said, "he becomes inclined to slip."

Dan groped for a polite rejoinder.

"Could your business questions with Anton wait until later in the week?" Michele asked.

"Sure."

"Then let's postpone the date. I'm afraid I've suddenly become quite tired."

"I know your name from the columns," Sandra said, taking Harvey Simpson's hat and coat. "You're in café society."

"I wouldn't claim that distinction." Harvey glanced around the one-room apartment and, instinctively avoiding the sofa-bed, chose the one armchair. "May I sit down?"

"I wish you would. Maybe I could get you a cup of coffee, or a drink."

"Neither, at the moment, but thank you. I'd like to talk first." Harvey settled himself in the chair. "Dan Robertson was in to see me this morning—"

"What a man!" Sandra exclaimed, perching on the edge of her sofa-bed. "Did you see this morning's papers?"

"I'm afraid so." Harvey realized his humor sailed over her head. "He told me about your meeting with him, Miss Masters. That's why I'm here, without his knowledge, although I intend to tell him about our visit, of course."

She wished she weren't wearing one of her oldest wool dresses and the quick makeup job she reserved for neighborhood shopping.

"I wonder if you'd let me see the documents you showed Dan.

Sandra momentarily forgot her appearance. "How do I know you're who you say?"

For an instant Harvey was puzzled; then he smiled and took

his wallet from his pocket. "You'll find my driver's license and a number of credit cards here," he said, handing her the wallet. "I'm also carrying several letters. Let me see. Here's one addressed to me from a literary agent."

She studied the cards, then read the letter.

Obviously, Harvey thought, she was a person who took no unnecessary risks.

"Is Helga Borg really going to write a book for you?"

"Well, I don't know. The idea is being discussed."

"I've seen every movie she's ever made."

Harvey retrieved his wallet and letter. "Do my credentials satisfy you, Miss Masters?"

Sandra nodded, looking embarrassed. "I had to be sure. You know how it is." She walked to a table at the far side of a room, unlocked a drawer and took out a sheaf of photocopies of letters. "Here they are."

Harvey looked through them quickly, not bothering to read them, but merely establishing their identity. Dan was right; these documents were all he had claimed, and the reference to Governor Herder's partnership in the contracting firm leaped out at him. "Dan Robertson is right," he said. "This data will be a very helpful addition to his book."

"I've just made up my mind to let him have it, but I'm not one hundred percent sure."

"Perhaps my methods of persuasion will help you reach a decision." Harvey took a checkbook from his pocket.

Sandra was on the verge of protesting that money wasn't her first consideration, but she quickly changed her mind. If a rich publisher wanted to pay her for the letters, she'd be a fool not to take all she could get.

"What would you call a reasonable sum, Miss Masters?"

Like her mother, she enjoyed driving a bargain. "That depends. The letters wouldn't be worth a nickel to a lot of people, but they seem to mean a lot to you and Mr. Robertson."

Harvey held a pen poised above the checkbook. "How does two thousand strike you?" He realized from her expression that she would have been satisfied with half.

"Three," Sandra said.

Smiling, he made out the check. "You might want to come with me to cash it," he said as he handed it to her. "My bank is only a few minutes from here by taxi, and we can wrap up the deal."

Sandra took the check, thanked him and went for their coats. Obviously he was determined to take no chances, and wanted the letters as soon as possible.

Harvey helped her into her coat, then struggled into his own. "Be sure you bring the papers with you," he said casually.

"You bet." She folded them carefully and put them into her handbag. In a few minutes she had made as much as it took her five months to earn; now she could take her time finding the job she wanted, and could splurge on a new wardrobe as well. There would even be enough to buy some new furniture for Mama and Buddy, once she got them out of the Fourth Street firetrap into a real apartment.

Harvey was satisfied, too.

"I'd never have made a good diplomat." Dan stood at the windows of Warren Hopkins' apartment, looking out at the city, with Warren beside him. "There are dozens of tactful ways to open a subject, but I don't know any of them."

Warren was curious, but slightly impatient. Carolyn was due to arrive in an hour, and unless he could get rid of his unexpected visitor within a reasonable time, he'd have to try to reach her by phone and warn her to wait.

"I'm here to talk about something that is none of my business—by any stretch of the imagination. I've been roped into it, and I'm not even certain how it happened."

"Fire away." Warren was prepared to discuss any aspect of Dan's fight with Jerry Solanz, and believed he could act successfully as a peace-maker.

"Your uncle had a little chat with me."

"Oh?" Warren stiffened.

"He told me he'd also talked with you."

"I suggest we drop it right there," Warren said.

"That's what I'd want to do if our positions were reversed. But put yourself in my place, if you can. I find it very difficult to refuse to listen to a direct order from your uncle."

Warren crossed the room to the hearth and threw a fresh log onto the fire. "You can go back to him," he said, "and tell him we had a long talk. An interminable talk. But I wouldn't listen to a word." He jabbed viciously at the log with a brass-handled poker.

"My private hell," Warren continued, "is that I've never

hated Edward. I've given him cause to think I'm the stinker of the world, but he's done nothing to me. Or to her."

There was no sound in the room but the crackling of the fire. "I wish I were wiser," Warren said at last.

Dan reached for a cigarette. "Well, so much for your uncle's insistence that I have a talk with you. Sorry to have taken your time." Dan stood.

Warren hesitated briefly, then said, "I'd invite you to stay. But Carolyn will be here soon."

"I've already had one very brief, unpleasant and abortive talk with her, some weeks ago. As she probably told you. I prefer not to embarrass her."

Warren accompanied him to the front hall, and took his hat and coat from the closet. They shook hands and Dan went out to the elevator.

He would report to Ben Hopkins that, although he had no idea what Warren would do, they had had their talk.

Anton sipped his highball as he watched his wife close the door of her bedroom behind them and draw the drapes, cutting off the daylight. "What's all this?" he demanded.

Instead of answering in words, Michele went to him and kissed him.

"Love at high noon?" he asked, amused. "This is a busy day."

"I told you I postponed our lunch date with Dan Robertson."

"Yes, but I have a few dozen other—"

"They can wait." She kissed him again, more fervently.

Anton remained unresponsive. "I should have guessed when you drove home as though you were behind the wheel of a fire engine."

He was too tense for her to tell him that she had seen the sure signs of a new homosexual involvement; he would listen to reason only when he was relaxed. So still smiling, she pulled out the tail of his turtle-neck shirt and, reaching up under it, began to brush her fingertips back and forth across his nipples.

"I have work to do!" Anton tried to back away.

Michele moved with him, stroking more rapidly, her touch still light. "You know you like it," she said briskly.

"Well, yes, but—"

"Relax and enjoy it. You've been celibate long enough." She maneuvered him toward the bed, and, pulling sweater higher, bent to kiss the nipples.

Anton made an effort to get away, but the attempt was half-hearted.

Michele increased her efforts and soon felt him respond. He would no longer try to free himself, she knew; he was in her hands, to treat as she pleased.

Unable to stop himself, he began to wriggle. "You're a clever bitch."

She raised her head long enough to murmur, "I think so, too." Then she undressed him and herself.

Anton helped as best he could, but was trembling.

Slowly, teasing him, Michele inched a hand up the inside of his thigh. He gasped, tried to sit up and then fell back, squirming.

She laughed. "Who knows how to make love to you?"

"You do." Anton's breathing was heavy.

"Better than anyone?"

"Yes."

She was dominating him completely, and there was a hint of cruelty in her voice as she demanded, "Then say it. The whole thing."

"You make love to me—better—than anyone else."

It pleased her that she was in command, that he would beg her to resume if, as she had sometimes done in the past, she stopped abruptly. But her one aim was to exhaust him sexually, at least temporarily, in the hope that he would resist his attraction to Teddy Howard.

Anton's eyes were glazed as he submitted to her caresses. When his movements became convulsive, Michele threw herself onto him.

His convulsions became wilder and he sobbed for breath before falling limp.

She kissed him, gently now, and stroked his face. "How was it?"

He opened his eyes for an instant. "Wonderful."

Michele remained close to him for a short time before disengaging herself. Her husband's steady breathing told her that he had dropped off to sleep; if he followed his usual routine, he would nap for an hour or two.

She crossed the room to get her dressing gown, absently picking up clothing strewn on the floor. This was the only form of love-making she had known for so long that she could scarcely remember how she felt when a man took the initiative. It didn't matter, really; her satisfactions went far beyond the physical, and the hope that Anton would not look at Teddy Howard provided a pleasure all its own.

"He's manic today," Jan Marek said in a low voice as Dan came into the main auditorium of the Repertory Theater. "Stay back here with me, out of the way."

Dan nodded and slipped into a seat at the rear, beside the playwright. "Any special problems?"

"Berenice again."

"Is she that bad?"

"The way Jerry is beating at her and riding her, even Siddons or Bernhardt would come unglued."

"Now what's the trouble?"

"Everything. Nothing."

"I'm afraid I'm not in a position to tamp him down. If I say a word to him, it'll make him worse. Can't you do it?"

Marek shook his head. "Not when he's operating on jet fuel. And I'm not sure I want to interfere, Dan. I feel sorry as hell for Berenice, but Jerry knows what he's doing."

"Are you sure?"

"Yes. I've seen him do this with others in the final days of rehearsals. I don't know whether his rages are deliberate— I'm inclined to suspect they are. He drives an actor to the thin edge of madness, and somehow gets the performance out of him that he's wanted all along. It's brutal, but it seems to work."

Julian Adams and two other actors were doing a scene from the second act of *Confessional*, and Dan, thoroughly familiar with it, looked around at the theater, into which the company had moved the preceding day. Even in the glare of the naked-bulbed work-light, it was lovely. The seats had been done in a deep red velvet, the walls and dome were a green that gave a feeling of clean spaciousness, and the gold trim added to the richness of the overall effect.

It was difficult to remember the early days of the square, when architects and decorators had been split into feuding camps. Those who had favored stark modernism had insisted that America's newest legitimate theater would look hopelessly old-fashioned, but they had been mistaken. The repertory had a late eighteenth-century air rather than the overly rococo that had been in vogue during the earlier part of that era and had been slavishly copied in nineteenth-century theaters. It was a compliment to everyone connected with the repertory that David Garrick would have felt as at home here as did the company that Jerry Solanz had assembled.

Berenice made her entrance, hesitated before crossing the stage and faltered as she delivered her first line.

"Here we go again," Marek muttered.

Jerry rose from his third-row seat and loudly clapped his hands together. "Hold it! Will you be good enough to step down to the apron, Miss Tolmey?"

Berenice reluctantly moved downstage.

"Tell me, Miss Tolmey, are you an imbecile or an actress? Are you an inanimate puppet with sawdust in your head, or are you a real, live woman?" Jerry's tone was as scathing as his words.

"You have me so rattled I don't know what I'm doing," Berenice said plaintively.

"By now the part of Paula should be inside you. By now you should be Paula. Every word, every gesture should be second nature to you. How in Christ's name do you expect to give a performance when there's an audience out front if you can't even remember your lines?"

Berenice started to reply.

But Jerry cut her off by clapping his hands together again. "And that god-awful business on your entrance, Miss Tolmey! What's your excuse for that?"

"I know I'm supposed to walk toward stage left," she said, "but I don't feel it that way. I keep wanting to move stage right."

"You want? Who cares what you want? I've told you where to move. I've told you until I'm hoarse, and it does no good!" Jerry was working himself into a rage.

The other members of the cast were embarrassed, but Julian Adams was the only one with enough stature to intervene. "It won't bother me if she wants to make her move stage right, Jerry. It's a valid interpretation, you know. When Paula sees Chuck she might want to keep her distance from him instead of—"

"I appreciate your help, Julian." There was only a hint of sarcasm in Jerry's voice now. "Either way is valid. But I'm thinking of how it looks from out here, and if she moves

310

stage right, it looks clumsy. Now, Miss Tolmey! Aren't you ashamed of yourself? You're fluffing your lines and stumbling through your business so badly that even your colleagues are forced to step in, hoping they can help you. I think you owe the rest of the company an apology, Miss Tolmey."

Berenice stood very still, rooted in misery.

"Goddammit, Miss Tolmey—apologize!" Jerry roared.

Dan started to rise from his seat. "This is too much."

Jan Marek hauled him back. "Don't interfere or he'll go berserk."

"Don't you have a voice?" Jerry was livid. "We're all waiting, Miss Tolmey!"

Julian Adams took pity on the girl. "She doesn't need to apologize, Jerry." He went to Berenice and put an arm around her shoulders. "Just ease up, kid, and everything will go fine. We're all with you."

Berenice looked at him in mute gratitude, then wrenched herself free, and started down the steps from the stage into the auditorium.

"Where do you think you're going?" Jerry screamed.

"I need some fresh air." Her voice was low, but carried.

"Come back here!"

She paid no attention and made her way slowly up the aisle.

"I'll apologize on her behalf, ladies and gentlemen," Jerry called. "And while Miss Tolmey gets her fresh air—or goes to the can—or whatever she's going to do, let's not waste our own time, which happens to be valuable. Try the next scene, please, from the top."

Dan exhaled slowly.

Berenice saw him with Jan Marek, and came toward him, slowly.

Dan saw she was trembling, and that her eyes were unnaturally bright.

She halted beside him, and a quaking hand touched his shoulder for an instant. "I don't know how much more of this I can take," she said, and fled into the lobby.

Marek reached out to hold Dan in his seat. "Don't follow her, or you'll give Jerry another reason to bray at her."

"He's a sadistic son of a bitch," Dan said bitterly.

"So he is. He's also the best director in the business. One of the toughest, roughest, no-holds-barred businesses in the

311

world. Nobody forced her to become an actress. Her own ego drives have brought her here, and if it's too much for her, she ought to quit."

Betsy Callison sat at the dressing table in her bedroom, and was combing her hair when a tap sounded at her door.

"May I come in?" her father asked.

"Of course, Daddy. Don't you look elegant! New dinner jacket?"

Charles Callison preened. "I'm just breaking it in tonight. I guess I don't look too bad for an old man."

"You're not old! You look distinguished. And handsome."

"And you're the prettiest liar in town." He sat on her bed, the ice tinkling in the highball glass he carried. "Don't let me interrupt you."

Bettina picked up her brush again.

"Going out tonight?"

"Mmm."

"Anywhere special?"

"Not really. We thought we'd try the new restaurant that's just opened on the roof of the Four Eighty-Three Building."

"The Golden something-or-other."

"That's it. And then we thought we'd drop over to Jefferson Square. There's so much happening there these days." She picked up a can of hair spray.

"By 'we' I assume you mean you and Warren."

Betsy nodded.

"You don't see much of anyone else these days."

"Of course I do!"

"This is the season when your mother and I seem to have something doing nearly every night, so I'm probably not caught up on the subject of your dates." Charles Callison sounded diplomatically apologetic. "I suppose it just seems as though you see more of Warren than anyone else."

"Oh, I do, but there's nothing serious between us." She started to spray her hair.

"That's good."

Her father's unexpected bluntness startled her, and she stared at him for a moment. "Why is it good?"

"When I was an ambassador," her father replied, "I always took pride in my ability to say nothing with great style. I liked to imagine I had the polish of Voltaire being interrogated by the bishops. A self-flattering conceit, but harmless. However, I never learned how to say something of substance with grace." He took a small cigar from a gold case. "May I?"

"Of course." She knew him too well to push, and waited impatiently.

He took a long time lighting the cigar. "Your mother tells me something that corroborates my own impressions, that you're in love with Warren Hopkins."

"I have been for a long time, Daddy."

Callison studied the glowing tip of the cigar. "I realize that adults—and I credit you with being a grown woman—don't use switches or buttons to turn their emotions on and off. All the same—"

"All the same," she interrupted, "I've pulled every switch and pushed every button."

Her father scrutinized her. "Then you know."

She nodded.

"Recently?"

"No, for a long time. It seems like forever."

"Your mother indicated something of the sort, but I found it hard to believe, since rumors were called to my attention only recently. The trouble with the women in my family is that they don't confide in me. Care for part of my drink? Or may I get you one?"

"No, thanks. I've been on a diet-cola kick lately."

"Surely you're not dieting! Even granting my prejudices in your favor, your figure is superb."

"It's all right. I just like the taste of diet-colas, that's all."

Callison dragged on his cigar, reflecting that young people, in spite of their surface sophistication, were as vulnerable and naïve as their elders had been at the same age.

"If Mother has talked to you about me, then she's told you that I'm—waiting."

"The climate here isn't conducive to that sort of thing. You might enjoy a Mediterranean cruise. A long one. Or a trip to the West Coast. You have a classmate living in California, I believe, and from there you might want to visit Acapulco—"

"Why should I go away, Daddy?" Betsy picked up a lipstick and began sliding its metal top off and on.

"I think it might be very helpful if you're not here when the bubble bursts. In fact, your mother is prepared to go with you if—"

313

"I don't need Mother as a chaperone or a hand-holder! Sorry. That didn't come out the way I intended it. But you still haven't answered me, Daddy. What do you know that I don't?"

"More things than either of us has time to count. I'm not preaching morality to you, Bettina."

"I'd be the last to say that a man has—lived well, as one might put it—would necessarily be a poor risk as a husband. Your mother and I have no major complaints, but I don't mind admitting that before I married her I lived a rather spectacular life for some years. If Warren were to ask me for your hand tonight—and that's a conceit that dates me, doesn't it?—I'd give him my blessings, or whatever it is that the father of the bride gives on such occasions. I know of nothing basically wrong with him except his money. He has too much of it."

"You have a reputation as a wit, Daddy." Betsy was annoyed. "And as you admitted yourself just now, you can apply great style to very little. I still haven't been told why I should go on a long cruise, with or without Mother."

"I went to prep school with Edward Emory." Callison rattled the ice in his glass. "My memories of those days are very vivid. He lives up to the proper image of a banker, but he was quite different then. He was an athlete—a rugged athlete, and he had one of the ugliest tempers I've ever seen. Everyone in the dorm was careful not to cross him."

"What are you suggesting?"

"The whole town is buzzing, Bettina. I can only tell you that within the last week the subject has been raised twice at lunch, at the Tennis and Badminton Club, and again yesterday afternoon at the Union-City Club bar. When everyone Edward Emory knows is whispering behind his back, someone is certain to say something aloud. And his hearing is excellent."

"I see."

"Do you? I wonder. In times of great stress most of us revert to childhood patterns. I'm remembering not only that he had a hair-trigger temper, but was also an excellent shot when we went on hunting trips together in later years. Now, have I said enough to satisfy you?"

"Yes, enough to keep me right here at home!"

Callison's mask of urbanity slipped. "Apparently I haven't made the situation clear."

314

"But you have, Daddy. I understand there may be a scandal, and that Warren might even be attacked by Mr. Emory. That's all I need to know." Betsy turned back to her mirror, and began to apply the lipstick.

Her father stood. "My candor deserves the same in return, I think."

She did not reply until she had finished with the lipstick and blotted her mouth with a tissue. "I've been a coward. For a long time. I've gone out with Warren, pretending life is normal, and hoping that if I waited long enough he'd come to me. I haven't allowed myself to feel humiliated, or even to resent him because he's hidden behind me. But I'm through with that. I'm going to talk to him tonight."

"You might be wise to think about this for a day or two before you do anything rash," Callison said.

Betsy flipped back her long hair. "For month after month I've been doing nothing but thinking. I've accomplished nothing, and I've made myself miserable. I've tried to forget Warren and put him out of my life, but I've failed. Now I want a little action, and I have nothing to lose."

Perhaps she was naïve, her father thought, but she was not lacking in courage.

"Even your generation," Betsy said, "can understand the expression for what I intend to do tonight. I'm going for broke."

The work pace of the Jefferson Square office staff was becoming frantic. The first two units were preparing for their openings, other buildings were being erected at a rate ahead of schedule, and demolition would begin soon on the last slum dwellings to be torn down in the vast plot that would encompass the culture center. A steady flow of papers moved across Dan Robertson's desk, and he received so many telephone calls that, although he had always made it a practice to talk to anyone who wanted to speak to him, he had been forced to instruct his secretary to screen his calls.

In spite of the staggering load, however, he was finding it difficult to concentrate. The preparation of his book took up every evening he could spare, and he was so tired that on Sundays, his only holidays, he found himself falling asleep after wading through the newspapers.

He had the ever-present feeling of falling behind, and it was aggravating to discover he was constantly distracted by thoughts of Berenice. But he did not love her, therefore he believed he could control his desire for her. On the other hand, she continued to intrude into his thoughts, and he repeatedly found himself picturing her as she had looked when she had fled from Jerry Solanz' rehearsal, her pride shattered, her sensitive feelings lacerated.

He could not rid himself of the idea that there was an element of tragedy in Berenice, and the notion made him uneasy, no matter how hard he tried to rid himself of it. It was a simple matter to tell himself she was a prisoner of her own ambitions, but no matter how true the observation, he knew she found herself in a situation far more demanding and viciously unpleasant than she had ever bargained for. He was plagued by a desire to help her, even though he realized there was nothing he could do for her.

"Hello, partner!"

Dan was annoyed when he saw that his unannounced visitor was Sandra Masters, who dropped in on him far too frequently. He knew the girls in the office whispered about her, and he certainly couldn't blame them. Her new three-piece suit looked as though it might be expensive, but the short skirt was far too tight, and the plunging neckline of her blouse was so low-cut it offended his taste. Even her new cape was theatrical, and she had as much makeup on her face as actresses wore on stage.

"How are you?" he muttered, rising from his chair for a moment.

Sandra took the most comfortable seat in the office and made herself at home. "Right this minute I need a stiff drink," she said. "How about taking me over to one of those jazzy new bars in the neighborhood?"

Dan murmured something to the effect that he couldn't leave the office.

"Then I'll take a slug right here, if you have a bottle handy." She pulled off her gloves.

He said he was sorry he kept no liquor in the office, and, to be polite, asked, "Is something the matter?"

"Nothing new. I've just been seeing my mother. What an oddball Mama is. You've never seen anything like her. She and some of her buddies are going to be squatters in the Fourth Street tenement you plan to haul down. Honest to God. She's torn up eviction notices, and she swears it won't bother her when they turn off the heat and water. What a

sketch she is! If nothing else drove me to drink, she would!"
Half-rising, she helped herself to a cigarette from an open
package on Dan's desk.

"Her attitude isn't unusual," Dan said. "There's been
trouble with tenants in every building that's been demolished.
Many of them, particularly the immigrants, fight the very
idea of moving."

"Why? I don't dig it!" Sandra was still upset.

"As I understand it, tenements represent the only security
they know."

"I've told Mama a thousand times I'll pay the rent on her
new apartment, for God's sake!"

"If she's like the others, she may feel intimidated by a
high-rise building."

The girl sensed his restlessness. "I didn't really come here
to bitch about Mama. How's our book?"

He averted his face so she wouldn't see him laugh. It was
ludicrous that she considered herself his collaborator, but he
supposed she had developed high-flown ideas after Harvey
had given her so much money. Harvey, he still thought, had
been unnecessarily generous.

"I'm making progress," he said. "I hope."

Sandra's face fell. "It isn't done yet?"

"I'm afraid not."

"How soon will you finish it?" she asked insistently.

"That depends on quite a few factors, including the time
at my disposal. I doubt if I'll be able to do much more until
the Repertory Theater and Symphony Hall have opened."

"And after that how long will it take?"

He found her prying attitude irritating, but tried to remain
civil. "Two or three months, if I'm lucky."

Sandra stared at him, increasingly disturbed. "Then Simpson and Smith will publish it right away?"

"More or less, but that depends on what you call 'right
away.' Harvey Simpson will edit it himself, and I don't know
how many other manuscripts are on his personal schedule.
Printers are jammed these days, too, and it isn't easy to buy
paper. So it usually takes six to eight months to publish a
book once it goes into production."

"Are you giving me a run-around?" she demanded hotly.

Her sudden antagonism startled him. "Certainly not. Why
should I?"

"If my arithmetic is right, it'll take a whole year before the book is published!"

"It will be approximately a year."

"Screw that," Sandra said. "I want those snotty bastards nailed to the wall now!"

Dan didn't know what to say.

"If I'd gone to the newspaper, the story would have been printed in the column the very next day!" She was glaring at him, her long nails digging into the palms of her hands.

"There's a great difference between newspaper and book publishing," Dan said. "I assumed you understood—"

"I might be dead by a year from now. All of them might be dead, too. I wouldn't have made a deal with you if I'd thought it would take forever."

Dan refused to be browbeaten by this thoroughly unpleasant young woman. "I'm afraid there's nothing I can do about it," he said stiffly.

"I want those letters back!"

He had no intention of giving them to her. "It was my publisher, not I, who bought them from you. And I have no idea whether he'd be willing to let you buy them back from him." He knew very well, of course, that Harvey would not entertain the notion for a moment.

"How can I buy them back when I've spent more than half the money? I don't find thousand-dollar bills in the gutter!"

"It seems to me you'll have to be patient," Dan said. "Talk to Mr. Simpson, if you wish—"

"Sure, I'll talk to him, but I'll get the same double-talk you're giving me. For all I know, you're trying to protect Governor Herder and the rest of that crowd!"

"I'm neither attacking nor defending anyone. I intend to present facts," Dan said, his voice becoming hard.

"Well, I'm not going to wait around. To hell with you, to hell with your book and to hell with Simpson!" Sandra stormed out, slamming the door.

Dan immediately reached for the telephone, called his publisher and told him what had just happened.

"Vindictive, isn't she?" Harvey sounded tranquil.

"She's intending to stir up trouble," Dan said.

"Are you forgetting the letters are stashed away in my safe, one of the most burglar-proof safes manufactured? If it will help you to sleep better, Dan, I'll take them to my safe-deposit box at the Metropolitan-National."

"It's obvious that, with the letters or without, she'll go to the newspapers now."

"Let her. They get letters and calls and visits from cranks every day. They'll do a little checking, and when they learn that she's a former secretary of Francis Dougherty's who was discharged, they'll dismiss her as a sorehead. You had a hard time finding concrete evidence to hang on the square's sponsors, Dan, and so will they. Fortunately, she doesn't know the one thing they could dig out without any real trouble, that the Governor is a silent partner at Harrison, MacFee."

"You make it all sound logical, Harvey, but I don't like this."

"I can't say I relish it myself, but I can assure you that without those photo-copies, the girl can do nothing. No newspaper will publish unsubstantiated charges made against some of the country's leading citizens by a disgruntled nobody."

"I hope you're right, but if you'd seen her just now, you'd agree that she has an unlimited, vicious ability to make mischief."

A subdued Anton Helsing slumped in the Jaguar's bucket passenger seat, paying no attention to other cars as his wife wove in and out of traffic. "Sometimes," he said morosely, "you make me feel dreadfully inadequate."

Michele swerved slightly to avoid a taxi that cut in without warning. Then, not taking her eyes from the road, she reached out and patted his knee. "Don't. If I have no regrets, you shouldn't, either."

"But I can't help feeling that it must be painful for you to be married to a—half-man."

"You're enough of a man for me." She knew, when he failed to respond, that it would be wise to elaborate. "I like things the way they are."

"How could you?" He stared disconsolately at the dashboard.

"Long before we were married I knew how it would be, and I'm not disappointed."

"That doesn't make sense."

"Few things do," she said forcefully. "I'm not analyzing myself or you. I know very little about other couples, but I suspect they're far less normal than they try to appear.

319

Whatever normal may be. But I can't lose sleep over them. You and I are satisfied, which is all that matters." She drew to a halt at a stoplight. "There's just one thing I can't tolerate."

"I know," Anton said, "and I'll try not to get myself into another of those messes."

Michele turned to him for a moment and stroked his hand. "You're really very good, darling. Most of the time."

He was only partly mollified. "When I've played around a bit, it hasn't meant anything. Inside me. But I'd be devastated if you did it. Not that I could blame you."

"I won't," she promised. "Let me worry about us, and you can concentrate on your work."

Anton moved higher in his seat. "I wish," he said, "that I hadn't signed a contract with the square."

"Are you crazy? Every other director in the business would have leaped at the chance."

"I'm tempted to turn the orchestra back to Broussard, with my compliments."

"Anton! You aren't afraid!"

"I can get more out of an orchestra, without rehearsals, than any other director can do after working with his men for a month." Anton forgot his depression, but there was a matter-of-fact calm behind his pride. "And my *Concerto* is good, so good the critics will say that no one since Mahler has written anything like it. The square may need me, but I can do quite nicely without it."

"Have you had a quarrel with someone that I don't know about?"

"No, the only unpleasantness was that ridiculous request of Carolyn Emory's that I give a preview concert for sponsors and contributors. She can be a ghastly nuisance, but she stopped badgering me when I spoke rather sharply to her."

"Carolyn is a frustrated woman, and I hate to think of what will become of her when she has no more fund-raising projects to justify her existence."

Anton was alert now, his energies restored. "I can't explain why I've soured on the square, Michele. It's subjective. Just a feeling; nothing I can put my finger on. They're more concerned about their carpets and gold-leaf and teardrop chandelier crystals than they are about concert programs and play schedules. The museum's purchasing committee is buy-

320

ing according to price, not taste. Everyone cares more about the square's physical plant than what will be done on its stages."

"I know what you mean, but after you and Max de Groot and Jerry Solanz take charge, the emphasis will change."

"I hope you're right, but I'm not depending on it."

The dressing rooms at the Repertory Theater were light, comfortable and large, each boasting its own private bathroom and built-in costume racks. The quarters at the end of the carpeted corridor nearest the stage, which were occupied by the stars, were positively sumptuous. The suite assigned to Julian Adams was particularly elegant, and consisted of a living room, complete with a piano, which had been installed for musical artists, as well as a very spacious inner chamber and bath.

Dan had not seen the suite since it had been occupied, and was impressed. On the mantel over an imitation hearth stood two Oscars, golden statuettes that Adams had won for motion picture performances, a pipe rack rested on the coffee table, and near it a large scrapbook was on prominent display. A bit self-conscious, Dan thought.

"I asked you to drop in for a purpose, Mr. Robertson," Adams said in his resonant baritone. "I'd have come to your office, but we don't dare leave the theater during these last days of rehearsals. Would you like a drink, or could I send out for a snack?"

Dan politely declined.

"I'm excited about the square, and the probability that *Confessional* will be a great hit. But I'm afraid we may blow our chances unless something is done."

"About what?"

Adams smoothed his hair. "I don't want you to think I'm coming to you behind Jerry's back. Far from it. For one thing, I have too much respect for him. He's a great director, really great, and—"

"How is he putting the square and *Confessional* in jeopardy?"

The actor carefully selected a pipe from the rack. "Jerry is an old pro, and he's used to dealing with pros. I've been in the business for eighteen years. Mary Hunter must have at least forty years' worth of credits. I could go through the company, one by one. We're accustomed to directors, especially Jerry. All of us have worked for him at one time or another before we came here. We have a great admiration for him."

It was useless to push, Dan realized, and decided to let Adams proceed in his own way.

"There's one exception. Tolmey."

Dan stiffened.

"She's a good little actress, Mr. Robertson, and she'll become better, no question about it. Between us, she may be miscast as Paula. The part may be too much for her to handle. Not that I'd presume to tell Jan Marek and Jerry how to cast the play, you understand."

"I think," Dan said, "that she may surprise a great many people."

"Of course. She has a great potential as an actress, as I just said. Simply great." Holding the pipe, Adams struck a pose. "I've already indicated that this is a confidential talk?"

"You have, Mr. Adams."

The actor dropped his voice, a mannerism that was particularly effective on stage. "She and Jerry simply aren't hitting it off together. Far be it from me to speculate whether there's something wrong in their personal lives. That's no one's business but their own. But what is my concern, and yours, and that of everyone at the square, is their professional association. Jerry climbs on her back as soon as we start rehearsals every day, and he stays there. The way he rides the poor child is brutal."

"I've sat in on a few rehearsals," Dan said.

"Then you know. And it's getting to her. Tolmey wasn't too bad in the part a few weeks ago. She was no Helga Borg, but she has youth and an elfin quality that might have carried her. Unfortunately, she had her own interpretation of the part, and Jerry knocked it out of her."

Dan said nothing.

"It's gone, I think, but he continues to whip her. And she can't take it. She fluffs her lines, she blows her stage business and she's making nervous wrecks of the rest of us."

"Have you spoken to Solanz?"

"Three of us went to him yesterday, and I was elected the spokesman. Jerry can be very obtuse when it suits him, Mr. Robertson. I couldn't be too blunt, of course. I merely tried to suggest that he treat her a little more gently. Not in so many words, you understand. But he didn't seem to know what I was talking about, and he changed the subject every time I came to the end of a line. It was very frustrating."

"Jan Marek has gone to him several times, and the results have been the same," Dan said quietly.

Adams registered surprise. "You've been aware of the problem."

"For some time."

"And Jan, too."

"I'm sorry to say Solanz has convinced Marek his system will get a good performance out of Berenice."

The actor rubbed his long, lean jaw. "He might, of course. Jerry's techniques are almost legendary. I've seen actors perform well over their heads for him. What do you think, Mr. Robertson?"

Dan had no intention of being quoted by Adams, and under no circumstances wanted his opinions carried back to Solanz. "I don't know. He's a director, and I'm not."

Adams was unwilling to let the matter drop. "I thought I might be able to help Tolmey by going over our big second act scene with her alone. So I stopped in at her dressing room this morning, Mr. Robertson—and I found her just sitting, staring at the wall. She looked as dazed and listless as if she had been drugged. That's when I decided to call you."

Dan hated himself for being evasive, but had no choice. "Her ordeal will end soon," he said. "The play opens the end of next week."

"Would you talk to Jerry?" Adams finally found the nerve to say what he really wanted.

"If it would do any good, I'd go to him at once. But he hasn't spoken to me for some time. I believe you were at the Sapphire Room one evening—"

"It was a great show." The actor chuckled, then sobered. "How stupid of me. You're handcuffed."

"I'm afraid so."

"Perhaps you could speak to Tolmey. I know she thinks of you as a friend, so you might be able to tamp her down."

"I will," Dan said.

Adams heard the reluctance in his voice. "You might wait a few days, Mr. Robertson. Jerry is flying out to the Coast for twenty-four hours later in the week—I believe he and his wife are working out a property settlement of some sort— and he can't delay it any longer. Maybe that's been bugging him. Anyway, a change of scene might put him in a better mood when he gets back, so maybe he'll stop riding Tolmey by then."

The Governor's official dwelling was a somewhat smaller version of the Executive Mansion in Washington, and was known throughout the state as the "little White House." It was almost as difficult for a visitor to gain admission, too, and Francis Dougherty sat impatiently behind the wheel of his car while two state troopers at the gate carefully examined his credentials.

"Governor Herder is expecting me," he said. "He phoned me less than a half-hour ago and asked me to come right over."

"The sergeant is calling about you right now, sir," one of the troopers replied, straining to be polite. "We'll give you the green light as soon as we get clearance."

Dougherty drummed on the steering wheel.

After a brief wait he was allowed to proceed, and drove around the long, semi-circular driveway to the main entrance, where he surrendered a numbered pasteboard ticket to another trooper, who took the car away to a parking lot. A plainclothesman escorted the visitor into the building, and they walked down a corridor lined with portraits, most of them stylized and inferior, of previous governors.

Herder was waiting in his version of the Presidential oval office, a room that was used as a study since the actual gubernatorial office was located in the principal state office building. Shelves lined the room, most of them filled with books that remained untouched from the term of one governor to the next, but the overstuffed chairs and the tables, lamps and other accessories were relatively new, since each incumbent furnished the room himself, as he pleased.

"I'd have been here fifteen minutes ago," Dougherty said, "if it weren't for your security system. What do you think this is, the Kremlin?"

The usually imperturbable Albert Herder was agitated. "Francis," he said, "I've got one hell of a problem, and you're responsible for it."

Dougherty sat and reached for a cigar-filled humidor on the table beside him.

"That redheaded secretary who worked for you is threatening to blow the top off this building!"

"Sandra Masters?" Dougherty halted in the act of unwrapping a cigar.

"She made several attempts to reach me today. Again. I was too busy to talk to her, but she finally told Eddie Brown she's going to tell every newspaper in the state that I'm making money out of Jefferson Square real estate unless I reach an understanding with her."

"Holy God!"

The Governor stood with his feet planted apart, gesticulating. "You knew she mentioned the matter to me when I gave her a lift some time ago, but there was no hint then that she was out for blood."

Dougherty was shaken. "It would seem she's changed her mind. Maybe she's working for Assemblyman O'Hara and the machine he's trying to build."

"Maybe. But it doesn't sound like it to me."

"The only other alternative I can think of," Dougherty said, "is blackmail."

Herder threw himself into a chair. "She can ruin me, Francis."

"Don't panic. How much does she know?"

"I have no idea."

"Is she familiar with the Harrison, MacFee situation?" the lawyer asked.

"That depends on how many papers are knocking around in your files," the Governor replied bitterly.

"There's very little in writing on anything," Dougherty said, trying to soothe him.

"But there's enough, obviously, for her to have found out more than she ought to know."

Dougherty was silent for a few moments. "It would be hard to hang you on the property deals, but you'd be smart to pull out of Harrison, MacFee."

"The damage is done by now, if she knows," Herder said. "What did she do, rifle your files?"

"Apparently."

"How can you be so calm?"

"It won't do any good if I tear out my hair, Al."

"You've got to do something!"

"I've been afraid for several years that there'd be a leak in the real estate situation. I've told you in so many words. I've warned Edward Emory. I've even told Mr. Hopkins I've thought it dangerous. But nobody listened to me. And maybe

325

you remember that when you accepted a silent partnership in Harrison, MacFee, I said that you were flirting with political suicide."

"Damn you, Francis, don't lecture me!"

"You took a calculated risk." Dougherty lighted the cigar and puffed on it. "Well, maybe you're in serious trouble, and maybe you aren't."

"Shut that woman up!"

"First let's find out exactly what she knows and exactly what she wants. Then we can deal with her."

"I can't afford to wait," Herder said. "Friends are lining up convention delegates for me in sixteen states, and I'm dead if there's even a hint of scandal. I don't think the President wants me as a candidate, and he'll use any excuse to throw me out of the running."

"We're not that far along yet. Did Sandra set any deadline? Did she tell Eddie specifically what she wants?"

Herder shook his head. "She indicated she'd be in touch with me again in a day or two, and she laid it on the line that she expects to deal direct with me."

"I could break her neck," Dougherty said, "but let's get her pitch straight."

"You're going to handle her," the Governor said. "She worked for you!"

"I'll do what I can, but I won't promise any miracles."

"Are you welshing on me, Francis?"

Dougherty became angry. "I'm trying to think and plan realistically!"

"Take care of it any way you like, but don't let that woman open her mouth to the press! If I'm destroyed, the rest of you are going to hell with me!"

Dan put his knife and fork on his plate and reached for a cigarette. He had taken only a few bites of his meat, and had left the rest of his meal untouched.

Phyllis wondered whether to pretend she was unaware of his lack of appetite, and finally decided that candor was the preferable approach. "What's wrong, darling?"

"Nothing."

"You aren't feeling sick?"

"I'm fine."

"This is the first time I've ever known you not to want steak and my cottage fried potatoes," she said.

326

"It isn't the cook's fault." Dan made a gallant effort to be pleasant.

"What is it, then?"

"If I knew, I'd tell you. I'm working on the last chapters of the book, and I suppose I'm straining to get it finished. There are all sorts of complications at the Repertory Theater, and they're getting worse as we approach the opening." He couldn't force himself to tell his wife about Berenice's problems. "That Masters woman is screaming because the book isn't being published tomorrow, and she's demanding the heads of the square's directors. Two factions have formed on the museum committee that's buying works of art, and they aren't speaking to each other. They communicate by sending memos—through me. The demolition of the last two tenements has been delayed because some of the people still living there are fighting eviction. I just heard this afternoon there's going to be a three-week delay in getting the marble for the façade of the new opera building. Shall I go on?"

"I think I've heard enough, thanks." Phyllis rose from her own chair, crossed to the opposite side of the dining-room table and bent down to kiss him.

Dan inadvertently drew back. The worst of his torture was that he loved Phyllis, even though his obsessive desire for Berenice was unabated, and his sense of guilt was so strong that love-making with his wife had become unbearable.

She managed to plant a kiss on his forehead.

"Thanks," he said, speaking with an effort. "Go finish your dinner before everything gets cold."

"I'll eat if you will," Phyllis said.

Dan picked up his knife and fork again, and she returned to her own seat.

There was a silence, and the longer it lasted, the more tense the atmosphere became.

"Tell me something," Phyllis said.

"If I can."

"Why haven't we gone to bed together once in this past month? I'm not complaining, honey. I know you're awfully tired these days—"

"I am."

"—but I can't help wondering whether I've done something to offend you."

"Like what?"

"I don't know, Dan. That's why I've been upset."

"I'm sorry. I don't mean to be so goddamned temperamental and remote and preoccupied. It's just that."

"Oh, Dan! You know I love you!"

"I keep telling myself that once the book is finished, and once the repertory and symphony have opened, I'll be human again. Are you willing to believe that?"

"All right." She tried to sound more hopeful. "Coffee?"

"Black coffee will suit me fine."

"I wonder if you should. You've been sleeping so badly."

"As long as I can't sleep," he said, "I might as well enjoy my coffee." He rose to help her clear away the dinner dishes.

"Go sit in the living room," Phyllis said. "I'll take care of cleaning up."

"I'm not an invalid."

"I'd rather do it myself. I'll bring your coffee in to you."

"I'll just take this pile out to the kitchen." He preceded her, put the dirty plates in the sink and then allowed himself to be sent off to the living room.

There he settled himself in his easy chair, opened his attaché case and reached for his ever-present paper work. If he spent an hour or two on square business, perhaps he might be able to turn out a thousand words of his manuscript before he became too tired.

Phyllis decided to wash the dishes before she left the kitchen, and twenty minutes passed before she brought their coffee into the living room.

Dan, with papers spread out around him, had dozed off.

"The food isn't bad here," Warren Hopkins said, "and I like the atmosphere. We'll have to come again."

Betsy had paid no attention to either. "Yes," she replied, "it's very nice."

He summoned their waiter, intending to pay the check.

The girl summoned her courage. "I wanted to talk to you about something," she said.

The unexpected gravity of her tone surprised him. "Shall we have a liqueur before we go?"

"No, I don't want to talk here."

"Name your spot," Warren said. "The bar at the Royal Hungarian isn't bad, or—"

"That's too public, too."

He had rarely taken her to his apartment since the start of

his affair with Carolyn, but Betsy seemed to be hinting that she wanted to go there. "How about my place?"

She nodded solemnly.

Warren tried several topics of conversation in the taxi, but she made only minimal responses, and he realized she was becoming increasingly nervous. He fell silent in the apartment building elevator, and didn't speak again until he took her beige beaver coat and put it on a hanger in his front-hall closet. "Now," he said, "we'll do something about that liqueur."

"Later, perhaps," Betsy flipped back her long, blonde hair and, thoroughly ill at ease, wished she had left well enough alone. But she knew she would not be satisfied to coast any longer, and braced herself. "I may not be staying very long."

Warren was bewildered by the change in her mood. She had been pleasant, even jovial, at dinner, but now she looked positively grim—and a little frightened.

Betsy could not look at him. She stood in the center of his large living room and stared at the portrait of his great-grandfather over the hearth, not really seeing it. "I've known about your affair with Carolyn for a long time," she said.

Warren was too stunned to reply.

"It was none of my business," she said, "so I've never mentioned it to you."

Warren made a great effort. "I hope," he said, "I haven't caused you any unpleasantness."

"You have, but that's beside the point. I've resented the way you've used me as a front, but I don't want to talk about that part of it."

"Just a minute," Warren said, and he, too, was distressed. "I've taken you out because—well, because I enjoy your company. Enormously. I guess I sound like a dirty dog saying this, but I have a very deep affection for you."

"I'd rather not discuss you and me, if you don't mind." Betsy's voice was high and thin.

He started to protest, but subsided when she suddenly turned to him and he saw the anguish in her face.

"My father has known Mr. Emory for many years," she said, her distress becoming greater because she was being too crude. "He thinks you may be shot when Mr. Emory finds out."

Warren was so startled he laughed. "That isn't civilized."

"What you're doing isn't civilized." Betsy blurted out the words before she could stop herself.

He turned red. "I suppose you're right. But I do think retribution of that sort is rare nowadays."

"I didn't come here because I seriously believed your life was in danger." Her voice broke, and she hated herself.

"Betsy, I—" Warren started again. "No matter what I say, you're bound to misinterpret it."

"Then it would be best to say nothing, don't you think?" Her smile was overly bright.

He looked miserable as he raised his hands in a gesture of appeal, then let them fall to his sides again.

"May I have my coat, please?" Betsy thought she was speaking normally but her voice was scarcely audible. "The doorman will get me a taxi."

"That won't be necessary. I—"

"I'd prefer it, thank you." She walked to the front hall and waited.

Warren fumbled as he took her coat from the closet and held it for her. "Not seeing you again will be very strange."

She said nothing.

"I realize that in a situation like mine there's no such thing as extenuating circumstances. But I've done nothing to use you in any way. I wish I could make you believe it."

"It doesn't really matter what I believe, does it?" Betsy spoiled her exit line when she remembered she had left her handbag somewhere in the living room and went to retrieve it.

Warren had the good sense not to follow her, and remained in the foyer. He stood directly in front of the door. "My position isn't defensible, but I wish you'd let me explain it."

"Good-by, Warren."

"I can't let our friendship end this way. You've got to listen!"

She brushed past him, opened the door and went out into the corridor. Not until the elevator started to carry her down to the ground floor did she begin to cry.

The rehearsal ended in a shambles. Berenice Tolmey became hysterical and left the theater, the rest of the company was dismissed for the day, and Jerry Solanz stood on the bare stage, surrounded by the members of his staff, talking volubly.

There Jan Marek joined him, blinking under the glare of the work light. "I want to talk to you, Jerry," he said.

"Talk away, sweetie." Jerry looked grim, and his subordinates reflected his mood.

"Alone," Marek said.

"I have no secrets from Milt and the boys. You know that."

"Alone," the playwright repeated.

Jerry shrugged. "Don't leave the theater, boys. We'll have a production meeting in a few minutes." He waited until the members of his staff drifted off. "Okay, sweetie. Your bowels are in an uproar, but let me do your worrying for you. The play is going to be great."

"I just called Dan Robertson," Marek said, "and asked him to join us here. Right away."

"Anything that needs to be settled we can do by ourselves, without him," Jerry said angrily.

Marek blinked behind his thick glasses, but was unmoved. "It's my privilege," he said, and took a package of cigarettes from his pocket.

"Don't smoke on stage, sweetie."

The playwright ignored the admonition, and peered up the aisle. "He's coming."

"I can hardly wait," Jerry said.

Dan had dropped everything when Marek had called him, but now, aware of Solanz' steady, hostile gaze, he wondered if he would have been wiser to stay in his office. He climbed the stairs from the orchestra pit, nodded vaguely in Solanz' direction and said to Marek, "I got here as fast as I could."

"You wasted no time. Thanks." The playwright removed his glasses and polished them. "I'm surprised you didn't hear the explosions all the way across the plaza. It was like Chinese New Year's Day in San Francisco."

"We're in fine shape," Jerry said curtly.

"That isn't the way I've heard it." Dan measured him slowly.

"Pay no attention to Jan. He's always flipping when we come down to the wire. I've guaranteed him a sensational production, and I guarantee him, right now, that *Confessional* will get a spectacular reception."

"You're full of bull," Marek said. "If you tear into Berenice once more you won't have a leading lady. Maybe she's shot already. And the rest of the cast is so jittery that even Julian is forgetting his lines."

"Did I tell you how to write your play, sweetie? Let me direct it!"

"Jan isn't the only one who's concerned," Dan said.

"Oh? I suppose Berenice has been bellyaching to you."

"I haven't spoken with her in days," Dan said truthfully. "But a great many people are worried, Solanz, very deeply worried."

"Either I'm in charge, or I'm not!"

"No one is questioning your authority," Dan said. "You were given a free hand to produce and direct *Confessional* as you see fit, and no one is interfering with your rights."

"Then I'll handle this in my own way, Robertson!"

"On the other hand," Dan continued, "it's my job to step in when I see the production being jeopardized. Jan says he's afraid Berenice will fall apart before the play opens."

"It'll be a miracle if she doesn't," the playwright declared.

"There are others," Dan went on, "who feel the same way. We're opening in nine days, the first three weeks are sold out, and theater parties are booked for at least four months ahead. We can't postpone, and we can't cancel."

Jerry jammed his hands into the pockets of his tweed jacket. "Tomorrow," he said, "I'm flying out to the Coast for twenty-four hours. I'm tempted to stay there. I'm tempted to send you a telegram saying, 'Screw Jefferson Square, screw all the people who want to tell me how to run my show, and screw you.'"

"I'm sure you're tempted," Dan replied. "But you won't do it."

"Why not?"

"In the first place, you have a contract—"

"I've never yet seen a contract that my lawyers couldn't get me out of!"

"Possibly. You've also put your reputation on the line, and that's something you can't escape. You accepted the challenge of forming a repertory company. You accepted Jan's new play, and no one, not even the almighty Jerry Solanz, can slap Jan Marek across the face."

The playwright smiled his appreciation.

"Most important of all, you cast an unknown actress in

the lead. Jan was against it, I was against it, everybody connected with the square was against it. But you insisted on having the last word. If you walk out now, Solanz, you'll be committing professional suicide. You can't do it to Jan, to Berenice, to the theater."

"You aren't telling me a goddam thing I don't already know." Jerry was angrily triumphant. "But I know things you don't. Any of you. All you see is Berenice whirling like a top. So you get panicky. You don't know her the way I do. She's responding just as I want her to. I'm building her for the performance of a lifetime."

"It appears to me," Dan retorted, "that you're driving her into a state of nervous collapse!"

Jerry drew himself to his full height and stared up at the taller man. "I discovered her when she was a nothing. I saw the potential in her as an actress when you—and you, too, Jan—were screaming she couldn't play Paula. I still believe in my own judgment, and I know it will be vindicated."

"Apparently you can't see it," Dan insisted, "but you're driving the girl up walls."

"He's right, Jerry," Marek said. "She hasn't gone through one full day of rehearsal for more than a week."

Jerry looked around, saw his script table standing at one side of the stage and brought the flat of his hand down on it with such force that an ashtray and several pencils fell off. "Do you think I'm an amateur?" he shouted. "Do you think I'm not keeping a complete log of what happens at rehearsals? For Christ's sake, I don't care how much time she misses! I don't care how often she leaves here with her mascara running down her face! Get this through your thick heads, both of you—and anybody else who tries to butt in! I'm creating something. I'm molding. I'm taking a little third-rate actress who has a potential she herself doesn't recognize, and in nine days from now she's going to be a star. Until then I don't care what she feels or thinks or says. I'm gunning for opening night. And when she's a hit—when she makes something of your theater, Robertson, and of your play, Jan, both of you will come to me on your knees to thank me. Which is just what she'll do. But don't bother! I don't want your thanks! By then I'll have my vindication."

A light snow was falling, whipped by a sharp wind, and Sandra wished she had worn something on her head. Shifting the weight of the groceries she was carrying, she pulled her fur-trimmed collar higher and walked more rapidly. This would be a good night to stay home; she'd fix some spaghetti sauce that was better than any restaurant made, and, after she ate, she'd relax with the evening newspaper columns and a few hours of television. She had been enjoying living a life of leisure, and the possibility that she wouldn't have to find another job appealed to her. Governor Herder would be sure to pay her plenty for keeping her mouth shut, and her only regret was that she hadn't demanded money from the start. Cash was the best of all consolations.

She opened the outer door of her apartment building and walked inside, stamping her feet. Suddenly she realized a man was standing in the corner, beyond the mailboxes. Wise in the ways of the city, Sandra shifted her bag of groceries, ready to throw it at him and flee, should it be necessary.

"I've been waiting for you," Francis Dougherty said.

He was the last person in town she had expected to see, but she instantly surmised he had come because of her threat to the Governor. "What do you want?"

"A little conversation. Nothing else, I can tell you that."

"Okay. Converse."

"I don't like the draught that blows in under the door," he said.

Sandra was torn. She wanted to be rid of him, but at the same time wondered if he might be acting as Herder's intermediary. It was even possible that he had come with a specific financial offer, and she hesitated.

"I have a suburban train to catch in a half-hour," Dougherty said, glancing at his watch.

She relented. "All right. You can come up for a few minutes."

He muttered under his breath and did not offer to hold the bag of groceries as she fished in her handbag for the key to the inner door.

When they reached the apartment Sandra retaliated by allowing him to dispose of his own hat and coat, and then took as long as she could in her tiny kitchen, putting away her groceries.

To her surprise Dougherty made no objection, and waited quietly for her.

"Well," he said when she finally rejoined him, "home again."

"Mine, not yours, so don't get ideas," she said.

"I want a lot of things in this world, but you aren't one of them."

"We're right in there with the wit and snappy comebacks, aren't we?" It didn't matter that she was wearing a shapeless wool sweater and skirt, her oldest boots and thick stockings. She literally didn't care what Dougherty thought of her, and if he found her unattractive, that was tough for him. "You're busy and I'm busy," she said brusquely. "What do you want?"

He hated being treated in a cavalier fashion, even by a former mistress who no longer interested him. "What I like best about you is your hospitality."

"If you think I'm going to swoon because you've shown up here, or fall on my back for you, think again."

"Don't flatter yourself."

Sandra ostentatiously glanced at her watch.

Dougherty seated himself in the chair that had been his favorite. "What's the pitch on you and the Governor?"

"That's between me and him."

"I'm here as an attorney, representing my client, Albert Herder."

"I've worked in enough law offices—including yours—to know that when one side is represented by a lawyer, the other had better do the same and do it quick."

"You won't get a lawyer to handle what you're trying to pull off." Dougherty became ugly. "Try it, and I'll guarantee to have him disbarred."

"Big talk."

"Is it?" he demanded. "You gained access to certain documents in my office when you worked for me—"

"There was no legal reason I shouldn't have seen them. You never told me to stay away from any material, and as your secretary I had the right to see anything and everything in the files. You've got a weak case, counselor." Sandra was enjoying herself.

"Sister, you're cockeyed. Working in a law office for a few years doesn't make you a lawyer. Maybe you don't know it, but there are laws against blackmail."

"Who says I'm blackmailing anybody?"

"The Honorable Albert Herder."

"Then it's his word against mine, and any court, even one that's friendly to him, is going to think a long time before deciding a case in favor of a rich politician trying to make a grease spot out of a girl who has no money, no influence and is just trying to do her duty as a citizen. Think of all the dirt that would come out in a trial, Francis. Think of all the things Herder and the rest of you want to keep hushed up."

"Your memory isn't very good. You've forgotten how many cases have been heard in closed court. And if you don't think the Governor has enough influence to insure that a case against you would be tried without benefit of either the press or the general public, you've got a shock waiting for you."

Sandra remained unruffled. "There won't be any charges made against me, and there won't be any trial. He knows and you know that I'll talk to the newspapers. There are enough of them in the state that would love to hang him."

"You don't want to go into court any more than the Governor does," Dougherty said.

Sandra was buoyed by the knowledge that she had won the first round.

"What do you want from him?"

"Enough money to keep me quiet."

"You have guts, or else you're stupid. The jobs of a lot of people depend on Al Herder. Some of them would play rough if they were told their own futures were in jeopardy."

Again she laughed. "The hood who runs the syndicate that handles horse parlors in this state is an old boyfriend of mine from Fourth Street. He never did believe in being nasty to women, and I'm sure he'd protect me if I went to him for help."

"You think you have every angle covered."

"I've been thinking of nothing else for days."

"Why pick on the Governor?"

"Because he has more to lose and more reason to make a deal than any of the others. Benjamin Hopkins is too big, and would tell me to kiss his ass. Emory is a cold fish who wouldn't even believe I was blabbing about him until something got into print. And you're too small for me to bother."

It was absurd to become angry because she didn't consider him wealthy enough to blackmail, but Dougherty was annoyed. "You're smart to lay off me."

"I might change my mind any time," she said airily.

He jumped to his feet, his manner threatening.

"If you touch me," she said, "I'm calling in the police. I'll swear I had to quit my job with you because you kept chasing

336

after me like a horny old tomcat, and I'll say—under oath—that you tried to rape me and started to get rough after I told you to peddle your brand of sex someplace else."

Dougherty was afraid he might become ill. His heart was pounding, the blood rushed to his head and he felt dizzy for a few moments. It was outrageous that a cheap little tramp could outsmart and outmaneuver him, but he felt certain she would not hesitate to bring a charge of attempted rape against him. Gradually, with great effort, he forced himself to subside, and finally sat down again.

"That's a good boy," Sandra said with a superior drawl.

"How much do you want from the Governor?" he asked.

"As much as I can get. As much as keeping me quiet is worth to him."

"I might persuade him to give you two or three thousand, just for the nuisance value."

"Ha! I'm thinking of ten times that much."

Dougherty's manner changed. "You've always been a greedy bitch, and this time you've put yourself out of the ballgame. No newspaper, not even one that hates Al Herder's guts, is going to print any of your allegations without proof. There are libel laws that protect citizens—"

"There's plenty of proof," Sandra said, refraining from mentioning that it was no longer in her possession.

"I'm afraid I can't take your word for that."

"I've got it. That's good enough."

"It isn't good enough for me. Or for the Governor." Dougherty shouted. "Nobody hands out money for the hell of it."

"Don't take my word for it. Ask Dan Robertson."

Dougherty was astonished. "You're a liar!"

She raised an eyebrow.

"I can't believe that a man like Robertson would be in on something like this with you!"

"Believe what you please, or don't. You say you want proof that I have evidence that the newspapers would find good enough to print. Okay, ask Robertson. That's as much as you're going to get out of me. But you can give your client a message for me. Tell him I'm not going to wait forever. I have lots of uses for money. I need it more than he does and I want a bundle in a hurry."

Dougherty stood, and, as he stared at her, tried to decide whether she was bluffing.

"Your hat and coat are on the chair over there," Sandra said. "I think you remember how to let yourself out."

Dougherty glared at her. "I could wring your goddam neck," he said.

"If you come near me, you won't be catching suburban trains to anywhere for years. Just for the hell of it, I'm tempted to bring a complaint against you and watch you squirm your way out. Walk softly around me, Francis, mind your manners and wipe your feet on the doormat." Sandra couldn't remember when she had enjoyed herself so much.

The private dining room in the governor's executive suite had a handsome ceiling with panels of oak, a thick carpet and indirect lighting. The table could seat thirty in chairs of brass-studded leather, the ceiling was sound-proofed and the tall French windows afforded a splendid view of the gold-domed Capitol across the street.

Only the food was inferior, as the guests of Albert Herder and his predecessors as governor could testify. Meals were carried to the private chamber, from the cafeteria on the second floor, and the elevator service was so bad that even the use of room-service tables, complete with spirit lamps, helped very little. Herder had wanted to hire a chef at his own expense, but had been afraid his political foes would accuse him of putting on a rich man's airs, so he suffered the cafeteria meals, and his guests had no choice but to do the same.

His liquor, however, was the best available, and his chauffeur replenished the supplies every week. No one, not even his worst enemies, had ever been known to raise a voice in protest against the quantity or quality of the alcoholic beverages that flowed through the gubernatorial inner sanctum. Albert Herder displayed his greatest charm as a host, too, and his guests frequently forgot they were being entertained in a shabby state office building.

"Have another bourbon, Dan," the Governor said jovially, "and then maybe we can order lunch."

"I'm a one-drink man at noon, Governor," Dan said, still wondering why he had been issued the insistent invitation.

"As you will, of course. But I hope you won't mind a bottle of Burgundy with our meal. I was very lucky a few months ago, and was able to buy several cases of 1959 vintage."

It would be ungracious to confess that wine in the middle of the day made him sleepy, Dan thought, so he replied with a pleasantry. He was learning to sip wine very slowly, so there would be fewer opportunities to refill his glass.

Herder pushed a button under the table, and his valet, who doubled as a waiter on occasions such as this, appeared at once, carrying two mimeographed menus.

Dan accepted one.

"Don't believe what you read," the Governor told him. "The beef goulash bears no resemblance to anything remotely Hungarian. And stay away from the fish. It takes a special knack to ruin broiled fish, but the cook here has a genius for never preparing it edibly. He's on civil service, so we can't get rid of him. I recommend the minute steaks. The odds are pretty heavy they'll look and taste like the old wallet you meant to throw out last year, but there's a sporting chance they'll be edible."

Not caring what he ate, Dan left the choice to the Governor, and then was drawn into a discussion of the latest developments at Jefferson Square, the success of culture centers in such cities as San Diego and Houston, and the increasing difficulties faced by individual communities in their efforts to obtain a fair share of the federal funds available for such projects.

The minute steaks arrived, half-cold, and were leathery but palatable, which was more than could be said for the overcooked and crumbling boiled potatoes, sprinkled with parsley, and the watery spinach. Finally, over melting raspberry sherbet, a subtle change in the Governor's manner indicated that he was ready to broach the topic that had caused him to issue the imperative invitation.

"I'm hoping you can be of some help to me in a rather strange and unpleasant situation, Dan."

"I'm at your service, Governor."

Herder studied him intently. "I wonder if you happen to be acquainted with a young woman called Sandra Masters."

Dan felt as though he had touched a live wire. He realized at once that something out of the ordinary had happened, and, guessing that Sandra had found some way to carry out her threats against the people she hated, he braced himself to protect and defend his uncompleted book.

"She was Francis Dougherty's secretary," he said.

Herder was still watching him. "That's the one. Have you seen her lately?"

"Now that you mention it, she's dropped in at the office several times in the last couple of months, or however long it may have been since she left Francis. She was job hunting."

There was no trace of joviality in the Governor's face now. "If you don't mind telling me, what's your impression of her?"

Dan felt increasingly certain that Sandra had been kicking up a storm. "I don't mind in the least, but I'm afraid my observations have been fairly superficial, since I scarcely know her. Intellectually she's no giant. Our personnel department ran a routine check on her, and as nearly as I can recall they found she was competent. I can send you a copy of the personnel report, if you like, but I'd think Francis Dougherty could tell you far more about her."

"I wasn't thinking of her as a secretary," Herder said. One of his most effective techniques was that of dropping a provocative and incompleted observation, then letting it dangle until the person from whom he was seeking information volunteered a comment or two.

"She's rather handsome, if you like the type." Dan knew the Governor had no desire to discuss her physical attributes, but blithely pretended that was what he meant. "She's a little too beefy for me, but I can see where others might find her rather attractive."

Herder did not smile. "Has she ever mentioned me to you?"

Dan went through the motions of pondering. "I seem to recall," he said slowly, "that she was very pleased, the first time she came to see me about a job, because she had been photographed with you by some newspaper or magazine."

The Governor, himself a master of evasion, was prepared to pursue the matter. "She had called me a number of times, but wasn't looking for a position."

"I suppose," Dan said politely, "that any public figure of importance is pestered by people who want to claim they've shaken his hand or spoken to him. I'm always glad I'm too much of an introvert for that sort of existence."

"The Masters woman," Herder said, "claims that you and she are working together in what I'd call an unholy alliance. She says the two of you have acquired some documents that my political opponents could use to harm me."

A complete denial might complicate the situation, but Dan wanted to learn more of what Sandra had said and done before admitting anything. "That sounds very strange."

"These documents concern Jefferson Square. I haven't seen them, and I don't know what they are, but they supposedly pertain to me."

"I'm afraid I don't understand," Dan said. "For what purpose have they allegedly been acquired?"

"I've been told that you and she are engaged in a scheme to blackmail me."

Apparently the Governor knew nothing about the forthcoming book, so Dan was able to laugh. "That's fantastic!" He paused and let the laugh die away. "Surely you don't believe that I—"

"There's no offense meant, but I've learned since entering public life that the biggest mistake I can make, ever, is to take any person or situation for granted."

"I lack the courage and finesse of a blackmailer," Dan said, deeply angry with Sandra for bringing his name into her scheme.

"Do you know of any documents that might be used for such a purpose?"

Again Dan went through the pretense of searching his memory. "On one of her visits to my office," he said, guarding his words with care, "Miss Masters did show me some papers that had to do with some property you and several others were either buying or selling in the vicinity of the square." He tried to sound as though anything he had seen had been of no significance to him.

The Governor nodded a trifle too rapidly. "That must be it! What sort of papers were they?"

"I had no more than a glimpse of them." Dan hoped he appeared as apologetic as he was vague.

"They didn't mean anything to you?"

"I assume," Dan said, "that there's a great deal of real estate buying and selling around the square. After all, the entire neighborhood is being redeveloped."

Herder couldn't decide whether he was naïve or a good liar. "Yes, more than eighty-five thousand residents of the area are being moved to new high-rise units. One of the oldest and most troublesome slum sections of the city is being transformed by a mammoth urban renewal project."

"There's no need to tell me what's being done, Governor.

341

I see the rebuilding every day of my life."

A secretary came into the room with a small stack of telephone messages, but Herder waved her out. "The Masters woman said nothing to you about blackmail?"

"Not a word. If she had, I'd have been on the phone to you at once!"

The Governor was becoming increasingly satisfied that he had nothing to fear from this man whose very position as a Vice-President of Jefferson Square was a symbol of respectability. "Why do you suppose she came to you with the documents?"

"I wondered at the time," Dan said.

It was startling to see the Governor give such a smooth performance. Under no circumstances was it possible to imagine that Albert Herder was unaware of the ethical impropriety of his real estate transactions; as for his partnership in Harrison, MacFee, a subject which he had not raised, his income derived from that source was possibly illegal as well as unquestionably immoral.

Burly and aggressive, personable and intellectually gifted, Herder was one of the biggest criminals holding high public office in the United States, and Dan couldn't imagine why he chose to jeopardize his political career for the sake of an additional fortune he didn't need. Perhaps he was greedy, perhaps he enjoyed danger. In any event, it would be unwise to attempt to analyze his motivation in the pages of his book. All that Dan could do was present the facts and let the reader judge Albert Herder, the man.

"She didn't leave any of the papers—or copies of them—with you, by any chance?" the Governor asked suddenly.

"No, I glanced at some of them for a few seconds, and then Miss Masters took them back." Dan contrived to look blank and slightly bewildered, hoping he was giving as convincing a demonstration as the Governor.

"I'm afraid," Herder said, "that I've dragged you over here on a wild goose chase."

"Not at all. I've enjoyed the lunch." Dan wondered whether to let the subject of Sandra and her documents drop, and decided it would do no harm to say an additional word. "I find it difficult to believe that Miss Masters is a blackmailer, and I hope there's been a misinterpretation somewhere."

"I hope so," the Governor said, and stood, ending the lunch.

They parted at the door of an anteroom, Herder insisting on sending Dan back to Jefferson Square in a trooper-driven limousine. Then, after his guest had gone, the Governor hurried back to his own office and picked up a private line. He dialed Francis Dougherty's unlisted number, and when the lawyer answered, told him in detail about the meeting.

"The one thing that I got out of him," the Governor said, "is that there are some papers. But he seemed so unconcerned about our real estate deals that I didn't want to arouse his suspicions by asking him too many questions about what he was shown."

"He claims he doesn't have any of the documents, Al?"

"He was very clear on the point. He says the Masters woman gave him a quick peek at them, and took them away again."

Dougherty was silent for a moment. "I'm wondering why she told me to corroborate her story with Robertson. Probably just to prove there are papers and that she wasn't bluffing."

"I suppose. I don't think we'll turn up anything through him, but I'm not taking any chances. I'm putting a tail on him."

"Good. You have Sandra covered?"

"Twenty-four hours a day. I stopped being reluctant."

"I wonder," Dougherty said, "whether it would do any good to bug Robertson's office and home phones the way you've had Sandra's tapped."

"I'd rather not. If they're working together, it'll come out through her. But if he's in the clear, as he seems to be, there will be hell raised if he discovered his phones were being tapped."

"Who'd do the hell raising?"

"Ben Hopkins, of course," the Governor said. "He thinks the property deals are honorable in every way, and I don't want him to change his thinking. What's more, he knows nothing about my Harrison, MacFee setup, and he'd stop supporting me at once if he learned about it. One wrong move with somebody as wide-eyed as Robertson, and everything will come into the open. Aside from the plainclothes tail on him, I propose that we treat him as innocent—unless and until he proves himself otherwise."

Base-ray heating units were operating in the Museum of Fine Arts to help dry the concrete flooring, huge panes of glass had been installed in the windows of its broad corridors, and only the empty galleries, which would be electrically illuminated, were dark. In another week the permanent flooring of wear-resistant cork would be laid, and soon thereafter workmen would start putting up the interior walls. The Jefferson Square Board had every reason to believe that paintings and sculptures could be moved in by April, and that the doors of the museum could be opened to the public no later than May.

Two pairs of footsteps echoed on the hard concrete, sometimes pausing for a moment, occasionally halting briefly. "I think," Warren Hopkins said, "that this gallery might be best for the Goya black and whites."

"It's too late to change now." The collar of Carolyn Emory's mink coat was raised, and her dark hair fell outside it. "I've already read the copy that Dan's educational pamphlet department wrote. The pamphlet says the Goyas will be in the north wing."

"Why is it too late to change?"

"The pamphlets have already gone to press. Don't you remember?" There was a note of irritation in Carolyn's voice.

"No, I don't," Warren said, "and what's more, I really don't care where they put the damned Goyas!"

Carolyn put a hand on his arm. "What's wrong?"

"We're not allowed to smoke in here yet, and I want a cigarette."

"Really. Tell me. Have I done something to upset you?"

"For the one hundredth time since lunch, you've been perfect, Carolyn."

"If we're going to bicker, let's do it over something specific. This nebulous quarreling doesn't satisfy anyone." She smiled, but her violet eyes were serious.

"I'm not going to quarrel. But I suppose I'd better tell you. Betsy knows."

She was silent for a moment. "It was inevitable, I suppose." She started walking toward the next gallery.

Warren said nothing more.

"Is that all you're going to tell me?"

"What else is there to tell? She was hurt."

Carolyn roamed the empty gallery restlessly. "I feel very

344

sorry for her. I hope she hasn't cared about you too much."

"I've been feeling about eighteen inches tall," Warren said bitterly.

"I'm familiar with the sensation." She halted and faced him across the gallery. "If you're bothered because of your relationship with a girl you don't love, with whom you have no formal tie, how do you think I feel when I think of Edward?"

"Betsy's reason for talking to me about it was that her father believes Edward will start oiling his pistols when he finds out."

A sudden chill ran through Carolyn. "That's absurd."

"Is it?"

"If you're afraid—"

"Of course I'm afraid. Not of his pistols. But of what he must think of me."

"Are you afraid you're losing your self-respect?"

"Yes," Warren said.

"Would you regain it if we said good-by to each other?"

"I'm not sure."

"I don't like all the talk that's been going around town, any more than you do. My reputation is ruined by now, so I have very little to lose, but I still hate knowing that people are whispering behind my back."

"Then you do want to end it?"

"I—I can't decide. One minute I despise myself, and the next I can't bear the thought of giving you up."

"We're a great pair."

"What I do know," she said, "is that I'm not any different inside. I don't feel like a loose woman."

"Society's values have changed. You'd look rather silly wearing a scarlet A on your mink coat."

Carolyn was not amused. "I've always thought of myself as strong. But I'd shrivel away to nothing if we stopped seeing each other."

Warren started toward her.

She indicated with a quick gesture that they could be seen through the huge panes of glass on the far side of the corridor. Beyond the windows stood the plaza, where there was a steady stream of people coming in and out of the Repertory Theater and Symphony Hall.

Warren drew her into the shadows deep inside the gallery.

There they embraced and clung together.

Clouds of blue smoke rose from Harvey Simpson's pipe. "I don't see why you should be surprised that Governor Herder knows there are papers that give away his real estate deals," he said.

Dan was unable to make himself comfortable, and moved from one chair in the publisher's office to another. "I'm not in the least surprised."

"Good. It was inevitable there would be a leak. So what's eating you?"

"I've been hoping we could keep the lid clamped down a little longer, Harvey. But this leak means Hopkins and Emory and all the rest will know soon, too. It won't be long before they find out what I'm doing, and trace the photocopies to your safe."

"Let 'em. Every publisher has had his share of people screaming, 'You can't print that.' "

"I'm not afraid of their anger—"

"Are you sure, Dan?"

"Quite sure, although I'm not looking forward to recriminations and scenes, naturally. I'd like to murder Sandra Masters. If she'd kept her mouth shut after you bought the letters from her, everything would have been all right."

"She's an unstable woman. You can't be responsible for anything she does."

"I feel no such responsibility." Dan lighted a cigarette, disliked its taste and stubbed it out. "All I need is eight more weeks, Harvey. I've been trying so damned hard to see the repertory and symphony through their openings, get the Museum of Fine Arts in shape and make sure the demolition work starts for the preparation of the new buildings. In another eight weeks the manuscript will be done."

"That's good news! When do I see it?"

"After it's done."

"You realize I'm anxious to read it."

"Be patient a little longer."

"I wonder if you realize that your refusal to give me as much of the book as you've written is nothing more than an attempt to persuade yourself that you aren't being disloyal to Jefferson Square."

"Possibly. I'm too busy and too tired for self-analysis," Dan said.

"Just keep in mind that I want to put the book into production as soon as possible. What does Phyllis think of it?"

"I haven't shown it to her."

Harvey raised an eyebrow. "I hope you two aren't having problems."

"Why should we?" There was a savage undertone in Dan's voice.

The publisher raised both hands. "I'm not prying. I'm concerned about friends, that's all. You aren't asking me, but I'm telling you, Dan. You badly need a vacation."

"I'm driving to get through the next eight weeks. I can't even think about vacations!"

"I've never seen anyone wound up tighter. You're asking for trouble. Your problem—"

"My problem is living up to my obligations!"

When Anton Helsing throws one of his temper tantrums, Dan had been warned, you'll wish you were working anywhere on earth except Jefferson Square.

Anton, it appeared, was having such an explosion now, but it was unlike what Dan had anticipated. The director of the symphony was seated at the piano in his new office, behind the auditorium of the nearly completed hall, and his rage was icy, contemptuous and completely lacking in histrionics. Talking rapidly in a controlled voice, Anton was accompanying himself on the piano, playing what was tantamount to background music for his coldly angry speech.

"I have certain principles," he said, "and won't deviate from them. No one dictates my programs to me. I demand a free hand in the matinees for teen-agers, too. And at no time will I permit anyone who is my self-proclaimed enemy to sit in the audience."

Dan wanted to reply, but the volume of the music grew louder, making it impossible for him to speak without shouting. Anton was deliberately making it difficult for him, he knew, so he sat in his tweed-upholstered chair and scuffed at the thick new carpeting. By exercising patience, he eventually would have his say.

The sound decreased as Anton resumed. "I appreciate the interest of the board, and I'm sure their wives would enjoy telling their friends they had a hand in selecting my programs. But I refuse! Just as I cannot tolerate Henri Broussard sitting out front on the night of the opening!" Suddenly he closed the keyboard cover and whirled on his stool. "I'm sorry

347

if my stand makes life more complicated for you, but I hope you realize there's nothing personal in any of this. I've got to think of myself! And now that everything is settled," Anton said, becoming amiable, "let's go to lunch."

"I'd like to bring up one or two points before we leave." Dan made no move from his chair. "Why couldn't you switch the Mozart and Beethoven from your third concert to the second? It would be a gesture to the board, and I really don't see that you'd be losing anything."

Anton's face stiffened. "I'm not obliged to explain, and if I were dealing with anyone but you, I wouldn't. I have my own sense of programming balance. I'm doing the Mozart and the Beethoven in my third because it will be a program completely devoted to the classics. I don't believe in mixtures that turn out to be musical chop suey!"

"Fair enough," Dan admitted.

"Also, I don't want the board—or anyone else—to get a foot in the door. I'll be pestered to death once I start making concessions."

"All right. I'll notify the board that you can make no changes in your programming schedule."

"Thank you." Anton went to the sliding panel that opened onto his clothes-closet, and took his jacket from a hanger. "Where do you want to eat? Some place nearby where I won't be annoyed by tourists who want my autograph."

"We'll find the right place," Dan said. "But before we go, there's one more point to be settled. This business of barring Henri Broussard and Helena Godoy from the opening."

"The issue is settled." Anton's joviality vanished, and he became remote again. "I won't allow them to be there."

He was being so petty, so unreasonable that Dan had to curb his own temper. "We have no intention of giving them house passes," he said, "and we can refuse to sell them any of the seats we're reserving. But if they choose to buy tickets at the box office or somewhere else, we have no legal grounds for keeping them out of the hall."

"If I see them sitting there when I come out to the podium," Anton declared, "I'll just keep walking and leave by the other side of the stage. I simply won't conduct if they're in the audience!"

"Then you'll be creating a tempest without reason. Every newspaper in the country will print something, and Jefferson Square will be hurt."

348

"Too bad," Anton said, then asked maliciously. "Will the publicity be any worse than the square got when you knocked down Jerry Solanz at the Sapphire Room?"

"I thought you'd get around to that." Even though Dan was prepared with an answer, he felt ill at ease. "Well, let me make it quite clear that I behaved stupidly. There is one difference, however. My fight with Solanz didn't take place at the square itself. If we bar Broussard and Miss Godoy from the hall, Francis Dougherty tells me they can sue us for a tremendous sum."

"Broussard might file a suit, just for the publicity, but he wouldn't follow through. He's having a hard enough time finding a new job, and he knows that no orchestra would hire him if he makes a real stink."

"You may be right, but I'd hate to take the chance," Dan said.

Anton looked at him accusingly. "It's obvious you've heard the same rumor I picked up this morning."

"What's that?"

"Don't play it so cool. You've heard that Broussard and that ugly cow of his may be coming to the symphony opening."

"As I understand it," Dan said, "they're going to a dinner party being given by one of the board members—someone who was friendly to him, no doubt—and will be coming to the opening with the whole party."

Anton's expression became venomous. "Then there'll be quite a crowd on hand to see them turned away. This gets better and better."

"I could pretend to go along with you," Dan said, "in the hope that someone might persuade you to take a more reasonable attitude. But I can take no risk of seeing a crisis erupt on opening night. No matter what you and Broussard may think of each other, and no matter how just you may think your right to hate him, he'll be admitted to the hall, like anyone else, if he has a ticket."

"Then I won't be there," Anton replied quickly.

Dan was exasperated. "In that case, you'll be the one who'll find it difficult to work elsewhere. I've been learning about the concert world ever since I came to the square, and I think I can promise you that you wouldn't be invited to take over one podium in the United States or Canada. I believe various people have enough influence to have you barred from performing in England and western Europe, too."

"I don't like threats."

"Neither do I, Anton. I'm not threatening, though. I'm telling you plain facts, and I'm sorry they're harsh. You're within your rights when you insist that no one interfere with your programming or when you set conditions for your teen-agers' concerts. But I can't permit you to do something that will be harmful to the whole square."

Anton suddenly crumbled. "You'll force me to endure the mortification of giving a concert with Broussard sitting out there, laughing at me?"

"I can't imagine why he'd laugh, and if anyone should feel mortified, it would be Broussard, not you." It was true, Dan thought, that artists sometimes were as short-sighted, emotional and inconsistent as children.

"That's what Michele told me at breakfast. Have you two been plotting all this together?"

"I haven't spoken to her. But if you'll think about it, Broussard is the one who'll want to squirm. You'll be direct-ing the orchestra that was his, and playing your own new *Concerto* as well."

"But he'll be criticizing everything—"

"Let him!" Dan said.

Phyllis still felt a little uncomfortable when she went to lunch at one of the city's smart restaurants. Crowding past the narrow bar just inside the entrance, she felt the men drinking there stare at her, but, as usual, she was ignored by their companions, young and would-be young women with dyed hair and false eyelashes. It was ridiculous, she thought, that these girls always made her feel out of place, even though her suit and shoes were expensive and her mink was appropriate anywhere.

After what felt like an endless walk, she reached the velvet rope that barred the entrance to the dining room itself, and at the far side, studying a reservations list in a book, was the inevitable maître d'hôtel in his snug-fitting black coat, gray vest and striped trousers. She waited politely, but he indicated no awareness of her presence.

Phyllis summoned the courage to be rude in the best big-city manner. "I'm meeting Mrs. Helsing," she said. "She's reserved a table, I believe."

The man came alive and a smile cracked the austere

lacquer of his face. "Of course, Madame," he said, bowing and removing the velvet rope. "This way, please." He led her past innumerable crowded tables. Serving carts had been rolled only inches from the backs of diners, and table captains were deftly boning fish, carving meat, stirring sauces over flaming spirit lamps and tossing salads. Their skill, bustle and enterprise, as well as the incredibly cramped working conditions, were familiar attributes of the fine art of dining in the final third of the twentieth century.

Michele was seated at a table in a far corner. "I'd have ordered you a drink, but I didn't know what you'd want," she said as Phyllis joined her.

"Nothing too strong."

"Try a Scotch mist." Michele indicated her own glass. "They last forever."

"I'm not much of a Scotch drinker." Phyllis allowed the table captain to help her remove her coat, and then turned to him. "Could I have it with bourbon?"

"Of course, Madame. One bourbon mist." He moved off, snapping his fingers at an underling.

"I'm sorry I'm late," Phyllis said, "but traffic was awful."

"I know. I just got here myself. On days like this I swear I'll move to the country, and then I remember how deadly it is at the weekend place we own downstate." Michele laughed.

Phyllis felt ill at ease with her, although she liked her. Perhaps, even now, she had not become accustomed to celebrities and their wives.

"I hope you don't mind," Michele said, "but I've asked Betsy Callison to join us. She phoned me just as I was leaving the house—too late to check with you. She sounded horribly in the dumps over something, and I thought we might be able to cheer her up."

"I'll be glad to see her, naturally. But I'm not much of a cheer leader these days."

"Ghastly, isn't it? I just hope all of us can survive until those—those star-spangled mausoleums are opened."

"I'm glad to hear I'm not the only one having it rough."

"Oh, there must be dozens of us. After the openings—and you have to sweat through all of them, don't you?—there ought to be a party restricted to the spouses of everyone connected with Jefferson Square. Just spouses. What a drunken brawl that would be."

"I'd be tempted." Phyllis' drink came, and she relaxed with

it. "But I just get sick when I have too much."

"Me, too. But this is once when I wouldn't. Here's Betsy." Michele studied the girl as she came across the room. "Every time I see her with that long hair, I'm glad I realized that at my age I've got to wear it short. It probably won't be long before I start buying hats."

"I bought two of them just yesterday," Phyllis replied, and they were both laughing as Betsy was conducted to the table.

"I'm glad everybody is so jolly," the girl said.

Phyllis noted that she was very pale and was wearing far more eye makeup than usual.

"I'll have a martini," Betsy told the table captain. "Make it very dry."

"Well," Michele said. "The tomato juice girl is changing."

"It's about time, isn't it?"

Both of the women heard the bitterness in her voice, but tactfully ignored it.

Betsy lapsed into a silence almost immediately, and their attempts to draw her into the conversation were unsuccessful. "Pretend I'm not here until I've had a drink. Or maybe two."

Michele took her at her word. "Doesn't it make you feel good all over to know that at this very moment our husbands are probably having a frightful row?"

"I didn't know they were having lunch together." Phyllis refrained from adding that she knew very little about Dan's activities these days. "Why are they fighting?"

"Oh, Anton wakes up every morning with some new little insanities that have to be knocked out of his head."

"Dan is very good at that sort of thing." There was a hint of malice in Phyllis' tone.

"He'll need to be a wonder at it. Because Anton will keep it up until the symphony has opened." Michele sighed.

They changed the subject and chatted about play schools, summer day camps and the exorbitant prices of children's clothes.

"You two are taking forever over one drink," Betsy said, and ordered another martini.

They pretended not to notice her obvious tension.

Suddenly, after drinking part of it, she said, "Phyllis, I'd like to ask you a very personal question."

"Of course, but I won't promise I'll answer it," Phyllis said lightly.

"What would you do if you discovered your husband had

352

been unfaithful to you?"

"Oh, dear. I don't know, really. It never occurred to me that he might be."

"Truth or consequences in broad daylight," Michele said. "And in a restaurant overflowing with kindly suburban matrons on their way to matinees. If I'd remembered the matinees, I'd have suggested that we meet somewhere else."

"I'm serious about this," Betsy said.

Phyllis looked at her, and realized that her makeup could not hide the hollows beneath her eyes. It was possible, even probable, that she had been weeping.

"What would you do?" Betsy persisted.

"Well, I suppose it would depend on the circumstances. And the woman."

"That's too vague."

"No, I know what she means," Michele said.

"I'm too idiotic, or too inexperienced," Betsy said. "Or both."

"I'll try to explain," Phyllis said. "If he went off somewhere and had too much to drink—"

"I didn't mean a quick fling. A real affair."

"I see." Phyllis thought carefully. "Knowing Dan, he wouldn't have that kind of relationship with anyone unless she meant something to him. Something important. So I'd have to say it would mean he didn't love me any more. But whether I'd leave him or not is another question. There are children to think about, and—It would be messy."

Betsy turned to Michele.

"I'd forgive him. And I suggest we order lunch," Michele said curtly, summoning the captain.

After a long discussion of the day's specialties they decided to eat poached sole and a mixed salad.

"You see," Betsy said, "I've broken up with Warren."

The two older women exchanged quick glances.

"You don't have to be diplomatic," Betsy said. "You and I have talked about it, Michele, and I assume you know, too, Phyllis."

"I don't actually know, although I've heard things," Phyllis replied carefully.

"Do you think I was wrong?"

"I'm not very good at giving advice to other people." Phyllis became slightly flustered. "It all depends on the way you feel, and on him, and on your pride—"

"To hell with pride," Michele said. "If you want a man badly enough, take him. Any way you can get him."

"If he had tried to stop me, I think I'd have weakened. But I was—well, firm, and he didn't put up much of a struggle." Betsy looked at what was left of her martini and, with a sudden grimace of distaste, pushed the glass away.

"You've never had him," Michele said crisply, "and it looks as though you never were going to get him. So the best thing you can do, it seems to me, is to forget him."

"How do I do that?"

"I have no idea," Michele said.

"My parents are trying to insist I take a trip."

"That's quaint, sweet and old-fashioned." Michele was vehement. "But I don't believe the old change-of-scene treatment has ever helped anyone."

"The best," Phyllis said, "is supposed to be falling in love with someone else."

"I wouldn't even know how to start looking." Betsy was morose. "I have no interest in any of the other men I know. They actually bore me. Besides, I don't want anyone else. I want him."

"Then go back to him. Better yet, find some way of making him come to you." Michele ticked off the points on her strong fingers. "Use tricks, strategy, anything to draw him to you. Be prepared to wait it out, but forget all the little niceties you were taught at finishing school."

"I can't compete," Betsy said, "when she's going to bed with him and I'm not!"

Michele flipped back her hair. "The belief that the woman who is sleeping with a man has the advantage is part of the male seduction conspiracy. When a man has a woman, he loses interest in her. Unless she finds new ways to attract and hold him."

Phyllis discovered she was learning something, too.

"The woman who hasn't gone to bed with him really holds the upper hand," Michele continued. "He wants her, but she's still a challenge, a mystery. The chase is always more important to a man—at least to most men—than catching the woman. I sound like an authority, which I'm not, and I may be completely wrong. But I'm telling you what I've seen."

Their food arrived, and they ate in reflective silence for some minutes. Then Michele managed to change the subject.

The insistent ringing of the telephone awakened Sandra, and she wearily lifted herself to one elbow as she answered it.

"This is Eddie."

Her mouth felt dry, her head was heavy and she remembered killing a bottle of wine before going to bed. "What do you want?" she demanded.

"Personally, not a thing. The Governor wants to see you."

Suddenly she no longer felt sleepy. "That's interesting."

"He'd like to have a little chat with you."

"I'm available."

"Sure, I know," Eddie said facetiously.

"You're a scream," Sandra said. "The Governor's time is more valuable than mine, so I'll be glad to suit his convenience."

"Good. He'll expect you here, at his office, at three this afternoon."

"He can expect until hell freezes." She swung her legs to the floor, her feet searching for her mules.

"I don't dig you."

"When did you find that out?" Her laugh was hoarse.

Eddie became annoyed. "First you tell me you'll meet him any time, any place, and then you refuse to come here."

"My, aren't we innocent today! Three o'clock will be fine, but I'm not going to meet him, or you, or anybody else for a cozy little talk where there's a chance that a tape recorder may be running."

"My God, you're cautious!"

"Slobs like you," Sandra said, "have made me that way."

Eddie's irritation grew. "Where will you be willing to meet the Governor? Please keep in mind that a man in his position doesn't go sneaking off to quiet little bars."

Sandra thought for a few moments. "Does he drive a car?"

"Of course, but he has a chauffeur."

"I want no third parties as witnesses. Here's what I'm willing to do." Sandra reached for a cigarette on the table beside her. "I'll come to his office in a rented car. I want to make this as easy and painless for him as I can. We'll go for a little drive, with him behind the wheel—and nobody else in the car. But in my car. If he wants an escort of troopers on motorcycles, that's okay with me. Agreed?"

"This is damned silly."

"I've told you my terms."

"If he weren't anxious to see you—" Eddie broke off, and there was a silence at his end of the line for a moment. "All right. You're sure as hell Miss Safety of the Month."

"Tell the Governor I can hardly wait until our date."

Jerry Solanz packed several shirts in his suitcase, then stood before his necktie rack. "While I'm gone," he said, "Milt will run rehearsals."

"You told me." Berenice Tolmey sat cross-legged in an easy chair, gazing out of the window. "It looks like it's going to snow."

"I've already called the airport, sweetie, and they've assured me that all planes are running. No snow is expected for at least three hours. I never take chances."

"I know," she said, sighing and running a hand through her short hair.

Jerry shot a glance in her direction, then returned to his scrutiny of the neckties, which he began to select with great care. "You can't afford to let up while I'm gone. With so little time left before the opening, every day is important. Every hour is precious."

She nodded listlessly and continued to stare out of the window.

"You aren't listening to me, sweetie!"

"I can't afford to let up while you're gone," Berenice said in a mechanical tone. "Every day is important and every hour is precious."

He put several neckties on the bed, went to her and ran his hands up her bare legs. "I wish I could light a fire under you," he said, reaching up under the top of her short, two-piece nightgown.

"Not again, Jerry."

He looked at his watch. "There isn't time."

Berenice refrained from telling him that his sexual advances had at no time inspired her.

"You've been in a dream world, and it's getting worse. Snap out of it, sweetie!"

"I'll try," she said obediently, relieved when he removed his hand and went back to the neckties.

"I wonder if you have any idea how much I've got riding on you in this play."

"First, your reputation as a director. Second, the success

356

of *Confessional*. Third, my future as an actress. My entire future."

He grunted, but did not turn as he packed the neckties.

Berenice knew he expected a running conversation before he left, but she had nothing to say to him.

Jerry transferred a suit from a closet hanger to one in the suitcase. "I'll order some breakfast sent up to you before I go."

"All I want is coffee."

"Goddammit, you've got to eat! You've been acting like you're on a starvation diet lately."

"I'm not hungry," she said petulantly.

"You can't afford to lose any more weight. Remember that you've got to sling your ass all over that stage. It's a symbol of Paula, a key to her whole personality, and you've got to get that across to the audience in your first scene. But to do it, for Christ's sake, you've got to have an ass to sling!"

"It won't melt away in the next week, Jerry, even if I'm not hungry."

"You'll have scrambled eggs and bacon," he thundered as he walked to the telephone. "Buttered toast. And a big glass of orange juice."

She knew it was useless to argue.

He made the call to room service. "That's settled," he said, satisfied. "There's just one more thing. Every minute you're not at rehearsals, I want you to keep yourself roped to that chair, studying your 'sides.' Go over your lines until you can pick up a scene anywhere at all. At the beginning, in the middle, no matter where."

Berenice was tempted to tell him she was already letter-perfect in her role.

"That goddam fluffing has got to stop. I want to hear no more of it by the time I get back tomorrow!"

She nodded, but saw that he wasn't looking at her as he put on his overcoat and the fur shako he always wore in cold weather. "I'll remember everything you've told me, Jerry," she said, resisting the desire to put her fingers in her ears.

He came to her, embraced her and ran his hands over her body as he kissed her. "You're going to prove that Solanz has a better eye for casting than anybody else in show business. You're going to justify my giving you the part—and the break of a lifetime, sweetie." He took the suitcase into the living room, where a bellboy would pick it up, and closed

357

the door behind him.

Berenice heard him leave the suite, and stretched. She made no move until the room service waiter arrived with her breakfast, and called out to him, asking him to leave it in the living room. After he had gone she wandered out, looking in distaste at the dishes under the silver covers, and poured herself a cup of coffee, which she sipped rapidly.

Then she poured another, carried it into the bedroom and took a cigarette from a new package. Lighting it, she went to the bedside telephone, picked up the thick city directory and flipped through it, searching for a number. Her listlessness was gone, and she hummed a snatch of a song beneath her breath. For a whole day and night she was free, and she intended to utilize every moment not spent at rehearsals.

She had been looking forward to this day, relishing it in advance, and her eyes were shining by the time she found the number she wanted and picked up the telephone.

Ann Dougherty was suffering from her usual morning hangover and lay quietly on the pillows, careful not to jar or move her head. And, following her routine practice, she began to reconstruct the previous evening, little by little.

Francis had telephoned that he wouldn't be coming home for dinner, which no longer surprised or dismayed her, and she vaguely recalled eating something before settling down to an uninterrupted evening of drinking. With a great effort she rolled over and saw that the other bed was rumpled, which meant it had been occupied. An equally painful twist in the opposite direction showed her the face of her bedside clock: it was only a few minutes after eight, which meant that Francis hadn't yet gone into the city. She heard no sounds emanating from the direction of the bathroom, however, so she wasn't sure whether he was still in the house.

Prodding herself, Ann struggled out of bed and stood, swaying and shivering, as she climbed into her robe. Then she staggered to the door, opened it carefully and listened. The odor of frying bacon drifted up the stairs, and she heard voices in the dining room. Suddenly she remembered having hired a new maid a few days earlier, and satisfied that Francis was being fed, was able to concentrate on herself.

Two aspirin and the prescription headache tablets that she took every morning had no immediate effect, so she went to the lingerie drawer of her dresser and fumbled for the bottle of vodka she kept hidden there for emergencies. The preceding evening was a blank, and when Francis learned she was awake he would want to talk, so she had to be ready for him. She took several long swallows from the bottle and returned to her bed; after a few minutes the throbbing in her head began to subside, and she was able to forget her queasiness.

By the time Francis came into the bedroom for his jacket, she had smoothed her hair and was able to muster a smile. "You were late last night," she said, having learned the value of taking the initiative.

"Not really. I was here by midnight."

She couldn't remember whether she had still been awake then, and decided to probe. As a rule, when he spent the evening in town with one of his girls, he didn't reach home until two or three in the morning. "Did you have a nice time?" she asked, her voice a shade too innocently sweet.

"I told you on the phone that I was staying in for dinner and a conference with Al Herder."

"Oh, yes."

"He sent me home in one of his staff cars," Francis said, and paused. "You really had a snootful last night." He knew he was breaking one of their cardinal rules: if he refrained from attacking her drinking too blatantly, she would make no insinuations about his evening's activities.

Ann retaliated at once. "I assumed you were up to your usual."

"Whatever that may mean."

"And I did not have a snootful, as you put it." She glared at him, and almost convinced herself she was telling the truth. "I wasn't feeling well."

"Sure, okay," he said wearily as he slipped a handkerchief into the breast pocket of his jacket. "This is no morning for a scrap. We've got something important to settle."

If he even hinted that she should go to a sanitarium for a cure, as he'd been doing lately, she would create a scene that would drive him out of the house and probably would cause the new maid to quit on the spot.

"Do you remember the dummy corporation I set up in your name about six months ago?"

Ann looked at him blankly.

"My God, don't you ever remember anything?"

"A great many things you'd prefer that I forget," she said,

becoming dignified.

"The corporation has been dormant, but I may have to bring it to life. Today. If I do, I'll bring some papers home for you to sign."

"What kind of papers?"

"What the hell do you care? Legal papers!"

"You know I don't like signing anything I don't understand. My father always—"

"I have no stomach for sermons about your goddam father this morning. I may be transferring my shares in Jackson Drive Realty to the dummy corporation, that's all."

She recalled at least one similar maneuver in the past, and knew at once that trouble was brewing. "What's the matter, Francis?"

"Nothing! I may find it convenient not to have my name associated with any of the Jefferson Square property deals, that's all."

His expression told her that his difficulties were even more serious than she had guessed. "I don't know anything about your business ventures—"

"Then why hound me with stupid questions?" he demanded.

"Because I can tell that something isn't going right. How bad is it, Francis?"

He hesitated, then sat down on the side of her bed and put his hand over hers. "I don't know. Yet."

When he wilted he looked old and weary, and she felt that, perhaps, he really did need her. "What's the worst it could mean—to you?"

Francis decided that candor was preferable to evasion. If there should be an explosion, it was better that Ann be prepared for the shock. "A nasty financial scandal may break into the open at any time," he said.

"And Albert Herder is one of the principals?"

"He's more deeply involved than anyone else, but some of the other big boys are in it, too. All the Hopkins clan. And the Metropolitan-National crowd. I'm just a punk who has a rooting interest, and I want to avoid complications. There are all kinds of angles to this thing, and wheels within wheels. Nothing that would cause the Bar Association to start proceedings against me, but it could be damned embarrassing. Ben Hopkins can afford to ride out any storm. I can't."

"You say you'll know today."

360

"Maybe." Francis sat in a slump. "Al is going to schedule a meeting for this afternoon, if he can, and then we may know more."

Ann picked up his hand and held it against her face. "I'll sign any papers you bring home," she said. "You know I'm always glad to help."

Warren wandered disconsolately around his apartment until he heard the electric coffee-maker stop perking. Then he went into his small kitchen to pour his first cup of the day, and carried it back into his living room. Ordinarily he enjoyed the view at breakfast, but today the drapes were opened only enough to let in a little daylight, and he had no interest in the newspapers, either.

It was absurd, he thought, that "one of the world's most eligible bachelors," as the tabloids insisted on calling him, should be so lonely. He was sometimes tempted to hire a butler or maid who would prepare a proper meal for him in the mornings, but, being a Hopkins, he was reluctant to spend his money ostentatiously. He ate so few meals at home that any servant other than a cleaning woman was unnecessary. It was no chore, certainly, to prepare himself a simple breakfast.

This morning, however, he had no appetite, and rejected both cereal and eggs. He was willing to grant that he was feeling sorry for himself, a state of mind which the family elders discouraged, but the truth of the matter was that he was lonely.

Occasionally Carolyn had arrived for an early breakfast with him, but it wasn't at all satisfactory when she came from the outside. A man should have his breakfast with the woman who had shared his bed the previous night. And he always felt a trifle uncomfortable when Carolyn puttered around the place. She left the kitchen in a mess when she insisted on squeezing fresh oranges, and his scrambled eggs were superior to hers.

Actually, Warren supposed, what continued to bother him was the knowledge that Carolyn was married to someone else. No matter how hard he tried, he couldn't forget it, and sometimes he had been relieved when she had been late. This morning he was grateful that he hadn't invited her to join him.

It was frustrating to recognize his own inadequacies, to

know he still couldn't decide whether he wanted to be married to her. Their marriage would cause a sensation, of course, and they'd have to avoid the gossip-hungry and lascivious, who would bombard them with invitations. The people who mattered to them would cause no such problem, and would simply cut them. Certainly no member of the family would speak to them, and Uncle Ben probably would insist that they leave town.

What really bothered him, Warren decided, was the nagging feeling that he didn't want Carolyn as his wife. He was very fond of her, of course, yet realized there was no way a man could damn his mistress with fainter praise. What distressed him most was the fear that she would become bored, and eventually would be unfaithful to him. Their romance was civilized, and he suspected that a woman who had cheated on one husband would find it easy to be unfaithful to another.

Starting back toward the kitchen for another cup of coffee, Warren paused when he saw an envelope on a table. It had slipped his mind that he had been sent two seats for a preview of an Austrian-made cinema, Mozart's *Don Giovanni*.

It was precisely the sort of evening that Betsy would love. He tried to rid himself of the thought and hurried out to the kitchen, but the envelope was still resting on the table when he returned. If he called Betsy, she'd probably refuse to speak to him, and he wouldn't be able to blame her.

The temptation to ask her to join him for the evening was so great, however, that he wrestled with it for more than a quarter of an hour. Finally, in exasperation, he looked up the phone number of a girl he scarcely knew, unaware whether she liked opera or hated it, and called her.

Dan stirred beneath the covers, opened one eye and saw daylight through the closed blinds. He turned when he heard a faint sound at the far side of the bedroom, saw that Phyllis was fully dressed and struggled to a sitting position.

"I'm so sorry, honey," she said. "I tried to be as quiet as I could."

"You didn't wake me up. This damn thing didn't go off." He pointed accusingly at his bedside alarm clock, but was still too groggy to see it clearly. "What time is it?"

"Nine o'clock, and I turned it off."

"Nine!" He started to climb out of bed.

"I've already called your office and told them you'll be late this morning." Phyllis went to him, and with a hand on his shoulder, gently tried to push him down. "Why don't you sleep for another hour or two?"

"I can't. I have too much to do."

"Can't it wait, just this once? You were sleeping so soundly this morning that I didn't have the heart to let you get up. It's the first time in weeks you've slept like that."

"I was slugged," Dan admitted, flexing the muscles in his shoulders and neck. Then, seeing her start toward him, he quickly pulled on his robe and headed toward the bathroom. The torture he endured when they exchanged intimate gestures was growing worse, and he knew he would not be free of his self-inflicted hell until he got Berenice out of his system. It was impossible, he discovered, for a man of his temperament to express his deep love for one woman while wanting another, and the dilemma he had created for himself, combined with the approaching opening of the square and the completion of his book, caused pressures that were becoming unbearable.

When he emerged from the bathroom after his shave and shower, he found Phyllis waiting for him with fruit juice and steaming coffee on a tray.

"I'll get your toast for you," she said, "and I wish you'd eat a couple of soft-boiled eggs."

"No toast, thanks. And I couldn't even look at eggs."

"You haven't eaten a real breakfast in weeks, honey," Phyllis said.

"I'll make up for it at lunch."

She could see his ribs when he crossed the room in his shorts to get a shirt from his dresser, and she couldn't remember a time when he had been so thin. "Is that a promise?"

"No," he admitted, inserting links into the cuffs of the shirt. "But don't hound me, Phyl."

She fell silent, and kept busy while he dressed, drank his fruit juice and started his coffee. But his change bothered her, and she could not remain quiet indefinitely. "Am I really such a shrew?" she demanded.

"Sometimes, maybe." Dan saw the hurt in her face, and tried to make amends. "Not really. I've been finding it so tough to live with myself that I keep shifting the blame, and I seem to elect you every time."

She nodded, relieved that, at least, he recognized his own pattern. "How much longer will this last?"

"If I could get rid of my jumping nerves today, I would. Believe me."

"Well, you're on the last chapter of the book, and then you ought to breathe more easily."

"It isn't the book itself that bothers me. It's good."

"When may I read it, Dan?"

He hedged slightly, not quite knowing why he was reluctant to let her see the manuscript. "Soon."

Phyllis knew he had been procrastinating for months, but reserved comment.

"What really eats into me is knowing what the reactions will be when men who have trusted me hear about it. I don't know what it will do to some of them, but it's one awful feeling to know that Governor Herder's political career will be ruined. By me."

"You're hardly responsible for what he's done, honey. He's destroyed himself."

"Even if he's committed public suicide, it isn't much fun being the undertaker." It was absurd to wish she were less understanding, less sympathetic, but he did wish it nevertheless. "I've decided," he said, "to show a copy of the completed manuscript to Ben Hopkins."

Phyllis stared at him.

"You think I'm crazy."

"Frankly, yes," she said.

"He's been decent with me, even if he is a pirate, and I don't want to do anything behind his back."

"Have you told Harvey?"

"To hell with Harvey."

"He'll have to know."

"Eventually."

"No," Phyllis said. "Before you give the manuscript to Mr. Hopkins. A man with his power could find some way to prevent publication. Legally, or through putting financial pressure on Simpson and Smith. I don't know how, exactly, but in some way. And I honestly think you've got to be fair to Harvey and give him warning, even if you won't listen to whatever he may say to you."

"I shouldn't have told you." Dan made no attempt to hide his irritation, and finished dressing in silence.

Phyllis turned away, wanting to scream. Every time she

managed to establish some semblance of rapport with him, it was spoiled by a wrong word or gesture. Even if what she had just said was right, and she believed it was, she should have known enough to remain quiet and let him handle the matter as he saw fit. On the other hand, what kind of a marriage had theirs become if she had to weigh every move, everything she said for fear of offending him?"

Edward Emory sat at the breakfast table, methodically checking through the financial and business sections of the newspapers in front of him, occasionally making a brief notation in a small leather book with a gold pencil. Even when scribbling, his handwriting was neat. He put his newspapers aside to eat his stewed fruit and poached eggs on toast, then turned to them again while he sipped his coffee, and was so engrossed that he failed to hear Carolyn come into the dining room.

"Good morning," she said.

"Good morning, my dear." He raised his face for a ritual peck.

She went to her seat at the opposite end of the table and rang the little ivory-handled bell for the maid. "Did you sleep well?" she asked, wrapping her peignoir around her.

"Not too badly. And you?" He found an item that interested him, read it more carefully, and wrote more extensively in the notebook.

"I'm afraid I wandered around my room half the night," Carolyn said.

"You aren't ill, I hope."

"No, it was just one of those nights."

"You seem to have had quite a few of them lately." Edward waited until the maid gave Carolyn her coffee, poured more for him and left the room. "This stuff may be doing it to you." He tapped his cup. "You might experiment with my system. Try some with reduced caffeine."

"I loathe the taste. Besides, I'm sure it isn't the coffee. Some nights I sleep beautifully."

He was absorbed in the newspapers, and some moments passed before he replied. "Have you thought of seeing a doctor?"

Carolyn smiled. "I'm not ill, dear."

"It does no harm to have a regular checkup, you know. They advise it, all of them."

"I'll do it when I can find the time," she temporized. "Once the square has opened, I'm positive my insomnia will go."

"I wish you wouldn't think of Jefferson Square as your personal responsibility. It isn't." Edward took a tiny gold knife from his vest pocket, opened it and neatly cut a clipping from the newspaper he was perusing.

"I wish I could become more detached," she said. "But after all this time my involvement is too great."

He raised his head and really looked at her for the first time since she had come into the dining room. "I'm well aware of your involvement."

Carolyn's heart pounded, but she maintained a calm façade. "I've worked much harder raising money for the square and serving on various committees than I ever did on the hospital drives or the other campaigns."

Edward was still looking at her. "You'll be far happier, I'm sure, when you've cut your ties."

She wondered how much he knew, whether he was warning her or whether his phraseology was just a coincidence.

He smiled, too, rather blandly. "You can't see yourself, my dear, so you probably don't realize how strained you've become." He paused. "I find I've got to make a trip to London, and thought you might want to come with me. I'm flying over, but I'd like to come back by ship."

"It sounds very pleasant. I always enjoy London." She was guarded. "When are you going, Edward?"

"I'm not quite sure. We've set no dates yet."

"I definitely want to be here for the openings of the repertory and the symphony."

"I think I can arrange my schedule to fit those dates. I wouldn't want to miss them, either."

Carolyn hesitated for an instant. "You couldn't wait until spring, I suppose. I'm thinking of all that needs to be done at the museum."

Edward folded his newspapers and put the notebook and pencil into his inside jacket pocket. "I'll have to leave soon after the symphony opening, I'm sure." He put his napkin on the table and rose. "If you want to come with me, you'll have to be ready then. And if you don't mind my saying so, my dear, the only way you'll ever divorce yourself from the square will be to take a deep breath—and do it."

366

Betsy had cancelled a shopping date with a friend and a beauty parlor appointment, and had announced that she intended to spend the entire morning in bed. Her window was open a half-inch, and the cold forced her to remain under the covers, but she was wide awake, staring at the ceiling. She supposed she ought to get up for some breakfast, or at least a glass of milk, but her lethargy was too great.

She needed sleep, but had been awake most of the night, and when she had occasionally drifted off for short periods, she had dreamed of Warren, which had made her doubly uncomfortable when she had regained consciousness. She was a big girl, she told herself fiercely, and the time had come to put Warren Hopkins out of her mind and keep him out.

The percentages had gone against her, she had lost, and now she had to learn to accept defeat with good grace.

But the prospect of going through life without Warren crushed her. Until her final meeting with him she had felt so certain that, if she waited patiently enough, he would break off his affair and come to her. It was bewildering as well as heartbreaking to find that he had done no such thing.

Her real trouble, Betsy told herself angrily, was that she had never before failed to get anything she had wanted. Her parents had indulged all her whims, and even though they and their friends considered her sensible, she didn't agree. She was spoiled, and couldn't accept her own failure.

Her musician friends, she knew, would laugh at her plight. She was wealthy, she spent more on a season's wardrobe than they earned in a year, and she could go where she pleased, do as she wished. Any one of them would be delighted to change places with her. She would be willing, if only such a transfer would bring Warren to her.

She wasn't the only person who had ever been disappointed in love, she knew, and she would survive. From all she had read she imagined the painful emptiness she felt would begin to subside one day, but until it did she would have to bear her suffering.

It was a waste of effort to tell herself she was behaving like a foolish adolescent. Scolding didn't help. Nothing helped. At least she had stopped weeping, but she could take no credit for self-control; she had cried herself out, and there were no more tears in her.

"I'll do anything to get him," she said aloud. "Anything!"

367

Fourteen very senior executives of the various Hopkins enterprises were gathered at the table in the private dining room high in Hopkins Tower, waiting. All of them had already eaten at home or in their hotel suites, but their Thursday morning breakfasts were an obligatory tradition, and only illness or absence from the city on necessary business excused them from attendance. Some were the presidents of major corporations, others were untitled, but in this room their stature automatically diminished. They conversed in low tones, and no one smoked, because that, too, was a tradition handed down since the first Benjamin Hopkins had inaugurated the breakfasts.

Halved grapefruits sat at each place, and in the pantry adjoining the dining room the members of the staff waited, too. At the appropriate moment the meal would be served; until then it had to be hot, in readiness.

At last Benjamin Hopkins came into the dining room, nodding to his associates.

All of them stood, a custom many privately detested, but not once in the span of three generations had anyone voiced his sentiments aloud to the group. By the time a man reached the top of the hierarchy, he appreciated the value of maintaining certain forms.

Ben Hopkins went to his place at the head of the table and bowed his head. *"Defend, O Lord, these servants with thy heavenly grace that we may continue thine for ever; and daily increase in thy holy Spirit more and more, until we come into thy everlasting kingdom."* Like his father and grandfather before him, he opened every Thursday morning breakfast with the same line from the *Book of Common Prayer.*

Then he and his lieutenants sat down to their grapefruit. "I'm sorry I'm a few minutes late, gentlemen, but I've been tied up on the overseas telephone." He passed a slip of paper to the man two places to his right. "Copper is moving up too fast on the London and Zurich markets today, Roland."

Roland F. Curtis, principal executive officer of the world's largest and most powerful copper consortium, studied the figures briefly. "I'll issue a statement this morning to the effect that our South American mines will increase production in the next six months. That should steady prices."

Someone farther down the table raised his head. "But we can't possibly increase the Andean labor force on such short notice."

"I doubt if it will be necessary to increase actual production," Ben Hopkins said. "The mere announcement should be enough for our purposes. Henry, welcome home. How was Tokyo?"

"Bustling, as always," said Henry W. Adams, President of World-Wide Trading. "All of you will find copies of my report to Ben on your desks. In a word, we're increasing our exports to Japan by an estimated four percent in the next quarter, and our imports from the Tokyo subsidiary will go up at least five percent. For the benefit of any of you who may be going over there in the near future, Tajo Soyoyami's new cook is a gem. He can do anything with steak."

The butler inadvertently chose that moment to send in the platters of creamed chipped beef on toast, and several of the gentlemen smiled. Everyone assumed that the dish was served at the Thursday morning breakfasts because, presumably, the first Benjamin Hopkins had liked it. Only Ben Hopkins knew for certain, and it had never occurred to his associates to ask him. None of them really liked creamed chipped beef, but grew accustomed to it after spending several years in the inner circle.

Like it or not, however, everyone ate.

Conversation was brisk and ordered. Each man made a short report, stressing matters he thought the others should hear, and there were a few comments before the spotlight turned to the next. The breakfast never lasted past ten o'clock, and those who wanted to discuss a problem in detail adjourned after the meal to the office of one or another for the purpose. The servants had withdrawn, every man poured his own coffee or tea from his individual pot, and there were no outside interruptions. Although there was no specific rule against the receipt of important telephone calls, no member of the group could recall hearing any of the instruments in the room ring during the Thursday breakfasts.

At 9:59 Ben Hopkins stood. "One final word in a somewhat lighter vein, gentlemen. Let me remind you that the Repertory Theater at Jefferson Square is opening next week, and I hope that those of you who can attend will be there. My wife is looking forward to the evening, and I dare say yours are, too. I'm taking the liberty of mentioning the opening only because most of us have made major contributions to the square, and the prestige of the Hopkins Fund is partic-

369

ularly committed. Henry, if you and Theodore can spare a few minutes, perhaps you'll join me in my office for a survey of the proposed tariff schedules the Common Market countries have just drawn up."

The desk clock in Michele's sitting room chimed ten as Anton sauntered in, resplendent in green silk dressing gown and matching pajamas. "I thought I smelled French coffee."

Michele, who had been writing a letter, stood and went to the tray to pour him a cup. "You said in the note you left me that you wanted to sleep late."

"I just got up a few minutes ago."

"That's hardly late."

"If I could have slept longer, I'd still be in bed," he snapped. Then, watching her, he added more quietly, "Just the *café*, please. Never mind the *au lait*."

Michele knew he liked the taste of the strong coffee and chicory after a hard night's work. "How did it go?"

He dropped onto the sofa and ran his long fingers through his close-cropped hair. "I've never heard worse."

"It couldn't have been that bad."

"Permit me to know my own musicians and my own composition. We'll need at least one more session, probably two, before we can record the *Concerto*."

Michele saw that his hand was trembling slightly as he picked up his coffee cup and saucer. "Were you late?"

"I kept them at it until almost two, with only one break."

It had been a far longer night's work than she had realized. "Any complaints?"

Anton sipped the bitter brew, shuddered and took another swallow. "The second violins bitched, as usual, but I shut them up. I must admit I felt sorry for the oboes. They must have done those long passages at least ten times. Bad as they were, I could see they were exhausted by the time I let them out."

Michele sympathized with the entire orchestra. When Anton was rehearsing for a recording of one of his own works, nothing satisfied him, and he drove his men as mercilessly as he drove himself.

"The *Concerto* is ghastly," he said abruptly.

"Just yesterday you told me again that it's the best you've ever done."

"I heard it for hours last night," he said, growing an-

370

noyed, "and I've changed my mind."

Michele knew that nothing she might say would ease his unhappiness.

"If I had time, I'd rewrite the second movement." He finished his coffee and, snapping his fingers, pointed to his cup.

She swallowed her own anger and refilled the cup.

"I'd take it out of the opening program if it hadn't been publicized so heavily. Either that or postpone the opening."

"You can't, Anton."

"I'm thinking of it," he said with stubborn petulance.

Michele could see a new storm brewing. "Discuss a postponement with Dan Robertson, not with me."

"I have. He sat through the rehearsal and brought me home. I told him when we had hamburgers sent in at the end of the rehearsal. I was ravenous, but he lost his appetite when he heard my idea."

"I dare say."

"He refused to let me postpone. Or drop the *Concerto*. But I simply can't play something that isn't right."

She forced herself to smile reassuringly and remain silent. Anton wanted a stiff argument, which would give him a chance to release his emotions in a temper tantrum, but she refused to give him the opportunity he sought.

"Either the entire orchestra is made up exclusively of men who play with their thumbs—which is possible—or I've written one of the worst failures of the decade."

She forcibly changed the subject. "Why did you have hamburgers sent in? There are enough places open in the square neighborhood these days."

"Obviously," he flared, "as you'd know if you'd been paying any attention when we've gone to one of those restaurants, they're filled with celebrity-hunters after midnight. How can I relax, how can I enjoy myself if they're sitting at their tables, staring at me and whispering? How I loathe them when they come up to me with their autograph books and simper, 'We've seen you on television.' As though that gave us a bond of kinship!"

Michele realized she could not point out to him that, more frequently than not, he loved being recognized in public places, that he signed autographs with gusto, and that he had sometimes sulked when people hadn't known him in public places.

"I told Dan—forcibly, too—that we ought to have a special eating and drinking place in the square for the use of no one but performing artists and their guests. They're putting in four restaurants and a cafeteria. Think of it! Five, in all! But in every one of them we'll be annoyed by the yokels. City yokels. Yokels from Crotch, Kansas. Yokels from all over the world. How in God's name can we unwind in front of people who expect us to behave as though we're on stage?"

"What did Dan say?" Michele refused to become entangled in the substance of his proposal.

"He was very decent about it. There's no provision for a performing artists' club in any of the blueprints, although God knows we have enough Green Rooms, recreation rooms, smoking rooms and all the rest. I refuse to submit to the indignity of getting a stale sandwich and a bottle of milk out of a machine!"

"You were telling me about Dan."

Anton finished his coffee, stood and began to roam around the room. "Yes. He's going to take up the whole idea with the board. He couldn't promise me they'd do anything, which is fair enough. He explained that we're over our budget now. Astronomically. He's a very decent fellow, you know." Suddenly he halted and looked at the clock. "I have three hours before I'm due at the hall. I think I'll do something about that second movement and see if I can make it less of a mess."

He would work himself into a frenzy before the day ended, she knew, unless she intervened. So she went to him, opened his dressing gown and, embracing him, reached under his pajama coat and began to stroke his back.

"Don't start anything," he said. "Please. I'm simply not in the mood for it today!"

Michele ignored his protests and her caresses became more insistent.

372

CHAPTER EIGHT

When Dan reached his office an hour and a half later than usual, he found a pile of telephone messages, among them one from Berenice Tolmey, saying she would call him again when there was a break in the *Confessional* rehearsals. He felt a twinge of uneasiness, knowing that Jerry Solanz had flown to California, but he became busier than usual, thanks to his tardiness, and forgot Berenice until he heard her voice on the phone at noon.

"I've been trying to reach you all morning," she said, "but I've been on stage nearly the whole time, and this is my first chance to call." She sounded a little breathless.

"How is the play going?"

"With Jerry not here, it's a ball! I'd almost forgotten that acting could be so much fun."

"I'll bet."

"I've been wanting to see you," Berenice said. "Could you meet me after rehearsals this afternoon? We'll be through at five."

"Let me check my calendar," he said. "That's a little early for me. How about five forty-five?"

"I'm so glad!"

"I understand there's a new bar that's just opened, about a block from the opera—"

"We aren't going to a bar today," Berenice said with a laugh. "Or to a museum garden. Or for a taxi ride."

He was apprehensive, and hoped, too, that his secretary or someone else in the outer office wasn't listening to their conversation.

"I have a surprise for you. Write down this address."

He picked up a pen, and jotted down a street name and number that meant nothing to him.

"It's 12C," she said. "Don't forget that, because it isn't in my name."

Dan's uneasiness increased. Apparently she was arranging a liaison in a friend's apartment.

"I'll meet you there at a quarter to six, sharp," she said. "Come straight up when you get there."

He stared at the slip of paper after she hung up. He reached for his telephone and quickly dialed a number. "Hello, Phyl," he said. "I'm going to be late tonight. I—don't know how late."

The rented Ford moved up Jackson Drive, preceded by two state troopers on motorcycles who, however, did not use their sirens. Behind the wheel Albert Herder was grim, his homburg pulled down on his head, his gloved hands gripping the wheel so hard the leather was pulled taut.

Sandra, lounging against the far corner of the front seat, looked at ease. Her fur-collared coat was open, her skirt was riding high, and she smoked nonchalantly, evidently enjoying the experience. Not even her mother would have known she was nervous.

"Let's start talking," the Governor said. "The leaders of the Legislature are coming to my office in an hour."

Sandra rolled down the window beside her.

Herder was disconcerted. "That's a cold wind. I can't afford to get laryngitis, I'm making an address at a banquet tonight."

"Just let me take a few deep breaths before I close it."

"Now then," he said curtly, "this is not my idea of the way to spend a winter afternoon. What do you want?"

"What's fair," she replied promptly.

He laughed. "I don't think our concepts of equity would coincide."

"If I'd gotten what I first wanted—"

"We can skip the justifications, too."

Sandra's voice became hard. "All I'm interested in now is cash."

"Before you point a gun at me, I've checked with Dan Robertson, and he doesn't have the papers that supposedly incriminate me."

"I never said he actually had them." Unless Dan actually double-crossed her, she felt she owed him and his publisher at least token loyalty. Even though it would be a long time before the book came out, she had been paid a good price

374

for the letters. "I'll bet he didn't deny he knew about them. And had read them."

"Well, no."

She was triumphant. "Then it doesn't matter where they are. It's enough that I can prove you're guilty, so what more do we need?"

"I don't consider myself guilty of anything! I have legitimate business interests—"

"Okay. If you want to let the voters decide, I guess we have nothing to talk about." The interior of the car was becoming chilly, and she wrapped herself in her coat.

"You say you want cash." An ugly note crept into his voice. "How much?"

"Fifty thousand would be fair." She managed to speak calmly.

Although the car was moving swiftly up the drive, he turned for a moment and stared at her. He had been willing to pay her a small sum in order to be rid of her, provided he could make reasonably certain she would not annoy him again, but fifty thousand dollars was far too much to give any blackmailer. "What makes you think I could raise that much?"

"Come off it. Everybody knows you're loaded. It was just this week I read that you gave your wife a diamond and emerald bracelet for an anniversary present."

Herder cursed the gossip columnists who allowed him no private life. "That was an exaggeration."

Sandra was silent for a moment. Once he showed a willingness to bargain, she would reduce her demand, but until then she intended to hold firm. "You asked me what I want. Now you know."

"I'm afraid," he said, "that you have a false idea of my personal finances." He touched the horn lightly, the troopers glanced around, and at his signal they swung over to the opposite side of the drive. He followed and they began their return to the center of the city.

She hoped he was bluffing; it seemed inconceivable to her that he would make no counter-offer to prevent her from telling her story to the press.

Herder wanted time to hash over the situation with Dougherty and Eddie and a few others he could trust. An initial payment of fifty thousand would mean, eventually, a tremendous outlay when she kept coming back for more, and he couldn't allow her threat to stand between him and his long-range ambitions. "I can't just reach into my wallet for fifty thousand dollars," he said. "No matter how rich you may think I am, I don't carry that kind of money around with me."

"I never thought you did!" Sandra retorted, her excitement rising. "But you're agreeing to pay it?"

"I haven't agreed to anything yet. You've just come to me, and I need to think about it."

"What's there to think about?"

"A great many things, which I'm under no obligation to spell out to you. You'll have to trust me to work this out to our mutual advantage."

"That's double-talk," she said scornfully.

"It's the best I can do at the moment. I'll get in touch with you, and we'll meet again in a few days."

"How soon?"

"I don't want this matter dragging on, any more than you do." He coughed slightly. "Now put up the window, please."

For a moment or two she made no move, then obeyed.

"That's better," he said in relief as warm air from the heater flooded the car.

Sandra let her coat fall open again. "I suppose you're going to the opening of the Repertory Theater at the square."

"I imagine we'll be there." The motorcycles turned off the drive and, heading into heavier traffic, began to use their sirens. The car did not lose speed. "Are you going?"

All the bitterness engendered by Sandra's futile dreams welled up in her. "Who'd ask me?"

Herder glanced at her briefly, and for an instant was intrigued by the quantity of thigh she showed. Eddie had indicated she "could be had," but hadn't gone into detail, and it was just barely possible that an affair might quiet her down.

But he rejected the idea almost as quickly as it occurred to him. A cheap mistress would be far more of a nuisance than a blackmailer, and could cause countless problems during his campaign for the Presidency. He couldn't recall who had said that politics and women did not mix, but he had always been careful to adhere to that rule of thumb.

"I don't give a damn if I never see the inside of Jefferson Square," Sandra said.

376

The apartment building was like a score of others in its immediate neighborhood, tall, solid and ugly. It was no more than three years old, but its façade of yellow brick was already turning a grubby city gray, and most of its windows, set in frames of uncompromising steel, were smeared with a thin layer of soot. The canopy extending from the entrance to the curb gave it a mild air of pseudo-distinction, but there was no doorman on duty, and its tiny lobby with its two small settees in red and white striped imitation velvet, had already acquired an air of shabbiness.

Dan had grown sufficiently accustomed to metropolitan living to pinpoint the economic level of the building's inhabitants. The majority, he believed, were in their twenties, secretaries and other office workers who shared apartments, young executives-of-tomorrow who did the same. He guessed the building had its share of newlyweds who, as their fortunes improved, would move into buildings of which this place was a relatively inexpensive copy, and there were undoubtedly some middle-aged couples in the place, too, childless men and women who had lost their dreams and even their hopes, but were clinging to a façade of middle-class respectability. A small, printed sign stood inside a frame at the entrance. *"One to Three Room Apartments,"* it read, *"with all modern conveniences. Some with terraces. No children or pets."* Below was the name, address and telephone number of the realty management company.

Dan pushed the elevator button and ascended swiftly to the twelfth floor in the tiny cage, and glanced at his watch. He was just five minutes late. His stomach was turning over, his nerves felt raw, exposed, and he could not rid himself of an unpleasant, furtive sense of guilt. He had come here for an assignation, and could no longer tell himself he was doing research for his book, or that he was motivated by a desire to help Berenice.

He found Apartment 12C without difficulty, and musical chimes sounded when he pushed the buzzer.

After a very brief wait Berenice opened the door. She was wearing a sleeveless turtle-neck blouse and slacks of thin, off-white silk jersey, a wide black belt, matching pumps with small heels and dangling jet earrings. Her makeup was so fresh it looked as though she had just applied it.

"Hi!" she said. "You almost beat me here, but I managed to get everything done."

As she helped Dan with his coat and hat he took in the entire apartment in a single glance. It consisted of a tiny living room, a smaller bedroom and an infinitesimal kitchen. On a coffee table before the divan that was the living room's one substantial piece of furniture stood a pitcher of martinis, a bottle of bourbon, a carafe of water and a bucket of ice. Judging from the cocktail glass near the pitcher, Berenice had already consumed the better part of a martini.

"Well," Dan said awkwardly. "Isn't this something."

"I borrowed it from a girlfriend of mine who used to be an actress, too," Berenice said. "She couldn't make a living at it, so she went into modeling, and now she has a regular job in a dress house. Over in the garment district. At least she eats regularly."

"It's very nice," Dan said.

"Let me show you around."

"I can see it all from here."

Berenice looked at him. "We've been waiting a long time, haven't we?" She went to him, and curled her arms around his neck.

As Dan embraced and kissed her, holding her close, he realized she was wearing nothing beneath her blouse and slacks. It no longer mattered what she had been earlier in life; her association with Jerry Solanz had transformed her into a version of the part she was playing in *Confessional*.

She rubbed against him, a lithe, young kitten, eager to be taken, and his kiss became more demanding.

Suddenly Berenice broke away. "Gee," she said breathlessly. "I don't know what it is, but when you and I start to make out, fireworks start exploding."

She went to the coffee table and sat down to mix him a stiff highball, her manner cozily proprietary.

Dan could almost imagine himself married to her. But apart from wanting each other, they shared so little. And the thought of leaving Phyllis was unbearable. The prospect of giving up the children altogether numbed him.

He had seen Saturday fathers exercising their rights of custody at the zoo and elsewhere in the park, their expressions wistful and tired and somewhat irritated, their manner over-indulgent and a trifle bored. It was all too easy to picture himself in a similar position, and the very idea frightened him.

"Here," Berenice said, handing him the glass. "I hope this is your brand."

"Any brand is fine."

She filled her martini glass. "At least I remembered that you drink bourbon."

"You've gone to a lot of bother."

She raised her glass in a silent toast.

Dan held his glass up to her, and sipped. The highball she had mixed was so potent he almost choked on it. "Did you do all this after rehearsals?"

"Uh-huh. What a rush. I got out a few minutes early, though. I set my watch ahead, as a gag, and all the others went along with it. That poor Milt, he didn't know any better, so he let all of us out at quarter of five instead of five." Her giggle sounded like a schoolgirl's. But her eyes were luminous. "Come and sit down."

"In a minute." He felt safer with the coffee table separating them.

She continued to pat the place beside her on the divan for a moment or two, but her hand slowed and then fell still, and there was a hurt look in her eyes.

"I wanted to ask you about today's rehearsal," Dan said hastily.

Berenice brightened. "What a riot we had. Poor Milt tries to act like he's Jerry, and he had us holding our sides. First we ran through the whole play once—"

"How did it go?"

"I didn't fluff one line or get one piece of stage business wrong!"

He was reminded of a small child bringing home a report card filled with A's.

"I just breezed through it. Without Jerry there, I wasn't scared or nervous or anything."

"That's great," Dan said.

She sipped her drink. "Julian Adams and that crazy Hank Grossman sat me on their shoulders and paraded around the stage. It was a kind of celebration, or something."

"You had cause for celebration."

"Milt didn't think so. He had to keep acting like he was Jerry, so he found a million things wrong. Especially with me, of course. So that started us. The whole company." She rocked with laughter for a moment before resuming. "We started to ad lib. And we emphasized all the wrong things in the regular lines. You know, to give them a dirty meaning—"

"Double-entendre."

"That's it. We kept breaking ourselves up. And the more we kidded around, the madder Milt got. But nobody paid any attention to him, and even Jan Marek thought it was a gasser. Every time I saw him sitting out front, he had his glasses off, and he was laughing so hard he was crying. It was the first day I've had any real fun since we started working on this play." Suddenly her face darkened. "But I've had it. Tomorrow the hell starts again."

"Will Milt tell Solanz he lost control of the rehearsal today?"

"Milt? He wouldn't dare. If he did, then everything that goes wrong between now and the opening would be Milt's fault. Jerry would skin his ass. Anyway," she said, "Jan would protect us, and it's too late for Jerry to fire us and get another company together by next week." She drained her drink, brooded for a moment and then, refilling her glass, looked up at Dan.

They had exhausted the one topic of conversation that was of mutual interest, and he had nothing to say.

The ringing of the telephone broke the tension. "Excuse me." Berenice stood and went off into the bedroom to answer it. The conversation was brief, and Berenice was smiling when she returned to her place on the divan. "That was Claire."

Dan looked blank.

"My girlfriend who owns this apartment."

Dan nodded and took a long swallow of his drink.

"Claire is great. We roomed together when we first went over to England to hunt for jobs in the theater."

There was a silence after that, which was broken by Berenice. "Dan," she said, "I need to be loved."

Dan felt as though a razor had slashed him across the face. The lie itself would be easy enough to perpetrate. He was sufficiently aroused to tell her he loved her, and could say it with conviction.

But the consequences would be catastrophic. She was not a girl to be used and thrown aside like a cheap one-shot pickup. If he committed himself, he would have to be prepared to follow through in the days and months ahead. The words stuck in his throat.

380

"I somehow get the impression," Berenice said, "that the party's over. Is that right, Dan?"

"That's a terrible way to put it, Berenice. But, yes, maybe it's better that way for both of us."

"I'm glad Claire drinks bourbon," she said. "I think we'll get stoned together."

Dan watched her as she moved off to the bedroom, to the telephone. When he heard her talking to Claire, he let himself out of the apartment.

Taxis were scarce, and it took him a quarter of an hour to flag one down. He gave the driver his address, and glanced at his watch; only an hour had passed since he had first arrived at Berenice's borrowed apartment.

Dan lit a cigarette, and an unfamiliar taste on his lips caused him to look at the butt end. There was lipstick on it, so he took a handkerchief from his pocket and scrubbed his mouth. When he next looked at the handkerchief, under the glare of a neon sign as the taxi halted at a stoplight, he saw it was smeared with pale pink.

He continued to hold the handkerchief in his hand until the taxi slowed to a halt at his own apartment building. Then he stuffed the crumpled square of linen into a corner of the upholstered seat.

Phyllis was in their bedroom as he came into the apartment and put his hat and coat in the foyer closet. "Well. Surprise!" she called. "I wasn't expecting you for hours."

"I guess I'm a little earlier than I thought." He raised his voice, too, and lingered in the living room, ashamed to face her.

"Francis Dougherty phoned you a little while ago," she told him as she joined him. "He said he couldn't get you at your office, and he wants you to call him at once. Here's the number."

Dan took the slip of paper from her. Turning away from her, he busied himself at the phone.

Phyllis was very much aware of his failure to give her even a token kiss of greeting. These days he frequently ignored what had been their virtually inviolable custom, and she wondered how much longer she could put up with his new indifference.

Dougherty answered his phone after a single ring, and

sounded grim. "I'm sure as all hell glad to hear from you, Dan," he said. "I want to get together with you as soon as you can make it."

"Suit your own convenience, Francis. I'm available."

"Would I get in the way of your evening's plans if I drop over right now?"

"We don't have any, but I can meet you some place, if you prefer."

"No, I won't impose on you any more than I can help. I'll hop in a cab and be there in a few minutes."

Dan turned to Phyllis after he cradled the telephone. "He's coming right over."

She stifled a sigh. The increasing tempo of activities at the square and of Dan's involvement in them had virtually destroyed their normal domestic life. "I ate dinner just before you came home because I didn't think you'd be here until late. Have you had anything?"

He shook his head as he started toward a living-room chair. "Not yet, but I'm not hungry."

"You've got to eat. Francis may stay for hours."

"I'll wait."

"Let me fix you a sandwich and some milk."

Dan shook his head. "Don't nag at me. Please."

Her own nerves were raw. "If that's nagging—"

"It isn't," he interjected wearily. "I just want to sit for a few minutes before he gets here, that's all."

Phyllis left the room. When the door buzzer sounded, she answered the summons. By the time Dan hauled himself to his feet, she had already admitted the Jefferson Square attorney to the apartment.

"I'm terribly sorry, Phyllis," Francis said. "I've probably interrupted your dinner."

"No, you haven't. Come on in," she replied.

Dan greeted his guest with as much cordiality as he could muster, and offered him a drink.

"Just one," Francis said. "I've had a snort or two at the office."

Phyllis, who had been intending to leave the room with a quick apology, paused at the door. "Haven't you had dinner?"

Dougherty was embarrassed. "Things have been a little hectic—"

"Dan hasn't eaten, either. I'll do something about that."

Both men protested.

But she was on firm ground and would not listen. "It won't take me long to broil some steaks and fix a salad." She disappeared in the direction of the kitchen.

"Great gal," Dougherty said.

"Wonderful. Too good for me."

The lawyer's grin was wan. "Then there's the other kind." He took a swallow of his drink and sat back in his chair. "Al Herder tells me you had lunch with him yesterday, I think it was."

"Yes."

"There's a god-awful mess brewing, Dan. It's that bitch who worked for me, as I believe you know. She saw Al this afternoon and put a blackmail bite on him! She wants fifty thousand dollars from him as the price of keeping her mouth shut."

Dan suddenly felt ill.

Francis smiled sourly. "Grand, isn't it?"

"I had no idea she—"

"That broad would slit her own mother's throat if it would help her. Now, I don't know where you stand politically in this state—"

"I don't," Dan said. "I haven't been a resident long enough to vote in a state election here."

"I keep forgetting you're that new."

"Is the Governor going to prosecute Miss Masters?"

"How in God's name can he, particularly if she has real goods on him that will burn him? That's why I'm here. I don't want the square involved, and I don't want you drawn in, but you can still be one hell of a big help. It's true, isn't it, that she showed you some documents that would incriminate Al in a real estate combine?"

"Yes."

"I'm assuming," Francis said, "they were papers she stole from my office or had copied."

Dan didn't answer.

"I wouldn't want to be caught in the middle either if I were you. But there's one thing I want you to know, and I want to stress it. Albert Herder is a dedicated, honorable statesman. He's done nothing wrong. No matter how bad this or that document may make him look, he's broken no laws, and he's done nothing unethical."

Dan didn't know whether Dougherty was familiar with the Governor's private association with Harrison, MacFee, but assumed he knew all about it. In that case the attorney was staging an act on behalf of his client. He did it well, Dan had to concede.

"But when a man is in politics," Francis continued, "he can be made to look bad, even though every move he makes is legitimate. I could cite you a lot of examples, but I don't think I've got to spell it out for you."

"No, I know what you mean," Dan said.

Francis emptied his drink, but refused a refill. "There's just one thing I want to know from you. Is Sandra Masters bluffing, or does she really have documents that will castrate Al politically?"

Dan hesitated once more. His book would do far more than any efforts of Sandra's to dig the Governor's political grave. "I'd say they're incriminating."

"That's what I thought. I didn't think she'd stick her neck out unless she really had her mitts on something juicy. Okay, I guess that's it. We'll have to take it from there."

"What will you do?"

"I'll tell you what I'd like to do. Gag and bind her, and then watch Al pump bullets into her."

"I hope that's a bad joke."

"Relax. He's not a hoodlum, and he doesn't hire them either."

Dan could only hope the lawyer was telling the truth.

Harvey Simpson leafed through the sheets of paper in the heavy manuscript box. "I've been waiting a long time for this."

Dan studied the pattern in his publisher's rug. "I can't take any pleasure in this book. I still feel as though I've stabbed people who have been decent to me."

Harvey searched through the box. "Here we are. In this chapter on Governor Herder, you've more than justified the whole effort. You've done a great public service to the people of the entire country."

"I'm his executioner," Dan said, "and I don't think that any executioner is ever very happy about his job."

"I can only hope that your perspective will improve." Harvey closed the manuscript box. "I'll have this completely read by day after tomorrow."

384

"Aren't you coming to the opening of the Repertory Theater tomorrow night?"

"Of course. I'd forgotten it, and don't glare at me. You'll have to give me an extra twenty-four hours to read the book."

"Take all the time you want," Dan said dispiritedly.

"I shall. In the meantime I'll notify the accounting department to put the check for your advance royalties into the works."

"Not yet, please," Dan said. "I want to wait until I've gone off the square payroll."

"When will that be?"

"Your guess is as good as mine, Harvey. It will depend on Ben Hopkins."

"You're still determined to let him read the book?" The publisher sounded resigned.

"You know how I feel. I can't spend the rest of my life knowing I acted behind his back."

"If you insist."

"I'm sorry," Dan said, "but I'm afraid I do."

Harvey replied forcefully. "I'm not afraid of Benjamin Hopkins. I wouldn't go out of my way to pick a quarrel with the Hopkins empire. I don't think anyone in his right mind would. But I believe you've written an honest book about Jefferson Square, and if he tries to get tough, I won't avoid a fight. My own guess is that Hopkins is too smart a man to harass us. Do you have an extra carbon of the script?"

"One. Phyllis has been hounding me, so I gave it to her to read just before I came over here this morning."

"I'll be interested in her reaction." Harvey glanced at his watch. "I wonder if she'd like to join us for lunch. We've got to celebrate the completion of the book."

"Celebrations will have to wait," Dan said. "The square has become a madhouse. Aside from the last-minute headaches, we're being inundated by the press, and our public relations people are swamped. I've never known such excitement."

"You don't think you ought to add something about the opening in a postscript of some sort?"

"The place for it," Dan said, "will be in the conclusion to the section on Berenice Tolmey. That part of the book won't be complete until I include her performance in *Confessional*, and I think that's the place for a few pages of summary on the opening itself."

When Phyllis emerged from her bath and returned to the bedroom in her robe, Dan was already half-dressed, putting studs in his dress shirt. "How soon are you leaving?" she asked.

"As quickly as I can get out," he said. "I'm sorry I've got to dash to the square ahead of you, but there's so much—"

"I understand, honey."

"The Helsings will come for you at seven thirty, on the button. And don't be upset if I'm not in my seat when the curtain goes up. I'll join you as soon as I can."

"I just hope you'll have the chance to enjoy at least part of the evening."

"I'll be glad when it's over."

Phyllis wanted to raise his spirits, and although she knew this was no time to talk about his book, she couldn't resist telling him, "I finished your manuscript today, Dan. I sat up half the night with it, and I went back to it this morning. I think it's good."

He turned to her, shirt-tails hanging out. "You aren't just saying the right things?"

"I hope you know me better than that." She paused. "Your best writing is in the chapters on Berenice Tolmey."

Dan was uncertain whether he really heard something indefinable in her voice or whether he imagined it.

"You showed her such compassion. She'll be very pleased with the book."

"I doubt if she'll read it."

"I would," Phyllis said, weighing her words with great care. "I'd be flattered if someone wrote about me that way."

"Be glad you aren't in her place," Dan said gruffly. "If she fails in that part tonight, it could be the end of her."

The press began congregating at the Repertory Theater early. Representatives of the local newspapers had been on hand all day, and the special out-of-town reporters, including correspondents from abroad, started to saunter in around seven o'clock. *The New York Times,* which was running a special series of articles comparing and contrasting Jefferson Square with Lincoln Center, sent three newsmen and a photographer. *Life* and *Look* also had photographers on hand, wandering around the entrance, corridors and staircases, and younger photographers, less certain of themselves, followed them.

In the Jefferson Square plaza the mobile television units were stationed. Each of the networks had sent a huge truck, and the local, independent stations had dispatched their own. For a time each had insisted on using its own lighting facilities, but the square's public relations department had effected a compromise, so joint facilities were being utilized, and the whole plaza was bathed in a glow as bright as that of midsummer sunlight.

Scores of police reserves were on hand, directed by captains and lieutenants with gold badges on their caps. There were almost as many state troopers, and a group of quiet, efficient civilians rechecked every approach, every window and height overlooking the entrance to the Repertory Theater. Only a few hours earlier word had been received that the President of the United States would attend with a party of eleven, and almost immediately thereafter a large detail of Secret Service men had arrived to take charge of all security arrangements.

The President's decision caused fresh problems for Dan and his staff, who had to find and set aside seats for the distinguished guests and, scattered at strategic points in the theater, Secret Service operatives. Members of the square's board and other prominent patrons had to be satisfied with inferior seats in a shuffle that resembled a complicated game of musical chairs, and a number of ticket-holders found themselves shunted to a row at the rear of the orchestra that had been reserved for just such an emergency. Scores of telephone calls were made, tempers were lost and the diplomacy of the staff was strained to its utmost.

"No," Dan told his director of public relations. "I won't make any statement before the cameras. I'm just a working man, as you are, and with people like the President, and Helga Borg, and five governors, and Anton Helsing, and that Yugoslavian prima ballerina whose name I can't pronounce, nobody will want to see or hear me."

He did not go on to say that, with a copy of his manuscript already sent to Ben Hopkins' office, it was almost inevitable

387

that he would be asked to leave his position at the square in the immediate future.

Mayor Burke arrived shortly after seven o'clock and summoned his police commissioner, the chief of the state police and the head of the Secret Service detail to an impromptu conference at the foot of the central staircase in the lobby. Photographers who had nothing better to do and were trying to obtain a complete pictorial record of the occasion snapped some pictures of them, but the security officers, not concerned about whether the mayor shared in the evening's limelight or not, abruptly ended the meeting. Burke was mollified, however, when two of the television directors taped interviews with him for later use.

Members of the cast drifted in, and the photographers converged on Julian Adams, whose inner tensions remained concealed as he smiled and posed for them. Berenice Tolmey, wearing her old polo coat and slacks, and so pale without makeup that she looked like a frightened adolescent, was unrecognized, and slipped off through the stage door to her dressing room without being stopped.

The arrival of Jerry Solanz and Jan Marek a few minutes later created the first major stir of the evening. Reporters and photographers crowded around them, and Jerry spoke fluently in a free-ranging interview, discussing the significance of repertory theaters in general and of Jefferson Square in particular, the symbolism to be found in *Confessional*, his future play schedule, his past and present films and the growing importance of the performing and creative arts. He also predicted, at some length, that his "find," Berenice Tolmey, would be a star before the evening ended.

The crowd of newspapermen had blocked the cameras, so Jerry gladly repeated the interview for the benefit of television audiences.

Jan Marek was tight-lipped and glum, and could be persuaded to make only one comment. "I hope," he said, "that my play speaks for itself." Refusing to answer other questions, he went backstage to wish the members of the company good luck.

One hundred and fifty additional policemen, summoned by Mayor Burke, strengthened the cordons guarding every approach to the square.

Dan, who had forgotten his promise to Phyllis that he would make time to eat a sandwich, turned a newly arrived newspaper correspondent over to the public relations director, answered three telephone calls in the box-office, and conferred with a White House aide on the propriety of the pit orchestra playing "Hail to the Chief" when the President came down the aisle. The aide doubted that the President would want such attention drawn to him on a night when he was a member of the audience, not a participant in the drama of the occasion.

It was seven thirty by the time Dan went backstage to give the company his good wishes.

Berenice's dressing-room door was closed.

Julian Adams' personal manager, press agent, wife and several friends were sitting in the small drawing room of his suite, chatting, but he was not there. So Dan made the rounds, stopping for a moment at each room along the long corridor.

As he retraced his steps he saw that Berenice's door was open. He increased his pace, and saw her in deep conversation with Julian, who turned away just as he reached them.

"I wish you everything wonderful, Berenice," Dan said.

She gave no sign of hearing or seeing him as she closed the door, and he heard a lock fall into place.

He shook hands with Julian, wished him luck, and then asked, "How is she?"

"I've seen all kinds of pre-opening jitters," the actor replied, "but she seems to be in a trance. Either she'll raise the roof off this new theater of yours, Dan, or she'll lay the biggest egg in history."

There was just time for a puff or two of a cigarette. Dan went to the Green Room where, to his surprise, he found Jerry Solanz pacing alone, drinking a chilled soft drink from a bottle. Both men halted and looked at each other, then Dan went forward, hand extended.

"Good luck," he said.

Jerry hesitated for an instant, then grinned. "What the hell. This is no night to carry grudges." He pumped Dan's hand vigorously. "After tonight, you won't be able to stop me from doing my Ben Jonson play. We've got a real hit on our hands. I feel it in my radar net."

"I hope you're right."

"Want a drink, sweetie?" Not waiting for a reply, Jerry dropped a coin into the dispensing machine, then handed Dan a cold soft drink bottle.

"Thanks." Dan hadn't realized he was thirsty, and the liquid eased the burning in his throat caused by too many cigarettes. "We can't ring up the curtain until the President and his party are seated."

"Has he landed yet?"

"There was no word from the airport five minutes ago."

"Shit. Not only do I want to establish the principle that Repertory Theater performances start on schedule," Jerry said, "but if we're late, the critics for the morning papers will be rushed writing their reviews."

"The police will do everything they can for us tonight," Dan said, "so if it's necessary, I think they'd take the critics off to their offices in squad cars."

"Sweetie, you're using your goddam head." Jerry's jubilation was brief. "Have you seen Berenice?"

"For a second, but she didn't know I was there," Dan said.

Jerry threw his soft drink bottle into a wastebasket and plunged his hands into the pockets of his dinner jacket. "She insisted on going off alone to some crummy goddam dump for a bite to eat, and now she's keeping her door locked. Oh well. Screw it. Either she's set in her part by now, or we've had it. All of us."

Sandra stood at the window of her mother's tenement apartment, adjusting the focus of a pair of binoculars as she looked down at the brilliantly lighted plaza of Jefferson Square. "Where did Buddy get the money for these glasses, Mama?"

Maria Mascaroni, who resented the festivities that were helping to drive her from her home, had retreated to her sink where she was washing the dinner dishes. "He bought them."

"Swiped them, you mean. When did he ever earn any money?"

"Buddy is a good boy!" The old woman roused herself. "Right now he's down there, parking the automobiles of the rich people."

Sandra was surprised. "He has a job in the square's underground garage?"

"Every day after school, and now the opera starts, every night, too."

"The Repertory Theater is opening tonight, Mama. Not the opera!"

Maria's sniff indicated her opinion of all Jefferson Square culture.

"There's Helga Borg!" Sandra's voice rose as she peered through the glasses. "I read about that white mink coat. Look at it, Mama. It cost twenty-five G's—"

"In my village, women like that did not stay. They went to Napoli. Your kind, too."

"What a coat! Is it gorgeous! And that Emory woman, the banker's wife, is wearing a dark one that cost almost as much. I don't know what any man sees in her, but she sure puts a fortune on her back."

"Men, money. Money, men." Maria began to scrub a pot.

"I wish to God you'd kept that TV set I bought you a couple of years ago." Sandra was rooted to the window.

"You see enough now."

In the distance sirens wailed, the sound growing louder, and soon a caravan of limousines screeched to a halt in front of the Repertory Theater. Police held back the surging crowds milling in the plaza, and cameramen, photographers and reporters surged forward.

"It's him," Sandra said. "The President." Suddenly she laughed scornfully. "Wouldn't you know. Governor Herder is with him, hanging on to the tail of his coat. For all the good it'll do him. I've got to hear this." She hurried across the room to switch on a dilapidated radio, then scurried back to her post at the window.

The radio hummed loudly.

"Christ, it takes forever for that thing to warm up!"

"In my house no one uses this talk," Maria said severely. "You stay here, you show respect."

Without warning, a familiar, mellow voice emerged from the radio speaker. "—so this is an occasion in which all Americans may share. Concentrated in these handsome buildings are great works of art, sculpture, music and literature, which will be enhanced by the performances of the greatest American and foreign artists. It gives me pleasure to welcome Jefferson Square to the growing ranks of America's culture centers, and I take pride in the knowledge that it will well serve this city and state, its neighbors and the nation at large."

"Thank you, Mr. President," reporters and announcers said as the crowd applauded.

"Governor Albert Herder, who is the President's host this evening, is standing beside him," an announcer said. "Would you care to add to the President's remarks, Governor?"

"Would he!" Sandra exclaimed. "Oh, this is great." She laughed as the President moved to the barricades to shake some of the many hands extended to him, while Governor Herder began to speak. "I'm happy to welcome the President to the Repertory Theater of Jefferson Square tonight, and to extend a cordial invitation to all Americans to visit the most complete, modern and beautiful of all culture centers."

"The *klutz*," Sandra said. "Listen to him rip through his speech." She went to the radio and snapped it off, then returned to the window. "He probably prepared a fifteen-minute speech before he knew the President was coming."

Maria made no reply, but a deep sigh indicated her disapproval of Sandra's lack of respect for authority.

Other automobiles began to disgorge their passengers as the President and his party disappeared into the Repertory Theater. The line of waiting automobiles was long, but some people in evening clothes were walking rapidly from points as far as a block from the entrance, knowing the play would begin once the President was seated.

"Look at those coats and dresses!" Sandra was entranced. "Isn't this something?" Suddenly she began to weep, her tears smearing the glass of the binoculars.

Members of the Secret Service detail unobtrusively held back the throngs in the lobby, but it was a difficult operation. Even men and women of sophistication were trying to inch closer in an attempt to hear the conversation near the huge marble masks of Comedy and Tragedy that filled the outer portion of the auditorium wall.

"This is grand, Ben," the President said. "If there had been places like this when I was a boy, I would have gone to fewer of those big movie palaces."

"We hope you'll come often, Mr. President," Benjamin Hopkins said. "And after the performance we'll be honored if you'll join us. There will be two parties."

"I'll come by for a short while," the President replied. "I'm flying back to Washington tonight, and I have some hours of homework ahead of me, so I don't want to get away too late."

Ben Hopkins assured him that that would be no problem. Then he escorted him and his party into the auditorium. At the emphatic request of the President, "Hail to the Chief" was not played, as his aide had predicted.

Dan stood against the wall at one side of the lobby, watching people gather at the two entrances to the orchestra, and there a Presidential aide joined him.

"You can start now, Mr. Robertson. He's sitting."

"I hope he doesn't mind waiting a couple of minutes," Dan said, "but he caused such a heavy traffic jam that these people couldn't get here any sooner. We won't be seating anyone during the first scene, so I'd like to give them a chance to get inside."

"Take all the time you need. When the boss is in a good mood, nothing bothers him. I just hope Governor Herder stops button-holing him, or the ride back to Washington is going to be pure hell."

Phyllis came through the lobby with the Helsings and Harvey and Esther Simpson, and Anton was fuming as Dan went to greet them. "We spent twenty minutes just sitting in the car," he said loudly, "about three blocks away, and it was too far to walk. The police stopped everybody short. And held us there."

People were staring at him and whispering, and Michele tried to quiet him.

"We'll make different arrangements for my opening, Dan," he continued. "I insist on it!"

"We haven't started yet," Dan told him soothingly, and murmured to Phyllis, "I'll be with you in a few minutes."

He deliberately waited until they reached their seats before pressing a concealed wall buzzer. Then the auditorium lights dimmed, the pit orchestra played "The Star-Spangled Banner," and Jefferson Square came to life.

The stage lights were extinguished momentarily at the end of the first scene, and Dan leaned toward Phyllis. "I'll be back. I hope," he muttered, and bolted up the aisle.

He found Jan Marek pacing up and down at the rear of the theatre, and the playwright greeted him with a fierce whisper. "What's got into Berenice?"

"She's giving the part her own interpretation. The interpretation she wanted from the start."

"That's sure as hell what she's doing. It's as though Jerry hadn't spent five minutes of rehearsals with her. My God, he's wild!"

"Has he gone backstage?"

"A few minutes ago," Marek said as they retreated toward the exit door, where they could continue to talk quietly while watching the performance.

"I've got to admit," Dan said, "that she's doing it well. She makes sense."

The playwright nodded. "I couldn't have visualized her version of Paula, but it does hang together. She's creating a Paula of her own and what scares hell out of me are the big scenes."

Dan felt cold, and rubbed his hands together. "Me, too."

Jerry Solanz materialized beside them, a film of sweat on his red face. "The goddam bitch wouldn't even talk to me. She kept her door locked while she changed her costume, and she brushed past me as she went on stage again. A split second later and she'd have missed her cue."

They managed to lead him into the lobby.

"I can't really get hold of her until intermission, and then I'll break her apart!"

Dan and Marek exchanged glances, and it appeared to both of them that the significance of what Berenice was doing hadn't yet dawned on the director.

"You've got to leave her alone," Dan said.

"Are you nuts, too? She's spoiling the play, and she's ruining all of us!"

"Listen, Jerry," Marek said. "Whether we approve or not, Berenice must be allowed to do the rest of the play in her own way. If she changes her interpretation for the second act, the contrast will make a hodge-podge of everything."

"Right," Dan said. "The audience will be completely confused."

"I know." Suddenly capitulating, Jerry removed his glasses and mopped his face with a handkerchief. "Maybe it's just as well I couldn't make her listen to me. Even though she's stinking up the stage, maybe the rest of the company can carry the play. But they sure can't hide what she's doing."

"She isn't as bad as you think," Dan said. "There's integrity in her interpretation."

394

Jerry glared at him as they started back into the auditorium. "If I ever find out you had a hand in this, Robertson," he muttered, "I'll kill you, too."

Carolyn and Edward Emory appeared directly in front of Warren Hopkins in the lobby crush during the intermission between the first and second acts of *Confessional*. "Good evening," he said.

At that instant Edward saw someone he knew off to his left, and fell into conversation with the man.

"Hello," Carolyn said, her hand lightly holding her husband's arm.

Warren glanced at Edward, uncertain whether he was being snubbed. "You look very lovely tonight. That's a splendid gown."

"Thank you," Carolyn was on guard, but her eyes were expressive. "I had it made, and I don't mind telling you I was frantic. It wasn't delivered until yesterday."

Warren was familiar with every detail of the crisis. "Really?" He hoped he sounded convincing. "It was worth the anxiety."

Edward was still occupied, seemingly unaware of the younger man's existence.

There was a momentary, awkward silence, and then Warren bowed and turned away. As he lighted a cigarette he discovered that his hand was trembling. He made his way across the lobby, stopping short when he saw Bettina ahead of him, animatedly conversing with a group of young people.

Her hair was piled high on her head, giving her an unexpected maturity that, nevertheless, blended with her youthful face, and her appeal was enhanced by a strapless evening dress with a close-fitting bodice.

Betsy felt someone looking at her, turned slightly and saw Warren. Her eyes met his for an instant, so she could not pretend to be unaware of his proximity. She could either recognize him or look through him. But before she could decide what to do, she began to smile at him.

The President remained in his seat during the intermission. Secret Service men quietly turned back patrons from the rear of the orchestra and balcony who wanted a word with him, his autograph or just a closer look.

Albert Herder kept seated, also. The other governors and the senators in the audience came to pay their respects to the President, and acknowledged Herder sitting beside the Chief Executive. But they understood too well that his seeming friendliness with the President had no real meaning. As governor of the host state he would be seated nowhere else, even if he were a member of the opposition party.

"Mr. President," Herder said hopefully, "the backstage areas of this theater are extraordinary, the last word in technical design and comfort. Would you like to inspect them?"

"Another time, Al, not tonight," the old man said. "One of the problems of being President is that the office turns people into stammering boobs. I wouldn't want to upset that fine cast of actors back there."

Herder smiled, wondering whether there was any inducement under the sun that he could offer in return for the President's blessings.

Berenice's first big scene came half-way through the second act, and immediately prior to it Dan shifted in his seat, unable to find a comfortable position, unable to hold his legs and arms still.

"What's wrong?" Phyllis whispered.

He shook his head and said nothing.

The lights dimmed between scenes, then brightened to show a motel bedroom. This was the scene that the company, in its first days of rehearsal, had called "the strip," and Berenice was required to undress as she quarreled with the man who would become Paula's new husband. In Jerry Solanz' version of the scene she had been deliberately provocative, flaunting her sex appeal until, after losing her temper, she broke down and wept hysterically.

But Berenice's concept of the character did not remotely resemble the director's. Her Paula was shy and diffident, and she gave the part a new dimension, a pathos that had been lacking. Only her walk was unchanged.

Julian Adams adjusted superbly to the change. Little of the stage business that had been rehearsed remained the same, but he moved freely, easily as he delineated the novelist who tried to dominate Paula but was in turn captivated.

Gradually Dan became conscious of the remarkable quiet

that pervaded the theater. No one coughed, no one whispered, no one moved; until the lights dimmed again after Berenice, instead of sobbing wildly, stood very still, with real tears streaming down her face. Then, all at once, a sustained roar of applause echoed through the auditorium, and many of the spectators cheered.

"She's done it!" Dan exclaimed, applauding more vehemently than anyone. "She's brought it off!"

Not until the applause subsided did he realize that Phyllis was looking very tired and strained.

"This is the most exciting evening I can remember," the young man in the overly elegant evening clothes said.

"The girl is marvelous, and I wouldn't have thought anyone could make you forget Julian Adams was on the stage, but that's just what she did." Anton Helsing was aware of his wife inching a trifle closer to him in the lobby crush.

"I've read about her," the young man said, "but I discounted all of that slush as Solanz' publicity. I'm delighted to say I was wrong. Not that she's my type," he added, and laughed.

Again Michele edged closer.

Anton became irritated. He knew as well as she did that the young man was a flaming gay boy, but he didn't need her constant protection. He was an adult, capable of taking care of himself.

"I know," the young man said, flirting with him, "that your opening is going to be even better. I've been hearing marvelous things about your *Concerto.*"

"Don't believe all you hear, but the orchestra will do its best." Anton felt the pressure of Michele's hand on his elbow, and could not free himself as she guided them back toward their seats. He glared at her, then said in her ear, "What did you think I was going to do? Run off to the men's room with him?"

"I've learned," she replied quietly, "not to take chances."

Dan and Phyllis managed to reach the outer lobby for a cigarette, and against the wall, a short distance from them, the show business crowd was paying court and tribute to Jerry Solanz.

Helga Borg, white mink artfully draped over her seductive shoulders, was speaking in an actress' voice that carried above the hubbub. "Oh, you're a sly one, Jerry! I couldn't have played the part the way Tolmey is doing it—my, God, who could? The point is, I wouldn't have tried! The part cries out for her approach, but from the advance build-up you gave her, I expected something quite different. You've turned all of us upside down. You're incredible, darling!"

It was impossible to hear Jerry's reply, but he looked smugly pleased.

Jan Marek came up to Dan. "Let's go outside for a minute. Where we can talk. You, too, Mrs. Robertson, if it isn't too cold for you."

"This coat wouldn't let me get cold," Phyllis said.

A cold breeze was blowing across the floodlighted plaza, where the policemen and state troopers were still on duty, with the cars of the Presidential entourage strung out in the driveway. A man in plain clothes approached the trio, and Dan waved to him. "Everything is under control, Lieutenant," he called.

"Nothing is under control," Marek said, "but I'm delirious. The President just sent for me and congratulated me."

"Isn't that wonderful." Phyllis beamed.

"Not particularly," the playwright said dryly. "He isn't a drama critic. It's funny how the holes and soft spots don't show up until you play before an audience. But it's Tolmey who is making me see what's wrong with the play itself. If she'd done it this way in rehearsals, I'd have rewritten the first act."

"Don't worry about it tonight," Dan said. "Enjoy the unique experience of a lifetime."

"Brother, I am. I keep wondering how much better she might have been if Jerry had turned her loose from the start."

"I think," Dan said, "that she's giving a complete portrait of Paula. The concept must have been growing in her all through rehearsals."

Phyllis was listening intently to every word.

"However she's done it," Marek said, "I'm eating crow. What really gets me is Jerry—you saw him in there. Watch him take all the credit."

Albert Herder was becoming desperate. If he could win the endorsement of the President, or, lacking it, could convince enough industrial and financial leaders that the President was backing him, he could ride out any scandal the Masters woman might create.

He remained standing when a senator came to say a word to the President, and as he caught the eye of one prominent citizen, then another, he flashed his famous smile and waved. For a moment he was tempted to put a hand on the President's shoulder, a gesture that dozens in the auditorium would be certain to notice. But he didn't quite dare. There was a chance the President would be sufficiently amused to tolerate the familiarity, but he might become resentful, knowing he was being used, and if that should happen, the Herder political career would end when he completed his present term as governor.

Damn his soul, Herder thought. All he's got to do is make one lousy sign, and I'm set for life.

Berenice's portrayal of a crushed, defeated Paula in the climactic scene of the third act was extraordinary, and her interpretation, still her own, was startling. Instead of using feminine wiles to prevent the collapse of her life, her Paula became a snarling animal at bay. Her voice soared to shrill heights, then dropped to a harsh whisper that carried to the farthest reaches of the second balcony. She cast aside all restraints, and in a frenzy that Dan thought might be real, she threw herself about the stage with such abandon he was afraid she would hurt herself.

At the end of the scene she staggered into the wings, and he had to prevent himself from going backstage to see if she had really collapsed.

The shouts and cheers of the audience was deafening. One scene remained to be played before *Confessional* came to an end. But the audience held up the performance for several minutes, and the drama critics for the morning newspapers left hurriedly before the conclusion.

Dan went out to make certain the squad cars were on hand to transport them to their offices, where they would write their reviews for the next morning's final editions.

By the time he returned to the auditorium the play had just ended and the cast was coming on stage for its curtain calls. He was relieved when Berenice appeared and, applauding her vigorously, noted that she looked exhausted.

The rest of the company joined in the applause for her when her turn came to step forward alone. And the President, forgetting that the audience would not be allowed to leave until he departed, remained in his place to pay tribute to a glowing performance by an inspired actress.

The cast party was being held on the stage, where the set for the last scene had not yet been struck. Long tables were laden with cold turkey and ham, several hot dishes that the caterer had provided, and a variety of salads. Bars set up on either side of the stage were magnets for dozens of people, and uniformed guards were on hand to prevent anyone from coming down from the stage into the auditorium with lighted cigarettes.

Dan and Phyllis were late, having attended the small, brief reception for the President in the Directors' Lounge, and both were tired as they made their way through the theater to the stage.

"I don't think I want another drink," Phyllis said.

"Some food will do you good," Dan told her.

"You, too."

"Before we go. I want another glass of champagne first. This joint is really swinging, isn't it?" He looked for Berenice, but couldn't find her in the crowd.

When the Robertsons reached the stage they were surrounded. Glasses were thrust into their hands, and Dan congratulated everyone he saw. He shared the unanimous opinion of everyone present: thanks to the luminous performance of Berenice Tolmey, the Repertory Theater's first play was sure to enjoy a great success.

Someone tapped Dan on the shoulder, and the moment he saw Jan Marek's face he knew something was wrong. They headed backstage together, neither speaking.

Benjamin Hopkins, making a token appearance at the cast party, loomed up before Dan, halting him. "Let me repeat what I said to you in front of the President, Dan. My knowledge of the theater is limited, but I appreciate efficiency. You've done a splendid job."

"Thank you, sir."

"I've been reading the document you sent to my office. With great interest." Hopkins' eyes were masked, as always, revealing nothing. "Call my secretary tomorrow, will you? You and I will have a talk."

"I will, Mr. Hopkins," Dan said, and they shook hands.

The silent Marek was waiting in the wings.

Dan followed him into the dressing-room corridor, and Marek headed straight for Berenice's suite.

The door was open, and in the corner stood Milt and another assistant, conversing in low but obviously agitated voices.

Jerry Solanz sat slumped on the sofa, the collar of his dress shirt open, his face ashen. He look like a man who had suffered a heart attack.

The two assistants stopped speaking.

Jerry roused himself. "Does he know?" he asked hoarsely.

"I haven't asked him yet," Marek said, and turned to Dan. "Have you seen Berenice?"

"No, I was looking for her on stage."

"She's disappeared," Jerry said. "Her door was locked for a long time, and when I came back a few minutes ago, it was open—just like it is now. But she's nowhere in the theater. On the night of the biggest hit an actress could make, the goddam fool kid has just plain vanished!"

The sirens of the motorcycle escort faded in the distance as the Presidential motorcade sped toward the airport in the suburbs. In Jefferson Square plaza the television lights were being turned off, and the crews were packing their gear before departing. The line of limousines in the driveway had thinned, but some remained, indicating there was still activity inside.

Sandra lowered the binoculars for a moment to rest her weary arms. She had read in the gossip columns about the glamorous backstage party being given at the expense of the square, and she intended to remain at her post for another half hour, maybe longer, to catch another glimpse of Helga Borg and the other celebrities as they departed. Just seeing that white mink was worth the wait.

It wouldn't be long, Sandra told herself, before she had a mink of her own. She'd wear it everywhere—to the Sapphire Room, backstage parties, all the nightclubs.

The snoring of her mother interrupted her daydream, and her face contorted angrily. In two more weeks, she thought, Mama and Buddy would be evicted from this dump when demolition work started on the tenement next door. The day couldn't come soon enough.

Someone appeared from the direction of the stage door, out the night was dark now that the television lights and the theater's marquee had been extinguished, and Sandra raised her glasses again.

She caught a glimpse of a very young girl with short, tousled blonde hair and no makeup. She was wearing rumpled slacks, low-heeled shoes and a polo coat, its collar turned up in the cold.

With nothing better to occupy her, Sandra kept her glasses on the girl, who walked up Fourth Street and, after a few moments melted into the night.

Lowering the glasses again and lighting a cigarette, Sandra settled down in her vigil, waiting for another look at Helga Borg's fabulous mink coat.

CHAPTER NINE

The drama critic of the *Examiner* summed up the reaction of the press and the reviewers from other media. He wrote: *A new play by Jan Marek is always an important event, and his latest, opening the Repertory Theater at glittering Jefferson Square, which well may be the most beautiful and technically modern playhouse on the face of the earth, assumed a special significance. Marek's* Confessional *is not his best, however, and although the Repertory Theater as a physical plant lives up to all that has been said and written about it, both were eclipsed last night.*

Only a few times in a generation—perhaps they can be counted on the typewriter-worn fingers of a reviewer's hand —does a star of the first magnitude burst comet-like onto the stage scene. Berenice Tolmey, an actress of rare talent, made her debut before a cheering, appreciative audience which included the President of the United States, and so great was her impact that it is impossible to write about her without using every superlative in the dictionary.

Hailed as a new "sex symbol," Miss Tolmey proved herself much more, combining beauty, sensitivity, discipline and the indefinable incandescence that marks the greatest of actors. It is the duty of the playgoer to see Confessional, *since even minor Marek is better than most of what we are shown on the boards these days. Everyone will want to become acquainted with the lovely Repertory Theater. But, far beyond all this, no one who enjoys stage productions can afford to miss the performance by Berenice Tolmey, who gives new life and meaning to an ancient profession.*

Newspapers were spread around the bedroom, all of them open to the drama pages, and Dan sipped a mug of hot coffee as he sat at the telephone. Haggard after an almost sleepless night, and unshaven, he chain-smoked as he drank his scalding coffee.

"When did you last speak to Jerry, Jan?" he asked.

"Just now, before I called you." The playwright sounded equally weary. "He said you'd talked to him about forty-five minutes ago.

"Apparently there's no sign of Berenice anywhere. I was sure she'd show up at the hotel eventually."

"So was I. God, what a mess!" The sound of a match being struck could be heard over the wire. "I keep hoping that she'll see one of the reviews. That ought to bring her around fast enough."

"I hope so." Dan was dubious. "It's possible she's left town."

"Why would she?"

"I don't know. Why did she go off in the first place?"

"It's insane," Marek said. "But between Berenice and my own reviews, I'm just about ready to take a powder myself."

"Your reviews weren't that bad."

"She saved the play for us, no question about it. But nobody put any laurel wreaths on my head. Crowns of thorns would be more like it. I suppose I deserve the beating I got, but that doesn't make it hurt any less."

"We'll be sold out for months," Dan said, trying to console him.

"If Berenice comes back. What are we going to do?"

"I told Jerry that if I don't hear from him by eight thirty this morning, I've got to notify the police. Since he refuses to do it himself."

"Then there will be front page headlines for sure."

"Maybe the police will cooperate with us. I've thought of talking to Governor Herder and Mayor Burke. If they're willing to help, we might be able to keep this out of print for a few hours longer, and by then, I hope, we'll have found her."

"Well," Marek said, "let's keep in touch."

Dan rang off, finished his coffee and went into the bathroom to prepare for what promised to be an exceptionally busy day.

Phyllis was waiting for him with fresh coffee when he returned to their bedroom. "Any luck?" she asked.

"Nothing, as of ten minutes ago. But I had an idea while I

was under the shower, and I want to follow it through before I get panicky." He began to drink the coffee as he dressed. "There's just a chance I may know where to find Berenice."

"Where?"

Dan realized he had said too much. It had occurred to him almost immediately to try Claire's apartment, but he was afraid of the implications in his knowing she might be there. Furthermore, he had reasoned, if she had gone there, Claire herself would have talked sense into Berenice and seen to it that she returned. But now, Dan was desperate and confused. He had no choice but to go there himself. "Let me see if I'm right first, Phyllis, and I'll explain later."

Phyllis' uneasiness, which she had felt so frequently in recent days, welled up in her again.

He hastily knotted his necktie and got into his jacket. "If anybody calls me, I'll be at my office in a half-hour. Better say forty-five minutes. And if any of the newspapers call, don't tell them anything." He kissed her absently and hurried off.

The conviction continued to grow that Dan's personal involvement in Berenice Tolmey's disappearance was greater than she knew.

Warren dialed the number rapidly, drumming on his bedside table with his free hand until Carolyn answered. "Can you talk?" he asked, his usual form of greeting.

"Yes, Edward left about ten minutes ago."

"Then I timed it right."

"Wasn't it marvelous last night? I've never seen anything as electrifying as that girl's performance."

"Yes, it was good," he replied in a monotone.

"You weren't having a very pleasant evening, I'm afraid."

"It threw me when Edward didn't speak."

Now it was Carolyn's turn to remain silent.

"Was it deliberate?"

Her calm façade cracked. "I don't know, Warren. I was as upset as you were, and I didn't dare ask him. I kept telling myself to leave well enough alone."

"I'm sure he knows something. It couldn't have been an accident that you and he were at the far side of the Directors' Lounge during the whole reception for the President."

"I don't think we should read too much significance into that."

"Coupled with his snub in the lobby, I think it has a great deal of meaning. I didn't get much sleep last night, Carolyn. I've been thinking. And I want to see you."

"I can't possibly come over this morning. I have two appointments, and then lunch—"

"Let's make it at three, if that's convenient. I think the museum would be best."

Carolyn hesitated for a moment. The risks became greater each time they met, and her apprehensiveness increased. "All right," she said, and could not even try to keep her lack of enthusiasm from her voice.

Dan fidgeted in the tiny elevator, but could not curb his nervousness. If his hunch proved right, it would solve only part of the problem, and he was certain his reception would be chilly. The elevator halted, and he walked down the corridor to Apartment 12C.

A redhaired girl, heavily made up and wearing a kimono-like robe, came to the door.

"I'm Dan Robertson, and you must be Claire." Dan didn't know her last name, and felt rather foolish.

She stared at him for a moment, and then her face cleared. "You're Berenice's friend."

He nodded, uncertain that the identification fitted. He realized immediately that Berenice wasn't here. "I'm sorry to barge in on you like this, but I wonder if you have a moment."

"Sure, come in. I don't have too much time, or I'll be late for work."

A fresh wave of guilt swept over Dan as he entered the room where he had last seen Berenice alone.

"Wasn't the *Examiner* just great this morning? I always knew she'd be a big star. Excuse me if I go and finish dressing, will you?" Claire retreated into the bedroom, leaving the door ajar.

Dan looked around. "I thought she might be here."

"Berenice? You must be kidding." Claire returned to the living room, buttoning a blouse over a low-cut bra. "She must be wallowing in a champagne bath just about now."

"You haven't heard from her?"

The girl looked into a wall mirror to check her hair and makeup. "Not for two or three days. She's been on a real blast-off into space."

406

"More of one than any of us realized, I'm afraid. She disappeared last night, right after the performance."

"Oh, God." Claire sat down on the sofa. "Have you got a cigarette?"

Dan gave her one, and lighted it for her.

"Doesn't Jerry Solanz—"

"No one has any idea what's become of her. I was hoping I'd find her here."

Claire shook her head and gazed glumly into space.

"Are there any other friends—"

"Not that I know of." She took another puff. "Well, I can't let myself cry. There isn't time to do my makeup over." She looked at her watch. "I'm going to be late for work as it is."

"Can I drop you off in a taxi? I'll have to stop off at the state executive office, and the garment district is on the way."

"Thanks, that'll be a big help. I'll be ready in a minute or two."

"May I use your phone while I'm waiting?"

"Help yourself," she called, and went off to her bathroom.

Dan called his office, then telephoned Phyllis to see if there were any messages regarding Berenice. There were none.

"Where are you?" Phyllis asked.

He could not tell her he was standing in the bedroom of a young woman he had never before met, a dress model. "I'll tell you about it later," he said, and put the phone in its cradle.

Claire knew where to find a free taxi in the neighborhood, and as soon as they were settled on its seat he began to question her about Berenice.

"She's never had many friends, and after she started living with Solanz, she stopped seeing all of them, except me. He didn't know about me."

"Could she have gone to a relative?"

"She doesn't have any." Frown lines looked incongruous on Claire's young face. "Berenice is a funny kid. I got to know her real well when we were in England together, as well as anybody could know her. She always had this big thing about being an actress. But there was something about her—there still is—that's kinky. I don't mean shacking up with Solanz, although I'd throw up if I had to do that. What

I mean is, she doesn't think like other people. Or behave like them."

"Is she the sort of girl," Dan asked, "who might jump off a bridge?"

"Yes."

Dan broke out in a cold sweat. Panic welled up inside him and, suddenly, he didn't know where to turn. "Oh, God," he said.

"That's the way she is," Claire said, and fumbled in her handbag for a tissue.

"She must have known she was making a big hit. The audience was shouting itself hoarse last night. I've never heard such tremendous applause."

"If it was me, Mr. Robertson, I'd flip. But I can't tell you what Berenice thought, because I honest-to-God don't know."

The taxi pulled to a halt at the entrance to the skyscraper in which she worked. "If I hear anything," Dan said, "I'll let you know. She needs a friend."

The cook and governess, sitting together over cups of coffee in the kitchen stopped speaking and listened to the piano music that flooded the house. When Anton Helsing was inspired, angry or upset, his playing was angelic.

Michele, talking on the telephone, cut short her conversation and walked quietly from her sitting room to the living room, where she sat in a corner.

Anton was completely engrossed in his *Concerto,* and seemed unaware of her presence. He swept through the final movement, and as he reached his last crescendo he halted abruptly, slammed the keyboard lid and stood. "That's the end of the stupid thing," he said.

Michele had rarely seen him in such a foul mood, and waited for an explanation.

"No one is going to hear it again," he told her. "I'm getting back the arrangements, and I'll cancel the pressing of the recording. I'm going to substitute something else at the opening concert. As far as I'm concerned, I never wrote the *Concerto.*"

She braced herself, but he surprised her by stalking out of the room, and she had to follow him to his bedroom.

Anton rolled down the sleeves of his shirt and busied himself inserting gold links in the cuffs. Seemingly he had regained his poise as he said, "I'll take a taxi to the recording company offices, and then I'll go straight over to Symphony Hall. The recording people are going to scream when they learn that I'm withdrawing the *Concerto*."

Michele couldn't decide whether to tell him that she knew his reasons or whether to coax him into telling her. In any event, she decided to ask. "Why are you withdrawing it?"

His look indicated a belief that she had lost her senses. "It's obvious."

"Not to me."

"How can I compete with Tolmey? I'm still haunted by that performance. She reminded me of a young boy who had just been badly wounded."

Michele hadn't thought of Berenice as a boy, and was certain that most of the previous night's audience would have been surprised by the analogy, but she kept her opinion to herself. "You aren't competing, Anton," she said calmly.

"This is once," he told her, "when you're not going to talk me out of something I know to be true!"

"I have no intention of it."

"There are two events at the square this year," he said. "I'm not counting the museum opening later in the spring, because that's in a different category. There was last night's opening, and now there'll be mine. They're sure to be compared."

"Not by music critics or drama critics."

"By the public, the people who buy tickets and records!" He raised his voice to a shout.

The ringing of Michele's telephone interrupted him, and she was glad to escape. "I'll take it in my sitting room," she said.

He made no reply as he continued to dress.

By the time she returned, he was adjusting the handkerchief in the breast pocket of his jacket, and, concentrating on the reflection in the mirror, paid no attention to her.

"That was Phyllis Robertson calling," Michele said.

Anton patted the handkerchief, then pulled it a small fraction of an inch higher.

"Berenice Tolmey vanished last night," Michele said. "They don't know if she ran away after the final curtain—or whether she was kidnapped—or what. As you can imagine, they're going wild."

Anton's enormous expressive hands dropped to his sides, and he stood very still. "This isn't a gag?" he asked softly.

"Hardly."

"What will they do?"

"Phyllis had no idea. Dan went off to search for her this morning, and I suppose they've called in the police by now."

Anton's fingers began to move, slowly at first, then very rapidly. "Will they close *Confessional?*"

"I don't know, and I'm sure they don't, either. I doubt if they can make any decision until they locate her."

He removed his jacket and carefully placed it on one of the padded hangers he had designed for his clothes. Snapping his fingers, he walked to the easy chair on the far side of the room and sat. "My visit to the record company can wait," he said.

Michele opened her mouth to question his sudden change in plans, then closed it again. Anton's tight, malicious smile told her all she needed to know.

"I'm sorry as hell, Dan," Eddie Brown said, staring up at a familiar crack in the dusty ceiling of his office, "but the Governor won't see anybody this morning. It doesn't matter what the emergency is."

"I need his help," Dan said. "Jefferson Square needs it."

"So does the whole state." Eddie removed his feet from the desk and sat upright. "Between the threats of that Masters bitch—you know about them—and the cold shoulder he got from the President last night, the Honorable Albert Herder isn't fit company even for himself. He chewed my ass out for nothing this morning, and if I know him, he'll spend the whole day brooding in his office. With the door locked and the phone turned off."

"I thought the President was very friendly toward him at the reception."

"If it had been you—or me—we'd have been happy. But not the Honorable Albert. He was sore as hell because the President didn't jump up on the stage and announce that he's supporting our boy for the nomination at the convention this year. And don't tell me its ridiculous, because I know it is. The Honorable Albert wants to be President so badly you can hear his ambitions all the way out here, even on a noisy day."

"Maybe you can help, Eddie."

410

"That's why I'm here. The Honorable Albert's chief fixer."

Dan told him the story of what happened the preceding night, and voiced the hope that the police could make a quiet search for Berenice.

"There are some smart young reporters on the police beats these days. How long do you want the story kept out of print?"

"A few hours, if possible. Long enough for us to assess the situation and decide what to do."

"Okay, I think I can manage it. Keeping the state police quiet is easy. I'll issue an order in the Honorable Albert's name telling them to give no information and no statements to anybody. If that gets the press down on the Honorable A., we'll handle that later. You go down to City Hall and see the Police Commissioner. I'll have talked to him—and to Mayor Burke—before you get there. Tell him all you know, and they'll start hunting for the girl right away."

"We'll have fewer problems if we handle all this in an orderly manner," Dan said, looking around at the group gathered in his office. "I realize that all of us are worried and frightened, but that doesn't help the situation out there."

Everyone knew he was referring to the Repertory Theater, where a line four deep snaked out through the lobby from the box-office. In spite of the cold, people waited patiently for tickets to see the young star whom the critics had praised so lavishly.

"I still don't see how she could do this to me." Jerry Solanz rubbed his bloodshot eyes.

There was a knock at the door, and the square's director of public relations came in. "Sorry to interrupt," he said, "but one of the newspapers got hold of the story through a precinct police sergeant, and now they're all down my throat— the wire services, the papers, the news magazines, the radio and TV people, everybody."

"Admit nothing and say nothing," Dan told him, "until we have a statement for you."

"Let me tell them we're going to issue a statement soon, Mr. Robertson, or they'll make this thing twice as bad by speculating."

Edward Emory, who felt ill at ease attending the conference, shook his head. "I don't see how the square could be in a much worse predicament."

"Do whatever you think best," Dan told the public rela-, tions director, and waited until the man closed the door behind him. "Now, gentlemen, we've got to approach this matter from where we sit, not from Berenice's angle."

Jan Marek slowly polished his glasses. "I've been saying one thing all morning. We close the show. We have no choice."

"I doubt that you would do that in the commercial theater," Dan said.

"With the future of *Confessional* depending on Berenice alone, you bet we would."

"But Jefferson Square is a culture center, not a private enterprise being operated for personal profit," Dan said, and couldn't help wondering, briefly, whether Edward Emory read other meanings into the comment. "It's our obligation to keep the play running."

"Even if the square loses money?" the playwright demanded.

"Yes," Dan said firmly, and Edward winced.

"Marek is a thick-headed Bohemian who won't listen," Jerry said, making an effort to pull himself together. "I've already explained all this, but I'll do it again. We put the understudy into the part tonight, and we let anybody who wants to exchange seats for a future performance do it. We hire Helga Borg, and I'll put her into rehearsal this afternoon. There isn't a quicker study in show business, and I give you my word she'll be up on the part in a week. One lousy week—that's all. Not everybody will want to exchange seats, so in one stinking week, how badly can we get hurt?"

"You're sure she'll do the play?" Dan asked.

"Not an hour ago she came to see me at the hotel to tell me how sorry she felt about this goddam mess. I threw the idea at her, and she agreed before the words were out of my mouth."

"It would be a very different interpretation," Dan said, "but the name of Helga Borg has drawing power."

"There's none bigger," Jerry replied. "I gave Helga her start, remember, so she's indebted to me. What's more, she'll do the part the way it ought to be played. Not that Berenice wasn't effective, but Helga will be the real Paula, the Paula who was in Jan's mind from the day he started writing *Confessional*."

412

Dan couldn't help feeling that he was speaking as though Berenice were dead.

"It's a great chance, our only chance," Jerry said. "Send out for some more coffee, will you, sweetie? I'm still pooped, but I'm getting my second wind."

Dan spoke to his secretary on the inter-office phone.

Edward Emory consulted some notes he had scribbled on a pad. "As I understand it," he said, "we would not be required to pay Miss—ah—Borg a larger salary than the usual repertory theater wages?"

"With me directing, Helga would do the part for nothing," Jerry declared.

"Where do we stand if Berenice shows up?" Dan wanted to know.

"To hell with her," Jerry said. "She can go screw herself up a tree."

Francis Dougherty entered the conversation for the first time. "I have our Tolmey contract right here. It's standard. There are the usual clauses. If she's ill or is otherwise prevented by forces beyond her control to appear in Repertory Theater productions for which she's been engaged, we're obliged to take her back within a reasonable period of time. But if she willfully and of her own volition walked out on us, she's broken the agreement."

"I don't want her," Jerry said emphatically.

"Just a minute," Dan said. "This is a theoretical discussion, since we don't know where Berenice has gone. But if she should appear at the theater tonight, let's say, or if she's ill and a physician certifies she must take a few days off, we've got to keep her. Is that correct, Francis?"

"Technically," Dougherty said, "all the square must do is pay her salary. The Repertory Theater isn't required to use her in a part on stage, any part."

"Then we pay her," Jerry declared, "and let her rot on her butt."

His vindictive short-sightedness shouldn't have been surprising, but it was. "If she comes back today—or tomorrow —or whenever," Dan said, "we've got to take her. We can't ignore the reviews. Earlier today both *Life* and *Look* approached us for feature stories on her, and *Time* has been talking about giving her a cover. So has *Newsweek*. And don't forget the line out there at the box-office has formed

413

for just one reason. Those people, and thousands more like them, want to see Berenice Tolmey!"

"She had her chance," Jerry said, "and she blew it."

Edward Emory was unaccustomed to such emotional vehemence in business dealings. "On financial grounds it would be sensible to take her back any time she wants to return."

"Helga Borg won't sign with us if she thinks we might heave her out," Jerry said, his annoyance growing. "She isn't some newcomer punk who can be pushed around!"

"Nevertheless," Dan said, "we've got to protect Berenice if she should return."

"What's this with you and Tolmey, sweetie?" Jerry demanded. "I've had my ideas about you two for a long time."

Dan felt himself redden. "Your ideas are mistaken."

"Maybe they are. Maybe they're not. Either way, she's had it!" Jerry pounded the arm of his chair.

"I'll cast my vote with Dan's," Marek said, still speaking in a subdued voice.

"Helga will insist—"

"Helga is a realist," the playwright cut in. "She knows she has us over a barrel. But she's got to be willing to do a little gambling of her own. I'm sure you could persuade her, Jerry."

"I refuse."

"Then Francis and I will do it," Dan said. "Aside from the unfairness to Berenice if we don't keep the door open for her, the public will demand to see her. Jefferson Square will be in operation for many years, and can't afford to antagonize the people on whom its future depends." He paused. "May I have your opinions, gentlemen?"

"I'll go along with you," Dougherty said.

"You appear to have the only sensible approach to the matter," Edward Emory declared. "I'll accept your proposal."

Jerry looked at each of them in turn. "The day Tolmey comes back here is the day I leave."

There was a long silence. "The square," Dan said at last, "will face the problem when it arises. Now, I think, we'd better tell public relations what to put into its statement."

The interior walls had been installed in one wing of the Museum of Fine Arts, brass and steel railings gleamed in the corridors, and a new, thick rug covered the concrete flooring.

The lighting fixtures were in place, and only the portraits on the freshly painted walls were needed to complete the gallery. Footsteps were muffled now, and Warren and Carolyn wandered from one room to another, both reluctant to discuss the subject that had brought them here. "The museum is beginning to look positively civilized," she said, and forced a laugh.

"Everything in life should be civilized," he replied.

"Just how do you mean that?"

"When Edward refuses to speak to me in public, I believe the time has come for us to evaluate our position."

"You make it sound like someone studying a portfolio of stocks and bonds."

"I sound like someone who is very embarrassed, and isn't being given much help."

"Do you expect me to say good-bye to you and saunter off into the twilight?"

"Not at all," Warren said. "I'm prepared to ask you to marry me."

Carolyn was silent.

"Will you?"

"I don't believe you want to marry me," she said.

"What you really mean," he replied, "is that you don't want to marry me."

She realized he was giving her the opportunity to make the initial break. "I enjoy my position as Mrs. Edward Emory," she said. "I don't know why but I do. I'd enjoy being a Hopkins-in-good-standing just as much, but I'd hate to spend all year, every year, traveling from the Riviera to the Alps to Acapulco and back. I couldn't enjoy that kind of life. I don't believe there are enough poor orphans in Switzerland who need to be helped by fund-raising drives."

Warren smiled painfully. Her humor was thin, but she was making the effort.

"Even if your uncle and the rest of your relatives—your uncle, really—accepted my marriage to you, I doubt that I would enjoy being older than my husband. It doesn't bother some women, I know, and their marriages are successful. But it would upset me. Besides I could never give you a family. My gynecologist told me years ago that my inability to bear children was mental. For years I claimed I wanted babies, and it took me a long time to realize I didn't mean it. I don't think that would make you very happy, now, would it? So my answer is plain and simple, and I hope it's direct. Thank you for your proposal. Every woman likes knowing she's wanted, and I'm old-fashioned enough to feel complimented when a man asks me to be his wife. But the advantages of the status quo outweigh those of a new life with you."

Her candor was shattering, and he could not reply. They started walking again, left the carpeted gallery and soon found themselves in an unfinished wing.

"It will probably take me a long time to become accustomed to—normal living again," Carolyn tried to smile.

They walked to the stairs, and paused for a moment near the well, where a four-ton statue of the Muses soon would be put in place. "At the right time," Warren said, "I hope you'll tell Edward I respect him."

"It won't be necessary. He'll know."

They left the museum and started across the plaza to a taxi stand. "I'm glad those eyesores are coming down," Warren said, gesturing toward the two tenements still standing on Fourth Street.

"Yes, by the time Edward and I come home from England, the new buildings should be going up. It will be wonderful when the square is really completed."

"I didn't know you were taking a trip," Warren said.

"Oh, I thought I told you."

"No. When are you leaving?"

"Soon after Anton Helsing's opening. I lack your appreciation of music, but it will be an interesting evening for me, since I think of the square as one of my babies. My favorite."

They reached the taxi stand, and Warren opened the rear door of the car that stood first in line.

"Good-by," Carolyn said, holding out her gloved hand.

"Good-by," he repeated as he removed his hat, shut the door and turned away.

The mid-afternoon rehearsal was frantic, and Jerry Solanz demonstrated that, under pressure, he could remain calm when others were jittery. Berenice's understudy was on stage with the rest of the company, running through *Confessional*, and Dan could see that she would be adequate in the part. Unquestionably, the ticket-holders who came to see her, and surprisingly few were exchanging their seats, would be short-changed, but not terribly.

416

Meanwhile Helga Borg, drab in a cloth coat, simple dress and no makeup, sat in the fourth row, simultaneously studying her lines and watching the stage business. Her concentration was complete, and occasionally, when Jerry came to her, she anticipated him, nodding quickly after he had spoken only a few words.

An assistant treasurer came from the box-office into the auditorium, tapped Dan on the shoulder and told him he was wanted on the telephone.

"Deputy Commissioner Sullivan," a deep voice said. "We think the Fourteenth Precinct may have found the girl, Mr. Robertson."

Dan found it was difficult to breathe.

"Do you want to identify her, or does Mr. Solanz?"

"What do you mean 'identify'? Is she—"

"No, no. Nothing like that. She's at City Hospital. Can you get over there?"

"Right away."

"Ask for Dr. Nathanson. He'll be expecting you."

Dan almost forgot to return to the auditorium for his coat and hat. Jerry was busy, Jan Marek was nowhere to be seen, and only a few production assistants were watching. So he told no one where he was going, and hurried out.

He smoked two cigarettes during the taxi ride to City Hospital, a huge complex of buildings, some of gray stone, some of red brick, that he had seen previously only from the outside. Any citizen too poor to afford treatment elsewhere was admitted to City, where there were entire wings for alcoholics, drug addicts and sufferers from venereal disease. There were more than three thousand beds in the place, the overcrowded conditions were so scandalous that every newspaper in town was demanding that federal and state as well as local funds be provided at once to build additional quarters, and, according to rumors that Dan had heard, an average of more than sixty patients died there each day.

The administration units were located in a section more than one hundred years old, and clerks in offices with hissing radiators sat dispiritedly at their typewriters, pecking away with a notable lack of enthusiasm. Dr. Nathanson, the assistant medical administrator, made his office on the second floor, where the atmosphere was somewhat livelier, and Dan was asked to wait in a small anteroom where the only furniture was a long wooden bench. The ceiling was dirty, the drab green paint on the walls was chipped and peeling, and the aura was coldly depressing.

Dr. Nathanson finally appeared, a man in his mid-thirties, dressed in a business suit, and looked, at first glance, like an unsuccessful garment district salesman. When the door of his office closed behind them, however, and he perched on the edge of a dusty table, his manner was incisive. "Two patrolmen in a Fourteenth District squad car picked up this girl at about one o'clock this morning at the entrance to the park where the hookers hang out, and that's what they thought she was, until they realized she was disoriented. So they brought her here instead of to the lockup. We've run a couple of tests that indicate no drugs or alcohol in her system, and she fits the description of your missing actress. Come along and take a look. She refuses to talk, so it'll save us trouble if you can identify her."

They left the office and made their way through an endless labyrinth of corridors, and Dan was surprised to see patients of both sexes wandering freely from ward to ward. Men and women wore the same drab hospital garb, gray two-piece pajamas, faded maroon robes of the wrong size, and felt slippers. Few had bothered to comb their hair, the men were unshaven, and almost all seemed to be suffering from City Hospital's most notorious disease, a feeling of hopelessness.

Dan glanced at his watch and saw it was almost five o'clock.

Dr. Nathanson appeared to read his mind. "You're wondering why it took so long before anybody notified you, Mr. Robertson. Maybe you've read of our shortage of doctors, nurses, technicians, everybody we need. If not, I'll make you a concise three-hour speech on the subject some time."

They halted before a leather-padded door, and Nathanson pushed a buzzer.

After an interminable wait someone peered out at them through a small glass window, the door was unlocked, and then locked again behind them.

Dan felt as though he had been transported to Bedlam or one of the other eighteenth-century hospitals for the insane. Men and women, most of them aged and obviously senile, sat on benches that lined both walls, staring blankly into space; some were unmoving, others plucked with almost nerveless fingers at their frayed robes. None spoke, and only a few bothered to raise dispirited heads and gaze in the direction of the two men walking briskly down the center of the lane. The only sound came from a television set blaring in a corner cubicle; a children's cartoon program was being shown on the screen, but the men and women sitting before it in dilapidated chairs looked at it with unseeing eyes.

The stench of urine was all-pervading.

The physician and Dan were admitted to another, inner, locked section, and here the atmosphere was even more depressing. The entrance to a men's ward was open, and the patients seemed to be strapped to their beds. A male attendant in white was sitting on an empty cot near the door, reading a comic book, oblivious to the high-pitched wails of a patient in a far corner.

Here, Dan noted, there was a grill steel mesh covering the outside of the grimy windows.

"We've got her in a security room," Dr. Nathanson said, and opened the doors of several wards, apparently looking for someone.

A young East Indian physician, small, slender and dark, dressed in white, came up behind him. "Did you want me, Dr. Nathanson?"

"Yes, this man may be able to identify your new customer."

The young resident led them through another maze of corridors, the last of which seemed to consist of private rooms. Using a key attached to a strong chain that was looped onto his belt, he unlocked a door.

After a moment's hesitation Dan opened it. The light filtering in through a high-set window protected by a steel mesh grill revealed a small cot with a single blanket on it. There was no other furniture in the cell, no object of any kind that a patient could use as a weapon or for self-destructive purposes.

Sitting up in the cot, staring at the smudged and cracking plaster of the opposite wall, was Berenice Tolmey. She turned her head slowly, and finally focused on Dan.

"Get out!" she said, and although her voice was low, it was filled with venom.

"We moved her by ambulance to a private sanitarium," Dan said, "and the red tape at City Hospital held us up for hours. However, she's in good hands, Mr. Hopkins. Jerry Solanz wanted to pay the bills, but I insisted that the square will take care of everything. The chief of psychiatric service has no idea whether she'll be there for a few days, a few weeks or months—it depends on how quickly she responds. But he's certain she'll need psychotherapy for a long time. Berenice can make her own financial arrangements for that treatment when she's herself again."

"I've always been fascinated by human reactions to pressures," Benjamin Hopkins said, resting against the arm of the leather sofa in his office. "Your own responses have been particularly interesting."

"I wanted to explain why I didn't come to see you yesterday."

"Oh, I understand. Besides, what's a day here or there?" Hopkins opened the cabinet of a lamp-table beside him and removed the box containing Dan's bulky manuscript. "This is an extraordinary piece of work."

Dan had rehearsed his speech for this point in their talk, but suddenly his mouth felt dry. "I've written an undated resignation. I'm prepared to leave today, if you wish, although I'd like to stay on until Anton Helsing has opened."

"The first thing I considered was your gesture in giving me this copy to read. It was a form of *noblesse oblige*, I presume."

"Well, my motives were more complicated, but I suppose it boils down to something like that."

"I enjoyed your portrait of the square itself, since I'm familiar with so little of what goes on there. Your section on the Tolmey girl was particularly good, and quite sympathetic," Ben Hopkins said. He paused, smiled and sat on the couch next to his visitor. "And your principal theme, what one might call financial shenanigans in high places, was most absorbing. However, with the exception of Governor Herder's secret partnership in the general contracting firm, I learned nothing new from your book."

Dan wished he would show emotion; anger not only would be preferable to his calm, but would clear the air.

"I don't condone what any of us have done, Dan, but on the other hand, I don't condemn it, either. You surprise me somewhat, you know, both by giving me this to read and by what you've written. You're still the naïve professor, I'm afraid."

"My concept of right and wrong—"

"Let's not play philosophical tennis, young man. You've

tried walking two roads simultaneously, which is impossible, and I can appreciate the difficulties you've suffered. If I didn't like you, I'd simply accept your resignation, let you publish your book, and damn you to Hell. But for your sake, and for another, far more compelling reason, I'd like you to see something, if you can. The book can't hurt me, Dan. Even if what you said about me were true. Far worse accusations have been written. Not only about me, but about my father and grandfather. What I wish you'd understand is that your whole approach has been ingenuous.

"Jefferson Square was founded and financed by men who wanted to bring culture on a mass scale to our people. They've succeeded, so far, and the square will be even more successful in the future. In return, some of these men have made a profit on their investment, so they haven't really contributed freely, have they? To the extent that federal, state and local funds have also gone into the square, they've cheated the taxpayer. There's no question about it, and I can't excuse them. But keep in mind that they've earned most of their profits by selling slum land to real estate developers.

"This is reality, the world as it is. Men with high motives have stooped to line their own pockets. I can't call them villains. I find it difficult to categorize people as good guys and bad guys. I've found both qualities in virtually everyone."

Dan was forced to agree.

"The one thing that disturbs me about your book is the loss of public confidence in Jefferson Square that its publication will cause. I'm thinking not only of the square, but of all culture centers in this country," Ben Hopkins said. "Look at them collectively, and you'll find a phenomenon unique to our time. Lincoln Center, Minneapolis, Houston, Los Angeles. Small cities like Albuquerque. There are more of them every year, and they're growing faster than talent can be supplied to them.

"The public appetite for culture is something new in the United States. We call it mass culture, which is a misnomer, of course. More people are being educated than ever before, and public tastes are becoming more refined. I needn't tell you all this. You told a great deal of it to me.

"But what you've apparently failed to realize is the personal involvement of the individual with his own local culture center—and with all the others, although indirectly. The man who buys a ticket to a ballet performance or an opera, the man who goes to see the paintings in *his* culture center feels he's a part-owner of the place. Which is precisely what he is, of course.

"What bothers me is the effect that your scandal—and it's juicy enough to create reverberations everywhere—will have on the entire culture center movement. The Hopkins Fund alone has spent many, many millions more promoting culture throughout the United States than my associates have earned in profits through their Jackson Drive Realty deals. When you add what the other foundations, Rockefeller, Ford and the rest have done, it's staggering. However, let's confine this to Jefferson Square alone." He thrust the box containing the manuscript into Dan's hands. "I'm not accepting your resignation today. You've been so busy working at the square and writing at the same time that you haven't had an opportunity to think. I wish you'd take a few days to do just that, Dan. Think. What are your real motives in publishing this book? What do you hope to accomplish? I can promise you that Edward Emory and the rest will neither be disgraced nor sent to prison."

"Governor Herder—"

"For the present, I'd rather leave him out of this. Weigh this question on its own basic merits. It seems to me that too many forces have been pulling you in two directions for too long, and I don't want to make your dilemma worse. I merely ask you to recognize human nature and human accomplishment—the reality of Jefferson Square, if you will—for what they are."

Betsy Callison was sitting alone at the dining-room table, sipping her breakfast coffee and leafing through the morning newspapers, when the maid came in to tell her that Warren Hopkins wanted to see her. Betsy's first thought was that she looked a fright in an old sweater and slacks, with no makeup and her hair in a pony-tail. In almost the same breath she decided to send back word that she wasn't at home, but by then it was too late.

Warren had followed the maid, and stood in the dining-room entrance, still wearing his topcoat, his hat in his hand. "It isn't accidental that I've found you here alone," he said. "I knew your mother was going to a committee meeting this morning, and I saw her leave about twenty minutes ago. I

422

also saw the blinds open in your bedroom windows, so I knew you were awake."

"You've had a busy morning, haven't you?" Betsy wished she could have dismissed him with a cool nod, which would have been so much more effective than her mild sarcasm.

"I won't disturb you for more than a minute."

She saw he was laboring under a great strain, and almost relented.

"I wanted you to know," Warren said, "that I offered to make an honest woman of a lady. Three days ago."

"Congratulations. I don't suppose you can set a date until she has her divorce. But why tell me? I could have waited until I read about it in the papers." Betsy wished she'd at least had the opportunity to put on a little lipstick.

Warren shook his head. "I made a gesture that was expected of me because I was brought up as a gentleman. The gesture was recognized for what it was—and she rejected it. Which is something both of us knew from the start. I guess it's a part of every Puritan's education to lose his balance because of a married woman. The illicit nature of the relationship is what makes it fascinating." He paused for an instant, then added somberly, "Not that it matters to you, but I really was a jackass."

Betsy noted his abnormally pale complexion and the hollows under his eyes. "As long as you're here," she said, "you may as well sit down. Leave your hat and coat somewhere—and do you want cream and sugar in your coffee?"

The wallpaper was cheerful, the flowered curtains matched the slip-covers on the chairs, and the little sitting room in no way resembled the stereotyped concept of sanitarium quarters. Nor did Berenice Tolmey look like a patient. The color in her cheeks indicated she had spent time outdoors, and although her face was free of cosmetics, there was a sparkle in her eyes. Clad in her usual turtle-neck sweater and stretch slacks, she seemed completely at home, in charge of the situation.

"The reason I came," Jerry Solanz said, watching her uneasily, "is because the doctor told me on the phone that you insisted."

"Of course." Berenice laughed quietly. "After all, you're my immediate employer, and—"

"Helga Borg replaced you in *Confessional.*"

423

"Temporarily. I have a letter from Francis Dougherty explaining my position. I intend to notify you in writing that I'm coming back to the play, but I owe the rest of the company, including Miss Borg, the courtesy of knowing where things stand. That's why I sent for you."

Jerry glanced around in annoyance. "Must this door be kept open, sweetie?"

"The door is open, sweetie, because I want it open," Berenice said. "Look. I want to show you something. The roots of my hair are showing. They're brown."

There was a hint of impatience in his voice. "Of course. I wouldn't expect you to get a bleach job here."

"But I could. If I wanted it. I'm letting my hair go natural again. And I'll wear a wig on stage when I'm playing Paula. My concept of Paula."

"Listen, sweetie, just because you got some pretty good reviews—"

"Just because I intend to be myself, sweetie. As long as I live. I'm lucky. I've spent hours with Dr. Gottlieb every day here, and I've seen Dr. McNaughton every morning, too. I could have gone all the way off the deep end, and stayed off. But we caught me in time. In less than two weeks I'm myself again, and by the time I leave here, next week, I'll be able to stand on my own feet forever."

"Don't be so cocky!" For the moment Jerry forgot he was in a sanitarium, and raised his voice.

"Oh, I'm not," Berenice said quietly. "I expect to be in therapy for a long time, as an out-patient. But I'll be strong enough to work, to live my own life in the apartment I'm moving into with a girlfriend, and to be myself. Maybe it was just a fluke that I became a star the night I cracked up, but it doesn't matter. After *Confessional* closes, if I fall on my bottom—on the ass you never for a second let me forget—that won't matter, either. I can always get a job as a model, or working in an office, or doing any one of a thousand things."

"I might have known you'd show this kind of gratitude," Jerry said bitterly. "You're still sick."

"I'm healthier than I've been in years, no thanks to you. You're a good director, Jerry, but you'd be better if you gave your actors their heads and treated them like intelligent people. If you're the genius you like to think, that's news to

424

me. Want to hear more?"

"I think I'll leave." He stood, stiffly.

"You can't go without giving me the satisfaction of telling you what else is on my mind. You have a genius, all right—for finding weaknesses in other people, neurotic weaknesses, and exploiting them to the limit. But you have a few weaknesses of your own. You need a girl who flashes sex to bolster your poor opinion of your own potency, which is why you have to hop into bed every other minute. But you're not the prime shit I thought you were when they first brought me here. You're too mixed up and miserable for that."

Jerry would not listen to any more, and left. Berenice watched him as he walked down the corridor, and after he disappeared from sight she went to the window and looked out at the serene, winter-stripped trees of the sanitarium lawn.

Sandra Masters was livid. She had forced an appointment on Governor Herder, who would see her within the hour, and she had no time to waste on her stubborn mother.

"Mama," she said, speaking loudly to make herself heard above the sounds of splintering wood and the crashing of debris as wreckers worked systematically, tearing down the adjacent tenement, "I'm not going to listen to another goddam word of your insanity. You and Buddy are getting out of this dump today. You and your nutty friend, Mrs. Elias, down on the ground floor, are the only people still living here."

Maria Mascaroni stood adamantly in her shabby domain, feet planted apart and arms folded. "I stay here," she said.

"I stopped off at the parking lot and told Buddy not to take anything along—except the pictures of Papa and the stuff you keep in that old carton. The new apartment will be furnished, with everything brand new. You'll have new clothes, new pots and pans for the kitchen—"

A deafening sound made her last words inaudible, and she blinked in surprise before she realized that a heavy metal ball used by the wreckers had smashed into the building next door. A fine layer of plaster dust sifted down from the ceiling, and a cheap reproduction of a medieval Madonna and Child that had been pinned to the wall adjacent to that of the other tenement fluttered to the floor.

"Christ, this is the limit!" Sandra went to the window,

teetering slightly on her high heels, then beckoned to her mother. "Come over here and look, Mama!"

Maria remained in the center of the room, refusing to budge.

"Look, so you'll know what the hell is going on out there!" Sandra went to the old woman and half-pushed, half-dragged her to the window.

The demolition crews were making rapid, thorough progress. The better part of the other tenement had been reduced to a hollow shell, and most of the outer wall was gone, which made it resemble a stage set. Odd pieces of furniture left behind by tenants who had been evacuated were still standing, an old kitchen table remaining in one flat, a dilapidated rocking chair in another. Plumbing pipes, most of them broken, jutted at crazy angles, and a chipped bathtub, most of its porcelain gone, was suspended between two floors by a single, rusted pipe.

"How can anybody live here?" Sandra demanded. "You don't have any hot water—"

"All I need I heat on the stove," Maria replied.

"By tomorrow, the next day at the latest," her daughter said, "they'll turn off the gas. And the heat. God, this dust is enough to choke you right now."

Maria, her face impassive, moved away from the window.

"If I didn't have an appointment, I'd haul you out of here right now."

Maria looked at her scornfully. "You go to see a man."

"That's exactly what I'm going to do. I'm seeing a slob who's going to pay me a lot of money, Mama, more money than you've ever seen in all your life. Either that, or else. Enough so I can support you and Buddy in your new place, and buy myself a lot of things I've been wanting for a long time, too. I'm coming back here for you as soon as I've seen him, and then you're getting out of here with me, if I've got to drag you by the heels!"

The old woman raised her head higher, and did not reply.

Again the heavy metal ball crashed into the other building, and this time the wall spewed a shower of plaster dust. Then, before the tremor stopped, the floor seemed to heave like the deck of a ship that was cutting through choppy seas, and Sandra felt a spasm of alarm.

"This place is coming apart at the seams!" she cried.

Suddenly the outer wall parted, and the window broke, the

glass disintegrating into small pieces. At the same instant the heaving of the floor became more intense.

The terrified Sandra opened her mouth, but could make no sound.

Maria remained calm. "God punishes you for your wickedness," she said, and began to intone a "Hail, Mary."

There was a cracking, ripping sound, and both women were thrown downward and toward the place where the window had been.

Sandra's long, agonized scream was heard above the crashing of masonry and falling timber. The demolition men heard it, as did everyone in the small crowd that had gathered across the street, and a police patrolman walking his beat the better part of a block away ran to his nearest Jefferson Square call box to ask that an ambulance be sent to the scene at once.

Barricades had been erected to keep back the crowds, and a deputy coroner had supervised the erection of an improvised rope fence in an area immediately surrounding the two crumpled, lifeless bodies. Uniformed policemen and detectives, insurance investigators and demolition workers, state policemen and a detail of the coroner's experts still milled around, ignored by official photographers and those from the newspapers, who continued to snap picture after picture.

A small group of reporters surrounded Governor Albert Herder, who had arrived on the scene a few minutes earlier and had just finished a hasty consultation with a city police captain and one of his own high-ranking state troopers. He held his homburg in his hand, and, his expression grimly sorrowful, he spoke slowly to the representatives of the press.

"I don't know, any more than you do, how there happened to be people in the building," he said. "Evacuation was supposed to have been completed a week ago. But I assure you, gentlemen, that we won't rest until we get to the bottom of the situation that caused this terrible tragedy.

"Once we know the facts, they'll be made available to you. Neither the state nor the city has anything to hide, and if anyone has been guilty of negligence, he'll be prosecuted. I'm shocked, as all our citizens will be."

Settling his homburg on his head, he walked to his waiting limousine while the photographers snapped his picture. He did not look at them as the car pulled away, the sirens of his motorcycle escort wailing. Not until they had moved several blocks from the scene of the tenement accident and Jefferson Square did he allow his shoulders to sag and his body to collapse. He was shaken; exhausted. He almost felt like a man who'd had a religious experience. Had fate intervened on his behalf to assure him the Presidency? Had Sandra Masters been destroyed by Divine Providence? The thought was utter nonsense, he knew. But it was frightening, nevertheless.

Michele Helsing sat behind the wheel of the convertible after parking near the stage door of Symphony Hall, the engine idling, the heater operating at full blast. Dusk came early, but the policeman on duty in the block had recognized her and given her permission to park, so she snapped off the car's lights and reached for a cigarette as she waited for Anton.

She was pampering him, of course, calling for him after his rehearsal instead of letting him take a taxi home, but she knew the accident would disturb him, particularly if he had heard, or had seen the evening newspapers' screaming headlines. Since the girl who had been killed once had enjoyed a peripheral connection with Jefferson Square, he was likely to regard her death as an omen, and would be so concerned about the fate of his *Concerto* that it would take hours to cajole and flatter him into a happier frame of mind.

Michele inhaled deeply, flicked the cigarette in the direction of the ashtray, but missed, and hastily rubbed the spilled ash into the carpeting with her shoe. Anton could be a perfect stinker about little things like spilled ashes when he was in a foul mood.

All artists were temperamental, of course, and Michele consoled herself with the thought that Anton was no worse than any other high-strung, creative person. And, as he was far more successful than most, it was easier to tolerate his temperament—provided one wasn't married to him.

Men began to emerge from the stage door, bundled in their overcoats, and Michele recognized an oboe player and a flutist. The rehearsal definitely was at an end, then, and Anton would appear soon. She glanced at the car clock and was relieved; there would be ample time for them to dress for the dinner party to which they had been invited. And, even if

Anton was depressed, his spirits would be sure to revive when admirers there made a fuss over him.

The stage door opened again, and when Michele saw Anton she started to lower the car window on the right side to call out to him, but halted herself abruptly. He was speaking to someone, a man she didn't know, and something in his attitude made her pause as they drifted a few feet from the entrance and stood, engaging in earnest conversation.

A beam of light from the open stage door reflected on the stranger's face for a moment, and Michele saw he was young and handsome, too ruggedly handsome, and she felt ill. It was difficult to stop watching Anton exerting his most persuasive, flirtatious charm on the man, but she forced herself to look away. The scene was so familiar that she could predict every smile, every gesture.

By now, she told herself, she should have become accustomed to Anton's habits, and it was absurd to feel the pangs of anger, disgust and panic she knew so well. Her alternatives were clear, and so were her limitations.

Partly for her own sake, in part for their son's, and, she liked to tell herself, because of what her husband could contribute to music, she had no intention of divorcing him. She enjoyed the prestige and affluence of being Mrs. Anton Helsing, and it made her feel good to believe her influence steadied him.

So much for the long-range situation. Her immediate choices were sharp: either she could break up his new romance with a combination of threats and love-making, or she could close her eyes to his latest infatuation and let him do whatever he pleased.

Her common sense, her pride and the protective instinct that had bound her to Anton for so long pulled her toward determined intervention. But she was weary, tired of acting as an ever-present buffer between him and his pretty boys. From time to time he undoubtedly had quick flings she knew nothing about, so what would it matter if she pretended to be unaware of this latest, budding affair? It took so much out of her to be his mother and mistress, lover and confessor and guardian, all at the same time.

Again Michele reached toward the window, then hesitated with her finger on the chrome button that would lower it.

If anyone at tonight's dinner party said as much as one

word envying the glamor and excitement of her marriage to a genius, she knew she would scream.

Edward Emory carefully poured two glasses of sherry, then carried one of them across the second-floor sitting room to his wife. "So much for the hospital expansion plans," he said. "I know the trustees are intending to ask you to become co-chairman of the fund-raising drive, but there's no need to give them an answer until we've come home from Europe."

"I wish they'd put me on some other committee, just for the novelty of it," Carolyn said.

"You've acquired too good a name as a fund-raiser." He recrossed the room for his own glass.

"Unfortunately." She laughed.

"Before I forget it," Edward said in the same tone, "I ran into Charles Callison at the club on my way home this evening. He tells me his daughter is being married."

"So I heard at the women's auxiliary tea this afternoon." Carolyn's calm matched his.

Edward raised his glass in his ritual, token toast. "To you, my dear."

"Thank you. I think it's high time I drank to you, Edward." Their glances met, briefly, then both looked away. "Are we dining together this evening?"

"I'm afraid," he said, "this is the night of my monthly dinner meeting with the bank's officers."

"How stupid of me to have forgotten. Donald Franklin is going, I presume?"

"Yes, I'm picking him up on the way."

"Then I think I'll call Margaret, and perhaps we can get together for an hour or so. She knows more about the hospital expansion plans than anyone, and once she's filled me in, I can get a head start on the fund-raising drive before we go to Europe."

Edward smiled. "Now you know why they always want you for the job. You begin to organize your committee before you've even received the formal invitation to take the position."

"Well," Carolyn said, sipping her sherry, "if I'm going to accept a responsibility, I believe in being thorough and efficient."

"Of course, my dear," he replied. "It's the only way."

430

Dan hesitated for no more than a moment at the dressing-room door before knocking firmly.

Berenice, who had not yet started putting on her makeup, was surprised to see him when she opened the door.

"I left word to be notified when you got to the theater," Dan said. "I just want to welcome you back—and wish you luck."

"Thanks. Won't you come in for a minute?" Berenice was cordial.

She looked, he thought, like one of the countless freshmen to whom he had taught his Introduction to the Humanities. It was difficult to believe she was a mature young woman, a theatrical star, the former mistress of a famous director and a recently released patient from a mental sanitarium.

"The flowers from you and Mrs. Robertson are lovely," she said.

Dan smiled as he saw vases of flowers filling every available space. "A lot of people had the same idea."

"People have been wonderful to me," Berenice said. "Including you when I went zilch."

"I don't deserve any medals." Dan accepted the invitation to sit opposite her.

"I don't believe you do, either," she said. "I've thought a great deal about you, Dan. While I was thinking about me, that is. I didn't really do anything except think about me in the sanitarium, and it was hard work."

"I've done some thinking of my own, without benefit of formal therapy, so I have a vague idea of what you mean."

"It's funny," Berenice said, "but I was never really in love with you. It isn't easy to remember exactly how I felt—that was when everything was all mixed up. But I believe all I did was lean on you. Which was your fault."

"I'll have to plead guilty."

"Not because you were on the make, which God knows you weren't. But you used me. You see, I've heard about the book you wrote, with a lot of it about me."

"The book isn't being published, and there are only two copies of the manuscript. The original is locked away at home with some other things that will never be printed."

Berenice had no need for his assurances and, in addition, misunderstood. "I don't want to read it. I know myself better than anyone, and I'm learning more all the time."

"This is a lame apology," Dan said, "but I tried hard not to

ou. Not hard enough, obviously. I contributed to your
down—"

Not really. I asked for everything that happened to me,
and I can't blame anybody but myself. Not even Jerry, most
of the time. Now that I'm learning to respect myself, I hope
he'll respect me enough so we can work together. If not, I'll
move on after the run of *Confessional*."

Her poise, Dan could see, was not simulated. "You'll do
just fine," he said.

Berenice raised a hand to run a hand through her hair before she remembered it had been set. "I'm finding out I don't
need anybody but myself. It's a new kind of feeling for me,
and very wonderful. It would be silly to say I won't become
frightened, sometimes. I do, and I will. But the doctors have
shown me that's natural and normal. It had never occurred
to me that other people are scared half their lives, and that's
why they often act as they do." She glanced at her watch,
then stood.

Dan knew it was time for her to start making up for her
return performance. He rose, too, and held out his hand.
"There won't be a vacant seat in the theater tonight, and
everyone out there will be rooting for you."

"I'll like that," Berenice said, "and I won't let them down."

He paused at the door.

"I'm growing up, Dan, which is what everybody must do,
eventually. I know what I want for myself, if I can get it,
which is a life as an actress—"

"Your career is set."

"If I keep getting the breaks. But you can be sure I'll be
doing my damndest to get what I believe is right for me."

Francis Dougherty caught a glimpse of his wife in the living room as he put his hat and coat away in the front-hall
closet, and began speaking to her, his voice raised slightly.
"I phoned you a couple of times," he said, "but the line was
busy. Anyway, I knew you'd realize I wouldn't be home for
dinner when I wasn't on the six thirty-one."

Ann had to be careful so he wouldn't hear the thickness in
her voice. "I wasn't worried, but I saved your dinner in case
you want it."

"Later, maybe." He came into the living room, smiling
casually. "I had a bite in town before I left."

"You stayed late at the office?"

432

"As usual, I'm afraid. Work piled up on me this afternoon." He went to the bar at the far side of the living room, and, as he mixed himself a highball, noted that considerable inroads had been made in a bottle of vodka he had put there the preceding evening.

Although Ann was feeling her drinks, her mind functioned well enough for her to know he was telling her a whole series of untruths. He hadn't called home, because the telephone had been silent since noon, except for her two brief attempts to reach him on his private line at the office after normal business hours, when no one had answered.

"Would you like a vodka and tonic?" he asked.

"No, thanks. I don't feel like drinking tonight. It's one of those days when I prefer coffee." Ann laughed, then made a surreptitious attempt to focus on him. Precisely as she had expected, his hair was combed carefully and the knot of his necktie looked neat. Ordinarily, when he came home from work, his hair was somewhat rumpled and his necktie knot had worked its way to the left side of his collar. Therefore, she felt positive, he had started another affair with one of his town girls, and had made himself presentable after taking her to bed.

"One drink won't hurt you," he said, aware that she was studying him and knowing that another stiff vodka would dull her ability to pick him apart.

"I really don't want one, Francis!" Ann's indignation was genuine. "There must be days when you don't feel like drinking!"

"Yeah. Sure." Rattling the ice in his glass, he crossed the room and lowered himself into his favorite easy chair.

"Tired?" she asked, concealing the malice behind the question.

"I'm beat. And people were still calling me about Sandra Masters. You'd think she'd been related to us."

"Poor Sandra. My flesh crawls whenever I—"

"Goddammit, stop thinking about her!" Francis refrained from saying that he preferred not to recall the bitch who was his former mistress and an employee he had discharged, and that, when others reminded him of her, his one feeling was that of relief. Ann often became maudlin when she drank too much, but maybe his sharp comment would silence her.

She reached for a magazine and concealed her face behind it. Positive that Francis had enjoyed an affair with his one-

433

time secretary, Ann wondered if he would react as callously when she, too, died. "Were you working on a new case?"

"No, just some complications with old clients." He wasn't stretching the truth too much, he told himself. He had spent months working on the divorce for the blonde he had unexpectedly laid early this evening after her return from Nevada. This time he'd really found himself a woman who would create a minimum of complications for him. Thanks to the settlement he'd won for her, she would be financially independent. Furthermore, she no more wanted to marry him than he wanted her as his wife, and her children were old enough not to get in the way when he stopped in at her apartment.

Ann saw his faint smirk, and knew she would be forced to endure the old, dreary routine in the months to come. Some evenings Francis wouldn't come home until eight or nine, as he had done tonight; on other occasions he would be very late, and there would be times, too, when he wouldn't come home at all. He would feed her evasions, half-truths and badly outrageous lies until she would be ready to climb walls, but he would remain convinced he was clever beyond compare. Then, when his affair came to an end, he would crawl back to her, expecting her to soothe him and rebuild his ego.

Her own patterns were as unvarying as his, and knowing she would do whatever he expected of her, no matter how great her loss of self-esteem, she loathed herself as much as she despised him. "I've changed my mind," she said. "I think I'll have that drink, after all."

Several dinner parties were in progress in the so-called Summer Room of the Tennis and Badminton Club, where ladies were admitted, and there the conversation was animated, the laughter prolonged and the atmosphere lively. But the corner dining hall traditionally reserved for men and known as the Members' Dining Room was virtually deserted. The habitués who enjoyed an hour or two of physical exercise preferred it for lunch, and the few who ate there in the evening were, as a rule, single men who lived at the club and, because of other plans, dined early.

So only the semi-private alcove table was occupied. It could not be seen from the Summer Room, and the chief steward, whose continuing employment depended on his ability to recognize the relative importance of members, withdrew his waiters and the lone busboy after cheese, crackers and coffee had been served.

Consequently Benjamin Hopkins and Governor Albert Herder were alone, their privacy unimpaired by potential or active eavesdroppers. They had chatted about everything from the state of the Union to the new corporate tax structure, the new eighteen-hole golf course at the country club on the river outside the city to the health of the eldest Hopkins grandchild, who suffered from asthma.

Ben Hopkins tested a wedge of Camembert with the tip of his cheese knife, found it a trifle too hard for his taste and concentrated on his coffee. "Albert," he said suddenly, "you seem to live under a lucky star."

One of the difficulties of dealing with the head of the house of Hopkins was that his manner, regardless of whether he was serious or in one of his rare, jovial moods, was always the same. "I suppose I've had a few good breaks lately," the Governor admitted.

"A few! Dan Robertson's book isn't being published, and the girl who could have ruined you is dead."

"Three different investigations are being made into the collapse of the tenement. We hope to know the full story very soon, Ben." Herder was appropriately somber. "I'd heard from Edward Emory that Robertson had changed his mind about bringing out the book, but I wasn't certain the rumor was true."

"It is. He came in to see me just today. So your reputation is safe, Albert."

Had Ben Hopkins been anyone else, the Governor would have grinned.

"I've found nothing wrong with the real estate sales made by most of the investors in the Jackson Drive group," Hopkins said. "Their ethical standards may be open to question, and they'd be criticized if the story became public, but they acted within their rights. Your own position is less tenable, since you hold a high public office."

Herder bristled. "You're being too harsh, Ben."

"As to your partnership in Harrison, MacFee, which you undoubtedly forced, I find it inexcusable in any man of stature, and in you, Albert, a violation of your oath of office." Ben Hopkins neither raised his voice nor changed his expression.

The sudden attack stunned the Governor.

"I've devoted a great deal of thought to you, Albert. Our families have been close for generations, and it was I who taught you to play tennis when you were a child. So it grieves me to see a man who will never know financial want behaving greedily. I recognized your political avarice long ago, but never knew it was financial as well."

Herder rallied from the initial assault. "I have no need to justify myself to you, Ben!"

"I neither expect nor want justification. I'm merely explaining my feelings so you'll know why I'm breaking with you, Albert. There's nothing wrong with earning money honorably, but service to society is an obligation that our wealth imposes on us. I'd assumed you were serving through holding office, and I'm unhappy because you were merely increasing your own fortune. Well, that's your business, but I won't support you for the Presidency, Albert."

The Governor took a deep breath. "I'm sorry that's how you feel, Ben, but there are others who will stand behind me."

Ben Hopkins sipped his coffee. "If our families hadn't been intimate for so long, I'd insist you give up office right now. But I was fond of your parents, and had great respect for your grandfather. So I prefer to let you retire to private life when your term expires."

Herder stared across the table at the impassive man. "You can give orders to your board of directors, Ben, but I'm not one of your errand boys."

"I neglected to mention," Hopkins continued, unruffled, "that although Dan Robertson's book isn't being published, he was kind enough to give me one of two copies in existence. I've already put it away for safe-keeping in my private vault, and I hope it will stay there. I wouldn't want to make a public scandal of your Harrison, MacFee partnership. I'd even be reluctant to take the one step short of that, passing along word to potential financial supporters looking for the right man to back for the Presidency that they'd be wasting their money on you."

"Do you want to destroy me, Ben?" Herder's voice was hoarse, and he had grown very pale.

"Not at all. I want to refrain from destroying you. I'm thinking of your children rather than you, it's true. Both of your sons will be going to college in the next year or two, and their inheritance, combined with the right education, can make them valuable members of society. I'm hoping to find places for one or both of them in the Hopkins Fund, so I hope you'll continue to impress them with the need to engage in public service that's imposed on men of their class and wealth."

"I'll follow through with the boys, Ben." The Governor stared down at his empty cheese plate. "But I'd rather have you impeach me than subject me to slow torture."

"Retirement from public life will give you the chance to readjust your standards, Albert. Think of what's ahead as an opportunity, not a deprivation. After all, the Presidency isn't everything in life."

"I left after the first act," Dan said. "It was obvious that Berenice picked up right where she'd left off, and she had the audience eating out of her hand. With her back in the company, the run of *Confessional* can be extended at least a month."

"Was Jerry Solanz at the theater?" Phyllis wanted to know.

"He was standing at the back of the house beaming from one aisle to the next. He'll make it his business to get along with her."

"From what I've read," Phyllis said, "that shouldn't be too difficult—for any man."

Dan looked across their living room at her. "What were you reading?"

"An unpublished manuscript. It was fascinating." She was silent for a long moment, averting her eyes, then forced herself to raise her face again. "Were you very much in love with her, Dan?"

He had half-expected the question in a more subtle form, and although her bluntness was surprising, he leaned forward in his chair. "At no time was I in love with her," he said slowly. "I've been trying to think through all that's happened since we came to Jefferson Square, and I know this is the truth. I've never stopped loving my wife, or being in love with her."

Phyllis studied him, but said nothing.

"For a short time I was infatuated with the glamor that Berenice Tolmey represented. And I felt desperately sorry for her, not realizing that her strength was greater than mine, ultimately."

"You're not weak, Dan!"

"I'm learning, partly from her example. You have no idea how tough it was to decide I wouldn't publish the book—"

"I knew," she murmured.

Dan grinned feebly. "Yes, I suppose you did, even though I deliberately told you nothing about the hell I was putting myself through. I figured I'd caused you enough problems in the past couple of years."

"Problems are part of marriage. Anyway, I was psychic, so I knew. It's strange, isn't it, how extra-sensory perception of some kind seems to work when people are close to each other?"

"Have you picked up any other messages on your E.S.P. antenna?"

"No, but I didn't need a telegram to tell me Harvey Simpson would be wild."

"He'll start speaking to me again. One of these days. I hope." Dan tapped a cigarette and reached for the table lighter. "It's just as well you haven't known the rest. Or guessed it. I put out some discreet inquiries indicating I might be available if a good college or university wanted someone to teach the Humanities."

"Is that what you plan to do, Dan?"

"Would you mind?"

"You're the one who has to be satisfied with his work, honey."

"Suppose the choice were up to you?"

"No fair," she protested.

"It won't influence me. I've made my decision," Dan said.

"All the more reason not to say a word," she replied with a slight laugh.

"I'm not quite sure when it jelled, but a day or so ago it finally dawned on me that I can't run away from myself. The book was a form of escape, you know, but it was just part of the move in the right direction. I'm staying right here at Jefferson Square."

The delight on Phyllis' face said more than words.

"I guess that makes it unanimous," Dan said, his own smile growing broader. "All the reasons that brought us here are still valid, but more so. The opportunities at the square, plus the personal advantages to us. There are differences now, of course. I really know my job, and can get things done—right —with fewer storms. I'll have the Repertory Theater whipped into shape in another six months, and the symphony is going to be the best in the country. I can see some problems ahead at the museum, but I know I can lick them. The next big headache will be the opera, but I'll manage. It's going to be easier, too, knowing I have the full support of Ben Hopkins. He's an honorable pirate. And that's a contradiction in terminology, but it's accurate."

"You sound happy, Dan, for the first time in months."

"I am. The square is going to fulfill its potential, and I'm going to live up to mine."

"I know," Phyllis said, and went to him.

How many of these Dell bestsellers have you read?

The Naked Ape by Desmond Morris   95c

Nicholas and Alexandra by Robert K. Massie $1.25

The Tower of Babel by Morris L. West $1.25

Pretty Maids All In A Row by Francis Pollini   95c

Jefferson Square by Noel Gerson   95c

The Brand Name Calorie Counter by Corinne T. Netzer $1.25

The Survivors by Anne Edwards   95c

The Doctor's Quick Weight-Loss Diet
by I. Maxwell Stillman and S. Sinclair Baker   95c

Stop-Time by Frank Conroy   95c

The Deal by G. William Marshall   95c

The Gospel Singer by Harry Crews   95c

Horse Under Water (A Putnam Book) by Len Deighton   75c

Three Into Two Won't Go by Andrea Newman   95c

The Ginger Man by J. P. Donleavy   95c

The Monkey Puzzle Tree by Nona Coxhead   95c

The Operating Theater by Vincent Brome   95c

Soul On Ice (A Delta Edition) by Eldridge Cleaver $1.95